The Life She Creates

A GRANITE SPRINGS NOVEL

Maggie Christensen

To my wonderful husband and soulmate who proved to me that it's never too late to fall in love.

Also by Maggie Christensen

Oregon Coast Series
The Sand Dollar
The Dreamcatcher
Madeline House

Sunshine Coast books
A Brahminy Sunrise
Champagne for Breakfast

Sydney Collection
Band of Gold
Broken Threads
Isobel's Promise
A Model Wife

Scottish Collection
The Good Sister
Isobel's Promise
A Single Woman

Granite Springs
The Life She Deserves
The Life She Chooses
The Life She Wants
The Life She Finds
The Life She Imagines
A Granite Springs Christmas

Check out the last page of this book to see how to join
my mailing list and get a free download of one of my books.

Prologue

Peta Forrest hugged her granddaughter tightly, but the young girl couldn't stop shivering. 'I want my mum,' she cried over and over again, just as she had each time she awoke during the long night.

Peta couldn't know how much Lily had seen or heard of the argument which seemed to have precipitated the violent outburst, the frenzy that led to the death of Joy, her daughter and Lily's mother. But at eight, she would understand her mother was dead, despite her denials and constant demands for her.

It had been a horrendous few weeks, and it had taken all of Peta's willpower to keep her granddaughter insulated from the news reports. It was bad enough the child had lost her mother, but at least Peta could protect her from the speculation which was rife in the media. With her own life on hold, her emotions in a whirl, she just hoped she could keep it together for Lily. The little girl needed love and stability right now.

Fortunately, it was school holidays, so it was easy to keep Lily home. And the little girl was too distraught to want to go anywhere, preferring to cuddle up with her old teddy bear in a corner of the sofa, shrouded in a blanket. She'd even started sucking her thumb again, a habit she'd long outgrown. The tragedy seemed to have made her regress; she was acting more like a five-year-old than the bright, confident, outgoing, eight-year-old she'd been only a few weeks earlier. Peta had taken leave from her job to care for her and had no idea how or when she could return.

When Lily was settled with a mug of hot chocolate, watching *The Princess Bride* on her iPad for the hundredth time, Peta picked up the letter she'd received two days earlier. Ann Baird! She hadn't thought of her for years. Ann was some sort of second cousin who lived in the countryside, in a small town called Granite Springs. Peta had never been there. They'd met several times when they were children and teenagers but in recent years had only exchanged cards at Christmas. Now she was offering them a room if they wanted to get away. Get away? Get away from Sydney, the city she'd lived in all her life, the city where she'd intended to spend the rest of it?

But life here had become impossible since Grant Holmes had been arrested for the cold-blooded murder of his wife. The papers and television stations had been full of the news about the respected Sydney doctor who had bludgeoned his wife to death while his daughter was asleep upstairs.

If only I could have protected Joy, Peta thought. *I should have known, seen the signs.* But who could have imagined the man Joy had loved with such devotion would turn out to be just like her father? They did say women chose husbands who resembled their fathers, but Grant had appeared to be the exact opposite. He was the product of one of Sydney's top private schools, came from a well-regarded family and was respected within his profession.

They'd met when Grant was a medical intern and Joy a student nurse. She'd wanted to follow in her father's footsteps but her grades hadn't been good enough for medicine. It seemed a marriage made in heaven. They married in a romantic harbourside ceremony as soon as Grant obtained his residency, and when little Lily was born, on Joy's twenty-first birthday, it seemed their happiness was complete.

Peta shuddered every time she realised how she'd been spared a similar fate.

It could have been her!

Her husband had been violent, too. But destiny had been kinder to her. Tony Forrest had been killed by a one-punch attack outside his favourite pub when he made the mistake of getting into an argument with the wrong person. Joy had been a teenager at the time, and Peta hoped she'd been unaware of the violence her mother had suffered at the hands of the father she loved.

If she could, Peta would have saved Joy. But she hadn't known. Despite their good relationship, meeting for coffee or lunch every week and talking almost every day, Joy had never told her. It was only after her death, one of Joy's best friends had revealed the prevalence of Grant's violent rages to a grief-stricken Peta.

Now, it was just her and Lily, and Peta was determined to protect her granddaughter, to ensure she led a safe and happy life.

Perhaps Granite Springs was the answer. Perhaps she needed to create a new life for them both in a place with no bad memories. She picked up the phone to call Ann.

One

'Are we there yet?' Lily's tired voice reached Peta from the back seat of her Honda Jazz. Peta sighed. It had been a long trip, but she had decided to make it without an overnight stop, unsure how her granddaughter would react to the strangeness of a motel room. Now they were almost at their destination.

'Nearly there, sweetie. We won't be long now. Do you need a toilet stop?' She glanced in the rearview mirror to see Lily shake her head violently. At the last stop there had been a family – a mum, dad, and two boys a little older than Lily. Lily had cowered away from the man and sent fearful looks in the direction of the two boys. Peta worried that the experience with Grant had given the girl a jaundiced outlook on life, especially where men were concerned. Hopefully, it was something she'd get over soon.

She remembered the conversation they'd had when Peta broached the subject of their leaving the city.

'Does that mean we won't ever see my dad again?'

'Is that what you'd like?' Peta asked.

Lily shuddered. 'He hurt my mummy. I hate he did that. Is he a bad man?'

Peta had hesitated, unsure how to reply. Finally, she'd taken the girl in her arms and said, 'He's sick, honey and his sickness made him do bad things. But your dad still loves you – and he loved your mum.' It hurt her to say those words, when she really wanted to mete out her own justice to him for exactly what he'd done to her lovely daughter.

But Lily was suffering enough, and if Peta could make life even a little better for her granddaughter, then she would.

'Look, here we are now,' she said, as the sign welcoming them to Granite Springs appeared out of the darkness. It was a relief to Peta. They'd left the city at dawn. It was now late, and fatigue had set in long ago. Her muscles were beginning to ache. She longed for a hot shower and a soft bed.

Following Ann's detailed directions, Peta found herself driving down a wide main street, now empty of traffic, lined with trees on both sides, past the inevitable war memorial and a sign to the botanic gardens. It wasn't long before she pulled up in a quiet street outside a red brick federation style home, from which came the warm glow of a welcoming light.

'Come on, sweetheart.' Peta helped the half-asleep child out of the car and, before they reached the gate, the door was flung open and a woman Peta barely recognised rushed out and enveloped them in a warm hug. Lily pushed herself against Peta.

'Sorry,' she apologised to Ann, 'She's a bit difficult with strangers at the moment.'

'Of course.' Ann sounded brisk. Peta tried to find the child she remembered in this grown woman, but failed. It had been too long. They had both changed. She was only grateful for the invitation, the reprieve from all they had left behind.

*

Peta awakened to the sound of a kookaburra cackling outside the window and the smell of coffee wafting in from the kitchen. She looked down at Lily's figure curled up beside her. Although Ann had prepared two rooms for them, Lily had refused to be separated from her grandmother. Fortunately, both had been sufficiently tired from the journey to fall into a deep sleep. For the first night since the tragedy, Lily hadn't awakened from a nightmare. It was a good sign. Perhaps this move was going to be for the best. Even if it had meant Peta leaving her own home, her job, her friends, Lily's peace of mind had to come first. Maybe they could both forge a new life here in Granite Springs.

'Good morning!' Ann greeted Peta when she entered the kitchen, a room filled with light, an oven and cooktop on one wall and a neat table against another. 'There's coffee, toast, or would you prefer a cooked breakfast?'

'Coffee and toast will be fine, thanks. This is so good of you. I'm afraid last night, I was too tired to make much sense.'

'No worries. You must have had a terrible time of it. How's Lily?'

'Asleep, thank goodness. This is the first good sleep she's had since...' Peta almost broke down remembering... visualising... 'Sorry.' She shook her head in an attempt to dismiss the images which arose unbidden at the most inopportune times.

'You don't have to talk about it if you don't want to, but anytime you need an ear, I'm here.'

'Thanks.' Peta couldn't imagine ever wanting to relive the horror of the past few weeks. She hoped that here, in this small country town, she and Lily could make a fresh start, create a new life and forget the horror of the past.

She helped herself to coffee and toast, spreading the golden bread liberally with the ginger marmalade Ann offered. The warmth of the coffee helped her become fully awake. She looked across the table at her cousin. 'This is so good of you, Ann. I don't know what we'd have done otherwise. But I don't want to be a bother to you. I can't remember when we last saw each other.'

'I think it was at your grandmother's seventieth birthday. I seem to remember travelling up to Sydney with Mum and Dad. It was exciting to visit the big city. You've always lived there?'

'I have. You were never tempted to move?'

'No.' Ann's tone was too sharp to invite any questions.

There was a story, something about... Peta tried to recall what she'd heard, but the details escaped her. She glanced at Ann again, but her face gave nothing away. Whatever it was, it had happened a long time ago, at a time when Peta was herself in the throes of young love. Like her daughter, she'd married young, pregnant with Joy. She'd often wondered if Tony had resented being tied down so young, if that was why he behaved the way he did. She'd never know.

'And you're no bother. It'll make a change to have some company. Since Mum passed, I've been rattling around in this old house.' She glanced around the kitchen which still showed signs of what must be her mother's taste, and her eyes dimmed. Then she seemed to pull herself together and morph into a businesswoman. 'I have to go to work this morning. I told the staff I'd be in a little later, but they can't always be trusted to get on with things if I'm not there to chivvy them along.'

'You still work at the university?' Peta didn't know much about Ann's life but she did remember her mother reading a letter extolling the praises of Ann who had gained a position at the newly opened university in town.

'For the past twenty years. I started as a lowly admin assistant and now I'm the office manager in the School of Education,' Ann said, a note of pride in her voice.

'That sounds interesting.' Peta knew she'd have to find a job here, too. Her meagre savings wouldn't last forever, and it would take some time for her Sydney house to sell. She didn't suppose there would be much demand here for her skills in interior design. She'd been sorry to leave her highly sought-after position with a top company in Sydney, but hoped the skills she'd honed there over the past years might stand her in good stead here in Granite Springs. Maybe she could even set up her own business.

'I have to go now. Help yourself from the fridge. I'll be back around half-five. You have my mobile number in an emergency.' From the expression on Ann's face, Peta deduced she couldn't imagine any emergency that would necessitate the need to use it.

'Bye.'

Ann left, leaving a gust of cold air behind her.

Holding her cup in both hands, Peta sat back in her chair and gazed around the kitchen. Now Ann had gone, she was able to examine it in more detail. She'd been right in imagining little had changed since Ann's mother passed away. Perhaps Ann led a busy life, too busy to change things, to modernise them. She couldn't help herself. She envisioned how the room could look with just the right… No, it wasn't her home. She had no business working out how it could be improved. No doubt Ann liked it just the way it was.

'Grandma!'

Peta looked around to see Lily standing in the doorway, still clutching her favourite toy.

'Good morning, sweetie. You had a lovely long sleep. Would you like some breakfast? How about a boiled egg with soldiers?' she asked, thinking the childhood treat might tempt Lily who had rejected most of her carefully prepared meals for days.

'Where's Auntie Ann?' Lily looked around, then slid into a chair.

'Auntie Ann's gone to work, so it's just us here. Let me get you some breakfast, then maybe we can explore the town. Granite Springs is a lot smaller than Sydney. I think it has only one main street. Imagine!'

Lily managed a weak smile.

*

An hour later, Peta and Lily left the house to explore the town. They walked up Main Street, pausing to gaze into shop windows, until they came across a bookshop. Lily's eyes lit up. She tugged on Peta's hand.

'Grandma, can we go in?'

Delighted to see some interest in the child who had been miserable for so long, Peta nodded and gave Lily's hand a squeeze.

Inside the shop, Lily dropped Peta's hand and made a beeline for the back of the store where there was a colourful display of children's books along with a couple of bean bags and a low table on which were displayed several recent titles. A large ginger cat came wandering towards her.

'She seems to know where she's going. I hope you don't mind Marmaduke.' A tall redheaded woman emerged from behind a row of shelves to greet Peta.

'Yes… no,' Peta replied, gazing after Lily, bewildered. This was the first time she'd shown interest in anything since her mother died. 'This is a lovely bookshop.'

'Thanks. Are you new in town or visiting? I'm Liz Pender. I'm familiar with most of the local kids. We have a regular storytelling for the littlies, plus a book club for the school age lot. They've all proved popular.'

'Peta Forrest.' Peta took the other woman's outstretched hand. 'We just arrived and are having a look around.' She was wary of giving out any more information.

'Welcome. Feel free to browse for as long as you like. As you can see, we're not busy this morning. The library has a host of school holiday activities going which keep a lot of the young ones occupied till lunch time.'

'Thanks.' Seeing Lily busy with a pile of books in the far corner, Peta took her time to browse the shelves for herself. She had brought her Kindle with her, but there was nothing quite like the smell and feel of an actual book and she loved finding new authors.

She was lost in a book set in Cornwall when she felt a tug on her leg. 'Can I have this one?'

Lily was standing there holding a copy of one of the Harry Potter series. Peta bit the inside of her cheek, remembering how Joy had bought the entire series for Lily and stored them in a special bookcase in her bedroom. They hadn't been back since the house had been declared a crime scene. All Lily's belongings were still there, just as they'd been that fateful night. No doubt they'd be allowed back to retrieve them sometime, but could either of them bear to enter that house ever again?

'Sure, honey.'

Peta paid for the book and the pair left the shop, Lily clutching the bag containing her purchase tightly, as if afraid it would be taken from her.

They wandered further along the street, with Peta becoming more certain with each step that this had been a good move. The wide street with cars angle-parked to the kerb was so different from the busy Sydney suburbs they'd left behind. Even the air seemed different – fresher.

It had been some time since breakfast and Peta felt in need of a pick-me-up when she noticed a sign for The Bean Sprout Café. 'How about a hot chocolate?' she asked.

Lily nodded, but the interest she'd shown in the bookshop seemed to have disappeared, to be replaced by her habitual miserable expression. Peta wondered how long it would take for Lily to regain her former cheerfulness or even to lose her fear of strangers. She had noticed how she sidled past Liz Pender as if afraid of her, though she had stroked the ginger cat.

Pushing open the door, they were greeted by a gust of warm air and the aroma of freshly ground coffee. The counter was manned by a smiling woman with dark hair who greeted them in much the same way as the bookshop owner.

'Good morning, I'm Marie. What can I get you this morning?'

As she smiled at Marie and gave her own name, Peta realised that here in Granite Springs everyone seemed to know everyone else. While that might have its advantages, it could also mean it was difficult to keep a secret, and she desperately wanted to keep the secret of how Lily's mother died.

Everything reinforced her earlier decision to legally change Lily's name to Forrest.

When their orders appeared – cappuccino for Peta and hot chocolate for Lily – they were served, not by the cheerful woman who'd greeted them at the counter, but by a tall, broad-shouldered man with greying dark hair and deep brown eyes. Peta wasn't sure why she noticed his eyes, but they twinkled with merriment and there was something gentle about them.

Lily shrunk into the corner of her bench seat when he placed the cups on the table along with a plate containing a couple of brownies.

'As you're new customers, I thought you might like to try Marie's brownies. Let me know how you like them. What's your name, little lady?' he asked the cowering Lily, who looked away.

'Sorry,' Peta said. 'Lily hasn't been well. I'm Peta.'

'Frank.' He was about to turn away, then stopped. 'Peta? Italian?'

'My grandmother was.'

'Ah!' But he didn't elaborate.

When he had left, humming to himself, Lily uncoiled and stretched out a hand to pick up the mug of hot chocolate on the top of which were floating three marshmallows. Then she reached for one of the brownies and began to nibble it.

Peta breathed a sigh of relief. Lily may have shown resistance to Frank, but her distrust didn't extend to the chocolate and brownie. It was good to see the tiny improvement in Lily's appetite, but she still had a long way to go.

Two

'It's about the house.'

Frank stopped cleaning the espresso machine and stared at Marie's flushed face. He'd guessed she had something to say to him; she'd been on edge all day. So, it was about the house. He'd wondered what she planned to do with it. Now she and the teenage Lucy had moved to live with Drew Hamilton in the mortgage belt up by the old quarry, the old house they'd lived in together was standing empty. He regularly drove past it to check for the For Sale sign he fully expected to see. But, so far, it hadn't appeared.

It had been a year since Frank finally had to accept Marie had moved on. Until then, even though they'd separated, and he'd moved into the tiny flat above the café, he'd harboured hopes that maybe one day they could rediscover the love they'd lost. They still worked amicably together in The Bean Sprout, the café which had belonged to generations of Frank's family and, when Marie became guardian to her niece, Lucy, his hopes were raised, only to be rudely shot down again.

'Let me make us a couple of coffees and I'll join you.'

Almost automatically Frank fixed the coffees and took them across to a table where he joined Marie. It was strange to think she would soon be married to someone else. He and Marie had never been legally married at all, even though they'd lived together as man and wife for almost thirty years. But, despite everything, they'd still managed to remain good mates.

'I suppose you're going to tell me you want to sell the old place,' he said, gazing down into his cup, unwilling to meet her eyes. He knew the corners of his own held a bead of moisture. That house was part of his past, part of their past. It held so many memories. He'd hate to see strangers living there, to think of strangers in the kitchen he'd so carefully planned, their children running up and down the stairs as he'd imagined his own children doing – the children who'd never been born. When he and Marie separated, he'd been happy for her to stay there. It was where she belonged. But now…

'That's just it.' Marie pushed a dark curl out of her eyes. 'I can't imagine strangers there, any more than I expect you can. So,' she clasped her mug in both hands, 'would you like to buy it – to buy me out?'

Frank felt his mouth fall open. He hadn't expected this. But could he afford it? House prices had escalated since he and Marie decided to split their possessions, due partly to an influx of city people seeking a tree change.

'I don't…' he began.

'I don't need an answer right away. But Drew and I have discussed it. I don't need to get the top dollar for it. If you want it – and I suspect you do – then, I'm sure we can come to some arrangement. We can bypass the realtor for one thing.' She chuckled. 'Lucy would like it too. She's attached to the old place and could keep her old room there,' she added, referring to her niece who was fond of her Uncle Frank.

Frank scratched his head, then took a gulp of coffee. This was the last thing he'd expected. But he had to admit it did have some appeal. While he was happy living above the café, it was a small unit and he often felt the urge to spread out more than was possible there. He missed the big family kitchen in his old home, even though he could always use the café kitchen if necessary. 'What do you want for it?' he asked.

'We'd have to get a valuation. So, you're interested? Perhaps you could rent out the flat.'

Typically, Marie was already organising his life and, while it used to amuse him, during the past year he'd become accustomed to making his own decisions. He was aware Marie felt he interfered with her life even after they'd parted, but in his mind, it was the opposite way around. Now, she had someone else to organise, and here she was, up to her old tricks. But the idea wasn't without merit.

'Let me sleep on it. Get a valuation. Then we'll see.'

'Okay,' Marie said, rising to leave. At the door she turned. 'Thanks, Frank. I know this last year hasn't been easy for you. But I want you to know I appreciate the way you've handled things.'

'Get away with you. You know I only wanted you to be happy. That's all I ever wanted.' *Even if that meant letting you marry someone else.*

Once Marie had gone, Frank locked the door behind her and made his way upstairs. Entering the small flat, he looked at it with fresh eyes, imagining how it would be to move back into what he still regarded as their family home.

But how would it be without Marie? Would he enjoy living there on his own?

Three

It was two weeks since they had arrived in Granite Springs, and Peta was becoming accustomed to the slower pace of life. It was pleasant staying with Ann, and although set in ways, her cousin was very kind. But Peta knew she couldn't stay there forever. She needed to find a place where she and Lily could put down roots, not two rooms in someone else's home, even one as comfortable as this one was – though it could do with a makeover. Peta thought longingly of the house she'd left behind on Sydney's North Shore – its open-plan design, its modern furnishings, the wide windows overlooking the harbour, the carefully tended garden where she loved to sit on summer evenings – and sighed.

'Do I have to go, Grandma?' Lily's petulant voice interrupted her reverie. School began today and on Ann's advice, she'd enrolled Lily in Granite Springs Primary. When they visited the school the previous week, Lily had looked around, her eyes wide with fear, though they had lightened somewhat at the sight of the beautifully designed and carefully constructed playground equipment, and she'd appeared interested when the tour of the school reached the library. Peta had been impressed by the friendliness of the headmistress and the youthfulness of the woman who was to be Lily's teacher. She'd been pleased to see Lily's face lose some of its sad expression when Allegra Moretti spoke to her.

'I'm new to this class next term, too,' Allegra said. 'I've been teaching in the infant school up till now. So, we'll both be new together.'

Peta knew Lily would be in good hands. 'I'm afraid so, Lily,' she said now. 'But remember how kind Miss Moretti is? I think you'll enjoy it. There will be other children to make friends with, children who…' She bit the inside of her cheek to avoid what she had been about to say.

But Lily knew. 'They won't know about Mum, will they?'

Peta gazed at her granddaughter. She looked so grown up dressed in the school uniform of blue pants, white blouse and blue cardigan. She wanted to take her in her arms and give her a hug, tell her she could stay home for a few days longer. But Lily had already taken a seat at the table and was pouring cereal into a bowl.

'A big day, Lily?' Ann walked into the kitchen, dressed for work in a smart grey suit with a pink shirt. As always, she looked immaculate.

Peta felt dowdy in comparison, though there was no reason why she should. Since coming to Granite Springs, she'd avoided her usual fashionable city wardrobe, preferring to wear comfortable jeans with a warm sweater. Perhaps she should make more of an effort.

'Yes,' Lily said in a small voice, shovelling up her cereal and managing to splash milk everywhere.

Ann didn't say anything, but Peta sensed her disapproval. It must be difficult for someone who was used to living alone, to suddenly have to get used to having another adult and a small child sharing her space. But Ann never said anything to make them feel unwelcome. Now she said, 'I look forward to hearing all about it tonight at dinner. Why don't we have something special? I heard you like pizza.'

To Peta's surprise, Lily's eyes lit up. 'Pizza? Could we? Mum always…' Her voice died away, and a tear trickled down her cheek. 'I'm finished breakfast, Grandma.' She slid out of her chair.

'Remember to clean your teeth, and you might want to give your face a wipe, too,' Peta called after her, as she ran out of the room. She had to stop herself from following, knowing Lily would want to be alone.

'It can't be easy for you.' Ann said, 'But I think you're doing well. I know you must be grieving, yet you manage to put on a brave face when Lily's around. Are you getting any sleep?'

Peta poured herself a cup of coffee and leant her chin on her hand, surprised Ann was so perceptive.

'I don't say much, but I can see how exhausted you are. Why don't you try to have a nap when Lily's at school today? I can understand how you've felt you needed to be with her all the time up till now. But once she's at school, she'll be someone else's responsibility. You can take time for yourself. I bet you haven't had that since your daughter was …'

Peta saw Ann flinch rather than utter the word, and her eyes filled with the tears that were never far away. She blinked rapidly.

'You're right. Thanks, Ann. Perhaps I will. I had intended to smarten myself up and try to find a job, though I have no idea what I can do here.'

'The local paper comes out today. Why don't you have a look in it? There may be something, though…' she tapped a manicured finger on the table, '…probably not what you're used to. I'd help if I could, but the university is cutting back on the budget. It's been all I can do to prevent my own staff from being cut.'

'Oh, I'd never expect your help.' It was kind of Ann to consider it. Maybe she wasn't as rigid as she appeared to be – and she was kind to Lily, having hunted out some of her own old toys and books for her. 'The paper is a good idea. Thanks.'

Ann finished her coffee and rose to leave. 'Have a good day,' she said from the doorway. And don't worry about Lily. I'm sure she'll be fine.'

Peta gazed after Ann. Her cousin was continually surprising her. She gave the impression of being strict and unbending, old for her years, but underneath Peta was beginning to see a softness, one she kept well hidden. She suspected Ann was a harridan at work. She wondered what had happened to the gentle cousin she remembered meeting on those few occasions when they were both not much older than Lily. There was something nagging at the back of her mind; something she'd heard her mother say; something about Ann; some bad luck. But it was a long time ago and her mind refused to process it. It probably didn't matter, though it could perhaps explain why she gave the impression she did. Peta had the feeling Ann didn't allow many people to get close to her.

*

By the time they left for school, Lily had recovered from the mood she'd been in at breakfast, though she still clutched Peta's hand as if it was a lifeline – a lifeline that was about to be withdrawn.

Peta left her with Allegra Moretti who promised to introduce her to one or two of her classmates before classes began. She felt bereft, as if she'd lost another member of her family. She blew her nose and took a deep breath. Lily was only gone until three o'clock.

Was this how all mothers felt? Peta tried to remember her own feelings when Joy started school. But the situation was entirely different. Joy had been eager to taste the delights of the private Sydney girls' school in which Tony had insisted on enrolling her. She'd been a happy child, adventurous and ready for every new experience.

Just as Lily had been a few weeks ago. She was so like her mother it tore at Peta's heart. Every time she looked at the little girl, she was reminded of what she'd lost. Joy hadn't only been her daughter, she'd been her best friend. How could Peta have been so blind to what was happening to her? Sometimes she felt so consumed with guilt it was like a torrent of shame engulfing her. Given her own experience with Tony, she should have seen all was not well.

Following Ann's advice, Peta headed to the newsagents to pick up a copy of the Granite Springs Advertiser then, reluctant to return to the empty house, decided to peruse it over a coffee. The café she and Lily had visited the day after they arrived was at the other end of Main Street, some distance from where she was, and she remembered seeing another close to the library. She should go there, anyway and join for both herself and Lily.

She walked towards the café which was called Mouthfuls. At this time of the morning, it was almost empty. She ordered a cappuccino and found a corner table where she could examine the paper in private. She didn't hold out much hope as she turned to the back pages containing death notices, ads for cars, trailers, pets and sundry other goods – but the only offers of employment were for cleaners.

Peta sighed and took a sip of her coffee, letting the warm liquid flow through her, but this morning it failed to bring the customary sensation of wellbeing. She supposed she could become a cleaner, but she had hoped for something more… more what? More satisfying, she thought, something where she'd be interacting with people. Though as a cleaner, she wouldn't have to explain herself, explain why she'd moved here, explain what she'd done before. She took out her pen and circled the ad, deciding to think about it later. She still had some funds. She could afford to wait a little longer.

Leaving the café, she made her way across to the library as planned, provided the requisite information, and was issued with two library cards, one for her and one for Lily. Afterwards, she spent a pleasant hour or so wandering around the library and browsing the shelves before selecting the latest Erica James novel and an old one by Elin Hilderbrand she hadn't read. On the way out, Peta paused in front of a large noticeboard on which there were several fliers and posters advertising local events and seeking volunteers for a variety of good causes. As her eyes scanned them, she noted there was a local choristers' group, another devoted to knitting for several different charities, and a Friends of the Library group seeking people to deliver books to the housebound. There was also a Friends of the Gallery group seeking volunteers, to man the local art gallery. It seemed that, even if she was unsuccessful in finding a job, there would be plenty in Granite Springs to keep her occupied.

Peta made her way back to Ann's house – she couldn't call it home. Home was in Sydney. But she knew, if this move was to succeed, she needed to find a place to call home here in Granite Springs and immerse herself into what people called *a tree change*.

Making herself a sandwich for lunch, Peta decided to settle down to read one of the books she'd brought home. She chose a comfortable armchair in a sunny spot in the living room and was soon involved in the drama set on a beach in Nantucket. The time flew, and Peta was shocked when she checked, to discover it was almost three o'clock.

Dropping the book onto the coffee table, she shrugged on her jacket and headed out, hurrying along the street towards the school. Once there, she joined the groups of mothers at the school gate, feeling strange to be back in a role she'd outgrown many years ago.

As the children began to emerge from the building in groups of two and three, Peta held her breath hoping Lily had had a good day. Although she'd managed to keep herself occupied, the little girl was never far from her thoughts and despite her reassuring words to Lily, she knew it would have been difficult for her to start afresh.

Back in Sydney, Lily had a group of close friends with whom she shared playdates and sleepovers. But she'd had to leave all that behind. In addition to losing both her parents, she'd lost her home and all her friends.

As several children appeared and were led off by their mothers, and there was still no sign of Lily. Peta wondered if there was a problem. Should she go into the building?

'Are you a new parent?'

Peta looked around to see an elegant woman with silvery-blonde hair piled on top of her head. She was wearing jeans and a cowl neck sweater topped with a heavy jacket – much like Peta's own outfit. 'Grandparent,' she said, thinking the woman looked too old to be a mother of primary school children.

'Like me. I'm Jo Ford. I haven't seen you around town before now.' She held out her hand.

Another one! Peta sighed inwardly. Why did everyone want to be her friend? But this woman looked kind. There was something about her face that invited confidence. 'Peta Forrest, she said, taking Jo's outstretched hand. 'I recently moved to Granite Springs with my granddaughter. We're living with my cousin at the moment. Oh, here's Lily now.'

To her relief, and preventing her from answering any further questions, Peta saw Lily walking toward her, talking seriously with two other girls. She exhaled. Lily had made friends.

'Is that your granddaughter?' Jo asked. 'She's with my two. Lottie and Livvy are twins. They're eight. Your one looks the same age. They must be in the same class.'

At that moment, the three girls arrived, Lily running up to Peta to take her hand.

Before either Lily or Peta could say anything, one of the twins started speaking. 'This is Lily, Grandma, Isn't it funny? Lottie, Livvy and Lily. Our names all match. We think that's why Legra asked us to look after her. Lily's new in Granite Springs, and we have Legra for our teacher again this term because Mrs Barker left to have a baby. Isn't it cool?'

Peta was bewildered. Her expression must have shown it, because Jo laughed and said, 'Steady on, twins. This is Mrs Forrest. She's Lily's grandma and she's not used to two boisterous eight-year-olds like you.' She turned to Peta. 'Legra is Miss Moretti. She took care of them when she was a student, before she was appointed to the staff here. But they know they must call her Miss Moretti at school. It's very naughty of them to share their nickname for her.'

While she was talking, the twins, two cheerful girls with identical freckled faces, their blonde hair tied up in matching ponytails, were playing tag around their grandmother, while Lily huddled close to Peta and looked on, eyes wide, a faint smile on her face.

'Gramma, can Lily come out to Yarran on Saturday?' one of the twins asked. 'You said we could ask a friend sometime, and she doesn't know anyone else.'

'Please,' the other added, grinning and hopping up and down in excitement.

'I don't know.' Jo looked apologetically at Peta. 'These two get so excited and don't know when to stop. Yarran is our acreage. It's a few kilometres out of town on the north side. Col and I love it there and we have a few alpacas which the girls love to feed and lead around. I'm taking care of Lottie and Livvy this weekend. You'd both be most welcome. But perhaps you have other plans? I'd understand it you don't want to. But why not?'

Peta was about to refuse. She wasn't sure she was ready to make friends, which is what an invite to Jo's home entailed. She opened her mouth to give a polite rejection when she felt Lily tug on the hem of her jacket. Looking down, she saw her granddaughter nodding furiously. 'Would you like that, Lily?' she asked in surprise. Lily nodded again, this time smiling.

'Looks like the answer's *yes*,' Peta said, smiling too.

'Let me have your number and I'll text you directions. Come around eleven and we can have lunch.'

'Oh, there's no need.' But she gave Jo her number before the other woman turned away at the urging of her granddaughters who were pulling her towards a large green SUV.

'Can we go home to Auntie Ann's now, Grandma?' Lily asked.

'What? Yes, of course.' Peta had the distinct impression she'd been manipulated whether by Jo, her twin granddaughters or Lily, she wasn't quite sure. But at least Lily seemed to be coming out of the shell she'd built around herself.

'How was school?' she asked, as they walked back the way Peta had come.

'Okay. Miss Moretti asked the twins to be my buddies. They're funny. They try to fool everyone into getting them mixed up.'

'They're very alike.'

'But they're really different. Livvy is noisier and Lottie is the quieter one. It's easy when you work that out.' Lily gave a smug smile and Peta realised the little girl had smiled more in the past few minutes than she had in the past few weeks. Something today had worked its magic. It may have been the school, Miss Moretti, or the twins. Perhaps it would all become clear on Saturday. And Jo Ford did seem to be nice and determined to be friendly. It was at this point that Peta realised she herself was smiling.

Four

Lily was quietly excited at breakfast on Saturday morning. Peta, while pleased to see her take an interest in something, was feeling hesitant about the visit. What would she find to talk about? Would Jo Ford want to know more about where they'd come from and why they had moved to Granite Springs?

The murder had ceased to make headlines, but surely even in Granite Springs, the news would have been full of the doctor who'd killed his wife in a fit of rage – the man whose pattern of behaviour should have alerted Peta her daughter was at risk. In her low moments, when sleep eluded her, she blamed herself for not seeing what was happening, fuelling her guilt. If only she'd been aware of the canker in her daughter's marriage, if only she'd seen her own life being repeated.

In the light of day, she knew it wasn't the case. Men like Grant Holmes were devious. He'd been careful to keep his violent behaviour hidden and, of course, Joy had been too ashamed to tell anyone, especially her own mother. Peta knew all about that – the shame, the guilt. But she wished there had been something she could have done. And she wondered how much Lily had been aware of. The little girl seemed to love her dad, and Peta had never seen him be anything other than loving towards her.

She looked across the table at Lily who was now happily munching on a slice of wholemeal toast piled with mashed banana.

'The twins' grandpa has alpacas,' Lily said, between mouthfuls, 'I looked them up and they look really cute. Livvy says we can feed them and lead them around on a rope. Her grandma has a dog too,' she said a yearning note in her voice. 'Mum said we couldn't have a pet. It would make too much mess.' Lily pursed her lips. 'Do you think it's okay for the twins' grandma to have one because they live on a farm?'

Peta felt her eyes moisten. She hadn't known of Lily's longing for a pet. If she had, she'd have… But what could she have done? Maybe we can have one here,' she said. 'Once we have a house of our own.'

'Really?' Lily appeared doubtful, but there was a glimmer of hope in her eyes, making Peta determined to make her granddaughter's wish come true.

She nodded. 'Now, she said, 'if you can get ready quickly, we can make a trip to the library before we go out to see the twins. I have your library card right here.' Peta placed the card on the table.

Lily scooped it up with a grin. 'That sounds good. The twins told me about the library. They have lots of activities in the school holidays. Maybe I can go in the next holidays. Will we still be living here?' Her voice dropped to a whisper.

'Of course we will,' Peta said with more confidence than she felt, sorry Lily was feeling so insecure. But it was no wonder. She'd been uprooted from everything with which she was familiar. 'You do like it here?' she asked.

'Ye….es. It's very different from Sydney.'

'Good different?'

Lily pursed her lips, seeming to give the matter serious consideration before replying. 'I think so.' She paused. 'I like the twins. And Miss Moretti. And the cat in that bookshop we went to.' She thought again. 'And I want to see the alpacas and Lottie's grandma's dog. He's called Scout.'

Peta felt buoyed by the youngster's enthusiasm. 'You're right,' she said, 'there are lots of nice things here and I can't wait to see the alpacas too.'

*

After a successful trip to the library, during which Lily found a bundle of books she liked, they headed out of town.

The directions Jo had texted were very clear, and Peta enjoyed seeing more of the countryside around Granite Springs. Sweeping paddocks stretched on either side of the road, some with sheep grazing peacefully, while in one Peta saw a tractor in the distance perhaps engaged in planting. It was a far cry from the city landscape they'd left behind and provided a refreshing change.

But Peta could understand Lily's uncertainty. At the moment, it was a novelty, but how would she adjust to living in the country permanently?

The mailbox Jo described appeared on the left-hand verge, and Peta turned onto the narrow dirt road, her little car bumping along the ruts made by numerous other vehicles. She could imagine how muddy it would get in heavy rain, but it was lovely out here away from the town.

They came to a white metal gate. Peta jumped out to open it then bumped the car across the cattle grid before getting out again to close it and drive towards the ranch-style house.

'Look, there are the alpacas,' Lily called from the back seat. 'Don't they look funny with such long necks?' She pointed to the group of brown, fawn and white animals grazing in a corner of the paddock under what looked to Peta's inexpert eyes like a large peppercorn tree.

'They certainly do.' Peta steered the car to park outside the fence which ran around the house.

Two blonde bundles of energy came barrelling towards them, causing Lily to open her door and jump out. With a whoop of glee, one of the twins grabbed Lily's hand and dragged her towards the house.

'You made it.' Jo emerged from the house to greet Peta with a hug which made her feel uncomfortable. She wasn't accustomed to receiving hugs from strangers and, even though Lily had made instant friends with the twins, Jo was a virtual stranger to her.

'It's lovely out here.' Peta moved out of Jo's embrace to gaze around her. It was indeed beautiful. The green of the paddock stretched almost as far as the eye could see, another house only just visible along the lane. There was what looked like a large vegetable garden and a stand of fruit trees.

'Isn't it? It's my little piece of heaven. But it's cold. Come inside to the warm.'

Grateful for the invitation, Peta followed Jo along the veranda, past a rose garden her mother would have envied, and into the house where the three girls were already fussing over an old Golden Labrador who was suffering their attentions with surprising patience.

'That's Scout,' Jo said. 'He's an old dog and will put up with a lot. But he'll soon move off when he's had enough. Does Lily have a pet?'

'No. She'd like one but…' Peta bit her lip. She didn't intend to give too much away about their situation. '…we're staying with my cousin at the moment. Perhaps once we have a place of our own.'

'So, you intend to settle in Granite Springs. What brought you here?' She was interrupted by the arrival of a tall man wearing the requisite jeans and heavy knit sweater over a checked shirt – much the same as Jo's outfit.

He had a big grin on his face, and Peta saw how Jo's face softened at his appearance. It was a surprise. They weren't a young couple. She judged they must be in their sixties. How had they managed to remain married – and happily too, if the looks they exchanged were anything to go by. It was very different from Peta's own experience. But a lot of things had surprised her since she arrived in Granite Springs.

'This is Col,' Jo said, linking arms with him.

'And you must be Lily's grandma,' he said, stretching out his hand. 'Welcome to Yarran, It's been Lily this and Lily that since the twins got here this morning. They're particularly amused by her name – Livvy, Lottie, and now Lily.' He chuckled.

Peta shook his hand, laughing too.

'Now, what can I get you to drink? We have beer and wine, or would you prefer something soft? I'm having a beer myself and I expect Jo will have a wine.'

'A glass of wine would be nice, thanks. But I have to remember I'm driving.'

'One glass, then.' Col took two glasses from a cupboard, then headed to the fridge to fetch a can of beer and a bottle of white wine. 'Jo's baked a quiche for lunch, so I thought white?' He held up the bottle for their approval.

The three settled in the large open living room with their drinks, leaving the girls with the dog.

'So, Col began, 'Jo tells me you're new in town and staying with your cousin?' His eyes held a question.

Peta looked down into her glass. Here it came, the interrogation she'd been afraid of. 'Ann Baird,' she said. Jo and Col probably knew Ann or knew of her. The town seemed to be like that.

But Jo shook her head.

Col looked puzzled for a few moments as if he was trying to place the name, then he slapped his leg. 'Of course, she'd be Meg Baird's daughter. I was a local solicitor for all my working life,' he said somewhat apologetically to Peta. 'There weren't many of the locals we didn't have contact with at one time or another. She was one of my partner's clients, but I remember the name. She died a few years ago now, I seem to recall. Gordon, my partner, probably knows your cousin too.' He nodded as if glad to have placed her.

The three small girls ran in at that moment following the dog, who slunk behind the sofa.

'I think Scout's had enough, girls,' Jo said rising to her feet. 'It's time for lunch, then I believe Col has plans for you with the alpacas.'

Three pairs of eyes turned towards Col who nodded and smiled. 'We have to show them off to your friend. Have you met any alpacas before, Lily?' he asked. The now shy Lily shook her head, and dropped her eyes to gaze at her feet which seemed to suddenly have become very interesting.

Lunch was a cheerful affair at which Peta was pleased to see Lily come out of her shell again and respond to Col's teasing and Jo's gentle questions about school and her opinion of Granite Springs. After apple pie for the adults and ice cream cones for the children, Livvy – or perhaps it was Lottie – pulled on Col's hand.

'Can we show Lily the alpacas now, Grandad?'

'Let your grandad finish his lunch,' Jo remonstrated, but Col rose.

'I'll have no peace till we do this. You two enjoy your tea or coffee and I'll take the three of them out into the paddock to see if we can entice my beasts to be friends.'

Peta half-rose, but Jo waved her back to her seat. 'They'll be fine with Col,' she said, making Peta realise Lily hadn't shown any of her now usual fear towards the twins' grandfather. There was something about the man that instilled confidence, something Lily must have felt. Jo had it too. It was an indefinable quality. And the whole house seemed steeped in it.

Jo prepared two cups of Earl Grey tea and the two women took them into a cosy sun-filled room at the back of the house, from which they could see Col and the three girls with the alpacas.

They sipped their tea, talking of generalities. Peta learnt Col was Jo's second husband, and although they'd been friends almost all their lives, they had only been married a few years. *Perhaps that explained their obvious affection*, Peta thought. Peta had relaxed, deciding there had been no need to fear any intrusive questions when Jo took her by surprise.

'You appear to be on your own with Lily. Her mother?'

'She died.' Peta knew her voice sounded harsh.

Jo wasn't deterred. 'Oh, my dear. She's so young to have lost her mother, and you lost your daughter. I'm sorry to sound intrusive. Was it recent?' Jo's gentle voice and concerned expression were too much for Peta.

She nodded, too full of emotion to speak.

'Her father?'

Peta felt her eyes fill. She shook her head. For the first time since coming to Granite Springs she was unable to hide her tears. 'I'm sorry.'

'*I'm* sorry. It's okay if you don't want to talk about it. But if you do, I assure you whatever you say will go no further.' She handed Peta a tissue.

Peta wiped her eyes and scrunched the tissue up in her hand. To her surprise, she discovered she did want to unburden herself. She had the distinct impression Jo Ford was a woman who kept her word – and kept secrets. She wondered idly how many secrets the older woman held in trust.

'I don't know where to start,' she said at last.

Jo didn't speak, but laid a gentle hand on Peta's arm.

After a long pause, Peta began. It all poured out, all the things she'd been bottling up, unwilling to speak about – Tony, Joy, Grant, Joy's death, her guilt. 'So, there you have it,' she finished. 'I chose to run away for Lily's sake – and my own. I had to create a new life for us, and when Ann wrote offering us a place to go, I jumped at the chance.'

'I remember the case,' Jo mused. 'I felt so sorry for the family, but I didn't expect to actually meet you. What you've been through – I can't imagine. You must find Granite Springs a godsend.'

'It is, and I'm truly grateful to Ann for inviting me. But we can't stay with her indefinitely. Now I'm here, I'm not sure what I can do. I need to find a job. My savings won't last forever. My Sydney house hasn't sold yet, and Joy's money, her life insurance… It's tied up.'

'Mmm. What did you do in Sydney?'

'Interior design – hotels, large office buildings and the like. There wouldn't be much call for that here, but I'm willing to give anything a try – as long as I can be there for Lily when she comes home from school.' Peta gave a wry smile, glad the topic of conversation had changed. She was more comfortable talking about herself and practical matters. Reliving the past had exhausted her. She took a sip of her tea.

'Mmm,' Jo murmured again. seeming to be considering what Peta had said. After a pause she said, 'I might be able to think of something. Leave it with me. My son, Danny, Danny Slater, is in the real estate business, mainly on the development side. Let me talk with him.'

Peta looked at Jo. Did the woman really know what she was talking about? She had said she'd be willing to do anything, but she couldn't see herself selling real estate. Didn't you need some sort of qualification for that?

She chose not to reply. It was kind of Jo to think of helping her, even if it could come to nothing. She looked out of the window to see Lily and the twins walking back across the paddock with Col. 'Oh, they're coming back now,' she said. Even from this distance, Lily looked happy, skipping along beside her two friends. It was amazing, Peta thought, how in one week, these two little girls had managed to do what Peta hadn't in all the weeks since Joy's death. Lily was almost her old self again, despite an underlying sadness which might never entirely disappear.

'Grandma!' Lily threw herself at Peta when they all returned. 'I love the alpacas. They let me stroke them – they're so soft – and they ate a carrot right out of my hand. I wish…'

'We couldn't have one in town,' Peta said, pre-empting Lily. 'They need wide spaces like Jo and Col have here.'

'But you can come to visit again,' Jo said with a chuckle. 'Lottie and Livvy can't take one home to the town either.'

'I suppose,' Lily said, her lip sagging. 'But I can get another sort of pet? You promised.'

'I did. As soon as we have our own place.' It was all dependent on her finding work, then somewhere for them to live. Peta knew it was something she needed to give more attention to.

It wasn't till they were driving home, with a re-energized Lily chatting ten to the dozen behind her, Peta remembered Jo's comment about her son. It was kind of her, but Peta knew she needed to work out something for herself.

Five

Frank couldn't stop thinking about Marie's proposal. He pictured himself back home again in the old house, sitting in his old armchair, his feet up on the coffee table – with no Marie to tell him to take them down – a beer in one hand, the newspaper in the other. His idea of bliss.

But it wouldn't come without a cost. He'd be on his own. It was nothing new. He'd been on his own for a couple of years now, ever since he and Marie decided to go their separate ways. He'd never expected her to find someone else. Always, in the back of his mind, there had been the chance they'd get back together and, while he'd been happy to move out, to live above the café, he'd always considered the old Federation house they bought in their early twenties to be his home.

It had seemed Marie did, too, inviting him there for meals on a regular basis and permitting him to retain a key so he could come and go as he pleased. Not that he did, of course, but the possibility was always there – until she met Drew Hamilton.

Drew Hamilton – the principal at Granite Springs High, who'd come into their lives and turned them upside down. The trouble was, Frank liked him. He was one of the good guys, and he made Marie happy.

Frank scratched his head and took a swig of beer from the can he'd opened after a makeshift dinner of café leftovers. His life hadn't turned out the way he expected. Growing up, he'd wanted a life like his parents had. They'd married young and Frank was their only child.

When he and Marie took over the café from them, he'd imagined seeing the family business continuing through the generations, just as he'd taken over from his father who'd taken over from his. Marie shared his vision and they'd been happy. But, somewhere along the line, discontent had set in, the passion of their early years disappeared, and life descended into a dull routine.

They continued to work the café together – still did – but it wasn't the same. Could he recapture some of his earlier enthusiasm by returning to the house they'd chosen together?

Frank crushed the empty can and went over to the desk he'd set up by the window. It was a good aspect looking out as it did on Granite Springs Main Street which, at this time of the evening, was empty apart from a few students staggering home from the hotel. Firing up the computer, he glanced at his emails, surprised to see one from someone called Bertolli – his family name. Opening it, his eyes moved quickly down the screen. The writer, who claimed to be a distant relative of his father, was seeking help with his son coming to Australia, ostensibly to get him away from an unsuitable match.

It was certainly the weirdest email to receive but wasn't something Frank wanted to consider right now. He had enough on his plate without worrying about some relative he'd never heard of.

He moved to the internet where he investigated local house prices, then checked his bank balance and current mortgage rates.

His phone rang.

'Hi, Frank here.'

'Uncle Frank!'

Frank settled back in his chair, delighted to hear his niece's voice. At seventeen, Lucy considered herself grown up, but she still enjoyed chatting with him and could play a mean game of Scrabble. 'What's up, Lucy? Stuck with your homework again?' he joked, referring to the one time he'd been able to help her with an assignment.

'No! Has Aunt Marie spoken to you about the weekend?'

'About what?' he asked carefully, knowing full well what this was about.

'Well! She will. She and Drew are planning to go skiing. They want to be alone.'

He could almost hear the smirk in her voice.

'She said she'd need to talk to you about the café and looking after Jess and me. But we think…'

Frank chuckled to himself, he could guess what was coming. He was right.

'We think we're old enough to look after ourselves. We're seventeen and…'

'…you want me to tell her that?'

'I knew you'd understand. You're the only one who does understand us. You will, won't you, Uncle Frank?'

Frank almost laughed at the wheedling note in Lucy's voice.

'I'm sorry, Lucy. This time, I agree with Marie. I know how grown up you and Jess are, but…' He held the phone away from his ear as there was a loud yell of denial. 'Steady on, Lucy. You know how your aunt worries about you, and about doing the right thing by your mum.' He paused to let his words sink in. Lucy's mother, Marie's sister, had died leaving Lucy in her care, a mission Marie took very seriously. 'I'm thinking of buying the old house from her. She's given me a key. Maybe we can check it out together?'

Frank waited. It was true Marie had given back the key he'd returned to her when she and Drew became an item. But he'd had no intention of using it. It was sitting in his desk drawer as a silent reminder of the decision he had to make.

'Cool! You're really going to live there? Can I have my old room when I come to visit? And can we set one up for Jess?'

'One thing at a time,' he chuckled. 'I haven't decided what I'm going to do yet.' But as he finished the call, the idea was beginning to take root.

Six

It was four weeks into the school term. Since Lily was having a sleepover with her new best friends, Livvy and Lottie, Peta decided to spoil herself. Ann was off at a conference in Canberra for the weekend, something to do with the university. She'd started to explain, but Peta had been too tired to take much in. It was enough to know she'd have the house to herself and a whole day to do as she pleased.

But she knew time would hang heavy on her hands. She still hadn't managed to find employment and was beginning to worry about outstaying her welcome with Ann, though her cousin was good with Lily. It was a pity she had never married and had children of her own. She'd have made a good mother, and it would have softened that outer shell she donned with most people.

It was bad enough on school days, but then she had the morning walk to school with Lily and the three o'clock deadline to keep her sane. Today there was neither. She rose – later than usual – took a leisurely shower and dressed in her now usual attire of jeans and a sweater.

About to make breakfast, Peta remembered the café where she and Lily visited and where she'd had cappuccino and a delicious brownie. She decided to treat herself to breakfast there.

After a bagel with egg, cheese and bacon and a large mug of coffee, Peta felt ready to face the day. She paid her bill, then, seeing several other customers heading towards the cash register, she picked up her dirty dishes and carried them over to the counter. As she was placing them on the surface, one of the other customers handed her a twenty-dollar bill saying, 'Keep the change.' Peta started to say, 'I don't work here,' but the woman had disappeared.

She stood there wondering what to do, waiting until the line in front of Frank had all been taken care of. Then she handed him the twenty-dollar note. 'Sorry, Frank. One of your customers thought I worked here. Marie not in today? You seem rushed off your feet.' She was about to turn away, when she saw a speculative look in Frank's eyes.

'You wouldn't like to help me out for a bit? I'll pay you. It would be great if you could clear some of the tables and wipe them down. I can't do it all and everyone seems to have been drawn out by the lovely morning. Marie has gone skiing.' His brow furrowed and Peta thought he was about to say something more, but he pressed his lips together.

This wasn't how Peta intended to spend the day but, seeing how frazzled Frank appeared to be, she hesitated. It was only for a moment, but Frank seized on her hesitation. 'You'll find Marie's apron on the back of the kitchen door. No sense messing up your lovely outfit,' he said, before turning back to his next customer.

Peta looked down at her jeans and sweater, not sure anyone could call it a lovely outfit, then, with a sigh of resignation, did as she was told. She went through to the kitchen and soon reappeared in the black apron with *The Bean Sprout* emblazoned on the front. Oddly enough, she felt quite comfortable in it. It was as if, by donning the apron, she'd become a different person; as if all the worry about Lily fell from her shoulders and the Peta who'd been a high-powered interior designer whose daughter had been murdered had become invisible.

In her new role, she discovered the customers barely noticed her. She moved swiftly between tables, serving coffee, removing plates as if she'd been doing it all her life. It was a task requiring little thought. She was kept so busy she didn't have time to think about anything other than to check which tables were empty and which required more coffee. The morning passed in a flash and it was almost three o'clock before Peta had time to draw breath.

'Thanks a million. I don't know how I'd have managed without you.' Frank took a handful of dollar bills out of the cash register and handed them to an exhausted Peta.

'Don't you have anyone else to help – to step in when your... when Marie's away?' she asked, unsure of the pair's relationship.

'Well, Marie's here most days and Saturdays I usually have a couple of teenagers to help out, but today they...' He scratched his head. 'I didn't think we'd be so busy so I said they could have today off. I guess I miscalculated. So, I'm doubly grateful for your help.' He folded his arms and rocked on his heels gazing at her as if he was seeing her for the first time. 'You must be hungry. Why don't you take a seat and I'll bring you something to eat? How about a black bean and vegetable enchilada, and a cappuccino?'

Peta looked around to see the café was now empty. She looked back at the man whose eyes were twinkling with kindness. It was really very good of him. 'Thanks, I'd like that,' she said. 'But let me pay for it.'

'Nonsense.' He disappeared into the kitchen.

Realising she was still wearing the black café apron, Peta drew it off over her head, folded it and laid it on the seat beside her. Then she took out her phone to check for any messages from Lily, but there were none. She'd promised to pick her up at four, so could only assume she was having a good time. Peta hadn't met the twins' mother who had picked up all three girls from school the day before, but the fact she was Jo's daughter had put to rest any qualms Peta might have had about letting Lily stay overnight with a stranger.

'Here you are. You don't mind if I join you?' Frank slid two plates and two cups of coffee onto the table.

Peta shook her head, surprised when Frank then went over to put the CLOSED sign on the door and lock it. For just a moment, she felt a hint of panic, then dismissed it. He was only being sensible and what harm could come to her here?

'You don't have your daughter with you today.'

'My granddaughter,' she corrected. 'She had a sleepover with friends. I have to pick her up at four.'

'You're fortunate. Marie and I didn't have any children, we parted and now...' he sighed and spread his hands, '...she's about to marry someone else.'

Too much information.

Peta gazed down into her coffee cup. When she looked up, Frank was regarding her with concern.

'Is something the matter?'

'No.'

'Granite Springs is a small town. Word gets around. I hear you're staying with Ann Baird. She's your…?'

'A cousin.' She should have known. But it seemed he didn't know who she was, who Lily was.

'It can't be easy.'

'What?' *Had he guessed? What had he heard?* But she was worrying unnecessarily.

'Living in someone else's home.'

'No.' Peta exhaled with relief.

'I know Ann can sometimes come on a bit strong, appear uncaring, but she has a kind heart. She hasn't had an easy life.'

There it was again – the suggestion everyone's business was public property.

'She's been very kind to us.' Peta didn't want to elaborate.

'Good.'

They'd been eating while they spoke. Peta chewed the last mouthful of her enchilada and finished her coffee. 'Thanks so much. You've been kind. But I mustn't take up any more of your time.' She rose and carried the apron to the kitchen where she hung it up and picked up her bag. When she returned to the café, Frank was still sitting where she'd left him.

'I guess you're looking for work, too?'

Was he going to offer her work in the café? No, he already had Marie and the two teenagers he'd mentioned. She nodded and slung her bag over her shoulder, hoping to distract him.

'If you like, I can keep my ears open. I'm sorry I can't offer you anything here. You did well today.'

'Thanks.' Peta wanted to leave. She was embarrassed with how everyone seemed to want to help her. It was good of them, of course, but she was accustomed to making her own arrangements and didn't want to be beholden to others for what smacked of charity.

*

Peta drew a sigh of relief when the door closed behind her. She got into her car and drove to the address given to her by the twins' mother. Eve Tait lived farther from the centre of town in a part that was unfamiliar to Peta. It was a newer area, a street of modern homes quite unlike the older part of town where Ann lived.

She pulled up outside the house and took a deep breath, readying herself for yet another round of questions.

'Hello, you must be Lily's grandma.' The woman who opened the door was a younger version of Jo, her blonde hair cut in a sleek bob, and wearing a pair of designer jeans and a smart grey tunic.

'Peta.'

'I'm Eve. Mum told me about you, and the twins have been talking non-stop about Lily. Come in.'

'I hope she hasn't been any trouble,' Peta said, following Eve into the house.

'Trouble? You'd know trouble if you had my twins and…' A smaller version of the twins appeared behind Eve. 'This is Emily Rose.' She smiled down at the little girl, who looked to be around three and was grabbing hold of the edge of her mother's tunic. Then she raised her eyes to meet Peta's again. 'But they've been very good. We went to the park this morning and they've been busy in the twins' bedroom since lunch. Does Lily have a bike? Perhaps next time they could go for a ride together with Brad – that's my husband. He and the twins often go riding on a Saturday afternoon. He loads the bikes up on the back of the car and they drive to somewhere quiet.'

'Oh, I'm sorry if having Lily spoiled their afternoon.'

'Not at all, but I'm sure Lily would enjoy it. Here are the girls now,' she said, as the three came scampering down the stairs.

'Grandma!' Lily ran to hug Peta, whose arms automatically clasped her. 'I've had such a good time. The twins have a little sister and…' Her voice paused as she saw Emily Rose staring at her. 'Can I come again?'

'That all depends on Mrs Tait,' Peta said, releasing the little girl who joined her friends again.

'Eve, please. Why don't you come through to the kitchen? I was about to make smoothies for the children. I don't know about you, but I could do with a drink. Why don't you stay to dinner? We have it early on a Saturday. Brad has gone out to pick up a takeaway. I can call him to cater for a couple of extra. Pizza okay with you?'

After the café and now this, Peta was beginning to feel her life wasn't her own. She wanted nothing more than to go back to Ann's and enjoy a quiet evening with Lily. But her granddaughter was looking at her with such a pleading expression, and Eve was clutching her phone waiting for her reply.

What was it about the people in this town? But Peta realised Eve was only being hospitable. In the past few months, she'd become so insular, she'd all but forgotten how to behave in a social setting and how to accept friendliness. 'Thanks,' she said, to see Lily high-five one of the twins.

'How can you tell them apart,' she said, when the three had disappeared again with little Emily Rose tagging behind them.

'It's easier now they're grown,' Eve said. 'And Mum has always managed it, but they've pulled the wool over their grandfathers' eyes many a time – both grandfathers,' she said, laughing. 'Now, will you have red or white?'

'White please,' Peta said, taking a seat in the light, modern kitchen, not unlike the one she left behind in Sydney. She'd have one like this again, she vowed, as soon as her finances permitted. But first – she made a sudden decision – she would look for something to rent. She – and Lily – needed to have somewhere they could call their own, where Lily could have friends to visit and she could… Peta wasn't sure what she would do, but it would be good not to be subject to someone else's whims. While Ann was kindness itself, it was her house, not Peta's.

Dinner was a riotous affair, making Peta glad she only ever had one child to care for, but it was good to see Lily's cheeks rosy again, her eyes glowing with fun as she chatted and argued with Livvy and Lottie. Peta was also glad to see how Lily seemed to feel comfortable around Brad. She'd been worried the little girl's anxiety about men was going to extend to every man she met. But now she'd seen her accept both Col and Brad, she felt she could relax.

It was as she was leaving, Eve took her aside.

'Mum said she'd mentioned you to Danny,' she said. 'He wants you to drop into the office on Monday. Any time. He'll be there all day. It's Granite Springs Realty on Main Street.'

'I know where it is, but…' Peta's voice trailed away. She had no idea what Danny Slater had in mind and didn't fancy the idea of selling real estate. But she had to find something soon and it would be rude to dismiss any offer of help. Although this family had done enough to help her and Lily already. 'Thanks,' she said, aware she was always thanking someone for something these days.

Seven

Frank locked the door behind Peta and watched her walk along the road to her car. There was something about the small, slight, blonde woman that brought out all Frank's protective instincts. He shook his head as he made his way back through the café and set about clearing up for the day. His arrangement with Marie was for him to pick up the girls and bring them back here for the night. He knew they'd be up for a meal out, perhaps a pizza or a visit to the Thai restaurant Lucy and Jess were so fond of. It would give him a rest from cooking, and he certainly felt he deserved one after the busy day he'd had.

Thinking back on the day brought Peta Forrest to mind again. There was a story there. He couldn't believe she just left Sydney to arrive in Granite Springs on a whim. With her granddaughter too. He wondered what had happened to her daughter – and the child's father. The child seemed shy when they'd come in together, wary almost. Was it him, or was she like that with all strangers – or only all male strangers?

Putting those thoughts aside, he cleared the cash register and calculated his takings for the day before heading upstairs to shower and change. He made himself a coffee and gazed out onto Main Street, now deserted in the lull between the sports groups going home and those setting out for an evening's entertainment. From here, he had a good view of the centre of town with its war memorial, and out beyond to the river where he and Marie had spent much of their teenage years. But there was no joy to be had in reminiscing. Time had passed. They had changed and were no longer the people they'd been then. He'd always love Marie, love the years they had together. But she'd moved on, and he knew he must, too.

He sighed, then picked up his wallet and keys.

The trip out to pick up the girls took around ten minutes. It was a part of town that made him feel uncomfortable; reminded him he'd come from Italian immigrants and didn't belong among the academics and high-fliers who chose to live here. His ancestors had come to Australia between the wars, escaping from political unrest and economic problems. They had settled here in Granite Springs, originally as agricultural workers. Then his grandfather had saved enough money to set up in a small business, changed his name from Bertolli to Beattie and The Bean Sprout Café had been established.

Frank was proud of his heritage, of his hard-working lineage but he sometimes wondered if his laidback attitude had prevented him from doing something more with his life.

'Here you are!' Lucy bounded out to greet Frank as he stepped from the car. 'We've been ready for ages. How was the café today – busy?'

'It was. I shouldn't have given you two the day off.'

'You could have called.'

'It worked out okay. One of my customers stayed to help.'

Lucy raised an eyebrow. 'A customer?'

'You don't know her. Peta Forrest. She's new in town.'

'A new lady friend?' Jess asked, appearing behind Lucy in time to hear the end of the conversation.

Frank felt himself redden, remembering how he'd been thinking about Peta after she left.

'No way!' Lucy said quickly. 'Uncle Frank doesn't have time for women.'

'You thought that about your Aunt Marie and men, before she met Dad,' Jess said gleefully, only to have Lucy bump her shoulder.

'Uncle Frank's different. Aren't you?' she asked, turning her face up to Frank's.

'That's enough from you two. Do you have your overnight bags?'

'Right here.' Jess kicked two bags lying on the driveway. 'I'll lock up and we can go.'

'Can I drive?' Lucy asked, as Frank put the bags in the boot and

Jess hopped into the back seat. 'I haven't clocked up my hundred and twenty hours yet. Please, Uncle Frank,' she wheedled in the voice he'd had trouble refusing all her life.

'Not now. Perhaps we can all go for a drive tomorrow. What about you, Jess?'

'Jess isn't so bothered about getting her licence. She has Ryan to drive her places.'

Jess blushed, and the two girls waved to a tall boy in the neighbouring driveway.

Frank recognised him as Ryan Kerr, one of the group of young people who normally visited the café on Saturday afternoons when the girls were working. 'Your friends didn't come to The Bean Sprout today,' he said, as they drove off.

'They knew we wouldn't be there. And we were all at the game. Granite Springs High was playing Doonside out at the university campus. A group of us went out with Ryan,' Lucy explained.

'Right. How about we pick up a takeaway?'

'Can we go to the Thai Kitchen?' Lucy asked. 'We love the food there. Then there's a movie we want to watch on Netflix later. That okay with you, Uncle Frank?'

Frank agreed and drove towards the river where the restaurant was located.

*

After the meal and the drive home, Lucy and Jess made hot chocolate and popcorn and settled down in front of Frank's wide-screen TV. After a quick look at the movie which wasn't to his taste, he retired to his bedroom with a good book and a glass of merlot, deciding an early night was in order.

He was pleased Lucy appeared to have recovered from the death of her mother only a year earlier and the unexpected appearance of the dad she'd never known. But the girl had her head screwed on and her recovery had been helped along by meeting Jess when she started school here in Granite Springs. There had been a few blips along the way, not least of which was a scare with the police, but she'd come out of it all right and was now a regular teenager looking forward to leaving school and going to university, although he knew from Marie she still sometimes awakened in the night crying for her mother.

It was the university thing that worried him. With no children of his own, he'd always regarded his niece – the daughter of Marie's sister – to be family. He'd assumed she'd be the one to carry on the family business, to take over The Bean Sprout when he and Marie were too old to manage. But now Marie was marrying Drew Hamilton, he was unsure of her continued presence in the café and Lucy, while apparently happy to work there on Saturdays, showed no signs of wanting to make it her career. Quite the opposite. Over dinner she and Jess shared their plans to study in Canberra at the Australian National University when they finished school.

'It'll be lit, Uncle Frank,' Lucy said, her eyes glowing. 'My teachers think I can get a scholarship to study Environmental Science. Wouldn't that be great?' she asked excitedly, adding in a quieter voice, 'Mum would be pleased.'

So, his ideas for passing on the café had gone up in smoke in an instant. It made him wonder what it was all for, why he was busting his gut every day for a business which would die with him. Maybe it was time to bite the bullet and make changes in his life. He was only in his early fifties. He had a lot of years ahead of him, years in which to make a fresh start.

As his eyes began to close, the last thing he saw was the image of a dainty blonde woman with curly hair and a vulnerable expression looking up at him, her eyes filled with… what?

Eight

Peta dressed carefully on Monday morning, even though she was determined to reject whatever offer Danny Slater made. She knew she couldn't really afford to be too fussy, but the thought of working in sales set her into a panic.

'You look nice, Grandma,' Lily said, as she poured too much milk on the Coco Pops that were her current favourite. They might not be the healthiest of breakfasts, but Peta felt Lily deserved some treats after what she'd been through. There would be time enough to clamp down and insist on healthier options later.

'Very smart,' was Ann's comment as she hurried out.

Peta wondered why her cousin was always in such a hurry. The woman never seemed to relax. Surely her life at the university couldn't be so demanding? She glanced down at the navy pantsuit and white roll-necked sweater, pleased with her choice. At least she'd make a good first impression on this Danny Slater.

She dropped Lily off at school, waved to Eve Tait in the distance and decided to walk to the real estate office. This was something she was coming to enjoy about Granite Springs – the ability to walk to most places. Another big difference with living in a small town.

There was a chill in the air, and Peta wished she'd thought to throw on a scarf. Instead she quickened her pace to arrive at her destination almost out of breath. She stopped in front of the large glass window to recover, seeing the number of homes for sale and rent. Hopefully she'd be here as a customer one of these days – if she decided to stay in town.

Taking a deep breath, Peta pushed open the door.

'Can I help you?' A pleasant dark-haired, round-faced woman walked up to greet her.

'I'm Peta Forrest. I have an appointment with Danny Slater.' Peta tried to sound more assured than she felt, not sure why her normal confidence was deserting her.

'Sure. I think he's on the phone right now. I'll check.'

A tall, dark-haired man exuding confidence emerged from a corner office. Peta couldn't help thinking he looked nothing like his mother or sister with his sharp features and smooth smile. He must take after his father.

'I'll handle this, Cathy,' he said. 'You must be Peta Forrest. Come through.' He led the way into his office and gestured to a chair, taking his own seat behind a desk. He picked up a pen and began tapping it on the desktop.

'My mother told me about you,' he began.

Peta's heart sank. While she didn't want to work in real estate, she also didn't want to be offered a job on the basis of favouritism. She pushed against the back of the chair, straightened her shoulders and opened her mouth to speak.

But before she could utter a word, Danny said, 'Mum said you've worked in interior design. Can you give me a rundown on what you've been involved in?'

Too surprised to speak, Peta stared at him for a moment then she began, explaining her role in Sydney and itemising the projects she'd worked on most recently. On familiar territory, she found her confidence returning. She finished by naming several companies including one major hotel chain, all of which could be contacted for references.

Danny had stopped tapping the desk and was gazing at her with what appeared to be admiration. 'Wow!' he said, after a long pause. 'When Mum said you had experience in interior design, I thought...' He appeared embarrassed.

Peta almost laughed. She knew exactly what he had thought – she was a bored housewife who'd decorated her own home and perhaps those of a few friends.

He recovered quickly. 'Given your experience, I'm surprised you chose to relocate to Granite Springs. But Sydney's loss is our gain. Mum was right. You'd be perfect.'

Perfect for what? But Peta remained silent.

Danny continued, 'I'm in the process of developing a new suburb on the outskirts of town. It's to be upmarket to cater for the inflow of city people seeking a tree change – modern but still with a rural flavour. The plan is to set up a few display homes to entice buyers to imagine how their new homes could look. I've been toying with how I can do that without importing city expertise. And here you are, already here.'

Peta felt a tremor of excitement. He wasn't about to offer her a sales position she'd hate. This was a project she could do really well – and enjoy.

'Just a minute.' Without waiting for her response, Danny leapt from his seat and went out into the main office, to return with large sheets of parchment containing street and house plans. He laid them on the desk and started describing the project which he was clearly excited about.

As he continued to talk, Peta could see why. It was an ambitious plan, and one which she'd love to be part of. Who would have imagined that, here in the middle of nowhere, she'd be offered such an opportunity?

Danny had been expounding the virtues of the project for some time when he stopped and looked at Peta, his eyes filled with concern. 'You will do it, won't you?' he asked.

'Of course. I'd love to. I'll need to know your timeframe and budget, and what products can be sourced locally.'

'Sure.' He dragged a hand through his hair. 'You'll probably have to go to Canberra or Sydney for some items, but I'm sure you're more familiar with suppliers than I am. And there's a local guy who recently started up a soft furnishings business who's keen to expand. Maybe you could start there. Hell, I can't believe you just walked in.'

They talked a bit longer, setting the parameters for Peta and agreeing she'd work on a freelance basis invoicing him for hours worked. Danny even suggested she might look at setting up her own business, something it had always been her ambition to do, but proved impractical in the city.

When she left the real estate office, Peta's mind was in a whirl.

Danny Slater's excitement was infectious, but she needed a clear head to set out her own plans. She had a lot to thank Jo for, and to think she'd considered her to be intrusive and interfering. Wanting time to digest this, Peta saw The Bean Sprout Café across the way and headed over. A coffee was exactly what she needed, and perhaps a slice of something to go with it.

She pushed open the door to see the café was almost full, groups of mothers with prams jockeying for space with older women taking a break from their shopping. She ordered a cappuccino and a slice of some delicious looking banana bread and, finding a free table in the far corner slid into it with relief.

This morning Frank was busy at the espresso machine and it was Marie who took her order and subsequently delivered it.

'You're looking happier today,' Marie said, as she set down the coffee and sweet treat. 'Are you enjoying life here in Granite Springs?'

Peta remembered, last time they'd spoken was just after she and Lily had arrived, when she was wondering if she'd done the right thing and worried their past would become common knowledge. 'Yes, thanks. I think I've just landed myself a job.'

'Congratulations! What is it you do again?'

'Interior design.'

'Here in Granite Springs?' Marie sounded dubious.

'With Danny Slater.' Peta didn't think there was any need to keep it secret. 'But I'm thinking of starting up my own business. Do you think I'll find any other takers?' She raised her eyebrows, eager to get Marie's opinion. She'd lived here all her life and would know the town and its residents really well.

'Well…' Marie glanced around and, seeing all the other tables were busily eating, took a seat opposite Peta. 'If you'd asked me a few years ago I'd have said no. But things are changing, the town is changing. There's a new vibe about the place, a lot of new people coming in from Sydney and Melbourne. I should know, I'm about to marry one.' She chuckled. 'I could use your services, myself. Drew's house badly needs a revamp. Men!' She thought for a moment. 'There's a new hotel going up on the road into town. Do you do them, too?'

If Peta's mind had been in a whirl when she walked in, it was now turning somersaults. 'I have done. But I can't think straight at the moment. I need to…' She mentally ticked off all the things she'd need to do to get started. And one thing was space, space to spread out, to keep her paperwork, samples, perhaps a few odd items to… But she was getting ahead of herself. 'I need to find somewhere to live before I can set myself up properly,' she said, almost to herself.

'I know!' Marie was off like a shot, leaving Peta gazing after her to see her chatting animatedly to Frank and gesturing towards Peta.

When she came back, Frank was with her.

'Tell her, Frank.' Marie nudged him with her elbow then, as a customer called from another part of the café, she left.

'Marie tells me you've found some work. I'm happy for you.' Frank's eyes twinkled in the way she remembered.

He was such a kind and considerate man. But this didn't explain why he was standing at her table looking awkward.

'Marie suggested you might be looking for somewhere to live and… I remembered what you said on Saturday.'

Peta racked her brain. What had she said? Saturday seemed so long ago. Was it only two days since she'd been here helping out?

'About living in someone else's space.'

Peta reddened. She hadn't meant to suggest she was unhappy at Ann's. Word seemed to get around Granite Springs so quickly. Ann had been good to her and Lily. She'd hate her to think Peta was ungrateful. What exactly had she said?

'Oh, you didn't say anything against your cousin. But now you've got this work with Slater, Marie thought…'

Get on with it.

'The thing is… I'm looking to buy Marie's house – what was our house – now she's moved on.'

Peta must have looked puzzled because he added, 'I'll be moving out of the flat above here. It's not much and is the same vintage as the café, but there are three bedrooms and a good-sized living area. If you're looking for somewhere to rent, maybe…' he said diffidently, as if expecting her to refuse.

Peta didn't know what to say. It was so unexpected. When she was gazing into the real estate office window, she'd scanned homes to rent but the few available were larger than she needed right now, and the rents were more than she was prepared to pay. 'How much?' she stuttered at last. Today was proving to be full of surprises.

'If the place suits you and your granddaughter, I'm sure we can settle on an arrangement that works. I can't let you see it now, but if you'd care to come back after we close, I can show you round.'

Peta just stared at him.

'We close here at three then have to clear up, so perhaps after four?'

When she'd finished her coffee, Peta paid her bill and left, still stunned by Frank's suggestion. Did she want to live above a café? It wasn't something she'd even considered. She'd been thinking more along the lines of a small townhouse or a unit in a small block. But there was nothing available.

She supposed it wouldn't do any harm to have a look.

Nine

'I'm not sure it's such a good idea.' Frank said to Marie when Peta had left. 'The poor woman seemed a bit shocked when I mentioned it.'

'It's a perfect solution.' Marie put a hand on Frank's arm. 'You are going ahead with buying the old place, aren't you?'

Frank gazed at the woman who used to be the centre of his whole existence, surprised to find those feelings had gone, to be replaced with ones of warm friendship. He remembered how visiting the old place, as Marie referred to it, with Lucy yesterday felt like coming home; how he'd decided there and then to arrange the finance to make it happen. He'd even set up an appointment with the bank for later today, planning to duck out after the lunch trade was over. But he hadn't decided what to do with the flat, not till Marie pushed him into it. It seemed that not content with forging a new future for herself, she intended to make over his life for him, too.

'I suppose,' he said, feeling she was taking advantage of the laidback attitude he'd always had to life. It was a good idea, but he'd have preferred to take his time about it, to mull it over, consider the pros and cons. The appointment with the bank was to be a token gesture. What if the necessary finance wasn't forthcoming, if he couldn't get a mortgage? Where would that leave him? He didn't want to appear a fool in front of Peta Forrest who had certainly perked up since he first saw her.

He sighed. Perhaps she'd find the flat too small for her needs, decide she couldn't bear to live in such a central location. He loved it here, but not everyone wanted to be in the centre of town, right on Main Street. It did tend to get a bit noisy on Saturday nights when the hotel patrons tumbled out, especially during the university semester.

'I've asked Gordon Slater to draw up the contract,' Marie continued, undeterred by his hesitation. 'I thought around the $500k mark, but you should get your own valuation.' She looked concerned. 'I really hope you can manage this, Frank. It would mean a lot to me – to think it wasn't going out of the family. It holds so many memories.'

For a moment, Frank thought he saw a wistful glint in her eyes, then it was gone. It was a bit rich for her to be sentimental about the house she'd been quick to leave, but it held memories for him, too. Good ones. And it would be nice to live there again. Despite being comfortable above the café, it had always felt temporary. It made sense to rent it out, and Peta Forrest was looking for somewhere to live.

He wished... Damn it! Frank wished he'd been the one to think of it first, not Marie. And he'd been disappointed in Peta's reaction. She was so vulnerable, he wanted to help her, her and the granddaughter who looked so like her.

The café became busier, and there was no time for Marie to make any other suggestions, or for him to think of anything but the job in hand. It wasn't till Gordon Slater, their solicitor, dropped in for a quick bite to eat and a coffee, that Marie nudged him again.

'I can let you have a copy of the contract tomorrow. Do you want to deal with Gordon too, or go to Bruce Jenkins?' she asked, referring to the other solicitor in town.

'Let me think about it.' This was all happening too fast for Frank, someone who tended to move slowly and surely. Once he'd made a decision, he didn't falter but he didn't like change. It had been a big deal when he and Marie broke up several years ago but, after an initial angst, he'd settled in above the café quite happily. To reverse the process – without Marie this time – wasn't something he wanted to rush into. But he had to be fair to Marie. The house was sitting empty and if he didn't buy it, he had no doubt there would be a line of others waiting to take his place.

'Don't take too long,' she said with a grin, as she collected a plate of calzone and salad and breezed off to deliver it.

The appointment at the bank had gone better than he expected, and he walked out with the assurance he was eligible for the necessary mortgage, though the size of the repayments caused him a few moment's anguish.

Three o'clock finally came. Frank breathed a sigh of relief as he placed the closed sign on the door and set about his daily task of checking the takings and cleaning the espresso machine, while Marie wiped down the tables and mopped the floor.

When she finally left with a knowing nod to the ceiling, Frank made his way upstairs to his present home. A quick glance around showed him it was in an unusual state of disarray. Living on his own, it was easy to keep the place clean and tidy. Being of an orderly mind, he liked it that way. But this weekend, he'd been entertaining two teenagers, so his normal immaculate living room and kitchen looked as if a bomb had dropped, while the bathroom still showed signs of their presence with wet towels lying across the bath and shower rail, and the remains of makeup in the sink. At least his bedroom and ensuite were undisturbed.

*

There was a timid knock at the door, and Frank could hear a high-pitched child's voice. He took one last look around the living room to check he'd managed to remove most of the mess before opening the door.

'Hello,' Peta said awkwardly. 'Are we too early?'

'Not at all. Come in. I've just been doing a bit of clearing up. I had my niece and her friend here all weekend and they're not the tidiest of guests.' He threw the door open wider to allow Peta and Lily inside.

They walked in and stood in the middle of the room. Peta looked around while Lily hung onto her hand.

Frank remembered how the girl had seemed afraid in the café and wondered what caused it. Was there something about him that instilled fear in her or was she naturally timid. He remembered what Lucy had been like at her age. She'd been lively and curious, into everything. She'd have been running around by now, chattering ten to the dozen.

Now, Peta said, 'Lily, this is Frank. Remember him from the café?'

He served us hot chocolate. He's a good person and he may be allowing us to live here in his flat.'

'Will he…?' Lily's eyes grew wide.

'He won't be living with us.' Peta smiled at Frank. 'Lily is a little bit unsure of men at the moment, but she'll get used to you.'

Frank smiled at the girl. 'I'm not a monster, Lily.'

But Lily flinched.

Frank continued, 'I have a niece who was just like you when she was your age,' he lied, in the hope of making her feel better.

'What's her name?'

'Lucy. She lives with her aunt who you met in the café, too. And she visits me sometimes.'

'How old is she?'

'She's seventeen now, quite grown up – or thinks she is.' He turned to face Peta again. 'Would you like to see the rest of the flat?'

'Yes, thanks.' She released Lily's hand, and the little girl, now seemingly feeling a little more at ease in his presence, ran over to look out the window.

'Look, Grandma! You can see right along the street from here. I can see that bookshop we went to, and the grocery store and…'

Peta gave a wide smile, making Frank wish it had been him who'd managed to generate it. She was pretty when she smiled. Her whole face lit up. He felt a tinge of something he hadn't felt in years, a tingling he used to feel when Marie… He stifled the memory. 'This way,' he said, leading Peta and a subdued Lily through the rest of the flat.

Back in the living room again, Lily said, 'Can we really live here? It feels safe.'

Thinking it was a strange word to use, Frank asked, 'Will it suit you, do you think? I know it's not to everyone's taste. But it is secure, and I'd only want…' he named the figure he'd worked out which would enable him to meet the requirements of his mortgage and which he hoped would be within Peta's budget.

'Would you like to live here, Lily?' Peta asked.

'Yes, please. It would be just us?' There was a note of concern in Lily's voice.

There was that fear again.

'Just us,' Peta confirmed.

'Could I…' Lily looked up at Frank, her wide blue eyes so like her grandmother's. 'Could I have a pet here or would it make too much mess?'

'Lily!' Peta's eyes signalled an apology.

'I don't see why not,' Frank replied, scratching his head. 'Though it would have to be one that didn't mind living cooped up. 'As long as your grandma agrees.'

Lily looked up at Peta.

'We'll see. We have to arrange to move in first. When…?'

Frank shuffled his feet. He hadn't thought so far ahead. 'Can I get back to you? I need to check out a few things.'

'Of course. Sorry.'

'No need to be sorry.' It suddenly occurred to him he wasn't sure what he was going to do with his furniture. The house was still practically fully furnished. Marie had only taken a few items with her, those she said she couldn't live without, but he had no idea what she intended to do with the rest. 'Furniture,' he said. 'I could probably leave some.'

'Could you?'

This time it was Frank who made her eyes glow. He felt something stir inside.

'All of mine is in my house in Sydney. The realter thought it would sell more easily if I left it. I will bring it here eventually of course, but…'

'Let me get back to you on that, too. There's a good auction place here if you need to buy a few pieces. They don't cost much.' He felt awkward talking like this about money, as if assuming she didn't have much to spare. But there was something about her, about the way she'd turned up in town, the way she seemed well-heeled and yet vulnerable. He wondered what she was running away from.

'Right. Thanks. I'll wait to hear from you, then?'

'Let me have your number and I can call or text.'

Peta reeled off her number, and Frank keyed it into his phone.

'We'd better be going,' she said, taking Lily by the hand again. 'Thanks, and I look forward to hearing from you.'

As he closed the door behind them, Frank could hear Lily asking, 'Why is that man letting us live in his house? Doesn't he want to live there anymore? It'll be fun living above a café. Can we eat there all the time?'

He smiled. He had a good feeling about this, a good feeling about Peta Forrest and her granddaughter. Who was he kidding? It was the grandmother, not the granddaughter he was interested in getting to know better, and what better way to do it than having them living right upstairs from his place of work?

He thought back to something Marie said that bothered him. She thought Peta looked familiar. But how could she? She said she'd never been to Granite Springs before now.

Ten

Lily skipped along beside Peta as they made their way back to Ann's house. She was full of questions about moving in above the café, most of which Peta was unable to answer.

'Wait till I tell Livvy and Lottie,' she said. 'They'll be so jealous. And can I really get a pet?'

Peta sighed but was forced to admire her determination. 'Perhaps,' she said. 'But I don't think a dog would enjoy being cooped up there. Dogs need space to run around.' She tried to think of a suitable pet, immediately discarding with a shiver the mice and guinea pigs which came to mind. 'Maybe a goldfish?' she suggested.

The look on Lily's face said it all.

'Well, perhaps not.'

'I know,' Lily said, hopping up and down. 'A cat. A cat like the one in the bookshop. I liked him and he liked me.'

'Mmm. Let me think about it.' A cat was certainly a possibility, but where would they find one? Peta hadn't seen a pet shop in town.

They arrived back just as Ann was getting out of her car.

'A successful day?' she asked.

'I think so,' Peta said with a grin. 'Full of surprises. We may not need to depend on your hospitality for much longer. I have a lot to tell you, but I'll wait till we're inside with a cuppa.'

Once inside, Lily ran to drop her school backpack off in her room, returning just as Peta was finishing telling Ann about her offer of employment and the flat. 'The flat is very nice,' she said. 'Although it's in the centre of town, it seems very secure.'

'It should be. I remember Frank Beattie's parents lived there when we were growing up and I know they were very security conscious. You should be right in the flat. There's no chance of…?' She raised an eyebrow.

'None.' Peta looked warily at Lily, but the little girl didn't appear to be listening, more intent on taking a carton of orange juice from the fridge. 'That's all taken care of.' Grant Holmes was safely tucked up in Long Bay having been denied bail. It could be many months before he was brought to trial – a trial she hoped would see him kept there for the rest of his life.

'And this work with Danny Slater – it sounds right for you. But won't it be short term?'

'Yes.' Peta felt her bubble of happiness begin to collapse, then reminded herself what Marie had said. 'But evidently there's a hotel chain which will be looking for someone to design their interior. Danny suggested I work freelance, set up my own company. It's something I've always wanted to do. *Forrest Interiors.*' She savoured the sound of the name.

'That's not a bad idea.'

Peta stared at Ann, surprised at her support.

'You probably shouldn't restrict yourself to Granite Springs. We're so close to Canberra and with your experience…' She waved a hand in the air. 'And I bet there are a few moneyed locals who'd give their eye teeth to say they've had their place professionally done over. You could become the new in-thing.' She chuckled. 'I think this calls for a celebration.'

Peta stared again at Ann who was taking a bottle of wine from the wine rack and two glasses from a cupboard. She was surprised to see this side of her normally stiff cousin. Was she seriously pleased for her, or just glad they were going to move out?

*

Next day, Peta had a lot to do. Before going to sleep, she'd made a list of things she needed to talk about with Danny Slater. But first, she wanted to drive out to the site of the new development to get a feel for the place. She'd always been of the opinion design had a lot to do with location. Her gut told her it was even more important in this instance.

After dropping Lily off at school, Peta drove out of town to where the large *Slater Development* sign might have been a blot on the landscape to some locals, but which signified a new start to her. She stepped out of the car and walked around the deserted area, work still to begin. It was a good location, the land flat, with a couple of dams which Danny intended to widen into manmade lakes, and a good stand of gums in one corner. The blocks would be equally distributed between residential and one acre lots, allowing for different tastes and budgets. It would be designed for the high end of the market.

Satisfied, Peta drove back to Ann's. Now she was alone, she spread the plans Danny had given her out on the dining room table, her heart quickening with the excitement a new project always gave her. She'd enjoy this one which, hopefully, would be the first of many for *Forrest Interiors*. Her excitement bubbled again.

Opening her computer, Peta searched to ensure the name hadn't already been taken, completed the necessary form to register her new business, then leant back taking deep breaths to savour the moment. How she wished she could share it with Joy. Her happiness dimmed and a tear came to her eye, grief threatening to overwhelm her again as she thought of the daughter who'd never know her mother was finally realising her dream.

After a hasty lunch, Peta spent the afternoon on the computer, making contact with suppliers she'd used before and researching those she could find locally. She wanted to have some firm ideas and samples of materials ready for her next meeting with Danny Slater. She guessed she should also set up an appointment with a solicitor to ensure she was doing all this properly. And there was something else she wanted a solicitor's advice on, something she hadn't thought of herself, but Ann mentioned last night after Lily was asleep.

'Have you thought of whether you need to adopt Lily?' she asked, as the two of them enjoyed a final glass of wine.

'Adopt? But I'm her grandmother. Surely I don't need to adopt her?'

'I'm not sure,' Ann said, 'But it wouldn't do any harm to find out. Though if, heaven forbid, her father managed to be declared innocent, I guess he'd have first call on her.'

Peta shook her head and folded one hand against her stomach, as if by doing so she could stop the flood of fear threatening to engulf her. She couldn't let Lily go back to her father, she just couldn't. If only Joy had confided in her, there would be no need for this. Her daughter would still be alive, they would all still be living in Sydney – Peta's house was big enough for all three of them – and Lily wouldn't regard strange men with suspicion.

'Well, it may never come to that, but it's best to be prepared.'

Ann was right. Peta had left Sydney with Lily without considering any of the possible legal implications. It wouldn't hurt to check it out. Ann had also recommended a solicitor. Gordon Slater was Danny Slater's father and Peta recalled Col Ford mentioning they'd been partners. Two recommendations for the father of the man who'd offered her work was good enough for her. She'd call to make an appointment.

*

By the time she picked Lily up from school, Peta was feeling pleased with what she'd accomplished. She had set up an appointment with the solicitor for two days hence and had a rough outline of the theme she'd settled on for Danny's display homes. Being on site had given her an idea. She planned to base her décor on the natural surroundings – the green of the gum leaves, the silvery-grey of the bark and the red of the soil. She could visualise it so clearly. It would provide the tranquil ambiance the out-of-town buyers were coming to the country to find. Hopefully, Danny would agree.

The sight of Lily bouncing out to meet her brought a tear to Peta's eyes. She had adjusted so well to the changes in her life, and now Peta was about to subject her to another. But she knew it was the right thing to do. They couldn't live with Ann forever and even though a move to Frank's flat was to be a temporary arrangement, it would give them breathing space.

Lily had almost reached her when her phone pinged with a text. Pulling it out of her pocket to take a quick glance, Peta saw it was from Frank.

All sorted this end. Can you come into the café tomorrow to finalise arrangements? Frank Beattie.

As Lily arrived to give her a hug, Peta thrust the phone back into her pocket. It was a relief to have confirmation her move could go ahead. As they walked back home, Lily chattered away about the day's events and the exploits of the naughty twins which had the entire class in laughter. While one part of her was listening to her granddaughter, another was trying to work out what needed to be done before they could move into the flat.

Armed with her news, Peta decided to cook a special meal for dinner as a way of thanking Ann for her hospitality. She also planned to take her out to dinner before they left, having noticed a few nice restaurants around town.

'This smells good, Grandma.' Lily slipped into the kitchen and peered into the dish on the stove. 'What is it?'

'I'm making a special dish your mum loved. It's chicken with red grapes and marsala. That's why we stopped off on the way home to buy chicken and grapes. Ann already had a bottle of marsala. What you can smell is the marsala bubbling in the pan with the chicken. When this part is done, we'll wait for Ann to get home, then pop it in the oven.'

'Yum. I don't remember Mum making it.'

'No, she probably didn't.' Joy hadn't enjoyed cooking as much as Peta did. She'd never been able to encourage her daughter to try out new recipes. And Grant had been a meat and two veg man who didn't like what he called fancy dishes.

'I like chicken nuggets. Is it like that?'

'Not exactly,' Peta stifled a smile, 'but I think you'll enjoy it. Maybe you'd like to learn to cook once we move?'

'I'd like that. Mum was going to teach me to make cookies before…' Her eyes filled with tears.

Peta pulled her granddaughter into a warm hug, her own eyes filling. It was damnable the way grief could creep up on you when you least expected it. And she'd learned it was best to give in to it. In the early days, immediately after Joy's death, she'd tried to put on a brave face for Lily but all it did was push the sadness further inside her where it sat like a canker waiting to erupt.

Now she said, 'It's okay to cry, Lily – to be sad. What happened to your mum was a terrible thing. But she wouldn't want you to be sad all the time.'

'I'm not.' Lily looked up at Peta, her eyes red and still filled with tears. In a broken voice she said, 'When I'm with the twins it's easy to be happy. Then I remember about Mum and I feel guilty for being happy when she can't be. Is that wrong?'

'No sweetie.' Peta hugged her tighter. 'It's only natural. But there's no need to feel guilty. Your mum wouldn't want that, would she?'

'No…oo.' Lily scrubbed her eyes with her fists making them redder than ever.

Peta dropped a kiss on her head. 'Why don't you go and wash your face. Then you can help me by setting the table. See if you can find some nice napkins and candles to make it special.'

'Okay, Grandma.' Lily brightened somewhat and trundled off to do as she was bid.

Peta watched her leave, her eyes still filled with unshed tears. If only she didn't look so much like her mother. But Peta knew it was one of the things she loved most about her granddaughter. It was as if she had the young Joy back again, only this time, there was no Tony to worry about, to have to protect her from. Though her husband had never been violent towards their daughter – it was Peta who bore the brunt of his anger – she'd always been afraid he might be.

Ann's arrival curbed her dark thoughts.

'Something smells good,' Ann said, walking into the kitchen and carefully placing her bag on a chair. She did this as meticulously as she did everything else.

Peta sometimes wondered if her cousin ever acted spontaneously. She seemed to keep herself under tight control.

'Are we celebrating again?' She glanced through to the dining room, where Lily was laying three places complete with red napkins and had placed a thick candle in the middle of the table.

'Looks like we've got the flat. Frank Beattie texted me and I've to meet him tomorrow to go over the details. So we may be out of your hair soon.'

'There's no rush. You're most welcome here.' But as Ann picked up her bag again before heading out of the kitchen, Peta noticed her eyes travelled to the corner where Lily had thrown her backpack.

Dinner was a cheerful affair. Afterwards, they all sat together in the living room, Peta and Ann reminiscing about their very different childhoods. Peta had grown up in the city and Ann right here in Granite Springs.

'You never wanted to leave?' Peta asked, as Lily listened wide-eyed to their stories.

Ann's eyes clouded over. She gave a bitter smile. 'No,' she said tight-lipped. 'I couldn't leave Mum.'

The mood was spoiled, and soon afterwards Peta sent Lily off to bed, promising to follow to kiss her goodnight. She took this opportunity to retire herself, claiming to be tired after her busy day.

But once Lily was fast asleep and Peta lay down, she couldn't rest. Who'd have thought the decision to come to Granite Springs would provide so much opportunity? On a whim, she drew a notepad and pen from her bag and began to doodle. Before long, she'd roughed out a logo for her business, using the same theme of gum trees as she'd chosen for Danny's display homes, this time including branches and leaves encircling the name of her new business.

Satisfied, she finally felt her eyes begin to close and let the pad and pen drop to the floor. She just managed to turn off the bedside lamp before falling asleep to dream of a big man with deep brown eyes smiling down at her.

Eleven

Frank pressed *Send* and stared at the blank screen. Had he been too abrupt, sounded too formal? He shrugged. He wasn't in the habit of sending texts to anyone but Marie and Lucy and his usual ending with x would hardly have been appropriate. But should he have included his surname or just signed it as Frank? He shoved the phone back into his pocket. He was overthinking this. It was only an arrangement to rent out his flat.

There was something about Peta Forrest that brought all his protective instincts to the fore. He knew nothing about her, but felt she'd suffered, was still suffering. It made him want to do whatever he could to make her happy. He'd seen how her face lit up when she smiled. He wanted to be the one to bring that smile back.

He returned to his daily task of cleaning up. People who fantasised about owning a café didn't consider all the mundane tasks involved. It wasn't all about serving coffee and chatting to customers. A lot went on behind the scenes. That was why he and Marie worked so well together. She understood, always had.

Not for the first time, Frank wondered if her marriage to Drew Hamilton would make a difference. Their relationship hadn't suffered up till now, but time would tell. He'd hate to have to work with someone else, someone he'd have to train up. He'd never had to do that with Marie. She'd slipped into her role in the café as if she'd been born to it as he had.

He paused, his hand on the espresso machine he was cleaning. He remembered how they'd returned from Bali, tanned and full of news of their secret marriage to find his dad had taken a turn for the worse and his mother, devastated at the thought of losing her life companion, was in no fit state to work. He and Marie had taken over the running of the café and continued to this day.

His father had died a few weeks later, and his mother had barely survived the year without him.

Frank had thought he and Marie would be like that, all the way to the very end. It wasn't to be. He was glad Marie had found someone, someone to love who loved her the way Frank had in the beginning. But it left him feeling so alone. Perhaps moving back into the house would help, or would it make it worse? Would he rattle around alone in the big empty space?

Frank sighed and gazed around the empty café. Marie had left early today, something she was doing more and more these days. It was only natural she wanted to be with Drew, Lucy and Jess, though the two young ones were more likely to be pursuing interests of their own. He turned off the lights and headed upstairs.

*

Frank felt excited as he set up next day, the thought of seeing Peta again filling him with an unexpected sense of anticipation.

'You're looking particularly cheerful this morning,' Marie observed, as she carried in the boxes of goodies she'd baked that morning. The home-baked concoctions were a popular draw for the café, and when Marie moved in with Drew, Frank had worried Marie wouldn't find time to bake before arriving for work. So far there had been little difference, even though some mornings she arrived empty-handed and set to baking in the café kitchen. He had no problem with that, the aroma from the oven filling the café just as it used to in the early years they were together, when they both lived upstairs.

'I'm meeting with my new tenant,' he said with a grin, trying to subdue the flutter in his stomach.

'Peta Forrest? She's taking the flat, then? That's good. When do you want to move back to the house? It's empty and there's no need to wait till it's all settled.'

'Really?' Now he knew it was going to happen, Marie was right, there was no need to wait. 'I could start moving things in tonight if that's okay.' Then, perhaps Peta could move into the flat on the weekend. It was strange how he liked the idea of her being upstairs while he was working down below. Although, of course, she wouldn't be there all the time. She'd be working too. Where did an interior designer work? Perhaps she *would* be working at home.

It was almost ten o'clock before the blonde woman he'd been looking out for finally pushed open the café door, walked in hesitantly and came up to the counter.

'Marie,' he called, 'can you manage on your own for a bit?' He glanced around to ensure everyone had been served. 'Take a seat and I'll get you a coffee. Cappuccino?' he asked Peta.

'Thanks.' She walked away to find a seat by the window. Today she was wearing a heavy grey cowl-necked sweater under a checked tweed jacket, perfect for the chilly morning. She looked quite… smart, Frank decided. He fixed a cappuccino for her and a long black for himself and carried them across. He took a seat opposite her and slid her coffee across the table.

'You said it was fixed?' she asked tentatively, wrapping her hands around the cup. 'We can have the flat?'

'You can and you can move in on the weekend if it's not too soon for you.'

'But you…?' She gazed at him, her brown eyes – unusual for someone so blonde – sparkling with delight.

'I'm moving back into the house Marie and I lived in. I think I said?'

'You did. Sorry, I forgot.' She looked down into her cup, then up again.

A man could get lost in those eyes, Frank thought, the now familiar flutter in his gut becoming stronger, along with the urge to make things right for this woman.

'You just need to sign the agreement and… Damn, I didn't bring the papers. Won't be a minute.' He pushed back his chair and went to the kitchen where he'd left the tenancy agreement he'd downloaded from the internet the night before. While annoyed he'd forgotten it in his excitement, he was glad of the opportunity to calm himself. Arranging for Peta Forrest to lease his flat had him in a spin. And he was smiling.

He picked up the document and, taking a deep breath, returned to join Peta.

His eyes never left her as she read through the document and signed it. She was such a little thing, and appeared so vulnerable it made Frank want to hug her.

'How would you like me to pay?'

Her question threw him for a moment then he regained his equilibrium. 'A credit card will be fine for now.'

'Right.' She opened her bag and held out a card. 'I can arrange for a direct deposit in future.'

'No worries.' Frank felt stupid. Couldn't he be more affable? He sounded like a dill. He cleared his throat. 'As I said, I'll be leaving most of the furniture, and I'll make sure the entrance from the café is sealed off. You don't need to worry about that. If there's anything you need, don't hesitate to ask. I'll be out by the end of Friday, so you can pick up the key...' His voice trailed away as he saw what looked like amusement in her eyes.

He picked up the coffee he hadn't touched till now and took a mouthful. He grimaced. It was cold.

Peta smiled and held out her hand. 'Thanks, I really appreciate this. You can't imagine how relieved I am to get it settled. We'll be able to move in on Saturday. I guess I can pick up the key from you then – here?'

Her hand was small and soft, his much larger one engulfing it. The feeling of her skin against his sparked feelings in him he'd thought gone forever. 'That'll be fine,' he said, his voice gruff to hide the flood of emotion threatening to overwhelm him.

Twelve

Peta stood outside the large wooden door. The words *Slater and Ford Solicitors* were engraved on a plaque, but Peta knew Col Ford had retired several years earlier. She supposed his partner had found it easier to retain the name. She took a deep breath and pushed the door open.

'Good morning.' The voice came from a motherly woman behind the reception desk. She wore a nametag showing her name was Dot. 'How can I help you?' she asked with a smile.

Peta immediately felt better. 'I have an appointment with Mr Slater – for ten o'clock.'

'If you would take a seat, he'll be with you shortly.' She smiled again.

Peta sat down at a small coffee table and picked up a magazine. But she had trouble concentrating. Before long, a tall grey-haired man who she recognised as Danny Slater's father, popped his head through the door beside Dot.

'Mrs Forrest? Come in.'

Inside his office, Peta took a seat opposite the large wooden desk behind which Gordon Slater had placed himself. He didn't appear too foreboding, but her experience in Sydney had made her wary of solicitors. Grant Holmes' sister had engaged one of the city's top criminal lawyers to defend her brother, and the media had been quick to jump on his comments about his client's innocence. But this was different, Peta reminded herself. It wasn't a criminal trial, and she was the one doing the hiring.

'Now,' he said, steepling his fingers. 'What can I help you with today? I understand you're new to town and are Ann Baird's cousin.'

How did he know? Did the whole town know?

He studied a sheet of paper on the desk. 'And I believe you're going to be working with my son, Danny?' He looked up.

Was nothing secret? This town!

'You seem to know all about me.' Peta's mouth went dry.

'Not at all, but you have to realise. Granite Springs is a small town, news gets around.' Then, perhaps recognising Peta's discomfort, he added, 'I had dinner with Danny last night and he mentioned you. It's as simple as that. I wouldn't like you to think you were the subject of town gossip. Danny did say he'd recommended you set up your own business. Interior design, isn't it? I dare say you've come to ask advice?'

Lost for words, all Peta could do was nod.

Gordon picked up his phone and asked Dot for coffee, then he looked across the desk at her again. 'Sorry if I'm making assumptions.' He drew a hand through his bushy hair. 'I've been in this business too long. Maybe it's time for me to hang up my spurs. But I have a young family.' He seemed embarrassed to have shared such personal details. 'Sorry, you don't need to know that.'

He was saved by the timely arrival of Dot with two cups of coffee.

Peta grasped hers gratefully and took a sip. 'I am here primarily about my business. I need to know I've done everything properly.' She proceeded to outline the steps she'd taken to establish her new endeavour, finishing with, 'Is there anything I've forgotten?'

While Peta was talking, Gordon had picked up a pen and made a few notes. When she finished, he tapped on his desk with his pen. 'Well done! You seem to have adequately covered everything. I imagine *Forrest Interiors* will be a popular addition to the town. I know my own wife would love to have a professional designer in. She's always reading home decorating magazines and loves the TV shows featuring house makeovers.' He frowned as if not too pleased at the idea.

'Oh, good.' It wasn't the type of commission Peta was accustomed to, but anything that would help get *Forrest Interiors* known would be a big help.

'Was there anything else?' Gordon made as if to rise.

Peta hesitated, but there was one more thing she wanted to clarify.

Ann's words had sparked a tinge of worry that hadn't been there before. 'There was something…'

Gordon sat down again.

'It's difficult.' She blinked to avoid the tears which she knew always threatened when she thought about or mentioned Joy. The words stuck in her throat.

'Take your time.' Gordon's voice became gentle.

Peta supposed he was used to dealing with all sorts of issues, perhaps even more complicated than hers.

She twisted her fingers in her lap and took a deep breath. 'I'm in Granite Springs with my granddaughter,' she began. 'I had to get her out of the city. You probably read about the case. Grant Holmes battered his wife to death while their daughter was asleep upstairs.' Her voice broke. 'The woman he killed was my daughter.'

'Oh, my dear!' He passed her a tissue.

Peta forgave the endearment which would normally have annoyed her. She took the tissue and mopped the tears which were rolling down her cheeks. 'Sorry.'

'Go on when you're ready. I remember the case.'

The case! That's all they were to people like him. Peta sniffed and continued. 'Lily's beginning to get over the dreadful grief of that time. I plan to settle here with her in Granite Springs, create a new life for us, where no one knows our past – her past. I thought that was all I needed to do, and change her name to Forrest. I've already enrolled her in school in my name. But my cousin suggested I should adopt her. Is she right? Isn't it enough I'm her grandmother?'

'I've heard my granddaughters – the twins – talk about their new friend, Lily. I didn't know…'

'I don't want anyone to know!' Peta said hotly. 'I'm trying to give her a fresh start. Jo's the only person I've told.'

'Jo? Would that be Jo Ford?'

Peta nodded. Of course, he was Danny's father which meant he was also Jo's ex-husband. This was such a small town. Everyone was connected in some way or other.

'They certainly won't hear it from me. Everything you say here is confidential. And I know how tight-lipped Jo can be.'

'What should I do?'

Gordon steepled his hands again. 'Well, adoption may be out of the question. As the father's still alive, you would require his agreement. I presume that wouldn't be forthcoming?'

Peta's heart sank. 'I doubt it.'

'Then we can apply for guardianship. It would be a temporary measure, you have to understand, while her father is unable to care for her himself.'

'Oh!' Peta's heart plummeted even further.

'The court will grant guardianship where the parent is unable, unwilling, or incapable of caring for the child. I would assume your situation would fit into all three.'

Peta remained silent, her hands so tightly clenched, her nails were cutting into her palms.

Gordon continued, 'The court will only grant an order which is, in their opinion, in the best interests of the child.'

'I'd have to go to court?' Peta gasped.

'Perhaps not.' Gordon's voice was still gentle. 'The first thing to do is to file a guardianship request. I can help you with the paperwork, but perhaps you'd like to take time to think about it?'

Peta didn't know what she wanted to do. This was so unexpected. She was Lily's grandmother. Joy would have wanted her to have her. But Joy wasn't here, and if she had been, the issue would never have arisen. And Grant... Well, he certainly couldn't look after Lily. But if what Gordon Slater was saying...'

'Do you mean to say, if he is found innocent, Lily will have to go back to her father?' She couldn't believe it, couldn't imagine her sweet little granddaughter living with that man ever again.

'That's what the law says.'

'Then the law's an ass!'

'You're not the first to make that judgement.' Gordon gave a wry smile. 'But, from what you've told me, and what I've read about the case...'

There it was again – that word. It wasn't *a case*. It was a death, the untimely death of a beloved daughter and mother which had led to her and Lily's escape from the media circus and all the sympathetic looks.

'...I think that eventuality is highly unlikely,' he finished.

What eventuality? He'd lost her. She felt a tightening in her chest.

'That your son-in-law would be found innocent,' he explained, clearly recognising her confusion.

'Right.' But what was she to do now? 'This application process, how do I go about it? Can you help?'

'I certainly can. I suggest you make another appointment. Come back when you've taken time to think this through, maybe talk it over with your cousin, with Lily?'

Peta stumbled out of his office, barely hearing Dot's farewell. Once out in the street, she looked wildly around in a daze. She wished she hadn't brought up the subject of Lily, of adoption. They were perfectly happy the way they were. But Ann was right. She should formalise the arrangement. But what if…? Could Grant take steps from prison to have her application for guardianship overturned? After all, he was supposed innocent until proven guilty, even though she knew what he'd done. Would applying for guardianship be stirring up a can of worms that was best left alone?

Thirteen

Frank was shocked to see Peta's ashen face when she stumbled into the café. He hadn't expected to see her until she picked up the keys on Saturday. He quickly fixed a cappuccino and carried it over to her.

'You look as if you need this,' he said.

'Thanks.' She picked up the cup, cradling it in both hands. Frank noticed they were shaking.

'What's wrong? Has something happened?'

'You could say that.' There was a defeated tone in her voice he hadn't heard before.

Frank glanced around. It was a quiet time of day and there were only two other customers, both of whom had been served. Marie was busy in the kitchen baking another batch of brownies and preparing filled baguettes for the lunch trade. He slid into the seat opposite. 'Want to talk about it?'

Peta shook her head, but he could see she was almost in tears. He hated to see a woman cry, and this woman was one who'd already touched him in a way he didn't fully understand. He stayed there, remaining silent while she sipped her coffee. When he judged she'd recovered somewhat, he asked again, 'Are you okay?'

'I just had some bad news,' she said, giving a sigh. 'Something I hadn't expected. But I'll be okay. Thanks for your concern.'

Frank knew that was the hint for him to leave, but he couldn't leave her like this. 'Can I get you anything else? Something to eat? A glass of water?' All he wanted to do was to see her smile again, that smile that lit up her face. And he wanted to punch whoever had upset her. His hands clenched involuntarily.

'Thanks. You're kind, but no. It was…' Tears began to run down her cheeks. She brushed them away, leaving her eyes red. 'I'm sorry. You don't…' She looked away.

Frank followed her eyes to see Marie emerge from the kitchen and raise her eyebrows. He shook his head. He racked his brains trying to work out what could have happened to cause Peta to feel like this.

'Your granddaughter,' he said at last. 'Has something happened to her?'

'No, she's at school. It's nothing really.' She wiped her eyes again.

Frank was sure that wasn't true. Some women cried at the drop of a hat. He knew that. But Marie hadn't been one of those, and he was pretty sure Peta wasn't either. But if she wasn't willing to share with him, there was nothing he could do.

To his surprise, he felt disappointed at her unwillingness to confide in him. But he was determined that one day he'd know her well enough to gain her trust. And he looked forward to that day.

*

After Peta left, saying she'd see him on Saturday, Frank took her empty cup across to the servery.

'She looked upset. Did you find out what was the matter?' Marie asked.

'No, she wouldn't say, but there's something wrong. She's still moving in on Saturday so it can't be too much.'

'I wonder,' Marie said.

'What?' Frank still had the image of the tearful Peta in mind and was wishing he could have comforted her.

'It may be too farfetched, but remember that murder in Sydney a couple of months ago? It was in the news and in all the papers.'

'What's that got to do with anything?'

'I'm just thinking aloud, but it would have been just before Peta Forrest arrived in town with her granddaughter in tow. There was a child, I seem to remember – a girl.'

'No – it couldn't be.' But if it was Peta's daughter who'd been murdered, it would explain a lot. It would explain why she was so buttoned up, unwilling to divulge anything about her past.

'She did say her daughter was dead – and that her granddaughter's father couldn't take care of her,' he mused. 'But, no, surely not?'

'It would fit. And I did say I thought she looked familiar.' Marie made a black coffee and handed it to Frank. 'You look as if you've seen a ghost.'

'Thanks.' Frank took the cup, but his mind wasn't on Marie or the coffee. All he could think about was the dainty blonde woman who today had looked as if she had the cares of the world on her shoulders, and the little girl who'd shied away from him. Could Marie be right? Frank vowed to check on the Internet later that evening.

'How's the move going?' Marie's voice brought him back to the present. 'Do you need any help? Drew and I could cart some stuff over to the house for you.'

'No, it's fine.' Frank might feel okay with Marie and Drew getting together, but he didn't want them muscling in on his move. 'I don't have much to move. I've told Peta she can have most of the furniture. You just need to tell me what you want from the house. I can buy the rest from you. I don't need much. I'll move the final batch of my personal stuff in tonight, and I've arranged for the flat to have a thorough clean tomorrow.'

'If you're sure?' Marie was looking at him with what he remembered as her concerned expression, the one she adopted when she was feeling sorry for some poor soul. He didn't need her pity.

'I'm sure.'

'She's pretty.'

'Who?' Frank felt himself redden.

'Peta Forrest, the one we've been talking about.'

'I suppose.' He tried to sound nonchalant.

'What you need, Frank Beattie, is a woman in your life. Now I've found a new life for myself, I wish you could too.' She bit her lip, as he pulled on his collar and moved his gaze to stare across the café. 'Okay.' She held up her hands in a defensive pose. 'I won't say any more, but she'd be good for you. And there aren't many women in Granite Springs I'd say that about.'

'You don't even know her.'

'But I like what I do know, and if what I think is correct, she'll be needing someone to comfort her. You're good at that, Frank. I don't know what I'd have done without you when Dee died. I know it was different but...'

Frank knew it was different too, but maybe not so much. When Marie's sister died suddenly, she'd left behind a teenage daughter, and it had taken a long time for both Marie and Lucy to find a way forward. Frustrated with the way this conversation was going, Frank pushed past Marie into the kitchen where he stood with his hands on the edge of the sink, staring into space. Was he so transparent?

*

With the last load of his possessions finally unpacked, Frank poured himself a glass of red wine and settled down in the room he'd earmarked for his study. It was the one they'd initially designated as a family room then, when he left, Marie had turned it into more of a sunroom and spent most of her time there. He'd probably find himself doing that, too. It was a light airy room, cosy now with the heating he'd turned on as soon as he arrived. He made a mental note to set it on a timer. He didn't want to come home to a cold house every day.

Settling down in the moulded desk chair he'd brought from the flat, he fired up his computer to do what he'd been planning ever since Marie made the suggestion. He googled the name he remembered – Grant Holmes – and began to scroll down the articles that appeared. At first, he didn't learn anything new. All of them rehashed the shocking murder of the lovely young mother, the arrest of the husband – the well-respected Sydney doctor – the shock and horror experienced by friends, neighbours and patients alike.

This wasn't what he was looking for. Then he found it, A tiny photograph of the family in happier times – Mum, Dad and daughter on a beach, all smiling into the camera. He enlarged it. It had been taken a few years earlier, but there was no mistaking the pert little face, the mop of blonde hair and the mother who looked so like a younger version of Peta Forrest.

Marie was right.

Frank leant back in his chair. So, this was what Peta was running from. He'd have left Sydney himself if he'd been her. The poor woman. How she must have suffered. And her granddaughter. The articles had noted she'd been asleep upstairs when the attack occurred. But had she? Would anyone be able to sleep through what must have been a noisy altercation? And no doubt it hadn't been the first time they'd had such a violent argument. A man who could lose control and kill his wife had, in Frank's opinion, been leading up to it for some time, years even. The papers were always full of cases of domestic violence and so many of them resulted in loss of life – usually the woman's.

Suddenly Lily's comments about the flat being safe made sense.

Thinking of what Peta must have been through, how she must imagine her daughter's final moments, made Frank even more determined to get to know her better, to protect her, to try to make up for what she'd experienced.

Fourteen

Peta was surprised to see tears in Ann's eyes as she hugged her goodbye.

'I'll miss you,' Ann said. 'You're being so brave about all this. I know I haven't perhaps seemed as warm as you'd have liked – as you and Lily deserved. I'm not good at showing my feelings. It doesn't mean I don't have them but over the years, I've become used to hiding them – from everyone. I'll try to be better. I hope you and Lily will come to visit. I've enjoyed having you both stay. But you're right, you need your own space, and Lily tells me she's going to get a kitten.'

'Hmm. She'll probably wear me down on that one,' Peta said, wondering what it was that had made Ann so wary of showing her feelings. She had the impression there was a dark secret there, but not one she was likely to discover. Maybe in time she and Ann would become closer. It would be difficult to live here without seeing her often, and she was family, the only family they had left. Peta tried to forget about Lily's father incarcerated in Sydney and his sister who claimed her brother's innocence. Grant and Celia Holmes were no family to Lily, not anymore.

'Ready to go?' Peta mentally checked they had everything, while Lily hopped up and down in excitement.

'Take those with you, Lily.' Ann produced a bag containing many of the games and books Lily had been enjoying over the past weeks. 'It's better they're with someone who appreciates them than mouldering away in my cupboard.'

'Thanks, Ann.' Peta's cousin had surprised her again.

'Ooh, thanks, Auntie Ann.' Lily reached up to plant a kiss on Ann's cheek.

Ann blushed. 'It's not much.' She waved away their thanks. 'If it doesn't work out, you know you can always come back here. And I look forward to seeing how you settle in.'

'You'll be our first dinner guest,' Peta assured her. Now it was time to leave, she was feeling warmer towards her cousin. Over dinner at The Riverside the previous evening, the other woman had unbent a little, allowed Peta to see the girl she remembered. She'd been surprised to find such a splendid restaurant here in Granite Springs, even more surprised to discover her new friend Jo was a co-owner with her son. It was Lily who, back to her usual chatterbox self, had innocently said, 'The twins said they come here all the time. Their grandma owns it.' When Peta glanced questioningly at Ann, she filled her in. It seemed to Peta that wherever she went in this town she ran into one or another of that family.

'Hop in, Lily,' Peta said. She closed the door behind her, slid into the driver's seat and drove off, Lily waving furiously to Ann till they were out of sight.

When they reached the café, Peta and Lily went inside where they found not only Frank and Marie, but also two teenage girls busily serving customers. The café was full at this time on a Saturday, many locals clearly following what Peta had thought was only the Sydney custom of going out to breakfast on the weekend.

Seeing Peta, Marie waved to her from the other side of the café, and Frank came out from behind the espresso machine to hand her a keyring. 'Would you like a coffee before you get started?' he asked.

Lily was tugging at the tail of her shirt. Peta looked down at the girl. 'Thanks, but I think I'd prefer to get settled first.'

'Well, if you want to pop down for lunch. It's on the house today.'

Peta felt her breath catch at the unexpected offer. He really was a kind and generous man. 'Thanks,' she said again. 'I'll see how we go.'

*

Once the car was unloaded, Peta left Lily to unpack the bag Ann had given her, while she stored everything away and made up the beds. She'd used the past few days to purchase bed linen and the few pieces of crockery they'd need while they were here. She now regretted leaving Sydney in such a rush. It would have been better to have taken more care and packed a few items they could use. Instead, Peta had merely thrown some of her and Lily's clothes into a couple of cases, stashed her laptop and personal documents into her briefcase and left the city that held all her memories.

She was closing the last drawer in Lily's bedroom when the girl wandered in.

'I'm bored. There's nothing to do here.' She pouted.

Peta checked her watch. 'It's after twelve. How about some lunch? Remember Frank suggested we have it downstairs. Then we might go to the park.'

Lily's face brightened at once. 'Yes please, Grandma. Livvy and Lottie might be at the park.'

When they walked in, the café was filling up again.

'Glad you came,' Frank greeted them. 'How are you settling in?'

'It's a bit early to say, but we've unpacked and I can see I'm short of a few items I'm going to need.' As soon as she unpacked her laptop, Peta realised she'd need a desk, a chair and a good light if she was going to set up the spare room as her office. She'd need to purchase a printer, too, cursing that she'd left a perfectly good one in Sydney. But it was easier to buy a new one than to go to the trouble of having her old one sent down – and she had no intention of returning there anytime soon. She supposed she'd have to make the trip when her house sold – and for the trial. The date for that hadn't been set yet. Peta wished she could forget all about it, but knew she needed to be there to witness her daughter's murderer sentenced.

After ordering toasted ham and cheese sandwiches with cappuccino for Peta, and Frank's recommended banana smoothie for Lily, they took their seats by the window.

'Can we do this all the time?' Lily wanted to know.

'Not all the time, honey. It would become too expensive.' As she saw Lily's lip drop, she added, 'But we can come sometimes. Perhaps we can invite the twins and their mum to meet us here one time.'

Lily nodded.

Their meals were served by one of the girls Peta had seen earlier. 'Uncle Frank said you don't have to pay for these today,' the blonde girl said with a grin. 'He says you've moved into the flat upstairs.'

'That's right,' Peta said, smiling back at her. She remembered Frank mentioning his niece. 'You must be Lucy.'

'That's me. And that's my sister Jess over there. Well, she's really almost my stepsister, but we're like real sisters now.'

Lily's eyes grew wider at this information. When Lucy had left, she whispered, 'What does she mean? Are they really sisters? They don't look alike.'

Peta looked across the café to where the two girls were now engaged in lively chatter with a group of young people. Although both girls sported the same short hairstyle, the one called Jess was as dark as Lucy was fair. 'I think what she means is that they're not really sisters, but when Jess's dad is married to Lucy's aunt they'll be just like sisters. Families are sometimes complicated.' Peta hoped she'd helped Lily understand.

'I wish I had a sister,' Lily murmured.

Peta winced. Lily didn't know, but Joy had been pregnant when it happened. Perhaps she would have had a sister if Grant Holmes had been a less violent man.

'Oh, sweetie!' Peta hugged Lily tightly.

'Can we go to the park now?' Lily asked, when they had finished eating and she had managed to drink all of the enormous smoothie.

'I guess we should.' Peta smiled. Lily was a delight when everything was going her way but now she was making a recovery from the worst of her grief, Peta was finding her granddaughter was subject to moodiness when thwarted. She'd been making allowances for her up till now, but knew the time would come when she had to be firmer.

She was trying not to think of the guardianship issue Gordon Slater had raised. It was all too difficult to contemplate right now. She had enough on her plate with the move and her new business. Peta knew she couldn't put it off forever, but needed time for the full implications to sink in. She'd get them settled into the flat, get her business up and running then… What she really wanted to do was to discuss the pros and cons with someone. Ann wouldn't do. She saw everything in black and white. And Peta had no real friends here – not yet.

At the park, there was no sign of the twins, but after her initial disappointment, Lily ran to take her place in the line waiting to go down the slippery dip, then raced over to claim a free swing.

Peta took a seat on a nearby bench, enjoying the gentle warmth from the winter sun. She watched Lily push herself higher and higher, remembering watching Joy do exactly the same. It only seemed like yesterday. Now everything had changed. She sighed, her eyes pricking with tears again. There was so much of her beautiful Joy in her granddaughter, it tugged at her heartstrings.

It had been kind of Frank Beattie to treat them to lunch. He was a good man – good-looking too. Peta couldn't dismiss the quiver, the faint attraction she felt when he was close. But nothing could come of it. She had the impression he was still yearning after his ex – the woman he worked with every day – even if she was about to marry someone else. And Peta didn't want to become involved with another man at this stage in her life. She didn't have a good record for choosing men. Tony had been a mistake, one it had taken her years to admit to. She couldn't imagine Frank treating a woman the way Tony had treated her. Though men could be devious, she'd learnt to her peril. Best to keep them all at arm's length.

'Hello!' Eve's voice interrupted her musings.

She looked up to see two blonde balls of energy racing towards Lily, their ponytails bouncing, each determined to claim the one free swing. They arrived at exactly the same time and a squabble ensued, resulting in all three girls choosing to go to the climbing frame where they clambered up the ropes and hung from the bars like monkeys.

'Phew! You're lucky you only have one of them.' Eve dropped onto the bench beside Peta.

'Emily Rose not with you this morning?'

'No. She has a birthday party with a little friend, so Brad offered to take her. I think he got off lightly. The twins have been driving me mad since lunch. They're missing their bike ride, so I decided to get rid of some of their energy by bringing them here. That reminds me,' she said, 'I asked you if Lily had a bike.'

Damn! Peta had forgotten all about that. And a bike would be good for Lily. 'She has one in Sydney but... we can't access it at the moment.'

Peta could see the question in Eve's eyes, but there was no way she could explain that Lily's home had been the site of a crime scene when they left – might still be – and she had no intention of setting foot in it ever again. 'Where would be a good place in town to buy one?' she asked instead.

'That's easy. There's a bike shop just round the corner from the library. It's next to a café, Mouthfuls. You may have seen it. The cyclists all tend to congregate there on a Saturday morning. It's become quite a hangout. Brad often ends up there along with a few mates after his ride.'

'I know Mouthfuls.' Peta remembered the café she'd gone to after her visit to the library. So much had happened since then, and she hadn't been back since. 'Perhaps I should get myself one, too. It's about time I had some exercise.'

'Just don't get fanatical about it,' Eve advised. 'Sometimes I wish Brad wasn't so keen.' She bit her lip. 'Anyway, the girls enjoy riding with him. They sometimes ride to school too, and there's a bike track in the national park outside town. You and Lily could ride there.'

'Thanks.' Lily was probably missing her bike, along with all the other belongings she'd had to leave behind. Peta wished she'd paid more attention to Eve's earlier remark. The roads and lanes here were a lot safer to ride on than those around her Sydney home. Peta seemed to recall Joy saying she had her heart in her mouth every time Lily took her bike out.

'The twins tell me you and Lily are moving.'

'We just did. This morning. We moved into the flat above The Bean Sprout. It's just until my house in Sydney sells, then we'll look for something more permanent.'

Peta could see Eve was trying to stop herself from asking the usual questions. But, unlike her mother, Jo, Eve didn't invite confidences.

Luckily, the three girls ran over at that point.

'Mum,' one of the twins yelled, 'Lily is living above a café. Isn't that amazing. She can eat there any time she wants.'

'Not exactly,' Peta laughed. 'But we did have lunch there today. And I promised Lily we could get together with you there sometime, perhaps in the school holidays.'

'That's ages away,' one of the twins said. Peta thought it must be Livvy who was doing all the talking.

'Only a few weeks,' Eve said with a sigh. 'The school terms seem shorter than I remember from when I was at school.'

Peta chuckled.

The girls ran off again.

'How did you manage to discover the flat was vacant?' Eve asked. 'I didn't know Frank was moving out.'

Peta reddened. 'He… Marie suggested it. It seems he's buying their house – or the house that was theirs. It appears to be a complicated arrangement.'

'More complicated than you could imagine. I shouldn't really be telling you this. Dad told me in confidence.' She paused.

Then don't, Peta thought, knowing Eve would tell her anyway.

'Dad says Frank and Marie were never really married. They thought they were, even went to his office to arrange a divorce. Of course, there's nothing shameful about living together these days, but back then, with Frank's Italian catholic family… Well!'

Peta flinched. She really didn't need to know this. It didn't help explain the bond she'd still sensed between Frank and Marie. Everyone had their secrets, though it seemed more difficult to keep a secret in Granite Springs. She shivered, wondering how long it would be before her and Lily's secret was revealed.

Fifteen

Frank couldn't stop thinking about Peta and her granddaughter, wondering how he could show his sympathy without giving away what he knew. It had been all he could do on Saturday to prevent himself from revealing his discovery. He knew it would be the wrong thing to do. Peta had come here to get away from the publicity, to avoid everyone who knew about their past. Although vulnerable, she was a proud woman who might flee at the slightest sign of sympathy, or what she might construe as misplaced charity.

All he could do was offer them a free lunch. What a miserable offering when he wanted to… Frank caught himself up. What did he want to do? Was Marie right about him, too?

Anyway, he'd managed to handle things well, he thought, and Lily appeared to be more comfortable around him. No wonder she'd shied away at their first meeting. Discovering your father was a monster at the tender age of eight would make a stronger person than her afraid of the entire male population.

He whistled as he busied himself with his daily tasks, happy in the thought that Peta was right there above him. Marie threw him a curious glance from time to time, but refrained from commenting on his good humour. He was grateful. Apart from telling her she was right about Peta and suggesting she keep it to herself, they hadn't mentioned the crime. From what he'd read, it hadn't gone to trial yet – these things could take months – but Peta's son-in-law was safely tucked up in Long Bay while the wheels of justice slowly ground towards their inevitable outcome.

The café was filling up for lunch, and Frank was making yet another batch of coffees when it hit him. The auction. Of course. He'd forgotten mentioning it to Peta when he showed her round the flat.

When the rush died down, he checked the local paper which listed the main items to be auctioned each week. He scanned the list, noting several lamps, coffee tables, and a desk were among those to be auctioned along with a plethora of other items which would have no interest to Peta.

Lost in thought, Frank was vaguely aware of the sound of the café door opening. Then he felt Marie nudge him. He looked up to see Peta standing awkwardly at the counter.

'I haven't come for coffee today,' she said. 'You mentioned something about an auction. I've figured out what I need for the flat and wondered if you could tell me where it's held. You did say Thursday, didn't you?'

'I did, and I can do better than that. Why don't I take you and Lily along? I was just looking at the paper.' He slid the newspaper towards her.

'Oh! I didn't expect…' She glanced down to scan the page. 'This is perfect. I should be able to get everything I need and more.' She smiled up at him and it seemed as if the day took on a brighter hue. 'But I can manage on my own.'

Conscious of Marie listening in the background, Frank lowered his voice. 'Have you ever been to an auction? These ones can get out of hand. You might be glad of some help.'

He could see Peta was about to refuse again and added what he thought might be a final enticement. 'I could load what you buy into the tray of my ute. Your Honda might be a tad small.'

She hesitated for a few moments then, 'I suppose,' she said slowly. 'If it's not too much trouble. You've been so kind to us already.'

Frank felt lightheaded. She'd agreed. They'd go to the auction together. It wasn't exactly a date, but he wanted to laugh with delight and pump a fist in the air. He made do with saying, 'That's settled, then. Thursday. I'll pick you both up at five-thirty. The auction proper gets going around six, so that should give you time to check out what they have and decide what you want to bid on. Okay?'

'Okay.' But her expression told him she wasn't as delighted about the arrangement as he was. Never mind. He could wait. For now, it was enough she'd agreed to spend Thursday evening with him.

'What was all that about?' Marie asked, when Peta had left. 'You look like a dog with two tails.'

'Nothing.' Frank took his place behind the coffee machine again and began to polish the stainless-steel device. 'I only arranged to take Peta to the auction on Thursday. She needs a few extra items for the flat. All her furniture is still in Sydney and she has a business to run.'

'Hmm. You found out a lot in a short time. Are you sure you're not interested in her? I'd be happy for you. As I said.'

Frank didn't know what to say. For so many years he and Marie had shared everything. There had been no secrets between them, not until Drew Hamilton came to town and she began to keep things to herself. Well, he could keep things to himself, too. Even though he wanted to shout to the world that he had an almost date with Peta Forrest, all he did was smile.

Sixteen

Had she made a mistake in agreeing to go to the auction with Frank Beattie?
Peta worried as she fixed a snack for herself and Lily on Thursday
afternoon. He'd already done so much for them, renting them this
flat, giving them a free lunch, not to mention the payment when she'd
helped him out in the café. It would be so easy to come to depend on
his generosity, to give up her resolve to do everything for herself, the
vow she'd made years ago when Tony died.

And it had worked. She'd single-handedly brought up Joy, bought
her own home, and made a name for herself in her chosen profession.
Now she was set to do it all over again with Lily and *Forrest Interiors*.
And, as soon as her Sydney house sold, she'd buy another here in
Granite Springs.

'When are we leaving, Grandma?' Lily appeared behind her. She'd
changed out of her school uniform and now wore the warm pants,
sweater and hooded jacket they'd bought on the weekend. Lily had
shot up in the few weeks they'd been here, necessitating a trip to the
shops, and Peta had spoiled herself with a couple of new outfits from
Eve Tait's boutique. She was wearing one this evening, not sure why
she felt the need to impress. The black wool pants, teamed with the pale
pink polo-necked sweater and the deeper pink quilted jacket seemed an
appropriate ensemble for a country town auction. She tried to dismiss
the small voice that said she wanted to look good for Frank Beattie.

'Soon. Mr Beattie is picking us up in half an hour. We'll be eating
late tonight so I've made ham sandwiches to tide us over.'

'Yum.' Lily hopped onto a chair and began to munch the white bread sandwiches she loved. Peta hadn't yet been able to convert her to the wholemeal bread she preferred.

'Have some milk, too.' Peta filled a glass, before joining her granddaughter at the table to eat her own healthier snack washed down with a cup of tea.

'Why is he coming with us?'

Good question.

'The items we need for this flat are being sold at an auction – where people bid. The price goes up till no one bids any higher and the highest bidder wins.'

'I know what an auction is. I've seen it on television.'

'Right. Well, I've never bid at one before and Frank offered to help. He has a ute which can cart what we buy back here, too.'

Put like that it all sounded sensible. Why did she feel there was more to it?

They had barely finished eating when there was a knock at the door. With a glance in the hallway mirror on her way past, Peta opened the door to see a different version of Frank.

Accustomed to seeing him at work in the café, a black apron over his everyday polo-necked shirt, she found herself staring at someone who seemed like a stranger. Tonight, it appeared to her as if he'd taken special care with his appearance, but perhaps it was just seeing him out of context. He was wearing a weatherproof jacket over a navy-blue sweater from the neckline of which a pale blue shirt collar peeked out. His hair was tidier than usual, and she could detect the fresh aroma of an unfamiliar men's cologne.

'H…hello,' she stuttered.

'Ready?'

'Lily!' she called into the flat. 'Almost,' she said to the stranger at her door.

'It's not far. We can walk. We won't need the ute tonight.' Frank looked somewhat shamefaced as he revealed that all items purchased were to be picked up on the following day. 'Sorry, I know I used the ute as an excuse to accompany you, but… well, I didn't want to see you being ripped off.'

'Hmm.' Peta knew she should feel annoyed at being duped, but instead she sensed his concern. 'I see,' she said. 'So, you thought I needed your protection?'

'Something like that.' He shuffled his feet and gazed at the ground as if wishing it would swallow him up.

Peta took pity on him and chuckled. 'Okay. You win. Let's go,' she said, as Lily appeared behind her.

*

The auction was a revelation to Peta who had never seen anything like the large room crammed with goods all waiting to be sold. There was quite a crowd of people rifling through a variety of objects ranging from good quality pieces of furniture to others which had definitely seen better days, and what appeared to be useless bric-a-brac.

Eventually, the crowd stilled and quietened, and the auctioneer began his spiel, knocking down one item after another. Seeing how quickly he moved, Peta was glad to allow Frank to bid for her and she was soon the proud owner of a desk, a large worktable, an ergonomic desk chair and an LED desk lamp.

She was about to try to make her way out of the room when she felt Lily tug at her jacket. 'Look, Grandma,' she whispered.

Peta moved her gaze to Frank who was bidding for another item, one which wasn't on her list. It was…

'It's a bike,' Lily said in a breathy voice. 'Look!'

Sure enough, the item being offered was a girl's bike complete with basket and streamers from the handlebars.

'It's just like the ones the twins have,' Lily said in awe. 'Why does Mr Beattie want it?'

'The bike?' Peta asked as they left, their purchasing finished and their items paid for.

'I thought Lily might like it. It's in good nick, just needs a lick of paint.'

'I…'

'My treat. You'd like a bike, Lily, wouldn't you?' he asked the little girl who nodded, wide-eyed.

'There was no need…'

'I know. But all the kids have bikes and this one looked the right size.' He grinned as if he'd just pulled off a coup of some sort.

Maybe he had, because Lily had forgotten her shyness with him and was gazing up at him admiringly.

'Now I'll be able to go riding with the twins,' she said smugly.

Peta felt guilty. She'd been meaning to go to the bike shop Eve mentioned, but had been too caught up in getting everything ready for her meeting with Danny on Monday, She didn't want to give him any reason to regret hiring her. 'Thanks,' she said belatedly. 'It's kind of you.'

Out in the street, Peta turned in the direction of the café and flat, but Frank remained standing outside the auction house.

'Now we've done that, why don't I introduce you both to one of Granite Springs' institutions?'

Peta glanced at him warily.

'I bet you haven't eaten yet.'

Lily shook her head.

'We had a snack before we left,' Peta said.

'A snack? You need something more than that. Let me introduce you to Jilly's Hamburgers.'

Peta was about to refuse and explain it was a school night, but seeing the anticipation in Lily's eyes, relented and agreed. 'As a special treat, Lily,' she said.

They made their way to the river and walked along the riverbank till they came to where an old-style caravan was parked. Peta and Lily found a seat at a picnic table while Frank bought the hamburgers. It was so peaceful here, Peta thought, watching the river swirl by, seeing the lights of The Riverside Restaurant in the distance. It was as if they were the only people in this little piece of a private world.

Lily huddled close to her grandmother. 'Mr Beattie's a nice man,' she whispered. 'At first, I wasn't sure. He's so big and strong but…' She cuddled into Peta's side.

'He is, isn't he?' Peta felt a warm glow suffuse her as she studied Frank. Standing with his back to her, she was aware of the breadth of his shoulders, the strength of the man, his innate goodness. She could picture the warmth in his deep brown eyes when he looked at her, the way his eyes crinkled up, the…

'Here we are.' The object of her musings was standing beside them, two enormous hamburgers in his hands. 'I'll go back for the fries and drinks,' he said, disappearing again.

They ate in silence and were almost finished when Lily said through a mouthful of fries,

'Lucy calls you Uncle Frank.'

'That's because I am her Uncle Frank.'

Lily paused and looked down at her shoes, seeming to study them carefully before raising her eyes again. 'Can I call you Uncle Frank, too? I don't have an uncle and my daddy…' She buttoned her lip as if afraid to say more.

Peta could see he was waiting for an explanation. 'Lily's dad had to go away,' she said after a long pause, so long she was sure Frank must know she was prevaricating. 'And we should be going too. It was good of you to take us to the auction and to introduce us to Jilly's Hamburgers. But it's getting late and Lily has school tomorrow.'

They walked back to the café together, to where Frank's ute was parked.

'I can pick those items up for you tomorrow,' he said, shuffling his feet and avoiding meeting her eyes.

'Thanks.' Why did she feel so awkward? He was just being kind. There was no more to it. Peta was sure he would do this for anyone, not sure why it made her catch her breath. She didn't want him to treat her differently, to think she was special, did she?

'Goodnight, then.' He turned abruptly and pressed the ute's control.

'Goodnight.' Peta ushered Lily around the corner and up the stairs to their new home, not sure why she felt so disappointed.

Seventeen

Frank cursed himself as he drove off. What was it about Peta Forrest that left him tongue-tied? She was so dainty, so vulnerable. He felt like a giant beside her. But it wasn't her size. Marie was a small woman, too. Peta carried her grief around with her, a grief so palpable you could almost touch it. It made him want to wrap her up and take her away to a safe place.

There was that word again – safe. Now he knew what had happened to her daughter, Frank felt even more protective of Peta and Lily. Was this why he acted so dumb in her presence? Marie would laugh if she saw how awkward he was, tell him to buck up.

It had been fine at the auction when he had something to do. He'd felt good bidding for the items she'd identified, then the bike – that had been good luck. He knew all the kids Lily's age had one, and he saw how Lily's eyes lit up when he bought it.

Frank sighed. If only it was all so easy. He was out of practice in dealing with women – women other than Marie. It was something he'd never thought he'd have to worry about again. He and Marie had rubbed along well, even after they separated. When she'd found love again, it had been a blow, but they were still mates, and there was Lucy.

Then Peta Forrest walked into the café and his life changed.

Arriving home, Frank turned off the engine, decided to leave the ute in the driveway and headed inside. He turned on the light, hearing his footsteps echoing in the empty hallway, and made for the kitchen, where he grabbed a beer from the fridge.

His phone rang as he was carrying it into his study, and he saw Lucy's face on the screen. Trust her to call just as he was feeling sorry for himself and wondering if he'd made a mistake in moving back to his old home.

'Hi, sweetie.'

'Uncle Frank! How is it being back in the old house?'

'Pretty good,' Frank lied. He dropped onto an easy chair and took a slurp of beer, the moisture from the can dripping onto his jeans, 'What's up?' Lucy rarely called without an ulterior motive.

'It's Aunt Marie's birthday soon.'

'It is.' How could he have forgotten? He'd celebrated Marie's birthday with her for more than thirty years. Had he been so caught up with the arrival of Peta Forrest in town he'd forgotten? 'It's a big one, too.' Marie would be fifty, a milestone however you looked at it. One he'd hit two years earlier. He remembered the trouble Marie had gone to, made him feel special, even if they weren't man and wife.

'What's Drew planning?' No doubt her new fellow would have a special celebration in mind, perhaps take her off for the weekend to an exotic location, or spoil her with flowers and champagne.

'I don't know, but I want to do something special for her. She's been so good to me. She didn't need to take me in when Mum…' Lucy's voice faltered as it always did when she mentioned her mother.

'What did you have in mind?' Frank knew whatever it was, he'd be part of it. That was the reason for Lucy's call.

'Well…' She let out a long breath. 'Jess and I thought… How would you feel about having a party at The Bean Sprout?'

'A party?' Frank put down his can of beer and scratched his head, making his hair stand on end.

Lucy appeared to take this as agreement. 'It'd be lit. Just family and a few of her friends. We could use the back room, decorate it with balloons and things. Jess and I can do that, and…'

'Whoa!'

'What?'

'You're going too fast for me. I haven't said yes.'

'But you will. Jess and I thought the Sunday after her birthday. I think she and Drew may go to Queensland for a few days around the actual date. Hasn't she spoken to you about it?'

'Not yet.' *Marie had been too intent on making hints about Peta Forrest.*

'Well, she will. So we want to get this set up.'

'Let me think about it.' Frank picked up his beer again, wondering why Lucy always managed to get around him. He guessed it was because she was the daughter he'd never had.

'Thanks, Uncle Frank. I knew we could count on you.'

He pretended to growl, but knew it didn't sound that way.

'Love you.' She hung up.

Frank shook his head, but suddenly the house didn't seem quite as empty.

*

As soon as he closed the café next day, Frank headed over to the auction house to pick up Peta's pieces and the bike for Lily. He whistled to himself as he stacked them into the bed of his ute, tying them to ensure nothing became dislodged on the way back. He smiled as he loaded the bike, anticipating Lily's delight. The poor kid needed a few treats after what she'd been through.

Back at the café, he drove round to the back entrance where the stairs to the flat were situated, turned off the engine and practically ran up them.

The door opened as soon as he knocked. It took his breath away to see Peta standing there with a big smile on her face, Lily peeking around her.

'Do you have my bike?' the little girl asked, before he had time to speak.

Frank laughed, any awkwardness he felt disappearing in the presence of her obvious pleasure. 'I certainly do,' he said, 'and the things your grandma bought, too. I'll just fetch them.' He turned away.

'Can I help?' Peta asked, following him out onto the landing. 'I'm not as weak as I look. Until I started to care for Lily, I used to run five k every morning and attended a regular ab class.'

'I'm impressed. Not just a pretty face, then?'

Peta blushed, making Frank feel guilty.

'Okay. Let's see how we can manage.'

As it turned out, she was true to her word, and Frank was grateful for her help as they manoeuvred the desk and table up the stairs and into the room she had designated as her study.

By the time they'd emptied the ute, both of them were breathing heavily and Peta's face was red with exertion. Frank assumed his was the same.

'I think we both need a drink now,' Peta said, closing the door behind them. 'Be careful,' she admonished Lily who was sitting on the stationary bike in the hallway. 'You can't ride it inside.'

'I know that, I'm just practicing. I told the twins about it and they said I should go riding with them and their dad tomorrow. Can I?'

'We'll see.' Peta rolled her eyes at Frank. 'You see what you've done now? But I did intend to get her a bike, I just hadn't got around to it. Thanks again.'

'My pleasure.' Entering the living room, Frank was surprised to see it transformed. Somehow, in only a week, and without additional furniture, Peta had rearranged the room, and with a few deft touches had put her stamp on it. He supposed that was what an interior designer did. He couldn't describe exactly what she'd done, only knew there were a few touches – a cushion here, a throw there, a few pictures, books, ornaments. It looked like a different place – like a home. 'Wow!' he said. 'I hardly recognise the place.'

Peta beamed. 'I haven't done much. Just a few odd touches here and there. I think it works.' She gazed around critically.

'It certainly does. Maybe I should get you to work on the house I've moved into. It was our home once – Marie's and mine – but now it feels like an abandoned old lady. Marie took a few pieces with her and those I took from here don't quite fit.' He rubbed his head.

For the first time, Frank saw Peta grin. 'I bet it doesn't need much to make it into a home again.' She led him into the kitchen. 'What can I offer you? Wine? Beer?'

'A beer would be good.'

Peta opened the fridge and removed a can of beer, which she handed to Frank, before taking out a bottle of white wine and pouring herself a glass.

'Can I have a juice, Grandma?' Lily asked wandering in, having become bored with sitting on a bike that wasn't going anywhere.

'You can help yourself. There's orange or mango in the fridge, and you know where the glasses are.'

An enticing aroma was coming from the oven. Frank's stomach rumbled. He'd been cooking all day and had packed up a few leftovers to take home for dinner but whatever Peta was making smelt delicious.

Lily said, 'We're having lasagne for dinner.'

'Sounds scrumptious,' he said, taking a gulp of beer and thinking how hard it would be to leave this warm inviting kitchen for the cold house that was waiting for him. Why hadn't he thought to turn on the heat before he left? He had still to get around to setting the timer.

'Would you like to join us?' Peta asked. 'There's plenty. I always make enough for a few meals.' She smiled at him across the table.

'Oh, I don't…' He knew he should refuse. She was only being polite. Had his thoughts shown on his face?

'Please do. It's the least I can do for all the help you've given us.'

'Well…'

'Good. Lily, why don't you set the table for three, while I get dinner ready?'

'Okay.' Lily finished her juice, took her empty glass over to the sink and disappeared.

'She's a good kid,' Frank said.

'Yes, despite…' She bit her lip. It seemed her grief was never far away.

Without thinking, Frank said, 'I know what you've been through.'

Peta's face turned white. 'Wh…what do you mean?' she asked, a tremor in her voice.

'Sorry, perhaps I shouldn't have said. It was Marie who mentioned…'

'Marie?' Peta's voice rose. 'What did Marie mention?'

'Calm down.' Shit, what had he done? He should have kept his big mouth shut. He'd only been trying to be understanding. 'She remembered seeing an article about a murder in Sydney that took place just before you arrived in town. She thought there was a child around Lily's age. It was me who looked it up and I found a family photo. I recognised Lily.'

'Oh! I suppose the whole town knows now.'

'Not from me – or from Marie. We know how to keep our mouths shut.' Which was absurd given he'd just shot his mouth off. 'Sorry.'

'We came here to get away from all that – the sly looks, the sympathy. I don't want what happened to her mother to determine how people relate to Lily. This was to be our new start.'

'It still can be. There's no reason for anyone else to find out. They won't hear it from me. You can trust me.' Frank silently berated himself for being such a fool.

'Sorry.' Peta took a long drink of wine. 'It was just… Perhaps I'm too sensitive about it, but…'

'It must have been dreadful.' The urge to take her in his arms was almost too much.

'It was. I had to get away – get Lily away.' She gazed down into her glass.

'All done, Grandma.' Lily bounced back in. 'Can I watch television till dinner is ready?'

Peta seemed to collect herself. 'No, I'll be serving it in a minute. Go wash your hands.'

Lily ran off.

'Anyway, I'd rather not talk about it right now,' she said, rising to lift the bubbling lasagne from the oven and place it on the kitchen bench. Then she opened the fridge to take out a large bowl of salad. 'If you go through, I'll bring this in.'

'Can I help?' Frank felt stupid for opening his big mouth.

Peta shook her head. 'But you might want to help yourself to another beer.'

'Thanks.' He took another can from the fridge and held up the wine bottle. When Peta nodded, he refilled her glass and carried both the can and the glass through to the dining table.

*

'That was divine, just like my Italian nonna used to make,' Frank said, when they had finished eating and Lily had disappeared to her room.

Peta blushed. 'You're the cook, not me. But it is from my nonna's recipe. I can't take all the credit.'

'That's your Italian heritage.'

The conversation, which had flowed freely during the meal, seemed to have dried up. Lily had kept them amused with her tales of school and her friends, the twins, who Frank quickly identified as being the two little blonde girls who often patronised the café with Jo Ford.

'I guess I should go.' But he was reluctant to leave. He'd been waiting for an opportunity to get to know Peta better and now it was within his grasp, he was acting like a tongue-tied teenager.

'Don't go yet,' Peta said to his surprise. 'I'll make us coffee, though it won't be as good as the blend you serve downstairs.'

'That would be great, thanks.' Frank tried to hide his delight.

When Peta returned with coffee and they were both seated in armchairs, one on either side of the gas fireplace, Peta said, 'I'm sorry I flew off the handle earlier. It's been so hard, trying to keep what happened to Joy secret. I should have realised. At first, Ann was the only person who knew, then Jo Ford managed to winkle it out of me, then I had to visit a solicitor, now you and Marie know. It seems it's impossible to keep a secret in Granite Springs.' Her forehead creased, making Frank want to smooth away the lines.

'Difficult but not impossible. And you've shared it with three people who are renowned for their ability to keep a confidence. I don't know why you had to see a solicitor – and I'm not going to ask – but any one worth his salt is trustworthy.'

'It was Gordon Slater I spoke to and he did assure me it was confidential.'

'There you go.' Frank wondered at her need to consult a solicitor. As far as he knew she hadn't sold her house in Sydney as yet, and surely the trial of her son-in-law didn't require her to seek legal help.

'I wanted to ask his advice about my new business and had to speak to him about Lily,' she said, pleating the edge of her shirt with shaking fingers.

Frank raised an eyebrow.

'I thought I was within my rights to remove her from the scene of the horror she experienced.'

'She didn't…?' Frank wondered if the little girl had been a witness to her mother's murder.

Peta shook her head. 'I don't think so. She was interviewed at the time. The poor mite was devastated. It took her weeks to stop sobbing uncontrollably. She still has nightmares. But what you're asking – I don't think so. No, she won't be called as a witness if that's what you were thinking. I talked to Gordon Slater about my continued care of her and he suggested applying for guardianship. Evidently adoption is out of the question.'

'It would be, since her father is still alive. I was involved in a slightly similar case with Marie and Lucy last year. Thankfully, it was resolved to the satisfaction of all parties. But it was touch and go for a bit. I'm sorry you have to deal with this.'

'I'm the one who should be sorry, I don't know why I'm telling you all this. I barely know you.' She looked away.

'Sometimes it's easier to talk to a stranger,' Frank said, feeling he was repeating something that had been said to him, or he'd heard. 'I wish there was something I could do to help.'

'You've listened,' Peta said. 'It helps me to say it out loud. I'm not sure what I'm going to do yet.'

'There's no rush, is there?'

Peta's lips pinched. 'Well, Grant Holmes isn't going anywhere at the moment, if that's what you mean. But it might be good for my care of Lily to have some legal basis. I need to look into it a bit more.'

'If there's anything I can do...' Frank had no idea of anything he could do to help, but he wanted to take the worry from Peta's expression.

She sighed. 'Thanks, you've been a big help already. I'm grateful. And Lily loves her bike. It was so good of you.'

Sensing the time for confidences was over, Frank drained his coffee and rose. 'This time I really must go,' he said. 'I have an early start tomorrow and I'm sure you have a lot to do, too.'

'You're right.'

At the door, they paused. Frank was tempted to take her in his arms and tell her everything would be all right. But he sensed any attempt to comfort her might be unwelcome, and he didn't want to risk spoiling the rapport he'd felt building. Instead he shook her hand, noticing again how small and fragile it felt in his big paw.

'Thanks for the meal,' he said. 'I'll be in touch.' Then he added daringly, 'Perhaps we can have another meal together sometime soon? My shout next time.'

He stood uncertain, waiting for her reply, relieved when she said, 'Thanks, I'd like that.'

Eighteen

Lily was excited as she got ready for her bike ride. They'd gone shopping that morning to buy her a helmet and the little girl couldn't wait to put it on. 'It's nicer than the one I had in Sydney,' she said, admiring herself in the large mirror in Peta's bedroom.

Peta flinched. It was the first time Lily had referred to any of the belongings she'd left behind. Did she think about them a lot? Peta wondered when they'd be able to retrieve them, if she even wanted anything from that house. She felt everything in it, everything belonging to Joy and Lily's life there, had been tainted by what had happened.

'When do you have to be there?' she asked.

'They're going to pick me up here. I told Lottie and Livvy it might be difficult to get my bike into your car. Their dad has a special roof rack, and he told them he can fit my bike on too.' She grinned.

'Where is it they ride again?' Peta asked, worried. Eve had told her but she'd forgotten and the thought of allowing Lily to go off without her filled her with dread, even though she knew Brad Tait could be trusted.

'In the National Park,' Lily said wearily. 'Livvy says there are special bike trails there among the trees. It's not like the streets back home.' Her voice faltered on the final word.

Home? Did Lily still think of Sydney as home? Peta gave herself a shake. Of course she did. It was where she'd spent her entire life until now.

'That sounds lovely.' Peta quashed her fears. She couldn't keep Lily cocooned for ever.

'What will *you* do this afternoon, Grandma?' Lily asked.

'Oh, I thought I'd pop round to see your Auntie Ann. I told her she'd be our first dinner guest, so I want to invite her to dinner this evening if she's free.'

'But she won't be the first. Uncle Frank came to dinner last night.'

'I don't think you should call him that,' Peta said without thinking. It made him sound as if he was part of the family when he was… practically a stranger.

'Why not? He said I could.' Lily pouted.

He had, and at the time, Peta had wondered at his easy acceptance of the little girl's request. There was no harm in it, but somehow, it made him seem more… more familiar than a landlord.

There was no time to discuss it further as they were interrupted by a loud rattle at the door and the sound of excited childish voices.

'Here they are!' Lily said excitedly, grabbing her helmet and running into the hallway to grasp the handlebars of her bike.

'There's no need to rush.' Peta opened the door to see the twins standing there with their dad.

'All set?' Brad asked.

He was dressed in the lycra outfit Peta recognised as the uniform of the avid cyclist. Back in Sydney, she and her friends had often laughed at the cohorts of the middle-aged men in lycra. She was pleased to see Lottie and Livvy were wearing jeans and tee-shirts similar to Lily.

'So this is the famous bike?' he asked, while the twins examined it carefully.

'It's just like ours,' one of the girls exclaimed. 'Only a bit scruffier.' She giggled.

'Uncle Frank's going to paint it,' Lily said defensively.

'I didn't know you had more family here,' Brad said, giving Peta a questioning look.

'He's not a relative.' Peta had known something like this would happen. 'Frank's our landlord, from the café downstairs. He said Lily could call him uncle.'

'Frank Beattie? Right.' Brad didn't appear concerned or interested. 'Well, I'll get these three out of your hair. I'll take good care of Lily and we should be back around four. That okay with you?'

'Perfect, thanks. Be good for the twins' dad, Lily. Remember to do what he says. And be careful. It's some time since you rode a bike.' She knew she was fussing but couldn't help it.

Lily threw her a scornful look before hugging her tightly, her little arms wrapping themselves around Peta's waist. 'See you later, Grandma. Give my love to Auntie Ann.'

There was a flurry as Brad collected the bike, fitted it onto the roof rack and he and the three girls left. Suddenly Peta was alone. She turned back into the flat. She'd intended to work on her plans before she visited Ann, but without Lily's chatter, the place seemed so empty she decided to leave earlier than she intended. She knew Ann's routine. Her cousin would be spending the afternoon with the weekend papers, then might busy herself in the garden. Peta hoped she'd be a welcome diversion.

*

Ann was in the garden when Peta drove up. She was with a woman Peta didn't recognise, though why would she? She barely knew anyone here yet. Whereas in Sydney she had a wide circle of friends, here in Granite Springs, apart from Jo Ford and her family, there was only Ann, and Frank and Marie, if she could call them friends. She had deliberately kept herself insulated as much as she could, but she recognised that had to change. If she was to build her business here, she needed to meet more of the locals. Although tempted to drive off again, she took a deep breath and stepped out of the car.

The two women turned at the sound of the car door closing, and Peta saw Ann's companion was a woman close to her and Ann's age with spiky blonde hair. She and Ann broke off their conversation as Peta walked up to the gate.

'Peta, how lovely to see you. This is Fran,' Ann said, then turning to her companion added, 'Fran, this is my cousin, Peta. The one I was telling you about.'

Peta flinched. What had Ann been saying about her? She felt her limbs begin to stiffen, then forced herself to relax. She couldn't allow herself to become distraught every time she thought someone might know her story. She smiled. 'Hello, Fran.'

Perhaps sensing her discomfort, Fran smiled again. 'Ann said you and your granddaughter have been staying with her and have moved into the flat above The Bean Sprout. Marie is a good friend of mine – Frank, too, of course.'

Peta breathed a sigh of relief. 'A week ago,' she agreed. 'It was good of Frank – and Marie. We're beginning to settle in. Ann was wonderful when we first arrived, but I didn't want to outstay our welcome.'

'Nonsense.' Ann brushed off her words. 'Fran and I were about to have a cuppa. Let's all go inside. I've spent almost all day in the garden. I'll be glad of the break. Just let me wash my hands and I'll be with you both.'

They moved inside, Peta and Fran heading for the kitchen while Ann disappeared into the bathroom.

'You haven't visited Granite Springs before?' Fran asked, filling the electric jug, before joining Peta at the kitchen table. She seemed to be very much at home in Ann's kitchen.

'No. Ann and I had lost touch until recently. I spent most of my life in Sydney. We saw a bit of each other when we were younger then grew apart.'

'It happens.'

There was silence, then Fran spoke again, 'Ann was very good to me when I first arrived in town. That was a long time ago. There's something nurturing about this place. It wraps around you like a comforting blanket.' She paused as if lost in her thoughts, then appeared to give herself a shake. 'Listen to me! You must think I'm losing it. But I was in a bad place when I landed here, and the town healed me. Strange how a place can do that.'

Peta gave Fran a curious look. This woman had suffered. But she appeared to have put whatever bothered her behind her and moved on. Peta wondered if Granite Springs could have the same effect on her.

Ann walked back in. 'Oh, good. The jug's on. Thanks. What sort of tea would you like? I'm going to have peppermint. Fran? Peta?'

Both women opted for peppermint, too, and sat down together at the table.

'How are you settling in?' Ann asked.

'Pretty well.' Peta told them how Frank had suggested the auction house and the items she'd purchased.

'Oh, I wish you'd told me you were going,' Ann said. 'I'd have come with you. It's easy to get ripped off if you don't know how it works.'

'Thanks, but I didn't go on my own. Frank Beattie came along to help.' As soon as she'd spoken, Peta wished she could take the words back. She saw the way Ann and Fran's eyes met at the mention of Frank's name.

It was Fran who spoke first. 'Frank's a good man. He took it hard when Marie met Drew Hamilton. I think he had hopes of a reconciliation when Lucy moved in. You do know Marie's sister died suddenly?'

'I didn't.' But it explained a lot – why Lucy was living with her aunt, why Frank seemed to be so protective of her. And, if he'd been hoping for a reconciliation with Marie, there was no chance he'd be interested in Peta. Why was she even contemplating the possibility?

'It was a difficult time for her – for both of them. I know Frank was a great support for Marie. It was a pity. But she met Drew and they're very happy. I felt sorry for Frank though. He helped her through it all, then...' Fran paused before continuing in a wistful tone, 'I'd love him to find love too. He deserves a good woman.'

Fran was going too far. She couldn't be suggesting...?

'Leave Peta alone.' Ann's voice broke into Peta's thoughts. 'Not everyone can find the same sort of happy ending as you did, Fran.'

Peta was surprised to hear a note of bitterness in Ann's tone. What had happened to her cousin to make her so disappointed in life? She had no time to wonder.

'But, Ann,' Fran said, 'you have to admit Granite Springs does seem to have that effect on some of us. I met my husband here a couple of years ago,' she said to Peta. 'I wasn't looking for love. When I met Owen, he was the last man I thought I could be interested in. But...' she laughed and spread her hands, '...here I am, married to an aging hippie, living on an acreage surrounded by goats, with a stepdaughter and grandson living in town. Life has a way of surprising you. Don't listen to Ann. She's set in her ways. I didn't want to listen to the advice *I* was given, but it was good advice. I was the one who was wrong. It sort of snuck up on me.' She chuckled.

'I'm not looking for a relationship,' Peta said stiffly. 'I have enough to think about without the complication of a man. I've never been lucky in that regard.' *And I have enough to contend with, too*, she thought.

'Of course not,' Ann was quick to say and changed the subject. 'Peta is setting up her interior design business,' she told Fran. 'She's going to be working on Danny Slater's new development.'

To Peta's relief, this led to a discussion on the pros and cons of the new homes which were springing up on the outskirts of town and the resulting effect on the economy. It appeared to be a hot issue, one Peta hadn't considered would be cause for debate.

The afternoon passed swiftly, and it was with regret Peta checked her watch to discover it was close to four o'clock. 'I need to go,' she said. 'Lily is out bike riding with the Tait twins and their dad and she'll be home soon.'

'I should go, too,' Fran said. 'It's been lovely to meet you Peta.'

'Likewise.' Despite her earlier reservations regarding the veiled hints about Frank Beattie, Peta had enjoyed Fran's company and knew she'd make a good friend. She was a warmer person than Ann, and closer to her own age than either Jo or Eve. She stifled the reminder that she was also a friend of Marie and Frank.

'You must come out to visit us at The Haven. I'm sure your granddaughter would enjoy seeing the goats, though I'm afraid they aren't very friendly most of the time. But they're fun to watch.'

'Thanks. We did visit an acreage soon after we arrived. I met Jo Ford and...'

'Jo and Col are our neighbours,' Fran interrupted with a laugh. 'You'll find this happens all the time in Granite Springs. Everyone is connected in some way. It bothered me at first, before I realised it's a good thing the community is so inter-connected. It's not like living in the city.'

'No, I've discovered that already,' Peta said ruefully. 'And thanks for the invitation. I'm sure Lily would love it.'

'You, too, Ann,' Fran said, turning to her friend. 'I'll be in touch.'

By this time, all three were standing outside. Fran got into her car and, with a wave she was off, leaving Peta with Ann.

'Fran's right, you know,' Ann said. 'There does seem to be something in the air in this town, though it's managed to pass me by.' She gave a wry chuckle. 'Or perhaps I'm just immune. But don't pay any attention to her. I've found to my frustration that those women who've found love in their later years are always eager to share the joy of their experience with others. It doesn't occur to them we don't all need a man to complete us.'

'Exactly!' Peta gave Ann a hug. She had more in common with her cousin than she'd thought. 'One reason I dropped by was to invite you to dinner. I did promise you'd be our first guest.' She conveniently ignored Frank's dinner the previous evening. 'What about tonight or tomorrow? Lily's looking forward to seeing you again.'

'Thanks, Peta. That would be lovely. Perhaps tomorrow?'

They agreed on a time and Peta drove off, arriving home just as Brad pulled up with the girls.

'I had such a good time, Grandma,' Lily said, as Brad drove off, the twins waving madly through the back window. 'Can I go with them again?'

'Of course, if you're invited,' Peta replied. While she was aware of Brad's offer to take Lily with them each week, she wasn't sure she wanted to take advantage of his good nature. Maybe she did need to buy a bike for herself. 'Guess what? Auntie Ann is coming to dinner tomorrow. Won't that be nice?'

'Mmm.' But Lily was already running upstairs and into the flat.

Peta manoeuvred the bike up the steps and into the hallway. It was comfortable here, and safe. It had been a good move, the right one. Lily was happy, and Peta herself was beginning to make friends. She smiled, thinking of her visit with Ann, then the image of Frank Beattie appeared in her mind's eye and she chuckled. Fran's comments about him had annoyed her, forced her into protesting she wasn't looking for a relationship. She wasn't, but there was something about Frank Beattie that made her heart beat a shade faster.

Nineteen

Peta gathered her notes and checked she had everything she needed. Even though she'd already been awarded the project, she wanted to impress Danny Slater. Something told her it wouldn't be easy. The meeting with his father had shown her how alike the two Slater men were, and Gordon Slater had given her the impression he liked to be in charge.

She glanced around the room before she left. It had been a good decision to move here, to have a place of their own. Although it was only a week since they moved in, Peta already felt at home in the flat, and loved the aroma of coffee which drifted up from the café below, tantalising her tastebuds. There was no time for coffee now, perhaps later. Her eyes fell on the desk and long table Frank had helped set up on Friday. They were perfect.

For a few moments, her eyes glazed over remembering the evening, the dinner, their conversation. Frank Beattie had surprised her. At first, she'd been wary of the big Italian man, reminiscent of many of her mother's family – a family of kind but chauvinistic men who believed a woman's place was in the home, preferably in the kitchen. Frank seemed different. He was big and kind – that was the only similarity. He'd proved to be a good listener too. It had been a shock to discover he knew who she was, but when the shock passed, she was confident he'd keep his word and their secret.

Peta knew her past couldn't remain secret forever. There was still the trial to get through. That would no doubt generate more media interest, and even if the journalists didn't find them here in Granite Springs, there would be headlines and photos. Peta hadn't forgotten how the family photos made their way into the journalists' hands at the time of the murder. They'd have a field day during the trial. Meantime, it was her duty to keep Lily as far away from it all as she could. If it meant applying for guardianship, then that's what she would do. But she needed to find out more first.

Peta's mind was still in a whirl when she reached the real estate office, so she stood outside for a few seconds to gather her thoughts. Then she took a deep breath, checked her reflection in the window and walked inside.

This time she received a warm smile from Cathy who directed her into Danny's office and offered tea or coffee.

'Coffee, thanks, white no sugar,' Peta said, as Danny rose to greet her.

'Looks as if you've been busy,' he said, gesturing to her bulging brief case and the swatches of material in her arms. She'd managed to obtain a few samples from the local supplier Danny had mentioned and was still waiting for some from a few others she'd found on the internet.

'I hope you'll be pleased with what I've come up with,' Peta said, a tremor of excitement in her voice. Her new venture depended on Danny agreeing to her plans.

'We'd better sit at the table. You look as if you need to spread out.' He indicated a table in the corner of the office.

Cathy returned with coffee just as Peta had spread out the swatches and was unpacking the sheets containing her proposal.

'Gosh, these look good,' Cathy said. 'They're so fresh. The design reminds me of a stand of gum trees.'

Peta smiled with pleasure. If Danny's assistant got what she was aiming for, hopefully he would too.

'Right,' Danny said, all business when Cathy left, closing the door behind her. 'Show me what you've got.' He leant back in his chair and folded his arms, waiting to be impressed.

Peta took a deep breath. She could do this. She imagined prospective buyers wandering around houses, admiring the interiors she'd designed.

By the time she'd finished outlining her proposal, Danny had abandoned his former restrained manner and was leaning forward, his eyes glowing with the same excitement as Peta was feeling.

He didn't speak immediately she finished, and a knot of worry began to curl in her stomach, then he grinned and said, 'Well done! You've caught the mood I want exactly. It was a lucky day for me when you walked in here. Mum was right.'

Peta glowed and released the breath she'd been holding. She'd been worrying needlessly. Everything was going to be all right.

She was on a high when she finally left, having arranged to meet with Danny every two weeks to fill him in on her progress. The houses still had to be built, so there was no immediate rush. She'd have time to work out where she was going to source all her materials and to fit in the couple of trips to Canberra she knew she would need. She wouldn't be able to find everything locally. She also intended to contact a few of the suppliers she was familiar with in Sydney, but had no intention of going back there.

It was still mid-morning and there was a chill in the air, suggesting a cup of something warm would be welcome. The coffee Cathy had made for her and Danny had been finished long before the end of their meeting. Peta glanced across at The Bean Sprout Café, but something made her hesitate. Would Frank Beattie think she was making an effort to see him if she arrived there for coffee only days after they'd had dinner together?

She remembered the café by the library called Mouthfuls so, instead of crossing the road, she loaded her samples and brief case into the car and set off.

'Cappuccino, please,' she said to the woman behind the counter whose name she couldn't remember, if she'd ever known it. She rubbed her hands together to warm them.

'Nippy this morning,' the woman replied. 'You settling in okay?'

'Yes, thanks.'

'I'm Melody. I don't think I introduced myself last time. You said you'd just arrived in town.'

'Peta wrinkled her brow. Had she told the woman that, or had Melody heard about her elsewhere? 'I'm Peta.'

'Take a seat, Peta, and I'll have your coffee in a tick. Can I tempt you with a muffin to go with it? We have strawberry and white chocolate this morning.'

Peta looked at the enticing display in the cabinet below the counter and made an instant decision. 'Yes, please, a muffin would be lovely,' she said and made her way to a seat by the window.

She had barely sat down when the door opened, and a familiar face walked in on a waft of cold air.

'Brrr, it's cold out there, Melody. I'll have my usual please and one of your special muffins,' Jo said, before catching sight of Peta. 'Peta! How lovely to see you. I thought I was going to have to enjoy a solitary cup of tea this morning. May I join you?'

Before Peta could reply, Jo had plopped herself down opposite and dropped a bundle of books on the floor.

'Library,' she said. 'I've been doing my deliveries this morning. I belong to Friends of the Library,' she explained to a bemused Peta. 'Delivering books to the housebound is my way of giving back to members of the community who love to read but can no longer get out to borrow for themselves. It's so rewarding to bring a little light into their lives. For some, Friends of the Library and Meals on Wheels are the only human contacts they have. I try to spend at least half an hour with my ladies on each visit. It's amazing what interesting lives they've led. Most have always lived here in Granite Springs or on surrounding properties, and often their families have moved away. Sorry, I'm rambling on. I tend to do that when I've been to see them. How are you?' Jo seemed to run out of breath.

'I saw a flier about the Friends group in the library,' Peta said, remembering how she'd considered becoming a volunteer, even gone so far as completing their form. But that had been before she met Danny and set up *Forrest Interiors*. She still couldn't quite believe how it all happened so quickly. 'I'm good,' she added.

'You spoke with Danny?'

'I did. I've just come from there. I'm going to design the interiors for his display homes.' Peta couldn't keep it to herself. 'It's all thanks to you. He suggested I set up my own business and work as a freelance. I can't thank you enough. It's something I've always wanted to do, but in Sydney...' She waved a hand dismissively. '*Forrest Interiors*.' She savoured the sound.

Their conversation was interrupted by Melody bringing over their orders. Then, as Peta was carefully dissecting her muffin into bite-sized pieces, Jo asked, 'Are you still living with your cousin?'

'No. Wow, this is delicious,' she said biting into a piece.

'We're fortunate to have two excellent cafés here in town – this one and The Bean Sprout. Melody wins prizes for her baking at the show each year. Where are you living now? I hope you found somewhere nice. Did Danny help you with finding a place, too?'

Peta blushed. 'I've moved into the flat above The Bean Sprout Café.'

Jo raised her eyebrows. 'Isn't Frank Beattie living there? I thought...'

'Oh, no!' Did Jo think she and Frank? She felt herself redden even more at the idea of her and Frank as an item. But was it really so ridiculous? 'He's moved back into what he calls his family home. I don't want to be the source of gossip, but I think he's buying it from Marie.'

'What a good idea. I wondered what they'd do about the house. You do know Marie is in a new relationship? It's a pity. Frank's such a good man. He deserves to find someone, too.' She gave Peta a speculative glance but didn't pursue it. 'And your granddaughter?' she asked instead. 'The twins talk about her all the time. She's settling down okay?'

'She seems to be.' Peta chewed on the inside of her cheek. Maybe she could talk to Jo about the guardianship thing.

'But...?'

Jo was too perceptive.

'There is something. I have to decide...'

'If you don't want to talk about it.' Jo tipped her head to one side.

Peta hesitated, unsure what she did want, then she looked at Jo. The older woman exuded confidence, and her husband was a solicitor, as was her ex-husband. She might be the perfect person to help resolve Peta's problem and offer advice.

'It's like this...' Peta outlined the issue as she understood it from what Gordon Slater had told her. 'So, I'm not sure what to do,' she finished with a sigh. 'I thought we were all right as we were, but perhaps I do need to make it all legal. But I don't want to rock the boat. It's all too hard.' Peta slumped in her seat. She'd been feeling on top of the world after her meeting with Danny. Now, reliving that earlier meeting with Gordon Slater, she was back in the quandary of not knowing what to do for the best.

'Well, I'm no lawyer,' Jo said, as Peta took a welcome drink of coffee, 'but I haven't been married to two of them without a bit of the law rubbing off. My advice would be to go down the legal route. I can see how you might feel it an unnecessary hurdle, but it would set your mind at rest to be sure.'

'Sure?'

'Sure you have the law on your side. I can't imagine any court would fail to allow you guardianship of your own granddaughter. If it was me, and Lottie and Livvy were at risk from their dad, I know how I'd feel.'

'Lily's not at risk from Grant at the moment.' Peta didn't know if she ever had been, but how could she countenance Lily having anything to do with the man who murdered her mother, even if he was her father?

'No, I understand that.' Jo fell silent for a few moments. 'Perhaps you should talk with Col. I know you've already seen Gordon – and he's a good solicitor – but Col can be more impartial. He could help you with the paperwork if you decide to go down that track. And he won't charge Gordon's inflated fees.' She gave a chuckle.

Peta thought for a moment. She would like a second opinion. Right now, she felt conflicted, just wished it would go away and she and Lily could get on with their new life.

'I think I'd like that,' she said.

'Good. Why don't you come out for lunch again? I can make sure the twins are there so Lily will have some playmates. How about next Sunday?'

'Thanks. Lily really enjoyed her last visit. It's kind of you. Are you sure Col won't mind?'

'He'll be fine. He likes to keep his hand in, and I'm sure he'll be able to offer advice and assistance if required. I can give him a heads up if you like.'

'Would you?' The thought of having the genial man who was Jo's husband helping her resolve this was a comfort. He was so much more approachable than Gordon Slater. She could understand why Jo was now married to him.

'Now,' Jo said, refilling her cup from the dainty teapot, 'tell me a bit more about what you're doing with Danny. I haven't been out to the development site yet, but he's been raving about it.'

The rest of the conversation was filled with Peta outlining her ideas for the display homes. As a result, by the time she left, she was back in the positive frame of mind in which she'd arrived.

As Peta walked back to her car, she saw Frank Beattie standing at the door of The Bean Sprout. He waved, the gesture surprising her with a glow of something she didn't recognise, her stomach churning with a feeling she had almost forgotten.

Twenty

Frank waved across the street when he saw Peta walking along. He was tempted to cross, to speak to her, but he couldn't leave the café. Even from this distance, he could see she had a smile on her face. He was glad things were going well for her. He'd noticed she often looked as if she had the cares of the world on her shoulders. No wonder with all she'd had to deal with – and it wasn't over yet.

'Everything okay?' Marie asked, when he walked back inside. She peered past him to see what had caught his attention.

'Sure.'

'Was that Peta Forrest I saw you wave to?' She grinned.

'It might have been.' Frank didn't want to discuss Peta with Marie, not again. But she wasn't so easily sidetracked.

'She's settled in upstairs?'

'Yes, she's made a difference to the place already. A woman's touch.' Damn! He hadn't meant to reveal he'd been there.

'When were you in the flat?' Marie asked with another grin. 'I knew you wouldn't be able to keep away.'

'I helped her with a few items from the auction house, picked them up and delivered them to her on Friday.'

'Delivered some items? And stayed to have a drink?'

'Dinner, actually.' While Frank didn't like where this was going, he was damned if he was going to hide from Marie of all people.

But Marie wouldn't let up. 'I told you she was a good prospect. When are you going to see her again?'

'I don't know.' Frank was being honest, but he knew he hadn't answered the intent of Marie's question. She wanted to know if he was going to see Peta again outside of any visits she might make to the café. And the answer was a resounding yes. He just wished Marie would leave it. There was something that felt vaguely incestuous about his former partner trying to push him into another relationship. Frank was perfectly able to find a woman on his own, if he wanted one. Though he hadn't realised he did, not till Peta Forrest walked into his life. And she had to be the one Marie had earmarked for him, too. It should have pleased him, made matters easier. Instead, it annoyed the heck out of him.

'Well, I think…' she began, her hands on her hips.

'Let it go, Marie. You have your life. Let me lead mine as I see fit.'

'Okay, if you're going to be like that.' She pretended to pout, but knowing Marie, any displeasure would soon disappear. She was the most even-tempered person he knew – until her ire was up. Then she could be as feisty as anyone, as her new partner learnt to his cost when they first met.

But Marie's comments prompted him to remember the dinner invitation he'd extended to Peta as he was leaving – and her acceptance.

After he arrived home that evening, he pondered on the wisdom of calling to arrange a date, trying to figure out how they could manage dinner without including Lily. While he had formed a liking and, he thought, a bond with the little girl, what he really wanted was to see Peta on her own. Maybe it was futile. Maybe he should forget the whole idea. Before he could overthink things, he picked up his phone.

'Hello, Peta Forrest.'

The sound of her voice conjured up the image of Peta as he'd seen her that morning, a smile on her face, her silvery blonde hair tossed by the wind, making his breath catch. 'Frank here, Frank Beattie.'

'Hello, Frank Beattie.' There was a smile in her voice. Frank pictured her sweet face, the way it lit up when she smiled.

'You looked pleased with yourself when I saw you today.'

She seemed to hesitate before replying, 'I was. I had a meeting with Danny Slater. He approves of my ideas for his display homes, so it's all systems go.'

'Well, that's good news, and if what you've done with the flat is anything to go by...' Frank knew he was waffling. He cleared his throat. 'I everything okay with the flat?'

'Yes, it's all good.'

He thought he heard amusement in her voice. Did she think he was going to be one of those controlling landlords? He cleared his throat again. This was even harder than he imagined. Had he found it this hard with Marie? It was so long ago he couldn't remember. Back then he was a teenager and thought himself invincible. Now he was in his fifties and knew better.

'I... I mentioned dinner.'

'You did.'

'And you agreed.'

'I did.'

She wasn't making this easy.

'I thought we could go to The Riverside if we can agree on a date.' He paused, wondering how to broach the subject of Lily.

Peta forestalled him. 'I'd like that. Were you intending to treat Lily, too? If not, Friday would be good. She's having a sleepover with friends. But if you wanted to include her, then it would have to be Saturday. I don't like her going out on a school night.'

Frank exhaled. He didn't know if she was being serious or trying to joke with him. 'Friday sounds good to me,' he said hurriedly 'I'll book a table. Can I pick you up? Say seven o'clock?'

'That would be perfect.'

When he hung up, Frank wiped the sweat from his brow. Who'd have thought making a date would turn out to be so stressful? Now he had the whole week to get through, he might manage to think of ways in which he could manage to avoid sounding like a dill and make proper adult conversation.

Twenty-one

Peta was smiling to herself when the call finished. Frank had sounded so uncertain, so tentative. She'd bet he wasn't in the habit of asking women out, and wondered if there had been anyone else since Marie. Not that it mattered to her. She was in no position to criticise others.

She'd been young when she met Tony, unsure of herself, impressed by the ambitious graduate of one of Sydney's best schools, on his way to become a top paediatrician. He'd fulfilled his dream, and she'd been there at his side, the wife basking in the glory of the successful man. Her own studies had gone by the wayside. He'd persuaded her there was no need for her to have a career. Then she'd become pregnant, and her days were fully occupied taking care of their home and daughter.

Later, with Joy at school, rather than rattle around in their harbourside mansion, Peta had enrolled in a course in interior design – deemed a suitable sort of hobby for a woman in her position. It had been a shot in the dark, fuelled by a liking for sketching as a child, and to her surprise Peta had taken to it like a duck to water. She'd found her calling. It had been a lifesaver when Tony died and provided her and Joy with a good income right up to the time she left Sydney.

'You look happy, Grandma.' Lily wandered into the kitchen where Peta was still sitting holding the phone and staring at the blank screen, lost in thought.

She looked up. 'I've been invited out to dinner, on Friday, when you have a sleepover with the twins.'

'Oh! What's for dinner tonight?'

Peta's news clearly made no impact on the little girl. She grinned inwardly and laid down the phone. 'Macaroni cheese sound okay?'

'I suppose.' Lily wandered off again, leaving Peta to wonder if Lily really was recovering from the worst of her grief. There hadn't been any nightmares recently, but that didn't mean the little girl wasn't lying awake remembering. She'd undergone counselling in Sydney immediately afterwards, but, of course, that stopped when they left the city. Lily seemed to be adjusting and her friendship with the twins certainly helped, but was Peta doing enough? It was difficult to know what to do for the best.

*

The week passed quickly and soon it was Friday. Eve had picked Lily up from school, so Peta had plenty of time to get ready for her date. It *was* a date, she told herself nervously as she tried to decide what to wear. Looking through the sparse wardrobe, she regretted once again that she'd left Sydney in such a hurry. She thought longingly of the designer garments languishing in the wardrobe in her old home. Then she sighed before pulling out the blue wool dress she'd worn for the meal at The Riverside with Ann. It was the nicest one she had here, one of the pieces she'd bought from Eve's boutique, and Frank didn't seem to be one for dressing up. Though he had brushed up well for their trip to the auction house, he had still been dressed casually.

Finally, she was ready, just as there was a knock on the door. She threw a pashmina around her shoulders, grabbed her bag and opened the door to see Frank standing there shuffling his feet.

*

'This has been lovely.' Peta held up her glass for a refill and gazed around the busy restaurant. It had been a good idea of Frank's to come here. The Riverside Restaurant was clearly a favourite with Granite Springs residents who were out in force tonight filling the downstairs room with their chatter. Earlier, a large group of people in their early twenties had snaked through and made their way upstairs to where Frank told her there was a large function room.

'We do all right here,' Frank said, toasting her with his glass. 'To more occasions like this.'

Peta laughed and clinked her glass to his, determined not to spoil the mood.

'Dessert, madam, sir?'

Frank raised an eyebrow in Peta's direction as the waiter handed them both a menu.

'I shouldn't, but…' Peta scanned the offerings, deciding she could just manage the specialty of the house – a concoction of vanilla cream, meringue and strawberry coulis.

Frank ordered apple pie with ice cream, and coffee for them both.

'I've enjoyed tonight,' he said, leaning back in his chair as they waited for their desserts and coffee to arrive. 'It's been good to spend time with you, to try to work out what makes Peta Forrest tick.'

'And what did you discover?' Peta asked, the wine she'd drunk making her feel more relaxed and uninhibited than usual.

Frank pretended to consider for a few moments, then he leant his elbows on the table. 'I discovered you're quite a complicated lady. You like to give the impression of being in control, but I suspect that underneath you're still suffering from the death of your daughter.' He cocked his head to one side.

Peta swallowed. She thought she'd managed to hide her grief, the grief that was never far from the surface. A lump came to her throat. She picked up her glass, but it was empty. She nodded.

'It must be hard.' Frank stretched a hand across the table to cover hers.

Peta looked at it. For a moment she let it lie there, his large hand covering her much smaller one. It felt good, comforting. Then she gently drew hers away, pretending she needed to push a stray curl behind her ear. 'It is,' she said, the joy she'd felt in the evening suddenly shattered.

'Sorry, perhaps I shouldn't have said anything.' Frank appeared embarrassed.

'No, I did ask. It's just… I can forget it for a while, then it hits me again. I don't expect it'll ever go away completely. It's something

I have to learn to live with. It's easier here in Granite Springs,' she said with a tentative smile. 'There's something about this place.' She waved her hands in the air, remembering it was what Ann's friend, Fran, had said. She was right. Already, Peta could sense the warmth of this community wrapping around her like a cloak, protecting her from her demons and helping her move forward. *Where had those thoughts come from?*

And Frank was part of it. Now, he was gazing at her, his eyes filled with compassion.

'Sorry,' he repeated. 'I didn't mean to bring it all back. Is there anything I can do?'

Peta shook her head. 'No, Frank. Your very presence is a comfort to me. Tonight has helped me realise there is a future for me here in Granite Springs. Oh,' she waved her hands in the air again, 'I know I already had that with my new business and the kindness I've been shown by everyone I've met, but somehow...' She tried to find the words to express her feelings. She didn't want to give Frank the wrong impression. She was no love-struck teenager, but she'd enjoyed his company. Tonight had shown her she'd been right to believe Frank was different from other men she'd known. He was a true gentleman, and there weren't many of those left. 'I've enjoyed your company,' she said at last, knowing it didn't convey enough of how she felt.

Their desserts and coffee arrived before Frank could react, and her words appeared to be forgotten as they finished their meals.

*

'Thanks for this evening,' Peta said, as she prepared to slide out of Frank's ute, wondering if it would be too awkward to shake hands.

To her surprise, Frank laid a hand on her shoulder. When she turned to face him, his breath was warm on her cheek. 'I enjoyed it very much, Peta. The food and the company. I hope we can do it again.'

Peta's breath caught, his nearness making her tremble.

Then his lips met hers in a kiss so brief, she wondered if it had actually happened. He reached over and opened the door of the ute for her. 'I'll call you,' he said gruffly, as if regretting the impulse that had resulted in the kiss.

Watching Frank drive off, Peta raised her fingers to touch her lips and smiled. It was the first time in years she'd felt this yearning, this ache for something more. There had been men of course. After Tony's death, after Joy left home, she'd re-entered the dating scene. It was a way of surviving, of feeling alive again. The touch of another human being, skin on skin. But there had been no emotional involvement, no desire for commitment. They were ships that passed in the night, providing the comfort her husband never had, a way of forgetting. But she could never forget entirely, never quite give her all to anyone, never trust. Why did she feel differently about Frank? What was it about him that made her feel she'd found a man who was different, one who she could learn to trust again, one who she could feel safe with?

She thought back to the conversation with Ann and Fran. Had she been too quick to dismiss Fran's words? Could she find room for a man in her new life or was her grief still too fresh for her to consider anything else?

Twenty-two

Frank drove off in a daze. He couldn't believe he'd kissed Peta. It had happened so suddenly, without any thought. She'd been so close he could smell the faint aroma of her perfume. It was a flowery fragrance, very different to the citrus based one Marie always wore. It suited her and made him think of his grandmother's garden – a scent of roses mixed with other more delicate fragrances. Delicate, like the woman herself. Her lips were soft, too, enticing. It had taken all of his self-control to draw back, wary of panicking her.

In Frank's mind, Peta was like a tender flower, one which needed care and nurturing, one which would bloom with the correct amount of attention. She brought out all his protective instincts and here he was mooning over her like a teenager in the throes of his first love. He forced himself to think of other matters.

It had been a week since Lucy's call about Marie's birthday and so far, he'd done nothing about it other than mark the event in the diary in the café where anyone could see it. Marie probably already had. He'd bring it up with her tomorrow. Lucy had suggested a small party. There would be Marie and Drew, Lucy and Jess... who else? He thought for a moment, trying to remember Marie's friends. There was Fran. She and Marie had been close for years. Now she was married to Owen Larsen and had moved out of town. He couldn't think of anyone else. He'd need to ask Lucy – or perhaps Marie herself.

For a wild moment he wondered if he could invite Peta, a thrill surging through him at the thought. They did know each other, and

Marie had been trying to steer him in her direction. He tucked the thought away for future consideration. There were two more weeks till the party. He had plenty of time.

*

Saturday in the café was the usual rush, the presence of Lucy and Jess adding to the general chaos and noise. They were good kids and had quickly picked up the routine. They also now had a following, had helped The Bean Sprout become the go-to Saturday afternoon spot for the local senior school students. It reminded Frank of when he and Marie started dating. One Saturday at the café had been when they first noticed each other *in that way*. Now it was Jess and Ryan Kerr who teamed up when she had a minute to spare and they thought no one was looking.

Nick and Kay Kerr. Frank mentally added them to the list for Marie's party. He supposed he should include Ryan too, and didn't Nick have a daughter? He wondered if she'd want to come or be too independent to be included. He glanced across the café to where the younger set were crowded around two tables. Despite being busy serving customers, both Jess and Lucy had joined in on whatever discussion was going on. There was a boy there he hadn't seen before. He looked older than the rest and seemed to be taking a particular interest in Lucy who was tossing her hair coyly.

His heart sank. His Lucy! He'd always known this day would come. She was seventeen after all. For a time, he'd thought she was interested in Ryan Kerr. The boy had kept both her and Jess as friends for some time before showing a preference for a delighted Jess. But Lucy hadn't seemed to mind, and Frank had been relieved to keep her as his little girl for a bit longer. It was crazy. She wasn't his little girl. She was his niece – not even that, really. But he'd always been her Uncle Frank, always would be.

His thoughts turned to the other little girl who'd asked if she could call him Uncle Frank. It would be a long time before Lily would be interested in boys, he thought with relief, his mind going to the little girl's grandmother. Last night had been wonderful, all he'd hoped for.

Now he needed to work out how to follow it up. Despite a natural reticence, Peta had agreed to see him again. He just had to work out when and where.

By the time the café emptied, leaving Frank and Marie with a still excited Lucy and Jess, Frank had gone through various scenarios in his mind, none of which satisfied him.

'Off you go, girls,' he said to Lucy and Jess who were gazing longingly after their friends, some of whom were loitering outside the door. 'We'll let you off your cleaning duties for once.'

'Thanks, Uncle Frank.' Lucy gave him a hug as she threw her apron onto the counter and rushed past, Jess at her side, eager to join the boys who were waiting outside.

'I don't like the look of that one who seems interested in Lucy,' he said to Marie, peering through the glass to where his niece and her friend had joined Ryan and the older boy. 'Who is he?'

'I don't know, haven't seen him before.' Marie joined him at the door. 'I suppose it had to happen.' She sighed. 'It would be crazy to think she'd manage to go through her teenage years without losing her heart to someone.'

'He looks too old for her.'

'Listen to yourself, Frank. You're sounding like a protective father. She's not your responsibility. Dee would...' Marie bit her lip, clearly remembering she was in *loco parentis* for her sister's child. It was a role she'd been thrust into when her sister died so suddenly and one she took seriously. 'Anyway, she's young. It probably won't last.'

'She's the same age you were when we got together,' Frank reminded her, only to see her eyes glaze over.

'That was different. Different times,' Marie declared.

Frank wasn't so sure. He determined to ask Lucy about the boy when he had the opportunity. Meantime... 'You have a birthday coming up,' he said.

Marie sparkled. 'You remembered.'

'Of course. Don't I always?' He conveniently forgot it had been Lucy who reminded him this year. 'Have you anything planned?'

'Drew wants us to go somewhere special for a few days. I was going to ask you about it. You know how I hate to leave you in the lurch, and I feel I've been doing that more and more since Drew and I got together.'

'No worries, I can manage. Though maybe…' Frank wondered if now was the time to mention what had been preying on his mind, '… maybe it's time to reconsider the café.' There he'd said it.

Marie looked shocked. 'Reconsider? What do you mean?'

'Reconsider the future. It seems to me that when you and Drew marry, you'll have less time for all this.' He widened his arms to encompass the café. 'And it's become clear to me that Lucy, while enjoying her Saturdays here, has no intention of making it her future. Perhaps it's time for me to look elsewhere, too.'

'You wouldn't leave the café?'

Frank shrugged. 'Maybe not, but if I'm to stay, I'll need to think about its long-term future. I had an email from Italy.' He tried to gauge Marie's reaction. It was the first time he'd mentioned the email which arrived three weeks earlier. Frank had put it aside, wary of the visa difficulties involved, and unsure if he wanted to be responsible for what might be a young man with problems. But it had sat there at the back of his mind. He wasn't sure why he'd mentioned it now. Perhaps it was seeing Lucy with what he deemed to be *an unsuitable match* that made him think of it.

Marie was still staring at him as if he'd lost the plot. 'All I did was ask for a few days off. I don't have any intention of leaving the café.' Her eyes roamed around the room. 'I love this place just as much as you do. It's been part of my life for what seems like forever.'

'Sorry.' Frank dragged a hand through his hair. 'Of course, you can take a few days. You do more than your share when you are here. Just let me know when. Fifty this year, hey?' He grinned.

'Don't! It makes me feel old. Lucy says…'

'About Lucy.' He pulled on one ear. 'She wants to arrange a party for you – in the back room – the Sunday after your birthday. I'm not sure if she wants it to be a surprise, but I need to know who you want me to invite.'

'Oh, the dear girl. She's so like her mother sometimes, it makes me want to weep. If Dee had been alive.' She swallowed. 'We always said we'd do something special for each other when we turned fifty. But she didn't make it.'

They were silent for a few moments, remembering Marie's sister, dead before her time.

Then, 'A party? That sounds fun. Who do you have on your list?'

Frank reeled off the names he'd thought of. 'Is there anyone else?'

'I don't think so. I don't want a big bash, just close friends. I wonder about Lucy's beau?'

'Leave that to me. I'll talk to Lucy.'

Marie said nothing but gave him a warning glance. He'd known her long enough to understand what she meant – don't upset Lucy.

*

By the time he arrived home, Frank was ready for a beer. A blast of warm air greeted him when he opened the door, making him glad he'd finally fixed up the timer for the heating. He placed the box of café leftovers on the kitchen table before taking a beer out of the fridge and dropping into a chair. He was glad today was over. Now he had time to think.

Images of the three women in his life filled his head – Marie, Lucy and Peta. He supposed he should include Lily, but she was too young to cause him problems. She was a sweet kid. Despite what she'd been through, she had retained the innocence he remembered in Lucy as a child, an innocence that seemed to disappear in the teenage years to be replaced by a worrying lack of inhibition.

Frank ate his dinner quickly, the leftover pasta making a dent in his hunger. Then he took another beer from the fridge and went into the study. Mention of the email from Italy reminded him he had yet to reply. He was in two minds. Did he want to be saddled with a shirt tail relative he'd never heard of? Would the young man provide welcome company, help fill the emptiness of this big old house, or turn out to be a liability? Perhaps he could suggest he come for a visit. That wouldn't commit either of them, and would give Frank a chance to judge whether there was the possibility of a longer term arrangement.

He quickly composed the email, satisfied he'd managed to sound welcoming while avoiding promising any permanent future arrangement. The lad probably wouldn't qualify for a sponsored work visa anyway. He supposed he could check it out, but he knew very well there was no skill shortage for hospitality.

The email done, Frank took a long draught of beer and decided he might as well use the time to send out invitations to Marie's birthday. When he finished, he sent a text to Lucy detailing what he'd done and asking if she wanted to bring a partner. He winced as he did it, but remembered Marie's warning. Almost before he'd pressed *send*, her reply pinged into his phone. How did these young ones manage to do that? He imagined Lucy's fingers flying across her phone. Frank smiled at the line of emojis Lucy had sent along with, *Well done, Uncle Frank. Thanks x* There was no mention of any addition to the list of attendees, so he heaved a sigh of relief the young man from the café wasn't of sufficient interest to warrant an invitation.

It was as he drained the can of beer Frank admitted to himself these had all been delaying tactics, delaying the call to Peta he knew he should make, wanted to make. He took a deep breath and nervously picked up his phone again.

Twenty-three

Peta had a smile on her face as she closed the phone. It hadn't taken Frank long to be back in touch. It was lovely to hear his voice again and to remember how much she'd enjoyed his company. It had occurred to her to pop down to the café today when Lily was off riding with the twins and their dad again, but she'd stifled the impulse lest he think she was keen to see him. She wasn't, but despite all the work she knew she had to do, the flat seemed empty without Lily. It was odd. It didn't feel that way on weekdays when Lily was at school. But this was Saturday, a day when families did things together.

Eve had invited her and Lily to dinner this evening, but she'd declined, making excuses. She preferred to stay home with the little girl. She didn't want to become dependent on the kindness of others. It was enough Eve's mother had invited them out to Yarran again next day. Lily was excited about the visit, remembering the fun with the alpacas last time. And of course, the twins would be there again.

'What's the matter, Grandma?' Lily appeared and climbed up on the sofa beside Peta. 'What are you thinking about?' She wrested the phone from Peta who was still clutching it and stared at the blank screen. 'Did someone call?'

Peta gave herself a shake, remembering Frank's suggestion. It was good of him to want to include Lily in their arrangements. 'It was your Uncle Frank,' she said, her voice stumbling over the name Lily had bestowed on him. 'How would you like to go to dinner at his house one day next week?'

Lily paused. 'Will you be going too?'

Peta laughed. 'Of course.'

'He must be a good cook if he makes all the food in the café.'

Peta laughed again. 'He's probably a better cook than I am.'

'Okay.' She dropped the phone into Peta's lap and slid to the floor. 'I can't wait till tomorrow,' she said. 'Livvy says her grandma's going to take us up the lane to see goats and horses. And there's a cat and more dogs.' Her eyes glowed in anticipation.

Peta winced. She'd done nothing about finding a pet for Lily, perhaps hoping in her innermost heart the little girl would forget about it. But she knew she wouldn't, and tomorrow's visit would no doubt only serve to reinforce her longing. 'Well, better have a good sleep so you'll have the energy,' she said, rising and tucking her phone into her pocket. 'Go and brush your teeth and I'll be through to kiss you goodnight in a little while.'

'Can I read for a bit? It helps me sleep.'

Peta hesitated. It was past Lily's usual bedtime, but she was aware of the nightmares that had plagued her and if a few minutes reading would help. 'Okay, fifteen minutes.'

'Thanks, Grandma.' Lily beamed and disappeared.

Alone again, Peta fingered the phone in her pocket. Frank's suggestion of cooking dinner for them had surprised her. When he mentioned seeing her again the night before, she'd imagined having to work out something for Lily or having to wait till her granddaughter had another sleepover. She couldn't imagine any other man including her granddaughter in a date. And to invite them to his home. But it would give her more of an insight into the man himself. Although she knew it had been Marie's home, too, and Marie's alone for the past few years, Frank no doubt had a major say in it at some point. The flat had been his, too, but had been impersonal, unlived in. Peta was sure the house would be more revealing.

*

'Time to get up!'

Peta was awakened by a bright-eyed Lily tugging at her shoulder. She opened her eyes and gazed blearily at the excited little girl. She sat up. 'What time is it?' She glanced at the bedside clock, surprised to see it was already eight o'clock. 'Okay. Why don't you have a shower and get yourself dressed while I do the same?'

Lily pranced off, leaving Peta to rise more leisurely and take herself off to the ensuite.

Dressed in a pair of jeans topped by a royal blue turtle-necked sweater, Peta was making scrambled eggs when Lily sauntered into the kitchen, a book in her hand. 'Can you pop a couple of slices of bread in the toaster, sweetie?' Peta asked.

'Mmm,' was Lily's muffled response, her head still in her book. But she did as she was bid before settling down at the table still engrossed in what she was reading.

'Good book?'

'Mmm.'

Peta smiled to herself, delighted Lily found such pleasure in reading. Joy had been the same at that age. Peta had often told her the house could be on fire and she'd never notice if her head was in a good book. Her love of books hadn't survived in her marriage, however, Grant refusing to countenance anything that took her attention from him and the running of his house. Why hadn't Peta tried to intervene? Why had she assumed everything would be fine? But it was too late now. All she could do was ensure Lily had a happy childhood.

'When can we leave?' Lily asked, when her plate was empty, and she'd drained the last of her juice.

'It's a bit early,' Peta said, checking her watch. 'We could go out to see if there's anywhere open where we can buy something to take to the twins' grandma.'

'We could get some brownies downstairs in the café.'

'No, honey. It's Sunday. The café's closed. But I'm sure we can find somewhere open. You'll need a jacket.'

Peta shrugged on her own wool jacket and picked up her bag, automatically checking her phone as they walked out. She had two texts, one from Ann thanking her for dinner and one from Frank confirming dinner on Tuesday. There was a missed call from Eve Tait.

She pressed return call as she hurried Lily out to the car. 'Hi, Eve, sorry I missed your call. We're on our way out. What's up?' As she pressed the control and Lily hopped into the car, she was hoping nothing had happened to stop the twins going to Yarran today.

'Thanks for calling back. I need to ask a favour. As you know, I was supposed to be taking the girls out to Mum's for lunch. They're excited about meeting up with Lily again. But Emily Rose has developed a temperature and I think I should keep her home. Brad's out on one of his mammoth rides,' she sighed. 'I don't want to disappoint the twins – life would be unbearable. So, I wondered if they could travel out and back with you.'

'Sure. No problem. I hope it's nothing serious with Emily Rose.'

'I don't expect so. I just want to be sure.'

'We're just off out. I can pick the twins up in an hour if that works for you.'

'Perfect. I'll let Mum know. Thanks.'

An hour later, after discovering a neat bakery on the bank of the river where Peta enjoyed a leisurely coffee and Lily a smoothie, they set off again. A delicious-looking pear and almond tart was sitting in a box on the passenger seat to leave room for the twins beside Lily in the back seat.

The car had barely stopped outside the Tait's home when the two girls rushed out and bundled into the car with delighted squeals. Eve waved from the doorway.

'I won't come out,' she called. 'Take care and enjoy your lunch.'

'Thanks, Eve,' Peta called back through an open window before ensuring the girls all had their seatbelts fastened.

Driving with three youngsters in the car was a new experience for Peta. Both Lily and Livvy were the chatterboxes with Lottie interrupting from time to time, but mostly remaining silent, content to gaze out the window, as Peta could see from her frequent glances in the rearview mirror. It was good to see them so happy, so free of the cares besetting their adult counterparts. Deep down, she knew she had to sort things out.

*

'Here you are!' Jo came out to greet them as soon as Peta pulled up. Scout was at her heel and all three girls made a big fuss of the old dog who clearly loved the attention. 'Thanks for bringing these two out,' Jo said.

'It was the least I could do.'

'Emily Rose is sick,' Livvy informed Jo, turning from Scout to give her grandmother a hug, 'so we got to come with Lily's grandma.'

Jo smiled. 'Why don't we all go inside so I can fetch a jacket and Scout's lead? I think Lily's grandma and your grandad want to have a chat, so I thought we could go for a walk. We'll have lunch when we get back. Lily hasn't met Owen and Fran's goats or Magda's horses.'

'Or her greyhounds or Fran's cat,' Lottie added. 'We told her about them. She's going to get a cat of her own.'

Jo raised an eyebrow in Peta's direction.

'I think I may have to give in to this one,' Peta said, still unsure how happy a cat would be in the confines of the flat.

When Jo had left, trailed by the three girls, Scout padding along beside them, Col turned to Peta. 'Let's go into the study. Would you like tea or coffee?'

'No thanks, I've not long had one.' Peta could still feel the effects of the caffeine from the coffee she'd had before leaving town, and her stomach was churning at the thought of what Col might have to tell her.

'Well,' he said, when Peta had outlined the issue as she saw it and repeated what Gordon had told her, 'I'm afraid my old colleague is a bit out of date. Guardianship Orders are rare nowadays. Most states and territories, including New South Wales, referred their powers re children, legitimate or otherwise. Children's issues are now dealt with under the Family Law Act. Proceedings are usually in the Family Court, or here in Granite Springs, the State Local Court. You do need to start proceedings as soon as possible for a residency order, final and interim.'

'I'm sorry. I don't understand.'

'Sorry, it's easy for me to forget I talk in what some people call legalese. To put it simply, you need to apply for the care of your granddaughter on a short-term and long-term basis. You need to apply for both at once and you need to apply to the court.'

'What will happen?' Peta began to tremble. This all sounded more complicated than she'd expected. She'd thought it would only be a matter of filling in a couple of forms.

Col leant back in his chair and steepled his fingers. 'The court will make an order for counselling, and almost certainly make an order appointing an ICL – that's an Independent Children's Lawyer – to represent the child's interest. The ICL would be from the Legal Aid Commission NSW or a private lawyer appointed by the Commission. The ICL would interview the child and anyone else who could help with information to decide the child's best interests.' He paused. 'Are you sure you wouldn't like a cup of something?'

'No.' But Peta was beginning to feel chilled. 'Will... will Lily be asked about this?'

'Yes, the court could take her wishes into account. What you must understand is they are bound to make their decision on what they deem to be the best interests of the child – in this case a child who has lost her mother and perhaps her father for a very long time.'

'But surely that's with me!' Peta burst out. 'Sorry, but I'm her grandmother, her mother's mother. She knows me. She's comfortable with me.'

'I have to ask, is there anyone else who might have a claim?'

A cold shiver ran up Peta's spine. 'There's her aunt, her father's sister, but...'

'Then you should contact her.'

Contact Celia? Contact the woman who'd sworn blind her brother was innocent, the woman who had never had any time for Joy, thought her brother had made a mistake, the woman who'd never paid any attention to Lily? She swallowed hard. 'Go on. I suppose Grant will have a say in it, too?' she asked bitterly.

'I presume Grant's the father? He would need to be served with a copy of your application. Is he close to his sister? He might contact her, and she might seek her own orders. That's why it's important to involve her. This could be done through the ICL.'

Peta could feel herself begin to tremble. What if...? She couldn't think straight. 'This... this ICL person. What's their role?'

'The ICL is obliged to consider the views of the child, but ultimately provide their own, independent perspective about what arrangements or decisions are in the child's best interests. Their main roles include arranging for necessary evidence, including expert evidence, to be obtained and put before the court.'

'Will I have to go to court?' Peta knotted her hands together to prevent them shaking. *This was sounding worse and worse.*

'Yes, at least for counselling, but as to hearings that would depend on whether the matter is defended.'

And knowing Grant, the bastard will defend it. He never liked me, always considered me an interfering old woman. But I didn't interfere enough to save my lovely daughter.

She exhaled loudly. 'So, what should I do now? Can you help?'

'I'm retired. You really need to go back to see Gordon. But I can have a word with him if you like, or....' He gave Peta a speculative look. 'Let me talk with him. I'll tell him about our little chat, suggest I look after you. I haven't entirely given up my profession. How would that be?'

'Oh, would you, Col? I'd be much happier working with you. Gordon was...' She hesitated, unsure how to describe how the other man made her feel.

'He's not always the most empathetic person in the world,' Col said, clearly understanding her dilemma. 'But he's a good lawyer. However, perhaps in this case...'

'Yes, please.'

'Okay. Let me talk with him and I'll have Dot ring you to set up a proper appointment to get things moving. You've met Dot?'

'Yes.' Peta remembered the motherly woman who'd put her at ease in the solicitor's office. 'That would be good. Thanks.'

'Now I think we both need a drink. Come through to the kitchen and I'll pour us both a glass of wine while we're waiting for the others to return. I know Jo has a roast in the oven which should be almost done.'

Relieved their talk was over, even though it hadn't gone exactly as she expected, Peta followed Col into the large family kitchen which was filled with the enticing aroma of roasting meat and herbs, mainly rosemary.

By the time Jo returned with the three excited girls, Peta was feeling calmer. She'd face whatever she had to do to retain care of Lily, even if it meant having to defend her claim in court. What a court case about her care might do to the still fragile Lily, she couldn't imagine, but according to what Col had told her, there was no way of avoiding this process.

'Grandma, it was so much fun,' Lily crowed, coming over to give Peta a hug.

Peta pulled her tightly towards her, wishing she could keep her safe from what was to come, but the little girl pulled away, determined to share her news.

'We saw goats. They were so naughty, and there was a black cat called Stormy, and then there were horses and *two* dogs.' She paused for breath, then demanded, 'When am I going to get *my* cat?'

'Sorry,' Jo mouthed to Peta, then said aloud, 'We called in on Owen and Fran – she says she's met you?'

Peta nodded remembering the friendly woman she'd met at Ann's.

'Then we visited Magda and George who live further up the lane. Magda's home was burned down in the last bushfire and she had to rebuild. But it seemed to be for the best as it brought her and George together. They're an older couple and really sweet together.'

'Magda said I was just like her granddaughter when she was my age,' Lily said. 'She showed me a photo, but I didn't think it looked like me at all.' She made a face.

They all laughed.

*

After lunch, Col allowed himself to be persuaded to take the girls to talk to the alpacas again, leaving Peta alone with Jo.

'I hope Col was able to help,' Jo said, when they were seated in a sheltered spot on the veranda with cups of tea.

'He was. It's more complicated than I expected. It seems like I'll have to go to court to claim my right to care for Lily – and her dad might defend it.'

'Oh, my dear!' Jo put a comforting hand on Peta's arm. 'But what is there to defend?'

'He has a sister,' Peta said bitterly. 'Celia Holmes never married and has always claimed Grant was falsely accused, that it was a burglary gone wrong. In her opinion, her sainted brother could do no evil. She has no idea what Joy had to suffer. She'd never believe it of him.'

'And you think he'd want her to have Lily?'

'I don't know what to think.' Peta could feel herself wilting, the anxiety which Col's words had created building up again. 'But he and his sister are very close. It wouldn't surprise me in the least.'

'Oh dear. I can see why you might be worried. Is there anything you can do?'

Peta gave a heavy sigh. 'I need to submit this application, then it's up to the court and someone called an ICL to decide what's best for Lily. I can only hope...' she took out a tissue to wipe her eyes. 'Sorry.'

'Nothing to be sorry about. So, you need to go back to Gordon?'

'Col has offered to work with me on the application. It's very good of him. I know he's retired and has all this to take care of.' She gestured across the paddock, to where Col and the girls were leading a couple of alpacas around.

'Oh, he does like to keep his hand in,' Jo said with a gentle smile. 'And I took care of Yarran for years before Col joined me. Though the alpacas are his baby. But he's a good solicitor, perhaps more careful than my ex, especially when it comes to family law. He'll be able to help you, if anyone can.'

'Thanks.' Peta tucked the tissue away and took a sip of tea.

It wasn't long before Col and the girls returned, and Peta determined it was time to leave. The three girls were full of energy on the drive back, bouncing around on the back seat and alternating between singing along to their favourite tunes and recounting their adventures with all the animals they'd met.

Peta was exhausted by the time she dropped the twins off, declining Eve's invitation to join them for dinner. She'd had enough company for the day and just wanted to be home alone with Lily. But, as she pulled into the parking space for the flat, she saw a figure outside the back door of the café. It was Frank Beattie.

Twenty-four

Frank had had a busy day catching up on the café accounts. He'd delayed working on his tax return, but as the deadline neared, he knew he had to get it done. Although he used an accountant, it was up to him to provide the details. Late afternoon he'd discovered a vital piece of information was missing and, rather than wait till next day, had headed out to The Bean Sprout where he found what he was looking for.

He was locking up again and preparing to leave when Peta Forrest's car pulled up. At first, he blinked to make sure he wasn't seeing things. Peta had been in his mind all day. He had to work out what he'd cook for the dinner to which he'd invited her and Lily. It was only two days away and he'd almost settled on a special roast lamb dish which had been one of his mother's favourites.

'It's Uncle Frank!' Lily's excited voice called out as soon as the car stopped and the door was opened. 'Guess what I saw today?' she asked, skipping across to where he was standing.

'Come here, Lily. Frank doesn't want to…' Peta began.

Frank grinned. He knew who he'd bet on if it came to a disagreement between Lily and her grandmother. He was right. Lily ignored Peta and kept on moving till she stood right in front of him, legs apart hands on her hips.

'What did you see?' he asked, ignoring Peta's tight lips.

'We saw goats, horses, dogs, alpacas and a lovely little back cat. Grandma still hasn't bought me my cat,' she complained, casting an irritated glance towards where Peta was standing at the foot of the stairs.

Frank glanced over towards Peta. He was still grinning at this unexpected meeting. He'd been thinking about her, and here she was. Not terribly unusual as she did live here, but a lucky chance. As he watched, she moved towards them.

'We've been visiting Jo Ford at her acreage,' she said. 'Her granddaughters were there too. I'm afraid Lily's still high on the excitement of it all. Sorry to bother you with it.'

'Not at all. It's lovely to see her so full of the joys of life. Sadly, we lose that capacity as we grow older. Don't you remember feeling that way about things? I do.' Frank could still remember his first sight of the ocean. He must have been a few years younger than Lily was now, when his parents had taken a break from the café to spend a week at Batemans Bay on the south coast. The vast stretch of sand and sea had been a revelation to the little boy accustomed to the arid country town. He'd taken off to run across the sand into the water without taking time to remove his shorts and shirt. His mother had been furious, but his dad had merely laughed.

It was a long time since he'd been to the coast. He should do it again. Perhaps he could offer to take Peta and Lily?

Peta was staring at him as if he'd gone mad. 'I don't recall,' she said. 'It's been a busy day. We need to get inside.' She shivered as a cool breeze blew up, sending a stray piece of paper flying across the parking lot.

'I'm sorry. Listen to your grandma, Lily. I'll catch you later.' He turned to walk away when he noticed the moisture in Peta's eyes. Immediately his manner changed. 'Are you all right, Peta? Did something happen to upset you?'

He thought she was going to crumble. For a moment she seemed to fade, then pulled herself up straighter. 'It's been a difficult day with one thing and another. I'll be fine.'

'You don't look fine.' Without thinking, Frank said, 'Why don't I come up with you and make you a coffee – or tea if you prefer? You look exhausted,' he added, noting the dark shadows beneath her eyes. Why hadn't he noticed them earlier?

He could see she was about to refuse, then she shrugged.

'Okay.'

Once inside, he filled Peta's coffee machine, glad to see she had a supply of a good brand, while she organised a reluctant Lily to have a bath.

'Here, this will perk you up.' Frank handed Peta a mug of coffee when she returned to the kitchen.

'Thanks,' she said, perching at the bench on one of the high stools Frank had left behind.

'Now, what's up?' Frank was standing behind the kitchen bench. He leant his elbows on the surface cradling his mug in both hands. 'Did something happen out at the Fords' to upset you?'

'No. Yes. Oh, Frank!'

Peta's eyes started to moisten again, making Frank want to envelop her in a warm hug and tell her he wouldn't let anyone hurt her. Somehow, he managed to resist the impulse. He waited, seeing she was having difficulty in deciding whether or not to share what was upsetting her.

Finally, she put down her mug and traced an invisible pattern on the benchtop with one finger, her eyes following it as if it held the answer to all her woes. When she raised her eyes again, they were filled with angst.

'It's Lily,' she said, her voice barely audible. 'Col says I need to go to court to keep her. There's to be counselling, something called an ICL and her father has the right to contest it. What if...?' Her eyes widened in alarm and she began to shake.

In an instant, Frank was around the bench and at her side. Without thinking and regardless of the wisdom of his action, he took her in his arms and hugged her tightly. She felt like a fragile little bird as he held her close, the floral fragrance that always surrounded her more potent now she was in his arms. He inhaled the heady aroma, feeling her move slightly. But she didn't try to move out of his clasp, instead seeming to move closer.

For Frank, time stood still.

'Sorry, I didn't mean to let go like that. It was so unexpected. I thought I was within my rights to bring Lily here with me. Now I have to prove I'm the best person to look after her.'

'Of course you are.' Frank held Peta at arm's length, seeing her deep brown eyes filled with tears. Taking one finger, he wiped away a drop which was trickling down her cheek. Her skin was as soft as he'd imagined. He gently stroked her cheek with his thumb.

Peta moved away. 'Sorry,' she said again, looking down at the floor.

'I've had my bath.' Lily's abrupt entrance interrupted what was, for Frank, a tender moment. 'I'm hungry, Grandma,' she added.

'Of course.' Peta wiped her eyes again.

The two mugs of coffee were still sitting on the benchtop. They'd be cold by now.

Frank cleared his throat. 'I guess I should be going. Will you be all right?' He didn't want to leave her like this, but what could he do? He felt so useless. This wasn't like the time Marie's sister died when he was able to take charge and make all the arrangements. This was something completely outside his responsibility – and knowledge. While he wanted to be the person to help Peta through it, he knew he had to leave it to the professional, to Col Ford.

'Thanks – for listening, for being here.' Peta managed a teary smile.

'I'm sorry I can't be of more help. But Col's a good guy and a sound lawyer, though he's retired now.'

'He can still practice. He's going to get the receptionist to set up a meeting.' Peta was still downcast, but Frank thought he could see her natural confidence begin to reassert itself. 'I'm sure it'll be fine. You just caught me at a bad time.'

'If there's anything I can do, you only have to ask. We're still on for Tuesday?' he asked at the door.

Peta nodded. 'I'm looking forward to seeing your house and to sampling your home cooking. An Italian dish, I hope.'

'Of course!'

He stood rocking back on his heels wondering whether to kiss her.

Peta solved his problem by standing on tiptoes to give him a brief peck on the cheek. 'See you then.'

The door closed behind her and Frank was left to stumble down the stairs wondering if he'd imagined their moment of closeness.

Twenty-five

Peta shivered as her feet hit the bedroom floor on Tuesday morning. While other parts of Australia seemed to be enjoying spring-like weather, Granite Springs was still in the thrall of an icy blast which felt as if it was coming straight from the Antarctic. It reminded Peta of a holiday she'd taken to Tasmania when she and her companion sought out motels with electric blankets and cafés with tomato soup. That had been a long time ago, before she and Tony married, but it had stuck in her mind.

'Is it tonight we're going to Uncle Frank's?' Lily asked, as she spooned up the porridge Peta had managed to introduce her to, albeit topped with brown sugar and maple syrup. It was a concoction too sweet for Peta who preferred low fat natural yoghurt on hers.

'It is. So, you'll need to do your homework as soon as you come home from school. It will be too late when we get back.' Peta took a gulp of coffee and checked the time. She had a lot to get through today, starting with a meeting with Col. True to his word, Col had spoken to both Gordon and Dot. The result was a call from Dot the day before and the meeting this morning. Peta supposed she should be pleased he'd acted so promptly, but part of her wished she had longer to get used to the idea. It was a bit like going to the dentist, she thought. You wanted it over, but were reluctant to make the appointment. This one had been made for her.

Waving Lily off at the school gates, Peta turned to see Eve smiling at her.

'Time for a coffee?' Eve asked.

Peta hesitated, about to refuse then, remembering how she'd refused both of Eve's invitations to dinner, nodded. 'I just have time for a quick one.'

'Me, too. I have to open the boutique at ten. Shall we go to The Bean Sprout?'

Peta hesitated again, but it was difficult to refuse as the café was the closest one to the school and along the road from Eve's boutique. It was also near the office where she was meeting Col at ten o'clock. She nodded.

To Peta's relief, there was no sign of Frank when they entered the café. Marie took their orders giving Peta what seemed to her like a knowing look. It was Eve who, when Marie served their coffees asked, 'Frank not in this morning?'

'He's shopping.'

Did she wink or did Peta imagine it? She kept her eyes glued to her coffee until Marie left.

'This is such a great café,' Eve said, oblivious to the exchange. 'I started coming here when I was in high school. We used to bunk off and come to the café to drink coffee and play cards – thought we were so sophisticated. It was run by Frank's parents back then, of course. Then his dad became sick, and Frank and Marie married. It's been an institution in Granite Springs for generations. Lucky you, living upstairs.'

'It's certainly very convenient,' Peta replied. She was watching the door, hoping Frank wouldn't arrive till after they'd left. For some reason she couldn't fathom, she was reluctant for him to see her having coffee here.

Fortunately, he still hadn't returned when they finished. The two women left the café and while Eve walked up Main Street to open her store, Peta walked in the other direction to meet with Col Ford and begin the process of submitting the paperwork for the interim and final residency order.

The rest of the day passed smoothly and, by the time Peta walked down to pick up Lily for school, she was pleased with her progress. Also, the hotel chain had replied to her query. They were impressed with her resumé and were eager to meet with her the following week, another possible commission for *Forrest Interiors*.

Lily skipped along at Peta's side, chattering about what had happened in school. She was a different child from the one who had been afraid of her own shadow when they arrived in town.

Suddenly, Lily stopped in her tracks and stared up at Peta. 'When am I going to get my cat?' she asked.

'Soon, as soon as I have time.' But Peta knew it was a weak excuse. She'd been procrastinating, unsure of how suited the flat was to an animal, even though Frank had given his approval.

*

Peta pulled up outside the red brick federation-style home. It was like many of the other houses in Granite Springs, including Ann's, with its typical elaborate gables, timber features, dominant roofline, and leadlight windows. It was exactly what Peta expected.

Peta and Lily walked up the path and knocked on the door. When Frank opened it, they followed him into the house, Lily hanging back a little, seeming to return to her former shyness. 'This seems like a lovely house,' Peta said, gazing around the wide hallway with its high ceiling, wooden picture rail and skirting board. The floors had been sanded and stained to give a warm appearance. 'Looks like you've done a lot of work here.'

'You should have seen it when Marie and I first bought it. But it was a labour of love.' He stroked the wall like an old friend. 'It's always felt like home. Even when Marie was living here on her own and I was in the flat. It's good to be back.' Frank led them into a large family kitchen filled with the aroma of cooking. She sniffed, identifying rosemary and thyme mingling with the smell of roast lamb. 'I thought we could eat here.' He rubbed a hand across his head, ruffling his hair.

Peta glanced around the kitchen. It was so well-designed, it could have been a restaurant kitchen, but it managed to have a homely feel, perhaps due to the scrubbed wood table which took pride of place in the centre. It was set for three. She wondered whether the kitchen design had been Marie or Frank's choice.

'A glass of wine?'

While she'd been lost in thought, Frank had taken a bottle of white wine from the fridge and was holding up two glasses.

'Thanks.'

Frank filled the glasses with wine, then another with juice for Lily.

'Do you live here all by yourself?' Lily asked when she and Peta were seated at the kitchen bench with their drinks.

Frank chuckled. 'Do you think this house is too big for just one person?' he asked.

Lily appeared to consider the question then said seriously, 'I think you need a dog to keep you company.'

'A dog? I'd never thought of that. But what would happen to it when I was at work?'

'Hmm. Maybe he could come with you and I could play with him when I come home from school. Grandma has promised to get me a pet, but it hasn't happened yet.' She threw a baleful glance at Peta.

'She's right,' Peta said. 'We decided on a cat as I think I told you, but I haven't a clue how to go about finding one.'

'I may be able to help you there. One of our customers mentioned she's looking for a home for her cat. She's moving and can't take the cat with her. It's not a kitten, which might be all to the good.'

Peta was unsure, but one look at Lily's beaming face decided for her. 'Maybe… if she's still looking for a home for it, we could meet her.'

'She comes in with a friend every Thursday. I can speak with her then and let you know.'

'Thanks. I seem to be forever thanking you for something. Why are you doing all this for us?'

Frank gazed into his wine. 'I want to make things easier for you both. You've both been through a lot. If there's anything I can do to help, then I'm happy to do so. It's a small thing.'

Lily beamed again. 'How soon can we get the cat?'

'Steady on, sweetheart, we have to find out if it's still available and check out its temperament. If it's an old cat, it might be set in its ways and difficult to adapt to a new home,' Peta said.

Lily's bottom lip drooped.

'Wait till Thursday, and we can find out. Right?'

'Your grandma's right,' Frank said. 'You need to make sure the cat's the right one for you. I'll talk with Vera on Thursday then let your grandma know. Perhaps you can go to meet the cat?'

With that, Lily seemed to be content, though Peta knew the girl would talk of nothing else for the next two days.

'It must be time for dinner,' Frank said.

They moved across to the kitchen table, and Frank carried over two large dishes which he'd removed from the oven.

Putting the discussion about the cat aside, Peta took another sip of wine and helped herself to the lamb and roast vegetables. 'This looks delicious,' she said.

'Mum's recipe.'

Peta smiled recalling how she'd dismissed her own cooking as her nonna's.

'Let me guess,' she said. 'Sunday Mediterranean roast lamb. It was my mum's standby, too. I haven't made it for years. My... Tony didn't enjoy lamb, and I became used to roasting beef or chicken.'

'You haven't mentioned your husband before now.'

'No, I... some other time,' Peta said, glancing at Lily out of the corner of her eye. The little girl appeared to be concentrating on her food, but Peta knew how Lily had the habit of listening when you didn't expect her to. She knew she needed to tell Frank about Tony if their relationship was going any further. It was part of her, a part she wanted to forget, but a part that had helped form her into the woman she was,

As the meal progressed, the conversation flowed with Peta and Frank sharing stories of their Italian parents. Both of Frank's had Italian heritage while, for Peta, it was only her mother.

Suddenly, Lily yawned and pushed away her plate.

'Oh, dear, I think it might be time to take Lily home.' Peta was sorry the evening was about to end. She was enjoying Frank's company, and it was good to learn more about him and his family.

'Perhaps we can do this again,' Frank suggested when they were standing at the door.

Lily was huddling into Peta's side to escape the cool breeze, or perhaps because she was tired. Maybe it had been a mistake to agree to dinner on a school night which had broken one of Peta's rules. 'Yes,' she said softly, feeling a warmth for this kind man.

As she drove home, Lily falling asleep in the back seat, Peta wondered if it was gratitude she felt for all the help Frank had given them, or if her feelings were of another sort entirely.

Twenty-six

Frank walked back through the house into the kitchen. As he cleared away the dishes and packed the leftovers into the fridge, he thought over the evening. It had been a success, and he now had a reason to contact Peta again. Next time, he vowed he'd invite her to Marie's birthday party. He whistled to himself as he stacked the dishwasher, then poured the remains of the wine into a glass.

It had been a godsend to think of Vera's cat. The poor woman had been distraught at the thought of having the animal put down if she couldn't find a home for it. But there was no way she could take it with her into the retirement home. They had a strict no pets policy. How wonderful if he could solve both her and Peta's problem in one fell swoop. He didn't think Peta was hooked on having a cat, but Lily was, and he knew she'd do anything for her granddaughter.

Taking his wine into the study, Frank fired up his computer, still on a high from Peta's visit. He scrolled down the emails he hadn't taken time to check for a couple of days, to discover a reply to the one he'd sent to Italy.

Frank's forehead creased as he read it. Alfonso Baldini was to arrive in Granite Springs in two weeks' time. It seemed his parents couldn't wait to be shot of him, which didn't bode well for Frank's peace of mind. The young man had obtained a twelve-month working holiday visa which permitted him to work in a regional area, remaining with one employer for no more than six months.

As he scanned the rest of the email, he discovered Al was purported to be fluent in English and keen to meet Cousin Frank. He'd been studying engineering at the Politecnico di Milano close to his hometown of Cesano Maderno. Frank pushed a hand through his hair. What good was an engineering student going to be in The Bean Sprout? Frank sighed. It seemed he was to be hosting – and employing – this unknown relative for the next six months.

*

It was a relief to Frank to see Vera and her friend enter the café as usual on Thursday morning. They ordered their customary pots of tea with a slice of banana bread to share and settled at their favourite table by the window where they could watch everyone passing by.

Frank waited until they'd been served and there was a lull in the busy morning before going over to speak with her. 'Morning, Vera. You're looking well, as usual. Have you found a home for your cat yet?'

Vera had been chatting cheerfully with her friend when he approached, but at his words her eyes clouded over. 'No, I haven't, and I don't know what I'm going to do. Archie's such a gentle, friendly cat. He's been my companion for so long, I can't bear to think...' She put a finger up to wipe her eyes. Her friend patted her arm and glared at Frank.

'I might have found a solution for you.'

She perked up. 'You have?'

'The woman who's living in the flat upstairs – Peta Forrest. Her granddaughter is eager for a cat and Peta didn't know where to find one. I mentioned you to her and...' Frank thought Vera was going to jump up and throw her arms around him.

'Oh, Frank, would she really give my Archie a home?'

'Perhaps, if Lily – that's her granddaughter – and he take to each other.'

'He loves children and was always a favourite with my grandchildren when they visited, but they're older now and there's no room for a cat in their lives. Not much room for me either,' she sniffed.

'What I suggest is that Peta and Lily visit you and Archie before anything is decided. Would that work for you?'

'Oh, yes! I can't thank you enough. I can move into Eden Gardens more easily if I know he's found a good home. When could they come?'

'Let me talk with Peta. She may even be upstairs now.' It occurred to Frank Peta ran her business from the flat. His heart surged at the thought he had a reason to pop upstairs and knock on her door. 'Let me check.'

Leaving the two women smiling their thanks, Frank headed over to let Marie know where he was going. He ignored her raised eyebrows and made his way outside and up the stairs. Once there, he realised he'd left in such a rush, he was still wearing his black café apron. He took a deep breath and raised his hand to knock.

Peta opened the door, a smile on her face. 'Frank!'

This morning she was casually dressed in a pair of black leggings topped with a long red sweater. She looked good enough to eat. Frank swallowed as a lump came to his throat.

'You've caught me in my work clothes,' Peta said apologetically. 'Won't you come in?'

'I won't stay, I need to get back.' Frank cursed inwardly. He was sounding like a lovestruck teenager. 'Vera's in the café now. The cat's still available. Would you like to come down to meet her?'

'I would. Let me finish what I'm doing. Five minutes okay?'

Frank nodded and Peta closed the door. He made his way back downstairs wishing he could restart the conversation, sound more sensible, intelligent.

Vera looked up expectantly when he returned.

'She'll be down shortly. Would you two ladies like another pot of tea?' he asked. 'No charge.'

'That would be lovely.'

Frank hurried off to make the tea, adding a cappuccino for Peta who arrived as he was finishing. She was still wearing her work clothes but had done something to her hair and seemed to Frank's uneducated eyes to be wearing more makeup.

Frank picked up the tray with the tea and coffee and led Peta over to Vera and her friend.

'Vera, this is Peta, the lady I told you about.'

'Hello, Vera. Frank tells me you have a cat that needs a new home.'

'I certainly do. My Archie's been with me for almost ten years, but

I can't take him with me where I'm going and I'd hate to see him destroyed.'

Peta dropped into a chair and Frank placed the tea and coffee on the table. 'Let me know if you need anything else,' he said, before leaving the three women to take care of another customer.

There was a rush of customers and while Frank was busy making coffee, he kept his eyes on the table by the window, pleased to see Peta and Vera seemed to be making friends. When the two older women finally rose to leave, Peta joined him by the espresso machine.

'Thanks,' she said. 'Vera's lovely. I feel so sorry for her having to find a home for her cat, and her family live so far away she rarely sees them. Lily and I are going over after school to meet Archie.'

'No problem.' But a warm glow spread through Frank knowing he'd been able to help Peta again.

'Vera says if Lily and Archie take to each other, we can bring him home right away. She has a lot to do to prepare for her move. She said her house has already been sold. The poor woman. So…' Peta gave a cheeky grin, '…why don't you pop upstairs when you close up. You can meet Archie too. I can't imagine us returning without him.' She laughed. 'You need to see what you've let me in for.' With a wave to Marie, she was off, leaving Frank gazing after her in surprise.

Twenty-seven

'I have a surprise for you,' Peta told Lily as she greeted her at the school gate, managing to extricate her from the twins.

Lily didn't immediately respond. Instead she said, 'Lottie wanted me to wait with her till her mum arrives. She has to go to the dentist and Livvy says…' Then she stopped chattering, and said, 'A surprise, not… Oh, it's Thursday, the day Uncle Frank was going to talk with that woman with the cat.' She grabbed hold of Peta's hand. 'Did he? Did he? What did she say? Can we have her cat? What's its name?'

'Steady on, Lily. The lady's name is Vera, and yes, Frank did talk with her. I did, too. She's a lovely lady and loves her cat very much. But she's moving into a nursing home where they don't permit pets. It's a boy cat and his name is Archie.'

'Archie.' Lily considered. 'I like it. But it's a funny name for a cat. There's a boy in my class called Archie. Why is he called that?'

'We're going to find out. That's the surprise. We're going to meet him right now.'

Lily started bouncing from one foot to the other and let out a squeal of delight.

'Now? I must tell Lottie and Livvy.' She dropped Peta's hand and dashed off to where the twins were standing, just as Eve's car pulled up.

'What's happening?' Eve asked, stepping out of the car and joining Peta. The three girls were dancing around by the gate and hugging each other.

'We're about to get a cat. Well, actually, we're going to meet the cat, but I can't imagine Lily agreeing to come home without him. He's an old cat and the present owner is unable to continue to care for him.'

'And how do you feel about it?'

'I'm resigned. I did promise Lily she could have a pet, and once she'd dismissed fish and other smaller animals, a cat seemed like the obvious solution. The twins don't have a pet?'

'No, thank goodness. There are enough small creatures in our house without any of the four-legged variety. But we go out to Mum's often enough for them to consider Scout practically belongs to them, and now Col has the alpacas, too.'

'Guess what, Mum?' Livvy asked, when the three girls ran over to join them. 'Lily's getting a cat.'

'So I hear.' Eve grinned and winked at Peta.

'Can we go now, Grandma?' Now she'd shared her news with the twins, Lily was eager to leave. She tugged on Peta's hand.

'I guess so. See you another time,' Peta said to Eve.

Peta packed Lily into the car and they set off. Vera lived in an older part of town Peta wasn't familiar with. When she turned into the street, she found it lined with homes much like Frank's, but they seemed to be still in their original condition. 'Look for number thirty-four,' she told Lily, as she drove slowly along the quiet street.

'There it is!' Lily yelled in a few moments. 'Stop, Grandma!'

Peta pulled up outside the house which boasted a well-kept rose garden and a line of low shrubs bordering a paved path. There was a For Sale sign in the front yard with a large SOLD sticker across it. As soon as the car stopped, the front door opened, and Vera peered out.

'I've been watching for you,' she said. 'Come in.'

They walked through a long hallway into a living room which was immaculate but smelt musty and damp. It was filled with the sort of furniture Peta remembered from her grandmother's home – a sofa and two armchairs covered in a floral print and a china cabinet containing china and ornaments which were no doubt the old woman's treasured possessions. The windows were almost completely obscured by thick lace curtains.

A large ginger cat sidled in and began to rub itself against Lily's leg. She jumped, then bent down to pat it. 'Is this Archie?' she asked, looking up at Vera.

'It certainly is, and he seems to have taken a shine to you, already.' Would you like a cup of tea?' Vera asked Peta.

About to refuse, Peta changed her mind. She remembered what Jo said about the ladies she delivered books to. The house had a deserted feel, almost as if no one lived there. Vera was probably lonely. Frank had said she and her friend met once each week in The Bean Sprout. Perhaps that was her only human contact. 'Thanks, Vera. That would be lovely.'

'And juice for the young lady?'

'I'm Lily. Look, Grandma, I think Archie likes me.'

Sure enough, the cat was continuing to rub himself against Lily and purring loudly.

'I think you're right.' Peta watched the two bonding.

'He's just like the cat in the bookshop. Why is he called Archie?' she asked Vera.

'He and the cat you've seen in the bookshop came from the same litter. They're brothers. As for his name. It would be before your time,' she said to Peta, then turned to Lily again. 'When I was your age, I loved a comic strip about a little boy with red hair called Archie Andrews. When I saw Archie as a kitten, he reminded me of the boy in the comic strip, so I decided to call him Archie after him.'

'There's a boy called Archie in my class, but he doesn't have red hair.' Lily bent down and stroked the cat again, then the creature shook himself free, bounded over to settle in a sunny spot by the window and proceeded to groom himself. Disappointed, Lily joined Peta on the sofa and watched as the cat licked his coat before lying down and stretching out to his full length.

'Did Archie get tired of being petted?' Vera asked, returning with tea, juice and a plate of shortbread. 'He's not as young as he used to be and likes to lie there in the sun. But he's a good cat, friendly. He's no trouble and is housetrained. I hope…' She looked across at Archie, her eyes moistening.

There was no doubt in Lily's mind. 'Can we take him home with us, Grandma?'

Peta looked across the room to where the cat was lying outstretched, then back to the anxious eyes of her granddaughter. 'I don't see why not, if you're sure.'

Lily nodded enthusiastically. 'Thank you!' She got up and went over to the window and dropped onto the carpet to join the cat. 'You're going to be my cat now, and I love you already.' The cat studiously ignored her and began grooming himself again.

'Are you sure too?' Peta asked Vera, who looked as if she was going to burst into tears.

'I'm so happy to have found a good home for him. I can see your granddaughter will love him like I do.'

'I love him already,' Lily said.

It took longer than Peta had anticipated to first finish her tea, then pack Archie, along with his bed, food and toys into the car. Luckily, Vera had a cat basket so there was no danger of the animal being loose in the car. Peta had had visions of the creature having to travel in Lily's arms and perhaps escaping to run around the vehicle.

'You must come to visit him,' Peta said to Vera as they were leaving.

'Thanks, my dear, but I don't think so. It's best if I don't. He's Lily's cat now, and I'll soon be moving on. It's enough to know he'll be loved and well cared for.' Her voice broke.

'Is Vera sad Archie is coming with us?' Lily asked, as they left the old woman standing waving at her gate.

'Of course she is. Archie has been her companion for a long time, her only companion. He's been like a member of her family.' Peta bit her lip as the memory of her own loss re-emerged, as it often did when she least expected it.

Fortunately, Lily didn't make the same connection. 'Well, you're part of our family now, Archie,' Lily told the cat. 'Can he sleep in my room, Grandma?'

'I don't think that's a good idea, honey,' Peta said with a sigh. 'We'll find a good spot for his bed and you can say goodnight to him there.'

Lily didn't reply but sat staring out the window.

It was almost five o'clock when they arrived back at the flat. Peta sighed, realising Frank had probably given up and gone home. While she didn't want to admit it, the man had got under her skin and she was excited at the prospect of seeing him again.

The last thing she'd expected to find in Granite Springs was romance, though perhaps that was the wrong word. It was hardly a romance. Then she remembered their kiss, the way her insides had melted, his strong arms around her. What else could she call it?

'There's Uncle Frank.' Lily pointed to the back door of the café as Peta parked in her usual spot.

Peta's heart leapt.

'I'd almost given you up.' He opened the driver's door and leant an arm on the roof of the car. 'Is that a cat I see?' he asked, peering inside.

'It's Archie and he's mine, though I may allow you to pet him.' Lily grinned.

'If your offer's still open…' he said hesitantly, '…maybe you'd like to share some leftovers I was about to take home with me. There's salad, ham and some satay chicken kebabs. I can leave them with you if…'

'No, come on up. It's good of you.' Peta had invited him to join them for a cup of coffee, not dinner, but it would have been churlish to refuse and the idea of having dinner with him again did have some appeal. But, coming so soon after her soul-searching about him, it was somewhat disturbing. 'This is becoming a habit,' she joked, to hide her awkwardness.

Frank helped to carry in the cat and his belongings. To Peta's relief and Lily's disappointment, he suggested the animal would feel more comfortable and secure if his bed was placed in the laundry. 'You can close the door,' he said. 'Then Archie will feel safe.'

Archie followed them through the living room, then into the kitchen, sniffing in all the corners, before jumping up onto one of the chairs and curling into a ball.

Lily made herself busy laying down the cat's food and water bowls in the kitchen, getting underfoot as Frank unwrapped the food and Peta took out three plates.

'So, it was a success? Vera will be pleased,' Frank said, when they were eating.

'I think so, though it was sad.' Peta laid down her cutlery, remembering the expression in the old woman's eyes. 'It must be hard to lose your home and your pet.'

'You understand loss.' Frank laid his hand on Peta's.

Damn the man! Why did he have to be so understanding? 'It's not the same.' But was it? For Vera, was losing her home and her cat as much a wrench as losing Joy had been for Peta? 'I guess we all think our own loss is worse,' she said.

'Can I go to play with Archie now?' Lily broke into their conversation.

'For a few minutes, then it's time for homework before bath and bed.'

'No homework tonight.' Lily slipped away.

Peta shook her head. 'Sometimes she can seem so grown up, then at others…'

'I remember what Lucy was like at her age, and you must remember your daughter.'

'Mmm. It was a long time ago.' She sighed. So much had happened since those days – days when she lived in fear of what Tony might do next, days which she wished would end. Then they did.

'What's the matter? What are you thinking about?'

'Nothing. It's…' But Peta knew she had to tell Frank about Tony at some time. She'd avoided it last night because Lily was with them. But now Lily was at the other end of the flat.

'Your husband?' he guessed.

Peta nodded, a lump coming to her throat. She took a sip of water, wishing it was something stronger. 'Tony… he… he wasn't a kind man. And Joy chose a man just like her father. But I was luckier than she was. He was felled in a one punch attack outside a Sydney pub when Joy was a teenager. A sad end for him, but a release for me and Joy. Though, I don't know if she saw it that way. She loved her dad.' She traced invisible lines on the table.

'And does Lily love her dad too?' Frank asked in a gentle voice.

'I think she's afraid of him,' Peta said after a long pause. 'She was wary of all men for a time – until she met you.' She smiled as their eyes met. 'You've been good to her – to us.'

'I hope you feel more than gratitude.'

Peta's breath caught in her throat. What was he suggesting? She wasn't ready for…

'Sorry if I spoke out of turn, if I took you by surprise. It's surprised me too… how I feel. Forget it. There was something I wanted to ask you.'

'Yes?' Peta raised her head to meet his eyes, wary of what he might be about to ask.

'It's Marie's birthday next weekend. It's the big one. She's turning fifty. Lucy has persuaded me to throw a party for her in the café's back room – just a few friends. I'd like you to come.'

Peta swallowed. She remembered her own fiftieth. There had been no celebration, no fanfare, no reckoning of the years. It was the week after Joy's death, and it had passed like any other day at the time. It was only later she realised her birthday had come and gone. 'I'm not sure. If it's close friends…'

'You will know some of them. I think you've met Fran Larsen. She'll be there with her husband and other friends, Nick and Kay Kerr. You know Marie and you'll get to meet Drew Hamilton, the man who ousted me in her affections.' Frank pretended to be annoyed, but Peta sensed he was amused. 'He's a good bloke. I'd like you to come,' he added with a winning smile.

Peta's stomach gave the now familiar leap at Frank's expression. What harm could it do? She did know Marie – though not well – and she would like to know Fran better. Her main worry was what it might say about Frank and her if she was to turn up at this party as Frank's partner.

You came here to create a new life, she reminded herself. This is part of it, albeit a part you didn't foresee. 'Lily,' she said weakly.

'Can't your cousin look after her for one evening?'

He had it all worked out! Ann would be delighted to have Lily for the evening, perhaps even overnight. They didn't see enough of her now they'd moved to the flat, and Lily was fond of her Auntie Ann. 'I'll ask her,' she said.

'Well, then.' Frank exhaled as if relieved a load had been lifted from him.

Had the poor man been worried about her refusing? Did he care more than she suspected? They barely knew each other but each time they met, she felt herself more drawn to him. He was a rock in the midst of all the uncertainty of her life – uncertainty about Lily, about the trial, the success of her new business, even about when her Sydney house would sell. She was beginning to rely on his comforting presence.

Twenty-eight

Frank wanted to dance and sing as he made his way down the stairs to where his ute was parked. It was something to look forward to, a step in the right direction. Perhaps Peta would drop into the café more often now, too. He'd expected to see more of her when she was living upstairs, but it hadn't happened. In fact, he had the impression that, for whatever reason, she was avoiding The Bean Sprout.

He knew he'd have to tell Marie Peta would be at the party. He wasn't looking forward to it. She'd teased him so much about Peta already with her hints and suggestions, but it would be good to have a partner for the evening. He'd hate to be the only one there on his own – not counting Lucy and Jess of course. He wondered if Jess would suggest bringing Ryan since his parents were coming. That left Lucy.

Frank remembered the long-haired lout he'd seen her with in the café. No way was he getting an invitation. He still hadn't asked Lucy about him, waiting for a suitable time. He sighed. Lucy wasn't his problem, but he'd been close to her and Marie for so long he felt some responsibility for the girl and who she associated with.

It was only when he arrived home, he remembered Al, who was due to arrive around the same time as the party. If he was there, Frank guessed the young man would have to come too. It would be rude to leave him alone in the house – and he was only a few years older than Lucy and Jess.

*

On Saturday morning, Frank rose early as usual and sent a text to Marie wishing her a happy birthday. It felt strange not to be seeing her on her special day as he had done for years, but Drew had swept her off to an exotic resort in North Queensland for the weekend. He'd have to wait till Tuesday before he could give his wishes in person. It was all part of the changes he was becoming used to.

As he stood in the shower, Frank mentally listed what he needed to do today. He'd have the assistance of Lucy and Jess who were turning into excellent helpers. As she'd promised, Marie had baked up a storm and, before she left, had delivered boxes of goodies to see them through the weekend. The weather was beginning to fine up and the busy weekend sports meant an equally busy day for the café.

'Hi Uncle Frank!' Lucy and Jess swung into the café almost as soon as he arrived. 'Aunt Marie asked us to get here early today since she wouldn't be here. What would you like us to do first?'

'Bless you both.' Frank instructed the girls to set up the tables and fired up the espresso machine to be ready for early customers. A group of local cyclists had begun to frequent the café on Saturday mornings, forsaking their usual trip to Mouthfuls. Brad Tait was part of the group, the father of the twins who Peta's granddaughter had become so friendly with.

The thought had barely passed through his mind when the door swung open and Brad and his mates flooded in, rubbing their hands and chatting about their recent ride.

'Morning, Frank,' they chorused, as they ordered coffees and slices of Marie's banana bread. Soon the place was bustling, giving Frank no time to think for several hours as he brewed coffee, and Lucy and Jess dashed around serving customers.

By three o'clock all three were ready to drop, but that didn't stop Lucy and Jess from joining the usual young crowd in the back corner for a heated debate. Frank peered across, trying to make out if the boy he'd seen the previous week was part of the group, but he couldn't be sure. Then they began to leave and, sure enough, there he was, an arm carelessly thrown across Lucy's shoulder.

'See you, babe,' he said to her, as he sauntered past Frank without making eye contact.

Babe! Frank winced. Lucy was no one's *babe*. Certainly not that guy's.

'Friend of yours, Lucy?' Frank asked, when the group had all left.

Lucy reddened. 'Rick? What's wrong with him?'

Sensing her defensiveness, Frank hesitated before replying. 'He seems older than the others.'

'He is. He left school a couple of years ago. He's doing an apprenticeship at the garage where Drew gets his car serviced. Jess and I met him there. He likes to tag along.'

Frank thought the boy liked to do more than tag along but kept quiet. He'd work out what to say to Lucy later.

'What are you girls up to tonight?' he asked, when they'd finished cleaning up and were ready to leave. The pair had managed to prevail on Drew and Marie to allow them to stay home by themselves this weekend. 'Want to have a bite to eat with your old uncle?' He knew he wasn't Jess's uncle, but the girl had recently taken to copying Lucy and calling him Uncle Frank. Just like Lily, he thought, a warm glow suffusing him at the thought of the little girl and her grandmother who were probably upstairs right now.

Lucy glanced at Jess and a message seemed to pass between them. 'We're going to a party later, but dinner might be good. Jess?'

Jess nodded. 'Dad and Marie know about the party. They're okay with it.'

It was Frank's turn to nod. He remembered a party the girls had gone to a year earlier which hadn't turned out well. But it had resulted in Marie meeting Drew and the rest was history, as they say.

'It's all above board,' Lucy reassured Frank. 'It's a friend's eighteenth and her parents will even be there.' She gave an exasperated sigh. 'So, yes to dinner. But we'll have to dash off afterwards.'

'No worries. I'll expect you around six. Pasta okay?'

'Yum. Love you, Uncle Frank.' Lucy gave Frank a peck on the cheek and the two girls left, the door slamming shut behind them.

'No leftovers tonight?'

Frank turned in surprise at the sound of Peta's voice as he was stepping into his ute empty handed. 'No, not tonight. We were busy. They cleaned us out. I'm just off home.'

Damn! He was tongue tied again. What was it about this woman that robbed him of any sensible thought? 'Have you and Lily had a good day?' he asked.

'We have.' Peta beamed. 'I finally bought myself a bike, and we've been riding along the river.'

Only then, did Frank notice Peta and Lily were both wheeling bikes and carrying their bike helmets. Peta's normally wild hair had been flattened and her face was redder than usual. Wearing a pair of tight leggings and a snug-fitting fleece jacket, she looked so amazing it was all he could do to stop himself from taking her in his arms. 'Sounds like fun,' he said instead.

'It was a lot of fun, Uncle Frank,' Lily said. 'I didn't know Grandma could ride a bike. You should come with us next time.'

'Frank can't do that. He has a café to run.' Peta blushed prettily. 'We should let you get on.'

But although only moments earlier, Frank had felt exhausted and eager to get home and shower before starting dinner, he was now in no hurry to leave. He drew a hand across the top of his head, wondering how he could prolong the conversation without sounding like an idiot.

'I talked with Ann,' Peta said. 'She's happy to have Lily so I'll be able to come to Marie's party. I wondered...' she hesitated. 'There's something... I'd like your advice. I value your opinion.'

A flush of pride started at Frank's feet and flowed through him. 'Anytime.'

'Would...? You're clearly going home now, but... perhaps later, when...' She gestured to where Lily was trying to maneuvre her bike up the stairs, indicating she meant when Lily was asleep.

'Sure. I'm having Lucy and Jess to dinner but they're off to a party. Around eightish?'

'Perfect.' She smiled. 'See you then.'

Frank hummed to himself as he drove home with a smile on his face. Things were starting to go his way. He wondered what Peta wanted his advice about.

*

Dinner was a cheerful affair, with the girls trying to outdo each other telling tall tales of growing up – Lucy in Canberra and Jess in Melbourne.

'But you don't regret coming to Granite Springs?' Frank asked, aware how much Lucy had missed her old school and friends when she came to live with Marie. He suspected Jess harboured the same feelings about Melbourne.

He caught a glance between Lucy and Jess. The pair were so alike in everything except looks. 'It's okay now,' Lucy said, and Jess nodded her agreement. 'But it was hard at first, and with Mum…' She broke off as she always did when she spoke about her mother. 'Anyway, I'll be back in Canberra next year if I get into ANU and Jess is coming too.' She grinned.

'Canberra's nice,' Jess said. 'Not as big as Melbourne but a lot bigger than Granite Springs. But it's okay here, too. Especially now we're in year twelve and part of the crowd.'

Frank thought of the group which followed them into The Bean Sprout on Saturday afternoons. He supposed that was *the crowd*.

'So, not such a bad place after all?'

'Dad likes it here,' Jess said.

'And it's Aunt Marie's home,' Lucy added. 'And yours,' she said as an afterthought. 'Did you never want to live anywhere else, you and Aunt Marie?'

'Not really.' Frank thought back to when he and Marie returned from Bali all those years ago. They were madly in love, imagined the world was their oyster and had no idea what was in store for them. Frank's dad died soon afterwards, and the young couple were thrown into running the café. There had been neither time nor opportunity to consider if it was where they wanted to live, what they wanted to do.

'Well, I wouldn't like to spend the rest of my life here,' Lucy said. 'Not when there are so many other places in the world. I want to travel, to see new places, and then settle down in a city somewhere.'

'Me, too,' Jess said. 'Perhaps I'll go back to Melbourne. I still have friends there, but I guess we have less in common now.'

'Look at the time.' Lucy pointed to the clock. 'Can you give us a ride, Uncle Frank? Drew made us promise not to drive when they were gone so we caught a cab here but…'

'You don't want to shell out for another when you have me on tap. Okay, then. Where is this party?'

'Oh thanks!' Lucy threw her arms around Frank. 'It's at Alison's home, close to where we live. We can walk home after.'

'Are you sure? I could pick you up. You could come back here.' Suddenly, Frank felt uncomfortable with the idea of the two seventeen-year-olds perhaps stumbling home from a party accompanied by someone like the hoodlum he'd seen Lucy with.

'Don't worry,' Jess said. 'Dad left strict instructions. Home before midnight, careful with the alcohol – we're underage – no drugs, no boys in the house. As if...' She grinned, then became more serious. 'We're not stupid. We learnt from that last time. We just want to have fun.'

Fun! What counted as fun these days? Back when he and Marie were seventeen, it meant hanging around down by the river, sometimes getting up to things that would have made their parents' hair stand on end. Then they'd gone to Bali and while there... Best he didn't think about it or he'd want to advise Marie and Drew to lock these two up till they were twenty-one.

'Well, off you go and have your fun. But be careful,' he said. 'Not everyone is what they seem.'

'Don't worry, Uncle Frank,' Lucy whispered into his ear as they walked outside. 'I know how to take care of myself.'

When he was back home and alone again, Frank shook his head. Who'd be a parent to a teenager? He forgot how, only a year earlier, he'd wanted to be exactly that. When Marie had suddenly been thrust into caring for her niece, his first thought had been to resurrect their relationship so he could be there to support her. He'd gladly have taken on responsibility for the young girl who'd lost her mother.

He thought he had a chance, then Marie chose Drew, and Frank knew there was no hope for him. It surprised him how quickly he'd accepted her decision. Perhaps subconsciously he'd known what he and Marie had was long gone. He sighed. He was glad now. Would he still have been attracted to Peta if he and Marie had reconciled? He shuddered. It didn't bear thinking about.

He loaded the dishwasher and poured himself a glass of red wine. He hadn't drunk any with dinner, preferring to stick to water with the girls. But now he was alone, he could indulge. It was only seven o'clock. He had an hour until he could go round to see Peta and discover what was troubling her.

*

Peta greeted Frank with a welcoming smile and led him into the living room where two glasses were already sitting on the coffee table along with a bottle of wine and a platter of cheese and biscuits. 'I thought…' she said, as if suddenly confused and regretting having set them out.

'Looks good,' Frank said, eager to put her at ease, surprised she was the one who appeared to feel awkward this time.

'Lily's asleep,' she said. 'I think our ride tired her out. I'm a bit unfit, too. I'm missing the gym I used to go to. The bike will do me good.'

They sat down on the sofa – about a metre apart.

'May I?' Frank lifted the bottle.

'Please do.'

Frank poured wine into both glasses and handed one to Peta who took a gulp.

'What's bothering you?' Frank asked, wondering why he had been chosen as the recipient of her confidences. She had a cousin here in town and must know other people, too, by now.

'I hope you don't mind,' she said, still holding her glass. 'I felt you'd be sympathetic. You've been such a help to me already, such a comfort.' She twirled the glass by the stem, almost spilling the wine. 'Ann would be too judgemental, would tell me what to do, and Jo is married to Col, who…'

Frank took the glass from her and placed it carefully on the coffee table. 'Why don't you tell me what this is all about?'

'Right.' Peta closed her eyes, then began. 'It's about Lily. As I told you, since it seems I don't have any legal right to keep her with me, I've applied for the residency order – Col Ford helped me. I found him to be easier to work with than Gordon Slater. Gordon was difficult to relate to.'

Frank nodded. He agreed with her. 'Has something happened?'

'Col has told me an Independent Children's Lawyer will be appointed and will want to talk with Lily. I don't know how to tell her.'

Suddenly it made sense to Frank. Peta was struggling with this new challenge, this chain of events, but Lily was still ignorant of what was going to happen.

'Oh!'

'That's where I thought you might be able to help.' Peta gazed at him, wide-eyed.

They were such beautiful eyes – brown, with a hint of green in a certain light. A man could drown in those eyes. But how could he help? He remembered the issue with Lucy the previous year when her father appeared out of the blue. But Lucy had been pleased to see him – at first, anyway. Lucy was much older than Lily, too, and this was an entirely different issue.

'I don't know if I can.' Frank picked up his wine again and stared into the glass as if it held an answer.

Peta's mouth drooped. Her eyes filled.

Frank wished he could help. But he had no children or grandchildren of his own to use for guidance. There was only Lucy.

Not knowing what else to do, but wanting to comfort Peta, Frank put his glass down again. He moved closer, stretched an arm around her shoulder and squeezed it, surprised when she leant into him. Frank held her gently, unable to believe his luck. She felt like a little bird in his arms, one which might take flight in an instant. He remained motionless, afraid to break the intimacy of the moment.

Time stood still.

Finally, Peta moved away. 'Sorry,' she said. 'What must you think of me?'

'I think you're a very courageous woman, one who's been through a lot recently and still has a challenge ahead. One which I'm sure you'll manage to overcome. I'm sorry I'm not the best person to advise you about Lily. This person the court is going to appoint. When will that happen?'

'Soon, I think. And there's talk of a counsellor. I did take her to one after… but it was to help her with her grief.'

'Maybe you can use that experience to introduce this one? Tell Lily about the order, the court and the need for her to talk to this person how it will help her to understand. Lily is a bright kid, you know. Maybe she'll take it all in her stride, with guidance from you, of course.'

'That might work. See, I knew you could help.'

Frank wasn't sure he had, but was happy to accept Peta's gratitude.

When he left, after another hour's conversation about unrelated matters, it seemed only natural to take her in his arms again and kiss her. It was different from the time he'd kissed her before, when he'd been afraid of being rebuffed. This time Frank knew she'd welcome his lips on hers. He trembled, suffused with desire as she melted into his embrace.

Twenty-nine

After Frank's visit last night, Peta felt calmer. She knew she had to talk with Lily and today might be the best time to do it. Frank was right, she was a bright kid and would hopefully understand the need for the court process, even if Peta didn't fully comprehend it herself. She just wished it would go away. But now the process was in motion, it would continue till it was over. Col said it could take months.

A pair of galahs alighted on the fence outside the window as she was filling the electric jug, their bright pink and grey plumage bringing a splash of colour to the drab metal railing. A church bell sounded in the distance breaking the silence. It was a Sunday morning in Granite Springs, so different to the hustle and bustle of the city.

Peta almost jumped as something rubbed against her ankles. There was a loud miaow. Drat! She must have forgotten to close the laundry door last night after Frank left. Archie was ready for his breakfast, but he'd have to wait till Lily surfaced. She'd been good at taking responsibility for her pet, rising early on Friday to look after his needs before going to school, and yesterday too. Peta wondered how long it would take for the novelty to wear off. But for now, she was content to let the cat wait till Lily awoke.

Sensing she wasn't going to feed him, Archie wandered off and Peta heard a squeal followed by a gurgling laugh, a sure sign the cat had discovered Lily's bedroom. She grimaced. So much for keeping the cat out of Lily's room and bed. But it was good to hear her so happy. Peta hoped what she had to tell her wouldn't spoil the happiness Lily had found here.

'Look who came to visit me.' Lily walked into the kitchen, carrying the large cat like a baby. He soon slithered from her grasp and headed to his empty food bowl where he stood expectantly. 'I think he wants his breakfast, Grandma.'

'I think so, too. Why don't you feed him, then wash and dress before you have yours? I'm making waffles this morning.'

'Yum.'

Peta waited till after breakfast, then said, 'Lily, there's something I need to talk with you about.'

The little girl looked at her warily. 'Is it about Dad?'

Peta's stomach churned. Had Lily been thinking about her dad? 'What makes you ask that?'

Lily shrugged. 'You sounded serious. You haven't sounded like that since we left Sydney.' She fidgeted in her seat. 'I don't want to talk about him.'

'This isn't exactly about him, it's about you and me. It seems that, for us to stay together, we need to get permission from a court.'

'That's stupid! You're my grandma. Who else would I live with?'

Peta cleared her throat and clasped her hands tightly together. 'You know I love you to bits and your mum would want you to stay with me.'

'I love you, too, Grandma.' Lily turned her sweet little face up to Peta's, a face so like Joy's it made her heart ache.

Peta almost wept. Lily looked so innocent. Why did she have to be subjected to all this? She sighed. 'I know, sweetie, but...' she took a deep breath, '...we have to do what the law says, and it says I need to apply for what's called a residency order for us to stay together.'

'Do we have to go back to Sydney?' Lily's eyes were filled with fear and she began to tremble.

Peta put an arm around her. 'No, honey. They have a court here, too. But it means you'll have to speak with someone who will ask you questions.'

'What about?'

'Probably about yourself, about your life in Sydney, about living with me.'

'Will she ask me about Dad? Like the other woman did?' Lily's eyes widened.

'Perhaps. And maybe about your Aunt Celia?' Peta held her breath.

'Aunt Celia doesn't like me. And she always said bad things to Dad about Mum when she thought I wasn't listening.'

Peta bit her lip but didn't respond. She hugged Lily tighter.

They sat in silence broken only by a loud purring sound coming from where Archie had chosen to park himself under the table.

Then Lily asked, 'Why will this person want to ask me about Aunt Celia?'

Peta bit her lip again before replying. 'She's your dad's sister. The person may want to know if you'd like to stay with her.'

'No!' Lily pulled herself from Peta's grasp. 'You won't let her, Grandma. You can't. I can't go back to Sydney, back to…' She broke into tears, slid from her seat and stormed off.

As she left, the cat emerged from where he'd been lying under the table and leapt up onto Peta's lap. Her hand automatically began to stroke his soft fur. 'Oh, dear, Archie. I was afraid she'd take it like this. What are we going to do?'

Deciding to leave Lily on her own till she settled down, Peta busied herself with clearing away the breakfast dishes. Seeing Archie grooming himself in a corner, Peta realised she'd soon be able to let him venture outside. She made a mental note to ask Frank if he'd object if she installed a cat flap to enable Archie to go in and out at will, once he'd become accustomed to his new home. Then she headed to her office to review the plans she'd started on earlier in the week.

The meeting with the hotel people had gone well. It looked as if the project was hers. They'd been impressed with her portfolio and previous experience and seemed happy to use a local business. It was a load off her shoulders. While the work with Danny had been the impetus to set up *Forrest Interiors*, it was only one commission. Peta knew she needed more to make a living from her new business.

After a while, she heard a noise behind her. Turning, expecting to see Archie slinking in, Peta saw Lily standing in the doorway. Her eyes were red, but she had stopped crying.

'I'm sorry, Grandma,' she sniffed. 'But I don't think I should have to speak to this person. Why do I have to? Can't you tell her I won't?'

'Come here, sweetheart.' Peta opened her arms, and Lily ran into them and buried her face into Peta's shoulder. 'I'm not sure when all this is going to happen. It may be soon, or it may take weeks, months even. But I'm always here if you need to talk about it again. It's not something you need to worry about. I'm sure the people who make the decisions will listen to you and to what you want to happen, who you want to live with. They only have your best interests at heart, you know.' She mentally crossed her fingers. She hoped that was the case. Her research on the internet – and Col – had indicated all decisions were made *in the best interests of the child*. Surely in this instance, it would be for Lily to remain with her.

'What does best interests mean?'

'Well…' Peta had to think, 'it means, they only want to see you safe and happy.'

'That's easy then. I'm safe and happy here.'

Peta had to smile. Lily was right, it should be that easy.

'What would you like to do today?'

Lily brightened. 'Can we go to see the miniature railway? The twins told me about it. It's in the Botanic Gardens. We didn't see it when we were there before.'

'I didn't know about it.'

Lily suddenly seemed to forget her earlier anxiety and became enthusiastic. 'Livvy says it's just like a real train only smaller and you can ride on it. It goes all the way through the gardens – though not where the playground is, of course.'

'And it's open on Sundays?'

'Only on Sundays. Can we go?'

'I don't see why not. Perhaps we can have lunch out, too.'

Taking advantage of Peta's desire to keep her happy, Lily added, 'And the playground afterwards?'

'We'll see,' Peta chuckled, relieved Lily had recovered so quickly.

Archie reappeared as they were about to leave, so Peta was able to ensure he had plenty of water before telling him to behave while they were gone. She wondered if she was mad to be talking to a cat like this.

*

To Lily's delight, the railway proved to be everything she'd imagined. Peta sat on a bench while the little girl set off on her ride with several others including a couple of adults with children younger than Lily.

It was nice, sitting there in the sun and Peta let her mind wander. A lot had happened since they arrived here, and there was a lot in store for her and Lily. Sometimes she was sure it would all turn out well, while at others she dreaded what the future might bring.

The one bright light on the horizon was her friendship with Frank Beattie. As she thought about the man, his image appeared in her mind. He was good-looking, there could be no question of that, with his dark hair which showed only a hint of grey and his deep brown eyes. But it wasn't his looks that drew Peta to him. Quite simply, he was the kindest, most dependable man she'd ever met. Put that way it didn't sound romantic but for Peta, who'd suffered under the thumb of one violent man, and lost her daughter to the cruelty of another, it was everything.

'Did you have a fun time?' Peta asked, when the little train reappeared, and Lily ran towards her.

'So much. I'm hungry now. Where are we having lunch?'

'There's a kiosk here in the gardens. How about we buy sandwiches there? Then you can spend time in the playground before we go home.'

Lily nodded eagerly and grabbed Peta's hand to pull her up.

After a lunch of ham and tomato sandwiches and flavoured milk, Peta allowed Lily to drag her towards the playground.

'Look, it's the twins!' she yelled, as they drew closer.

Peta's eyes followed Lily's pointing finger to where two blonde girls were climbing up the steps of the slippery dip.

Lily immediately dropped her grandmother's hand and raced over to join them, leaving Peta looking around for Eve. But it was Jo who was sitting on the nearby bench watching the girls.

'I'm on grandmother duty today,' Jo chuckled. 'But you're on duty every day. It can't be easy. How are you managing?'

Peta sat down and sighed. Jo was the first person to recognise it wasn't easy to be suddenly thrust into caring for an eight-year-old when you thought your child rearing days were over. She was glad to see her. 'I'm getting used to it,' she said, her eyes on Lily who had already come down the slide and was racing back towards the stairs on the heels of the twins.

'Col told me you'd submitted the application.' Jo put her hand over Peta's. 'Do you want to talk about it?'

Overcome, Peta shook her head. Since talking with Lily earlier, she'd been trying to put it out of her mind. There was nothing she could do. She just had to wait till she or Lily was summoned.

'Emily Rose has another sniffle today, and the twins were agitating to come here, so Eve called me,' Jo continued, as if she hadn't asked the question. 'It's a bonus to meet you here. The gardens are a great place for them on the weekend.'

'We've been to the miniature railway then had lunch.' Peta paused, then despite her denial continued, 'I had to tell Lily today – about the court business. Col said we could hear from the court any time, so I had to prepare her.'

'Oh, my dear! How did she take it?'

'Not well.' Peta relived Lily's sudden exit. 'But she appears to have got over it now.' She gestured to where the three girls were playing chasey with another group of children.

'They're resilient at that age,' Jo murmured, 'but she's already had to suffer more than most.'

'Mmm.'

'And a little bird tells me you're seeing Frank Beattie. Hmm?' Jo tilted her head to one side.

Peta blushed. She'd known this would happen. Ann had warned her about the gossip mill in Granite Springs. But she hadn't expected Jo to hear.

'I don't mean to be rude and I don't normally listen to gossip. But Frank's a good man. He deserves to find happiness. He and Marie always seemed happy. I never thought… But I guess we never know what goes on in other people's lives. Their split was amicable. They continued to work together, still do. But when Marie met Drew… anyone with half a brain could see the way it would go. You could do a lot worse.'

Peta stared at Jo in astonishment. She hadn't expected this. 'He's been very kind to me and Lily.'

'That's Frank all over.'

'But I'm not looking to have a man in my life. There's enough going on with Lily and setting up my new business.'

'How's that going? I hope Danny isn't too difficult to work with. He may be my son, but he and I have had our disagreements over the years. I know what he can be like.'

'No, everything's good there. He seems to like what I've suggested. And I have another project in train with the new motel being built on the edge of town.'

'Ah! You got that one, too. Good. Word will soon get around, and I'd be willing to bet you'll be rushed off your feet. I even hear my ex-husband's new wife has a mind to commission you.' She snorted. 'Sorry. I don't mean to denigrate what you offer, but Carol always had ideas above her station.'

Peta smiled, remembering how Gordon suggested much the same about his wife.

The girls came running back before any more could be said, and the two women said their goodbyes, promising to catch up again soon.

Peta was glad to have met Jo. It had made the time fly by, and she liked and respected the older woman. Driving home with a still excited Lily sitting behind her, Peta pondered Jo's comments about Frank. He seemed to be liked by everyone, everyone she met, anyway. And they all reaffirmed her own opinion of him. But was she ready to allow another man into her life – and was he ready to forget Marie?

Thirty

Frank checked himself in the mirror wondering if he'd pass muster with Peta. He thought he looked okay in the pale blue shirt, taupe pants and navy blazer. He'd shown the outfit to Lucy when she dropped in the previous afternoon after the café closed, and she'd whistled her approval. But he felt Peta might be more discerning. She'd be accustomed to the city slicker types he despised. Though he had to admit she hadn't given him any cause to feel inferior, quite the reverse. He remembered the way she'd leant into his embrace, the touch of her lips on his. He shivered in anticipation of the evening ahead.

It was almost six-thirty when he set off to walk to the café. He, Lucy, and Jess had spent most of the afternoon setting up the back room with streamers and balloons, including a large one in the shape of the number fifty. Lucy and Jess had moved tables to form one large one which they'd set with decorative flowers and fancy napkins. He'd prepared the food, which was ready to be heated, and the cake Lucy had ordered from the local patisserie was sitting in the fridge, along with several bottles of champagne. All that was needed to complete the picture were the guests.

In his pocket, Frank carried a gift which he knew Marie would love. It was a replica of a locket she owned as a girl and had lost on holiday one year, much to her dismay. For this milestone birthday, Frank had scoured the internet to find exactly what he wanted. He hoped Drew wouldn't consider it too personal a gift.

Lucy and Jess were waiting at the door of The Bean Sprout when he arrived.

'Where have you been?' Lucy asked, hopping from one foot to the other. 'We've been waiting for ages.'

'We said six-thirty.' Frank checked his watch. He was only a few minutes late. 'Anyway, I'm here now. Let's get this show on the road.'

By the time the first guests arrived, the room was sparkling with the fairy lights the girls had insisted on, the champagne was ready to be poured, there were platters of nibbles set out on a side table and the sound of Crowded House, Marie's favourite band, was blasting from the sound system.

'Wow!' Marie walked in, hand-in-hand with Drew. 'I didn't expect all this.' She gazed around the room in awe.

'All down to Lucy and Jess.' Frank gestured to where the two girls were standing beaming. 'I think champagne?' He headed over to pour three glasses then, tilting his head toward the two girls, half-filled two more. 'I know you two are still underage but it's a special occasion.'

They nudged each other and giggled, confirming Frank's suspicion they were no strangers to alcohol. He and Marie had been the same at their age – they couldn't wait to be grown up. But being grown up wasn't always what you expected. He'd never expected he and Marie would break up. Now here she was with her new man, and he was eagerly looking forward to Peta's arrival. Life had an odd way of delivering what you least expected.

'To a wonderful lady.' Frank raised his glass as the door opened and Kay and Nick arrived, an unusually tidy Ryan following them. He brightened up when he saw Jess and Lucy and hurried over to join them.

It wasn't long before Fran and Owen arrived, leaving Frank on tenterhooks until Peta's small figure appeared in the doorway. 'You came!' Frank's voice shook as he greeted her with a peck on the cheek, her smile lighting up the evening for him. Until now, he hadn't been sure she'd turn up.

'I said I would.' She looked around tremulously. 'But...'

'Let me introduce you.' Frank took Peta by the elbow and led her over to where the others were drinking and chatting. 'You already know Marie, and Lucy and Jess. And I think you've met Fran. Marie and Fran smiled warmly at Peta, but both Lucy and Jess were too busy talking with Ryan to notice. 'This is Drew... and Owen...'

Peta smiled.

'And Kay and Nick. The young fellow with the girls belongs to them.'

The introductions over, Frank poured Peta a glass of champagne which she sipped delicately. Fran immediately engaged her in conversation, leaving Frank free to check on the food.

In the kitchen, he stood motionless for a few seconds, his hands on the benchtop, taking a deep breath, before reaching to take the roast turkey and ham out of the oven and fetching the salads from the fridge.

'Can we help?'

Frank looked round to see Lucy, Jess and Ryan join him in the kitchen. 'Okay, guys. You can carry those out.' He pointed to the platters now sitting on the bench. 'I'll be out in a sec.' When they'd gone, he took another deep breath, not sure why he was feeling nervous. He belonged here. He and Marie had run the place for the last thirty years. Was Peta's presence affecting him, making him unsure of himself?

The evening went well. Marie was delighted with her gift, throwing her arms around Frank in a warm hug which brought back memories of their life together. Drew's grin as she extricated herself only served to confirm the strength of her new relationship. But Frank noticed a frown etched on Peta's brow. She couldn't be worried about his relationship with Marie, could she?

Suddenly it was over, and people began to take their leave. Only Frank and Peta were left in the empty room.

'Can I help?' she asked.

'Nothing to do. The young ones loaded the dishwasher and put the leftovers in the fridge. I can shut this room up and take care of it in the morning.'

'Thanks for inviting me. I enjoyed the evening more than I expected.' Peta's smile lit up her face. 'It was good to get to know Fran better. Her husband is quite a character.'

'Thanks for coming.' Frank felt tongue-tied again. Peta's presence had made the night for him. Seeing her sitting across the table set off a flare of pleasure which started in his toes and moved up through his body, keeping him in a state of excitement throughout the meal. Now all he wanted to do was take her in his arms. He hesitated. 'Would you like another glass of something or a coffee?' He didn't want this evening to end, for Peta to disappear upstairs and leave him to go back to his empty house.

'Why don't I make you a coffee?' Peta asked to his surprise. 'It may not be as good as yours, but I do have an espresso machine upstairs.' She grinned.

Did she feel the same way he did? 'Thanks. Good idea. I'll just lock up this place.'

A few minutes later, Frank was following Peta up the stairs to the flat. As soon as they walked in, they were greeted by a loud complaining yowl from Archie who leapt out of the open door.

'Oh, dear! I've been meaning to ask you for permission to install a cat flap,' Peta said, as they made their way into the living room. 'It would make it easier for him.'

'And you. No problem. I can install one.'

'Oh, I didn't mean for you to…'

'Honestly,' Frank said, 'it's not a problem.'

'Well, thanks again. It seems to be all I'm doing lately, thanking you…'

At that moment, the cat, having decided the inside of the flat was really where he wanted to be, flew back in again to join them, becoming so entangled in Peta's legs she clutched Frank to avoid losing her balance.

Suddenly afforded the opportunity, Frank grasped it – and Peta – with both hands. As his arms went around her, his lips found her hair and he inhaled her unique scent. Her body felt soft and pliable against his. His heart began to pound and, before he knew it, his lips found hers in a searing kiss.

When they finally came up for breath, Frank stroked a strand of hair away from Peta's face. A flood of desire threatened to overwhelm him as he held her close. 'I… I didn't mean for this to happen,' he stuttered.

'Coffee,' Peta murmured, her lips still so close to his, their breath intermingled.

Coffee? How could he think of coffee when all he wanted to do was carry her off to bed? Taking a deep breath, he dropped his arms to release Peta from his grasp. 'Coffee,' he agreed, beginning to experience the effect of the champagne he'd been drinking all evening. Was their embrace merely the result of too much of the celebratory drink?

'Wait here. I won't be long.'

Frank collapsed onto the sofa, suddenly exhausted. He could hear Peta talking to the cat in the kitchen, the rattle of pellets being poured into a bowl, the splash of water, then his eyes began to close.

Thirty-one

'Here it is. Sorry I took so long…' Peta's voice trailed away as she saw Frank asleep on the sofa, dead to the world. A tender smile tugged at her lips. The poor man must be exhausted. She was sure he'd worked hard to prepare for the evening, to ensure the party for Marie's birthday went off without a hitch. And it had. It had been a triumph, concluding with everyone singing Happy Birthday as Lucy carried in the cake, then gave a touching speech about how Marie had taken her in and cared for her like her own daughter. It brought tears to Peta's eyes.

She placed the two mugs on the coffee table and went over to give Frank a gentle shake. But he only grunted and slid further down into the cushions. She looked at him closely for the first time, taking in the now familiar face, the lines around his eyes and mouth, the greying hair. In the short time she'd known him, Frank Beattie had become an important part of Peta's life. She relived their kiss, revelling in the memory of his arms holding her, knowing she'd wanted more. For a brief moment she'd forgotten where she was, forgotten Lily, forgotten everything but the man in whose arms she was. Then common sense had reasserted itself and she'd pulled away. But for that moment, time really had stood still.

What was she to do? Archie crept in behind her and leapt up to join Frank on the sofa, curling up beside him and tucking his head against Frank's legs. Peta sighed. There was no way she could waken him. She took both mugs through to the kitchen and fetched a blanket from the spare bedroom. Placing the blanket around the sleeping figures of both man and cat, she crept back out to find her mug of coffee which she took to her bedroom and closed the door.

*

Peta slept like a log, wakening only when a pair of kookaburras began their morning chorus outside her window. She stretched lazily then stopped, suddenly remembering Frank, sleeping in the other room. Was he still there? Pulling on a towelling robe, Peta crept out and peeked into the living room. Frank was still sound asleep.

Sensing her presence, Archie leapt down from his spot and stretched his legs before padding over to greet her with a loud meow. At the sound, Frank stirred, blinking rapidly and gazing around as if trying to work out where he was. Conscious she was wearing a robe and little else, Peta withdrew into the kitchen to feed and water the cat, then to her bedroom where she had a quick shower and dressed in a pair of leggings and an oversized sweater.

Feeling more respectable, she returned to the living room, where she found Frank sitting upright, but still looking woozy.

'You look as if you need that coffee now,' she said with a grin. 'Sleep well?'

'Have I been here all night? I'm so sorry. What must you think of me?'

'Only that you were exhausted. Archie spent the night with you, too.' She chuckled. 'You know where the bathroom is. There's a fresh towel if you want to shower. There'll be coffee and breakfast in the kitchen when you're ready.'

'Thanks.' He dragged a hand through his already mussed hair and yawned.

Still smiling, Peta went to let Archie out, then back into the kitchen where she stood indecisive. It was a long time since she'd prepared breakfast for anyone but herself and Lily, and she didn't think her usual muesli or porridge, or even Lily's favourite pancakes or waffles, would be the right thing to feed Frank. She turned the espresso machine on, then, taking bacon and a few eggs from the fridge, set to making scrambled eggs and frying up several strips of bacon, before dropping slices of bread into the toaster.

'Something smells good.'

Peta turned from the stove to see a freshly showered Frank in the doorway, his wet hair plastered to his head and a huge grin on his face.

'Don't know when I last had time for a cooked breakfast,' he said. 'You didn't need to go to all this trouble.'

'No trouble.'

'I bet you don't do this every day.'

'No, but I thought…'

'You thought a man needed feeding up?'

Peta winced, embarrassed to have her thoughts so easily read.

'We don't all fall into the macho category, you know. I normally down a bowl of cereal before going to the café, though I may have something more there once I get things going.'

'Oh!' Blushing, Peta turned back to the stove.

'But it's most welcome.'

'When do you have to be at the café?'

'Not till later. I have to be out at the airport at ten, but I need to go home to change first.' He glanced down at the outfit he'd worn the night before. 'I can't go into work dressed like this.'

Peta thought he looked very nice – smarter than usual. But decided not to comment. 'The airport?'

'I have to pick up this young fellow, a distant cousin. He's from Italy.' He frowned.

'Nice for you. Have you met before? Is he going to be here for long?' She wondered why Frank didn't appear more excited at the prospect.

'I don't know him at all, and he has a twelve-month visa – one of those working holiday things. His family wanted to get him away from some girl, so they thought of me.' He frowned again.

Peta envisaged what effect the introduction of a young Italian male to The Bean Sprout Café might have on the youth population of Granite Springs and smiled.

'You may smile, but it could well be a disaster. As far as I can tell, he knows nothing about the hospitality business. He's studying engineering.' Frank said it as if it was a dirty word.

'But he's family,' she said, handing him a mug of coffee and placing a plate of eggs and bacon in front of him.

'Thanks.' Frank took a gulp of coffee. 'Family I've never met, never even been in communication with till now. But I suppose it may work out.'

Peta joined him at the table. It felt odd to be sitting having breakfast with him, almost as if they were a married couple, when they were only… what? She blushed, remembering the scenes which had filled her dreams, scenes in which she and Frank had done more than kiss, from which she'd awakened and stretched out her hand in the expectation of finding him lying there beside her. 'I hope it does work out,' she said hurriedly, lest he could read her mind.

Archie chose that moment to wander back in, attracted by the smell of bacon.

'Not for you,' she said, as the cat let out a loud meow, before taking up position under the table.

'How's he working out?'

'So far, so good. He's a well-trained cat. I can't complain. And Lily has taken the responsibility of caring for him seriously.'

'That's good.' Frank pushed away his empty plate and rose. 'I need to go. I'll try to fix that cat flap for you sometime this week. Thanks for being so understanding when I fell asleep on you.' He twisted his neck from side to side. 'I'm feeling a bit stiff. Serves me right. I'm too old for that sort of thing. Too much champagne. Next time…' He drew in a breath. 'Next time, I'll try to stay awake.'

'I hope so.' Peta was aware of an unspoken agreement that *next time* would be different in more ways than one.

Thirty-two

'Frank?' The tall dark-haired young man's eyes twinkled as they met his. The family likeness was unmistakable. Frank could have been looking at his father at eighteen or nineteen.

'You must be Alfonso.'

'Al, please.' The young man grinned and shook Frank's hand as the other disembarking passengers milled around them.

'Welcome to Granite Springs, Al. Let's find your luggage and get you out of here.'

The young man grinned again, his teeth sparkling white in a tanned face. His black hair had an errant wave that fell over his face forcing him to continually push it back.

As they left the airport, Frank could feel all eyes on them. Al was going to be an exotic addition to the town.

'I'll take you straight home. You'd probably like a rest after your trip.' But Al didn't appear at all tired.

'Can I see your café? My father, he say I am to work there, no?'

'That's the plan. Do you know anything about the hospitality business?'

'*Ospitalità?*' Al looked puzzled. 'Oh, you mean *alberghiera?*'

Frank racked his brains for the little Italian remaining from his childhood. 'That's right,' he said. 'Okay, the café it is.'

He stacked Al's two suitcases into the tray of the ute and headed into town, with his companion giving a running commentary on the way. Frank learned that although Al had been studying engineering, his dream was to become an actor.

'But my parents…' Al waved a hand in the air. 'They do not approve. They do not approve of me very much at all, I think.' He chuckled. 'It is different here? Yes?' He leant back in his seat and gazed out the window.

Frank winced. *What had he let himself in for?* Thank goodness he hadn't arrived in time for Marie's birthday bash.

On the way into town, Frank pointed out the local landmarks, eliciting very little comment from Al. But when they finally drove down Main Street, the young man seemed to come alive. He gazed out the window, twisting his head around to look at the street lined with shops, and the war memorial in the centre of the street.

'I think this Granite Springs it is not a big town,' he said, with a note of disappointment.

'We consider it to be a fairly large regional centre,' Frank said defensively. 'How big is your town?'

'Small.' Al dismissed it with a wave of the hand. 'But I live at the university in Milano. It is a city.'

'Here we are.' Frank pointed to The Bean Sprout before turning up the lane to park.

'This is The Bean Sprout? My father, he say…' Al fell silent, perhaps realising he'd said enough. Then, as they got out of the car, he asked, 'You have many staff?'

'There's only me and Marie. She…'

'Ah, yes. She was your wife. My father said. It is strange to continue to work together. No?'

'It works for us,' Frank said shortly. 'Come in and I'll show you around.'

'You must be Alfonso. Welcome to Granite Springs,' Marie greeted the young man. 'I thought…' She glanced at Frank, a question in her eyes.

'Al wanted to see the café. He tells me he doesn't need a rest.'

Marie raised her eyebrows. Their years together meant she understood from his tone Frank wasn't entirely comfortable with young Alfonso Bertolli. 'Well, why don't you fix him a coffee and he can see how we run things? Okay with you, Al?'

'I think it is a good plan.' Al took a seat in the back corner of the café and leant back surveying the scene.

Frank chuckled and went through to fetch his apron before taking up his customary position behind the espresso machine. While he was fixing coffee – a short black as Al requested – Frank could hear Marie chatting to Al. He couldn't hear what they were saying, but could see from her gestures she was trying to explain the history of the café. He was glad to leave it to her. The trip into town had shown Al to be rather full of himself. He only hoped the young man's condescending manner wasn't typical. Otherwise, it was going to be a long year.

Al was on his second cup of coffee and had managed to devour three of Marie's brownies, declaring them to be as good as those his mother made, when the door opened and Peta walked in, sending Frank's blood pressure up.

'Good morning, again,' he said with a twinkle in his eye, as she arrived at the counter. 'Cappuccino?'

'Please. I thought... I wanted to say...'

Frank held up a hand. 'It's okay. I know it was a bit awkward this morning. Did you see Ann?'

'Not yet. I wanted to see you first. Your cousin arrived?'

Frank gestured to the back table where Al was drinking coffee.

'Wow! He'll break a few hearts. Sorry.' She bit her lip. 'But there aren't many like him in Granite Springs. And with the addition of an Italian accent...'

Frank looked over at Al again. He'd thought him exotic, but now he could see what Peta meant. The lad had heartbreaker written all over him. He wished now he'd asked for more information about the *unsuitable match*. How far had it gone? Had he got some girl pregnant? How many reasons could there be for a family to want to send their son to the other end of the earth? 'Maybe,' he said, exhaling and thinking of Lucy who was at a vulnerable age. Or perhaps it could be a good thing to have someone like Al to make her forget the fellow who was sniffing around her.

'Okay if I join you?' he asked, as Peta turned away.

She gave him one of her special smiles. 'That would be good.'

'Can you manage for a bit, Marie?' he asked, when two cappuccinos were ready. At her nod and wink, he winced, but carried both cups across to where Peta was sitting at a window table.

'So,' Peta said, when he sat down. 'Is he what you expected?'

'Not exactly. He seems…' Frank didn't want to malign the young man on the basis of one car trip, but…

'He's probably feeling a bit strange and missing his home and family.'

'You're right.' Frank sighed. Peta was such a calming influence. He'd been embarrassed this morning when he realised he'd fallen asleep, had spent the night in the flat. It wasn't how he wanted to spend their first night together.

Peta was grinning as if she could read his thoughts. 'Last night…' she said.

Frank met her eyes. Did he see what he thought was in them, or was it wishful thinking?

'There's Lily.'

'And now Al.'

They broke into laughter.

'It's not as easy as it was when we were eighteen,' he said, remembering making out with Marie in the back seat of his dad's car. They were both too old for that even if the opportunity arose.

'There's no rush.' Peta put her hand over his, her little one looking odd on his large one.

'No.' Frank smiled. They had all the time in the world.

Thirty-three

Peta had a smile on her face as she left the café. It had been a spur-of-the-moment decision to drop in and she was glad she had. She didn't know why she'd been avoiding it for so long. Both Frank and Marie had been pleased to see her, and it had been interesting to get her first glimpse of Frank's Italian guest. She could see Frank would have his work cut out there, if the boy's looks were anything to go by. For Frank's sake, she hoped it would work out.

Driving across town to where her cousin lived, Peta gave thanks again for Ann's generous gesture of offering her refuge. It was so like Ann, she now realised. The woman gave the outwardly impression of being cold and uncaring, but underneath there was a heart of gold, albeit well-hidden. She wondered again what had turned the open, friendly teenager into this uptight middle-aged woman, but would never dare to ask.

Ann was in the front garden when Peta arrived. 'Lovely to see you,' she said. 'I'm glad you were able to come today. I usually spend my day off alone in the garden, but it's nice to have company.'

They went inside. The house was cold after the warmth of the sun on their backs. Spring was coming and the weather in Granite Springs was beginning to warm up. Peta was looking forward to her first summer here. She knew the heat would be different from Sydney. Granite Springs would be hot, but not plagued with the humidity which she hated and for which Sydney was renowned.

'Now, tell me what you've been doing,' Ann said, when they were enjoying a coffee after lunch.

Determined to cut down on her caffeine intake – this was her third today – Peta sipped the coffee slowly before replying. 'Working. There's the project with Danny Slater and now I have the new motel to work on. Then I really need to market myself. These two commissions won't last forever. I need to plan ahead.'

'I think I may be able to help you there.'

Peta cocked her head to one side. How could Ann help? But she'd forgotten. Ann had lived here all her life. She either knew, or knew of, all the people in Granite Springs and probably most of those in the surrounding townships, too.

'Susie's coming home,' she said.

Peta's mouth fell open. Susie was Ann's older sister, more than ten years older. From what Peta had heard from her mother, the older girl emigrated to England with her husband and family years ago. She must be in her sixties now. It would be nice for Ann, but how could it help her?

'She and Adrian have retired. He did well over there, but Susie misses the Aussie summers. Their children are all grown and have their own lives, so she and Adrian have decided to return home.' Ann squared her shoulders. 'She's asked me to find her a house – she's been very particular about what she wants – and to have it all done up for her. I thought of you.'

Peta almost choked. It was nice of Ann to want to help but she couldn't imagine what her cousin meant by *done up*.

'Oh, I know it may not be what you're looking for. You probably want something more commercial, but believe me, there are a lot of people in and around Granite Springs who like to think they're better than they should be. Susie's become one of them,' she said in a bitter tone.

'But…' Peta was about to voice her objections when she remembered someone else saying much the same thing. Maybe Ann had a point. 'What would you like me to do?'

'Nothing yet. I've asked Ken Thompson to look out for a suitable property – he's the senior partner in Granite Springs Realty. He's semi-retired now, but I trust his judgement. Ken's been in the business longer than young Danny Slater and knows the local market. He'd remember Susie too. They were all part of the same crowd when they were teenagers. Jo Ford was part of that group too, along with her husbands – both of them,' she said, her lips tightening in what Peta took to be disapproval. 'But once the property is purchased, I expect you could fit it out to suit Susie's taste. I have her email address. She wants a large old Federation home and has the idea of remodelling the inside in the original style. Does that sound like your thing?'

'I can do that. Yes.' It would make a change from the modern upmarket interiors Peta was accustomed to and would present the sort of challenge she enjoyed.

'Good. That's settled.' Ann leant back and fixed her gaze on Peta. 'And how is it living above the café? Is Lily settling in there? She seemed happy last night. I hear you have a cat.'

Peta chuckled. 'Word gets around. Are there no secrets in Granite Springs? I suppose Lily told you. She's over the moon about it.' As she had many times before, Peta wondered how long it would be before her own secret was common knowledge.

'And a house guest?' Ann gave her a sceptical look.

Peta's eyes widened. 'No, I don't have any guest, there's just Lily and me.'

Ann's eyebrows arched. 'So there's no truth in the rumour a certain landlord was seen departing in the early hours of the morning?'

Peta blushed. How had Ann heard? It had only been this morning.

'I heard when I was in the newsagent's this morning. Old Jenkins saw Frank Beattie drive off when he was taking in the morning papers. He didn't make anything of it, but I didn't think Frank had spent the night in the café. Was I wrong?'

'We didn't …. he… He spent the night in the flat because he fell asleep.' Even as she said it, Peta knew it was a weak excuse. Who would believe her?

'I don't blame you,' Ann surprised her by saying. 'I may look like a dried-up old spinster, but I wasn't always this way. I had my own romantic moments.' Her eyes took on a faraway look and Peta wondered again what had happened to that young woman to embitter her.

Peta tried again. 'We'd been at a birthday party in the café – for Marie's fiftieth. He came up for coffee afterwards and fell asleep while I was making it. The poor guy was exhausted.'

'Of course he did. He's a fine man, Peta. And, with Lily to look after, you need someone. It's not good for a woman to be alone. I should know, though I've grown used to it over the years. And, unlike me, you have a family to take care of.'

Peta flinched, reminded of the residency order and all it entailed. 'Did Lily say anything about the court?' she asked.

'The court? No. Is there something I should know?'

Peta sighed. It was hard, and each time she spoke about it she felt as if a nail was being driven into her heart. But Ann was family and deserved to know. 'Remember you mentioned my adopting Lily?'

Ann nodded. 'You said you were going to check it out. Did you?'

Peta started to explain, almost in tears by the time she finished.

'Oh, my dear. I wish I'd never mentioned it.'

'No, it's good you did. Col told me I should have done this right away. But I had no idea. All I could think of was getting Lily away from the place which held such bad memories for her.'

'Good ones, too,' Ann said in a gentle voice.

Peta took a tissue from the box on the table and wiped her eyes. 'Yes, from when Joy was alive. But now she associates Sydney with her mother's death. I still don't know how much she heard – or saw.'

'I expect she's blocked it out. It's what we do with the things we need to forget.'

Peta peered at her cousin's face, but it was as blank as usual. Ann gave nothing away.

'Anyway,' Peta scrunched up the tissue, 'we have to be prepared for this to drag on. Then there'll be the trial to get through.' Peta felt all the worry build up inside her head again, till she thought her head would burst.

'Will you go back to Sydney for it?'

'Of course.' Peta didn't hesitate. 'I need to see him convicted, see his face. But I don't want Lily there.'

'No. She can stay with me.'

'Thanks. But it won't be for months yet. These things take so long.' She sighed.

'Have you heard anything from the sister?'

'Celia? No. Why would she contact me? I only met her a couple of times – at Joy's wedding and again when Lily was born. I think she considered Joy – and therefore me – beneath her.'

'I just wondered. You said she believed Grant to be innocent?'

'She put him on a pedestal and thought he could do no wrong. Even if he did commit murder, she'd consider it was Joy's fault. Her and her damned brother,' Peta fumed.

'Finished?'

'What?' Peta had been lost in memories of the past and hadn't noticed Ann rising and picking up her mug. 'Oh, yes. It was lovely, thanks. I should pick up Lily's things and get on.'

'You'll find her overnight bag in the hall. She's a very tidy little girl. Joy did a good job there.'

'She did. She was a good mother.' Peta experienced a flood of regret at what might have been – if Joy hadn't been killed, if she'd had the child she was carrying.

'Let's do this again,' Ann said as they parted, 'and remember what I said. A good man is hard to find. You should hang on to Frank Beattie.'

Hang on to Frank Beattie. Ann's words reverberated in Peta's head as she drove home. She hadn't come to Granite Springs to find a man, but it seemed everything and everyone was pushing her towards Frank, not least the man himself. Should she accept what seemed to be the inevitable and follow the direction her heart seemed to be taking her, or take notice of the past and remain the solitary woman she'd been for more years than she cared to remember?

Thirty-four

At three o'clock on Friday, Frank was about to close the café for the day, when the door opened and Lucy bounced in. 'It's the start of the holidays and they let the senior students out early today. Aunt Marie said...' Lucy's voice faded as her eyes fell on the young man behind the coffee machine. 'Is that him?' she mouthed.

'This is Al, Lucy. A cousin of mine from Italy. I told you he was coming to stay a while.'

'Yes, but...' The normally talkative Lucy seemed lost for words.

'And this is the Lucy I hear so much about.' Al's eyes sparkled as he wiped his hands and came around the counter. 'You did not tell me she is so beautiful,' he said to a startled Marie.

Lucy grinned.

'Are you finished there?' Frank asked Al who'd been instructed to clean the espresso machine. To his surprise, the young man had proven to be a fast learner, completing even the most mundane tasks with a willingness unusual in someone of his age.

When Lucy and Jess started working on Saturdays, they had been full of complaints, eager to serve customers instead of the cleaning tasks they'd been hired to do.

'*Si.*' Al removed his Bean Sprout Café apron to reveal a skin-tight tee-shirt bearing an Italian logo.

'Oh wow!' Lucy said, standing as if struck to stone.

'Luce!' Marie intervened. 'Now you're here, you can help me out in the kitchen. Now!' she said, when Lucy didn't move.

'Sorry, Aunt Marie.' Lucy came to her senses and followed Marie into the kitchen.

'Did I do wrong?' Al asked, his eyes following the two women.

'No, but we don't tend to pay such lavish compliments here. It may be all right in Italy, in Milan. Here in Australia, in Granite Springs, we prefer to be more… more restrained.'

'But why?' Al's eyes widened. 'When you see a beautiful woman, it is only natural to tell her, no?'

'No. Lucy's only seventeen. She's not accustomed to men telling her she's beautiful. She… It might turn her head.'

'What is *turn her head*? I don't understand.'

Frank didn't know he did, either. It was a saying. One he couldn't explain. He had to try. 'It means it might make her think she's different, special,' he said weakly.

'But why? Is she angry with me?'

Frank ran a hand through his hair. 'No. I suspect she's delighted.'

'Then it is good. She is beautiful. I tell her. She is pleased. Yes?'

'Yes.' Frank decided he couldn't win, so changed the subject. 'You've done well this week, Al. I must admit I had my doubts, but you've fitted in very well. We'll make a barista of you yet.'

'A barista. I like barista.' He grinned. 'You use a lot of our words in Australia. But it surprises me there is no wine here in your café?'

'We have different licensing laws in Australia. Wine is only served in bars and restaurants. Speaking of which, why don't I show you a bit of Granite Springs nightlife one of these days, and take you to dinner at our best restaurant?'

'I would like it. And thank you for your kind words. I have tried to make my father proud of me. You will tell him?' Al's forehead creased, making Frank realise how much the young man relied on his father's good opinion.

*

It was two weeks before Frank made good his promise to show Al Granite Springs' finest restaurant. Their meal at The Riverside proved a success, with Al impressed with the menu and surroundings. They were driving along Main Street on their way home, when Frank saw a crowd of teenagers hanging around the door of one of the less salubrious bars, and thought he recognised Lucy among them. He steered the car over to stop several cars away from the group.

'I need to see what's going on,' he said to Al. 'I think that's Lucy.' They watched for a few minutes as one member of the group appeared to be arguing with the others. Lucy seemed to be trying to calm him. It was the lout he'd seen in the café. Frank swore under his breath. He wanted to get out of the car and drag Lucy away, but she wouldn't thank him for getting involved. She believed herself old enough to take care of herself.

As they watched, the boy she'd said was called Rick brushed off Lucy's restraining hand and lifted his in a threatening gesture. Before Frank had time to think, Al leapt out of the car and raced towards them, inserting himself between Lucy and the guy. All three spoke together, Al and the guy gesturing wildly, the other members of the group looking on silently, and Lucy with a restraining hand on Rick's arm. Then, as suddenly as he'd joined them, Al left and returned to the car.

'I couldn't persuade her to leave,' he said with a rueful expression. 'They'd been drinking. I think they have been thrown out of this bar.'

'Shit!' Frank punched the steering wheel with his fist.

'They're moving on, now,' Al said, peering through the windscreen.

Frank glanced up to see the group had split. Lucy was walking slowly along the road entwined with Rick, while the others were going in the opposite direction. He clenched his teeth. This was his little Lucy, with Rick's arm around her, his face turned into hers. Frank couldn't bear it. He released the door intending to go out to confront them.

'This *giovinastro*, he is her *suo ragazzo*?'

'I hope not!' But it seemed Al was right. And the Italian words were so much more evocative than the English. How could Lucy choose to become involved with a young thug like Rick? He'd talk to Marie. Lucy was her responsibility, hers and Drew's. But Frank couldn't let it go. He needed to do something now. Making a U-turn he headed for the upmarket suburb where Marie now lived with Drew.

'She is young, Lucy. A schoolgirl?' Al asked, as Frank tried to subdue his anger.

'Seventeen,' Frank said through tight lips. 'Sorry, Al. I need to see Marie, to talk with her. I wouldn't be able to sleep if I didn't do it tonight.'

'It was not nice, outside the bar. I think there might be a fight.'

'An argument, yes.' Frank drove on in silence, remembering the younger Lucy who had been her Uncle Frank's little shadow when she came to visit with Dee. It was hard to believe she'd turned into this obstinate teen and formed a relationship with someone who thought nothing of taking her into a bar, getting her drunk and involving her in a fight.

'*Bella.*' Al said when Frank pulled up outside the two-storey modern house.

'It's a bit different from my place.' But Frank was distracted. Now he was here, he was regretting the impulse that brought him. But it was too late. Al was already getting out of the ute.

Frank followed him and led the way to the front door where he rang the bell.

'Frank! What brings you here on a Friday evening? Marie!' Drew called into the house. 'And this must be…'

'Al,' Al said, when Frank didn't immediately respond.

'Welcome. I'm Drew. You'd better both come in.'

'Who is it?' Marie appeared in the hallway, a champagne glass in her hand.

'I'm sorry. I've interrupted your evening. I shouldn't have come.' Frank could see from the champagne glass, the dull glow of light and the soft music emanating from the living room that Marie and Drew had been enjoying a quiet evening together – the sort of evening he used to enjoy with her when they were a couple. He felt a tug of what might be jealousy, before reminding himself of the reason for his visit.

'Don't be silly. You know you're always welcome. I thought you and Al were going out to dinner.'

'We were. We did. It was when we were driving home… We saw Lucy.'

'Now you're here how about a drink? We're celebrating.' Drew picked up the champagne bottle.

'You saw Lucy in town?' Marie asked. 'So? She said she was meeting friends, Jess, too.'

'Thanks,' Frank said to Drew who, without waiting for an answer, had poured out drinks for Frank and Al. He turned to Marie. 'She wasn't with Jess. She was with that Rick guy and his mates outside the King's Arms.'

'What?'

'What was she doing there? Not exactly a good choice.' Drew put an arm around Marie's shoulders.

'Sorry,' Frank said again. 'Al got out and tried to reason with them. They were in an angry crowd and they'd both been drinking.' He pushed his free hand through his hair. 'They went off together to God knows where. I wanted to do something... I thought... Anyway, I wanted you both to know.'

Marie gave Drew a worried look. 'Drew...?'

'I agree with Frank. We needed to be informed. But there's nothing we can do right now. Sorry you were drawn into this, Al. Families!'

'I have a family too – a father who disapproves and a mother who worries.' Al smiled. 'Your Lucy. She is young. She is flying her wings.'

Marie nodded with a faint smile.

'Please sit down.' Drew suddenly seemed to notice they were all standing in the middle of the room.

'Thanks.' Frank gratefully took a seat. Then he remembered. 'You said you were celebrating?'

Marie and Drew shared a secret smile.

'I just heard today. My divorce is final. We can set a date for the wedding.' Drew clasped Marie's hand.

'Congratulations!' Frank held up his glass, stifling the ache he still felt at the loss of Marie's affection. Even the knowledge of his own growing feelings for Peta failed to extinguish it completely. 'When's it to be?'

Marie smiled at Frank. 'We haven't decided yet, but soon. We've still to tell Lucy and Jess. They were in such a rush to get out tonight. We'll announce it to them tomorrow. It'll be a small wedding, a few close friends. Maybe those who were at my birthday, plus a couple of Drew's mates from Melbourne.' She tightened her hand in Drew's.

Frank was glad for them. Marie deserved to be happy and if Drew was her choice, then he wished them well. Could he find the same happiness with Peta? Was that what he wanted? He took a gulp of champagne, coughing as it went down the wrong way.

Al thumped him on the back. 'A wedding? Elisa and I wanted to marry. It is why my father sent me here.'

His words fell into a well of silence.

It was broken by Marie. 'Tell us about her, Al.'

'She is *cosi bella* with the long black hair and the eyes, like deep pools of chocolate. We met in Milano where she is hairdresser.' His face lit up. 'She first cut my hair, then we eat dinner together. But my father, he thinks she is not good enough for me, for the budding engineer who will join his business.' His lips turned down. 'So I am here, with my cousin and I learn how to be a barista.' He gave a wry grin. 'It is not so bad, and perhaps she will join me. What my father does not know…'

Frank shifted uncomfortably in his seat. This was the first he'd heard of the possibility of Al's girlfriend joining him. This hadn't been part of the deal. How would he explain it to Al's dad if he encouraged the romance? But time enough for that later – if the girl did arrive.

Marie took a different view. 'How romantic! I'm a sucker for stories of young love. Did you know Frank and I…' she threw an apologetic glance at Drew, '…met when we were at school and married on a beach in Bali?'

'*Daverro?*'

'Yes, really,' Frank said. He remembered the event as if it was yesterday – the white sand, the marriage celebrant, Marie wearing a bright pink floral-patterned sarong, a garland of pink and white frangipani crowning her long dark curls, the sound of the waves, and their excitement. They'd been so much in love. 'It was very romantic, but it didn't…' he hesitated, '…last.' He'd been about to tell Al the marriage hadn't been legal but decided to keep that between Marie and him. It was something they'd kept secret, though he suspected Drew knew. They'd thought it legal at the time and had lived together for years as a married couple. It was only when the marriage fell apart and they sought a divorce they learned they had never been married at all. The romantic beach wedding in Bali wasn't recognised in Australia. There was no marriage certificate.

Marie sent him a rueful look. 'But we had some good years. I don't regret them. If you really love this Elisa of yours, you should grasp your happiness with both hands. Even if it might be fleeting,' she said to Al.

The young man looked down into his champagne glass. 'It is hard,' he said. 'When I am here, and she is so far away.'

'You're in touch?' Marie asked.

'Of course.' Al's eyes lit up again. 'We talk every day – on Facetime. But I miss her so much.'

This was news to Frank. Instead of a lady killer, he was hosting a lovesick guy pining for his Italian sweetheart. What would Al's father say if he knew, if he thought Frank was aiding and abetting his liaison? Then he wondered if Lucy knew. But Lucy was enamoured with Rick. His mind went back to the scene outside the King's Arms. His lips tightened again.

Marie recognised his concern. She knew him so well. 'Lucy will be all right. We'll talk with her. We may not be able to convince her to drop Rick, but she's not stupid. She'll see reason – eventually.'

'Mmm.' Frank wasn't so sure. He suspected Lucy was flattered by the attentions of what she saw as an older man – he must be all of nineteen. He drained his glass. 'We should be going. We've taken enough of your time and interrupted your celebration.'

'No problem. Thanks for coming.' Drew rose and clapped Frank on the shoulder. 'I'll give both girls a talk about inappropriate friends and behaviour – and about frequenting pubs before they turn eighteen. It won't do Jess any harm to hear it too.' He rubbed his chin. 'We think once they're old enough to fend for themselves our job's over, but it doesn't get any easier.'

'Thanks, Drew. I know Lucy's not my responsibility, but…'

'She's your niece. You've known her all her life. Marie and I are glad you keep an eye out for her. I know… if things had been different… you might have had more say in her life.'

'Right. Thanks.' Why did the guy have to be so nice about everything? But that was what had endeared him to Marie, and Frank had liked him from the start too, ever since he walked into The Bean Sprout.

Al was quiet on the drive home, no doubt thinking of his girl back in Milan.

Frank was glad. It gave him time to think, to consider why the news of Marie and Drew's impending wedding affected him the way it had. It wasn't something new. They'd been planning to marry ever since Marie told Frank there was no future for them together. He'd been foolish to think there was, there was no going back, but a man could hope.

It was only as he pulled into the driveway he identified the emotion he'd experienced. It wasn't distress at their announcement. He was jealous. Not jealous of Drew marrying Marie He was jealous of Marie finding happiness, of Marie setting a wedding date, when Frank was still trying to discover his own feelings for Peta Forrest and work out whether she felt anything for him in return.

Thirty-five

Peta awoke with a start. It was still dark. She peered at the bedside clock to see it was almost one o'clock. What had wakened her? Then she heard it again. The breaking of glass from outside. Pulling on her robe, she crept out, first checking Lily was still asleep. They'd had dinner with Ann the previous evening and Lily had been permitted to stay up beyond her usual bedtime, playing the card games she loved. The little girl lay curled up, clasping her favourite toy. Peta sighed with relief, then made her way to the living room and peered out the window.

The street was deserted, not unusual for this time on a Sunday morning. The Saturday night revellers would all have gone home, conscious of Granite Springs' respect for the sabbath. Here in the Australian countryside, the churches still ruled the community.

What had caused the noise? Had it come from behind the building? She went to the back of the flat, to where the door led to the outside landing and the courtyard behind both the flat and the café. Opening the door warily, Peta peered out. That was strange. There was a light streaming out from the café. Surely Frank couldn't be working there at this hour?

Then she heard a noise again. This time it was a clashing, as if a pile of pans had fallen. There was definitely someone inside the café, and Peta was almost sure it wasn't Frank. Trembling, she closed the door gently, went back to the bedroom and picked up her phone.

*

After calling both Frank and the police, Peta knew there was no sense in going back to bed. There was someone in the café downstairs, someone who had no business being there. What if they decided to come up here, to burgle her too? She knew the inside entrance from the café was boarded up but quivered, imagining the door being broken open and a masked man charging in, brandishing a weapon.

Peta went to the kitchen to make herself a cup of tea, forcing herself to think calmly. She added more sugar than she normally did and carried her cup into the living room. She picked up a book, then put it down again unable to concentrate. Her head was spinning. Her mouth was dry. She checked the time. How long had it been since she called? How long would the police take to respond? Every little sound made her jump. She couldn't bear it.

A scratching sound make her heart leap. Then she heard a yowl coming from the laundry. She gave a sigh of relief. Archie! She'd forgotten the cat. Putting down her cup, she went over to open the door. Archie immediately began to purr and rub himself around her ankles. It was so comforting to feel his warm body against her. For the first time, she was glad Lily had persisted in her demands for a pet. She picked him up, his fur tickling her face as she hugged the little creature. 'Oh, Archie, I'm so glad you're here.' She pressed her face into his thick coat. 'Help will be here soon.'

As she spoke, she heard the siren of a police car followed by the sound of running feet, then cars stopping, shouts, a scuffle, then more voices. She held the cat tighter, worried he might try to escape through the recently installed cat flap while she was standing close to the door in an attempt to figure out what was going on. Then there was a pounding at the door. She almost leapt out of her skin.

'Peta, are you there? Are you all right?' Frank's voice had never been so welcome.

Peta dropped Archie who gave an annoyed wail, opened the door and fell into Frank's arms.

'It's all over. You can relax now.' Frank patted Peta on the back, then stroked her hair, his firm, reassuring hand sending shivers down her spine.

She immediately felt all her worries dissolve. 'Oh, Frank!' she murmured into his shoulder. 'I was so scared. Did the police catch them? What happened? There was such a noise. Did they do much damage? What did they take?'

'Come and sit down.' Frank took her over to the sofa and settled her there. He picked up the cup of now cold tea and sniffed it. 'Tea's no good. You're in shock. Do you have any brandy?'

Without waiting for a reply, Frank headed for the kitchen where she heard him opening and shutting doors. There was brandy on the top shelf of the pantry, leftover from cooking and kept for emergencies. Peta supposed this was an emergency.

Frank returned and handed her a glass of neat brandy. 'Drink this.'

Peta gulped it down, the fiery liquid burning her throat. She coughed.

Frank refilled her glass and poured one for himself.

Peta sipped this one more slowly. 'What happened? You didn't answer before.'

Frank ran a hand over his hair. 'A storm in a teacup. The police caught him red-handed. I recognised him straight away. His name's Rick. He's been sniffing around Lucy. I knew he was no good, warned Marie and Drew about him. Now even Lucy will have to accept what he is – a petty criminal. He's been in the café a few Saturdays, seen the crowd, probably assumed there'd be cash. As if I'd leave anything in the cash register. He's a fool as well as everything else. I don't think he'd have come up here, unless...'

'Unless he thought there was cash here, too.' Peta shivered.

'Anyway, he's locked up now. And if he gets bail, I don't expect him to show his face near here again. Come here.' Frank drew the still shivering Peta towards him.

She moved closer, comforted by his nearness, the warmth of his body. A throb of desire pulsed through her, forcing her to lose any inhibitions. She felt his lips on her hair, his hand on her shoulder, heard his breath quickening.

He drew away suddenly, as if remembering something. 'I don't intend to take advantage of you. But you're still in shock. I don't think you should be alone. I can doss down on the sofa. Unless you have a better idea.'

Peta knew what she craved, and it wasn't to have Frank doss down on the sofa. Lily was asleep. She would never know. Neither would anyone else. It was after two o'clock on a Sunday morning. 'I know somewhere more comfortable,' she said.

In her bedroom, Peta wondered if she'd made a mistake. They'd both had brandy. She'd had two glasses. What if their desire was alcohol-fuelled, what if…?

Frank's arms around her quickly dispelled her doubts. His lips met hers, reminding her of their earlier embraces. His lips weren't cursory, demanding, like Tony's had been. They were warm, tender, seeking hers as if with a question, moving gently from her mouth to her neck, to her breasts, making her ache for more.

Their lovemaking was a revelation to Peta who'd only ever made love with her husband before now. Frank was practiced in discovering what pleased her, in taking his time, sending quivers of pleasure through her, bringing her to never before imagined heights of delight, to a place from where she thought she'd never return.

*

Peta and Frank were whispering in the kitchen as he was about to leave when Lily's voice surprised them.

'What is Uncle Frank doing here?' she asked, rubbing her eyes.

Frank gave Peta a warning glance before crouching down in front of the girl. 'There was a burglar in the café last night, so the police came to arrest him. I stayed here overnight to keep you and your grandma safe.'

Lily's eyes widened. 'A real burglar? The police were here? And I was asleep.' There was more disgust than fear in her voice. 'Wait till I tell the twins. Are we safe now?'

'Quite safe,' Frank assured her.

'You'd better stay for breakfast now,' Peta said. 'How about I make pancakes?'

'Yes, please! Then can we go to the park? You too, Uncle Frank.'

'Sorry, honey. I need to get back home. Al will be wondering where I am. In fact, I'd better let him know.' He took out his phone and started to text while Peta set to making pancakes.

'Go wash your face and get dressed,' Peta said to Lily who was standing in the middle of the kitchen. 'And don't forget Archie.'

Despite Peta's gratitude for the cat's company in the early hours, she didn't intend to let Lily shirk her responsibility.

'I'll do it now, Grandma.' Lily disappeared into the laundry and Peta could hear her talking to the cat as she poured food into his bowl.

'That's done.' Frank slid his phone back into his pocket. 'Maybe I could join you at the park later?'

'I don't think...' Peta blushed, imagining what everyone would think if they saw the three of them together at the park. She knew very well how quickly word got around in Granite Springs and didn't want to be the target of gossip.

'Only joking. I know what this town is like. It would spread like wildfire. Let's keep this to ourselves for now. There'll be time enough to go public with our relationship.'

Was that what it was? Were they in a relationship? Peta dropped a spoonful of pancake mix into the pan with more force than was necessary. She'd been grateful for Frank's company last night – well, this morning. It had seemed only natural to spend the night in his arms. But... She sneaked a glance to where he was now stroking a purring Archie, the cat arching his back in pleasure. Much as she had responded to Frank's touch in her bed, she realised, blushing at the memory.

But a relationship? Peta didn't know if she was ready for a relationship. And she wasn't a free agent. There was Lily to consider. As she told Fran, she didn't want or need a man in her life. But that was before she discovered how Frank affected her. It wasn't the wild passion she'd felt when she first met Tony. And look how that had turned out. It was a gentler feeling, a sense of comfort and security, the knowledge she could trust him with her life and with Lily's. She nodded, her eyes downcast lest he see the doubt in them.

'Are the pancakes ready?' Lily bounced in. 'Do you think the twins will be at the park today? I need to tell them...'

'That's enough, Lily.' Peta's voice was firmer than she intended. 'Can you help set the table?' she asked in a gentler tone. 'The pancakes are almost ready.'

When they were seated around a table filled with pancakes, fruit, milk, juice, yoghurt and maple syrup, Frank sighed. 'I've missed breakfasts like this. Even when Marie and I were together, it was just the two of us – except when Dee came to visit with Lucy.'

'You're very fond of Lucy, aren't you?' Peta asked.

'I am. It's going to be hard to tell her about Rick.'

'He's her boyfriend?'

'I think so. Al and I saw them outside the King's Arms last night. It looked as if they'd been thrown out. She's underage and he was drunk. Not too drunk to break into the café, though,' he said, a hard edge to his voice.

'It'll be difficult for her.'

Frank sighed. 'Too true. I knew he was no good. I told her, but...' He sighed again.

'She's a teenager. I remember what Joy was like at seventeen.' Peta conjured the image of her golden-haired daughter, full of life, in the throes of her first love. He'd been the son of a friend, and the relationship had petered out when they both started university. Then, after a string of different boyfriends, she'd met Grant. And her beautiful daughter had fallen headlong into the passionate affair which would result in her death.

During the rest of the meal, Lily pestered Frank with questions about the burglary until Peta called, 'Enough! Leave your Uncle Frank alone. It was an unpleasant experience, and he doesn't need to rehash it for your benefit.'

'But...' Lily saw the expression in her grandmother's eyes and fell silent.

'What your grandma is trying to say, Lily, is it was pretty scary for her to be up here alone while someone was moving around downstairs and making a lot of noise. It was good you were asleep, or you'd have been very scared too. Luckily, the police came quickly and caught the burglar.'

'Is he in prison now, like my dad? He's a bad man, too.'

'Like your dad,' Frank agreed, raising an eyebrow in Peta's direction.

It was Peta's turn to sigh. Lily didn't often mention her dad, but this showed she still thought about him. Peta wondered how Lily pictured him in prison. They'd never talked about it. Should they have? She shrank from the idea. When Grant was first incarcerated, he'd asked to see Lily, but the little girl had refused and Peta had never mentioned it again, then they'd left Sydney.

'Time to go. Thanks for breakfast,' Frank said.

Peta walked with him to the door where they paused. Lily was still in the kitchen talking to Archie.

Seemingly emboldened by the fact they were alone, Frank folded Peta into an embrace. 'Last night was unbelievable. I never thought it could be that way again for me. I hope… it wasn't just the drama of last night, was it? It meant something to you, too?' He buried his face in her hair.

'Yes, but I don't know. I didn't mean to… I have a lot going on, Frank. I'm not sure I have much to offer someone like you. You're a good caring man. You deserve someone who…'

Frank stopped her words with his lips. 'Let me be the judge of that,' he said, releasing her lips to place a kiss on her brow. 'I need to get back to Al, but I'll be in touch later.'

Peta smiled and nodded as she waved him off. Frank wasn't going to give up easily and she didn't really know if she wanted him to.

Thirty-six

Frank was whistling as he let himself into the house where Al was playing the sort of music that could burst your eardrums. Frank didn't say anything, but Al immediately lowered the sound to an acceptable level. 'It was bad, the robbery?' he asked.

'There wasn't any cash in the place, so he threw a few pots and pans about, broke some crockery and the back window – and damaged the lock. Nothing that can't be replaced. It was Rick, the fellow we saw earlier with Lucy.'

'The boyfriend of Lucy? I should have…' Al bunched up his fist.

'No. We don't do with fisticuffs here.'

'What is this fisticuffs?' Al stumbled over the word.

'Sorry. What I mean is we don't resolve our differences with our fists. The police have arrested him. He'll be charged with breaking and entering, probably get off easily since nothing was taken.'

'Okay.'

But the reminder ruined Frank's mood. He needed another caffeine hit to get it back. He headed to the coffee machine. 'Coffee?' he asked Al.

'Sure. It is what you say, is it not?'

Frank nodded his agreement. 'Have you had breakfast?'

'I make toast with the avocado in the bowl. It is okay?'

'Sure.'

Both smiled.

'How would you like to have a look around the countryside?' Frank asked, when they were both seated with mugs of coffee. 'It's pretty around here and we could have lunch somewhere in a country pub.'

'I would like it very much. It is very different here from where my parents live, from where I grew up.'

'What is Cesano Maderno like?'

'It is a city,' Al said with some pride, unlike his previous contemptuous comment. 'It was so small when I grew up, but now the tourists… You do not have them here?'

'Sometimes. But there isn't much for them in Granite Springs. We'll drive out of town and I'll show you the real Australia, or as much of it as we can reach in an afternoon.' He grinned. He was looking forward to showing off to his Italian cousin, wondering what a city boy would make of the wide-open spaces and paddocks of sheep. A thought occurred to him. He'd give Owen Larsen a call. Maybe he and Fran would be willing to play host to them for a bite of afternoon tea.

*

As Frank expected, Al was stunned into silence by the vast paddocks on both sides of the road. The sight of the odd kangaroo nibbling on grass at the far end of one had his eyes out on stalks.

'It is true,' he said in wonderment. 'These creatures, they hop around free everywhere.'

'Not exactly,' Frank chuckled. 'They are wild, but it's unusual to see them grazing in the middle of the day. You wouldn't find them so cute if the ute hit one at dusk. They can make a mess of a vehicle. Look there!' Frank pointed out a 'roo carcass lying at the side of the road. 'Some poor soul must have hit that one.'

'Did you?'

'No, I've been lucky so far. I've heard they're difficult to avoid as they follow the headlights. That's a small one. They can grow to one and a half metres and are heavy as shit to move, especially the males. There's a nature reserve in Canberra. I should take you there one day. They have kangaroos, koalas, platypus, emus. They're all there.'

'Koala. Is it the little bear, like a toy? They are real?'

'They sure are, lovely little creatures. They're endangered these days. The population is diminishing in the wild due to disease and the devastation of bushfires.'

As he spoke, it occurred to Frank there was someone else who'd enjoy a trip to Tidbinbilla. He hadn't been there himself since Lucy was little, when he and Marie had joined Dee and her for the day. Lily was the age Lucy had been then and would love it. He'd suggest it to Peta and the four of them could make a day of it.

As planned, they stopped for lunch at a typical country pub where Frank insisted Al try the counter lunch special, which was a meat pie with fries, washed down with a glass of beer. He pretended not to notice Al's grimace at his choice, grinning as the young man manfully hid his distaste and finished the lot.

'Now we're going to visit a friend of mine,' he said, as they left the pub. 'A friend of Marie's actually, or his wife is. Owen has only been in Granite Springs a short time. He's a good bloke. You'll like him. He runs goats on his place.'

'Runs? He runs with the goats?'

'Sorry.' Frank kept forgetting English wasn't Al's mother tongue and lapsing into Aussie vernacular. 'He keeps goats on his property. I think he has around twenty acres.'

'It is big here?'

Frank laughed. 'No, very small for an acreage. It's what they call a hobby farm, meaning it's too small to make a living from, so the owner is farming as a hobby. Owen and Fran Larsen both work at the university.'

'I see on the Internet there is a university here in Granite Springs. Larsen. It is not an English name, I think.'

'You're right. His family come from Denmark, but he's as Australian as I am.'

Al seemed to digest this. 'But your family are from Italy.'

'Right again. We're a multicultural country.'

'Not so much in Italy, but we do have many migrants.'

Before Frank could think of a suitable response, they reached the turning to the Larsen property, The Haven. He was glad he'd had the forethought to call Owen earlier, ensuring they'd receive a warm welcome.

'What is that?' Al pointed to the upturned milk churn serving as a mailbox.

Frank chuckled. 'Out here, people tend to use a variety of containers to receive their mail. The milk churn is Owen's. The others belong to his neighbours.' He pointed to the pair of buckets, one on top of the other, and the more recognisable mailbox which had obviously been purchased in a store.

Frank turned down the dirt track, the ute rattling on the uneven surface.

'This is a road?' Al asked in surprise.

Frank sighed. He was becoming tired of Al's interminable curiosity. While it was good the young man wanted to learn about Australia, his continual questions which sometimes sounded patronising, were somewhat wearing. He decided not to reply.

'Can you hop out and open the gate?' he asked, when they stopped at the rusted white metal gate. 'Make sure none of the goats escape, and close it when I've driven through,' he added, as he saw a couple of the creatures eyeing them curiously. He'd never visited Owen and Fran here before, having only met Owen a few times in the café then again at Marie's birthday party.

'Welcome!' Owen greeted them as they stepped out of the ute.

Al gazed around in astonishment. 'It is so dry here,' he said, looking at the stretch of soil and weeds which had once been grass. The goats were grazing on whatever they could find, stretching up to reach low-lying branches of the gum, wattle and pepper trees in the paddock.

'Not much pasture for the animals,' Frank said.

'No, it's been a hard year. I lay out pellets regularly and it seems to keep them happy. They'll eat anything. That's why we have to keep the house and the vegie garden fenced off.' Owen gestured to the high fence Frank hadn't noticed earlier.

'You escaped the bushfire? I noticed some charring on the fence as we drove in.'

'We were lucky. Not so our neighbour up the lane. Poor Magda lost the lot and had to rebuild.'

'I heard about that.' Frank remembered hearing how the elderly woman's home had been destroyed by fire. It had been the talk of the town. Everyone had expected her to go to live with her son in Melbourne, but she'd rebuilt and returned a year later to start again. 'Wasn't there some story…?'

'She's a feisty old bird. She and old George Turnbull got together. Both in their seventies, too. Seems like it's never too late to fall in love. Come in and meet the love of *my* life. Fran's been making afternoon tea for us and is looking forward to meeting you, Al.' Owen pushed open the gate in the fence surrounding the house, and ushered Frank and Al across the wrap-around veranda and into the house.

At their entrance, a black cat leapt down from a chair next to the Aga and slunk out the door, rubbing against their ankles on the way.

'Don't mind Stormy.' A bright-eyed woman with short blonde hair came forward to greet them. 'Good to see you again, Frank, and you must be Al. I'm Fran.'

When they were all settled around the large kitchen table with coffee, tea and slices of a fruit cake still warm from the oven, Al said, 'Frank tells me this property of yours is small, what he calls a hobby, but all this...' he gestured to the stretch of paddock they could see through the window, '...it is the size of our farms in Italy.'

Owen chuckled. 'I'd guess the soil is better in your country. I discovered that when I spent time in Spain. Australia is a big country, but much of it is uninhabitable, then there's the weather – it's either drought or flood. But we love it, don't we?' he asked Frank and Fran.

They both nodded.

As they were chatting, there was a flash of colour outside as a flock of pink and grey galahs flew past, then they heard the cackle of a pair of cockatoos who'd decided to perch in a large eucalypt by the fence.

'The birds here are so noisy,' Al exclaimed. 'There are more here than in the town, I think.'

'You're right there. It's one of the things I love about this place. Has Marie told you how I found it?' Owen asked Frank, stretching out his legs to reveal a pair of tatty trainers Frank hadn't noticed before.

'Didn't you rent it for a time?' Frank asked.

'That's right. When I came here, I was desperate to live on an acreage, and Jo Ford, who's our neighbour, told me about this one. Then the owners were forced to sell. Their misfortune was my good luck. I'd fallen in love with the place – and with this woman.' He looked fondly across the table at Fran who blushed.

Frank felt his stomach clench. It was such an intimate look, a look which spoke volumes, a look which told them all how much love the couple shared. What he'd give to have Peta look at him with the same expression.

'Might I go to walk around?' Al asked, when he'd finished the excellent coffee Owen had provided.

'Of course, I'll...' Owen made to rise, but Fran shook her head. He sat down again. 'Don't worry about the goats,' he said. 'They won't harm you, probably won't even come near, but they'll be curious. If you go out into the lane, make sure you close the gate after you.'

'Thank you.'

'Don't be too long,' Frank said, conscious of overstaying their welcome, but Owen and Fran were very pleasant company. He wished he'd made the effort to get to know them better before now, especially Owen who proved to be an interesting companion.

They watched as Al made his way across the paddock and tried unsuccessfully to get close to a couple of goats before going out through the gate and heading up the lane.

'It's a whole new experience for him,' Frank said, watching the boy saunter along. 'He's used to city living, grew up in a small town close to Milan then went to university in the city. Granite Springs has been a revelation to him, now this.' He stretched his arms wide. 'Thanks for allowing us to visit. I wanted to give him a taste of the real Australia.'

'Don't know about that,' Owen chuckled. 'The farmers on the broad acres around here would say there was nothing real about what Col and I do out here with our beasts. But it's real enough to us. And you're welcome to visit any time. Right, Fran?' His eyes met Fran's with another of the looks which made Frank ache to have someone of his own.

As if sensing his thoughts, Fran asked, 'What's this I hear about you and Peta?'

'Peta Forrest?'

'Marie tells me you're...' She paused as if not sure how to put her thoughts into words.

Frank shifted uncomfortably in his chair. Fran knew they were together at Marie's party. Had Marie been gossiping... about him and Peta? Had she guessed he'd spent the night there? No, he realised, even Marie's antennae didn't reach far enough to know about the burglary and how his actions in comforting Peta had ended up with them in her bed.

'Peta's new to Granite Springs. She arrived with her granddaughter and is renting the flat above the café. We…' How did he describe what they had together? It was all so new, so tentative. 'That's how I know her.'

Fran raised one eyebrow and appeared to be about to say more, when Owen intervened.

'Leave it, Fran. We had enough gossip about us when we got together. I thought you of all people wouldn't want to subject anyone else to idle chitchat.'

Fran bridled. 'I only asked. Marie…'

Owen glared at her, and she fell silent again. 'So, what's the story with young Al?' he asked.

Frank filled him in on what he knew about the boy, finishing with, 'He's proving to be a big help to us, but I doubt he's made to be a café owner, any more than he is to be an engineer. He tells me his dream is to be an actor.'

'His, and that of many others. But he's welcome to audit some of our drama classes if you can spare him.'

'How does that work?'

'He can join the class but there's no assessment and no qualification. He could also become involved in our end-of-year performance in some capacity. It might rid him of the notion when he discovers acting isn't all about prancing around on a stage.'

'Good idea.'

'With those looks he'll have all the girls falling at his feet,' Fran put in.

'Won't do them any good,' Frank said. 'It seems he has a girl back home – the one his dad sent him here to get away from. Al tells me she intends to join him. I'm not sure what to tell his father if that happens.'

'As the father of one who made what you called an *inappropriate alliance,* I'd suggest you say nothing. My daughter, Pia, was involved with a scumbag. She wouldn't listen to a word against him, then he threw her out when she fell pregnant.'

'And as a good dad, you were there for her.' Fran put her hand on Owen's. 'I agree with Owen. Sometimes parents know best, but sometimes they're wrong. Either way, it's best to let things take their course. It usually works out in the end, one way or another. Pia has a lovely little boy now and is settled here in Granite Springs. She's made friends here and one of them is the new vet. We're hoping…' She glanced across at Owen. 'Sorry, honey, I'm doing it again.'

Frank thought of Lucy and how she'd shrugged off any criticism of Rick. Surely, after last night, she'd finally see him for what he was?

'Be glad you don't have any of your own to worry about. See all these grey hairs?' Owen pulled a lock of hair out of the scrunchie that was keeping it tidy. 'I guess it might be time to get this mop cut again.' He looked at Fran with a rueful expression. 'Fran tries to keep me looking like a respectable university professor, but she has her work cut out. Don't you, sweetie?' Fran chose that moment to rise from her chair and he gave her a loving slap on the rear end, causing Frank to avert his eyes in embarrassment.

'There's Lucy,' he said. 'I can't help feeling some responsibility for her, and she's got herself mixed up with a bad lot.' Frank found himself telling them about the previous night, seeing Lucy and the ensuing burglary. 'I just hope that's the end of it,' he finished, remembering how upset Marie had been when he rang her earlier. She had the difficult task of telling Lucy.

'I hope so too, for your sake and Marie's. What a mess. It's a pity Al is already taken.' She gave a cheeky grin.

'Don't even think about it! He's only here on a twelve-month visa. A relationship with a guy who's going back to Italy wouldn't be any sort of solution.'

'As I once told Pia, she'll have to kiss a few frogs before she finds her prince. Let's just hope no more of them turn out to be criminals,' Owen said. 'Look, here comes your guy back again.'

Frank looked out the window to see Al crossing the paddock.

'Seen enough?' Owen asked the young man when he walked in.

'Wow! It is a different world out here. I see alpacas in the field down where I walk.' He shook his head.

'They belong to my neighbour. Col Ford is a retired solicitor and wanted something to keep him occupied. They're a lot easier to manage than my animals. But I love my goats, even if sometimes I could see them to yonder.'

They all laughed. Frank wasn't sure Al understood what Owen said but he got the sense of it. 'Ready to go home, Al?' he asked.

'Sure.'

'Thanks so much for the afternoon tea, Fran,' Frank said, as he rose to leave. 'I haven't seen you in The Bean Sprout recently.'

'Some of us have to work,' Fran said with a smile. 'I see Marie regularly and she keeps me in touch with what's going on.'

With what she thinks is going on with me and Peta, Frank thought, forgetting Marie was right in her assumptions.

'They are nice, your friends,' Al said, when they were on their way home. 'Their farm – you call it a hobby farm? Is the one with alpacas a hobby too? I think there are many like it.'

'You're right on both counts. Remind me to show you a book I have which features stories about large Australian properties – many running sheep or cattle. They stretch for thousands of kilometres.'

'*Caspita!*'

The two fell silent, giving Frank time to consider how, seeing Owen and Fran together, he'd had the sense of something missing in his life. He missed having someone to love, had for some time, even before he and Marie went their separate ways. He now understood what she meant when she said she loved him, but like a brother. It was strange how it happened, how the passion they once felt had gradually disappeared and they'd become more like brother and sister. There had been happy years. Frank wanted to remember those times. But now he was ready to move on.

Thirty-seven

'Is it today I have to see her?' Lily was more subdued than usual as she slid into her chair for breakfast. 'Do I have to? I think I feel sick, Grandma.' She looked up with such a woeful expression, Peta wanted to tell her she could stay home, didn't need to meet Brenda Kable, the Independent Children's Lawyer who'd been allocated to Lily.

But there could be no excuse. When Col contacted her to let her know the appointment was scheduled for that afternoon, Peta's initial feeling of alarm was replaced by one of relief, relief it was beginning. The sooner it began the sooner it would end, and she and Lily could get on with their lives. 'Sorry, sweetheart. We have to go. But this Mrs Kable sounds like a kind person. Mr Ford knows her and he says she often talks with children just like you. We're to meet her in her office. I don't expect I'll be in the interview with you, but I'll be waiting right outside.'

Peta wasn't sure if Brenda would want to talk with her too, either today or at another time. But she was prepared, whatever the outcome. What she wasn't prepared for was to give up Lily without a fight.

But Lily sat toying with her breakfast, even ignoring Archie who, sensing something was wrong, was trying to leap up onto her lap.

'Archie!' Peta didn't have the energy for him this morning. Since his comforting presence in the early hours of Sunday morning, she'd become fonder of the cat, but her fondness didn't extend to allowing him liberties which he knew were forbidden. At her tone, he immediately slunk away into the living room to his favourite spot under the window which caught the morning sun.

'I'm not hungry,' Lily said, pushing away her bowl of cereal.

'Well, at least drink your milk.'

Lily drank the milk, wiped the back of her hand across her mouth and slid from the table.

'Leaving in ten minutes,' Peta called after her, finishing her coffee.

The appointment was set for after school, so Peta had the day to herself again. Now she was ahead with her projects, she planned to contact the local paper and a regional magazine which featured local identities and businesses and was published monthly. It was Ann's suggestion and, grateful for her advice, Peta had added them to her marketing strategy. Her cousin was now proving to be the good friend Peta remembered from their childhood.

And she had lunch with Fran to look forward to. Peta had been surprised but pleased to receive a call from Fran Larsen a couple of days ago. It seemed Frank and his Italian cousin paid Owen and her a visit on the weekend and it reminded her she hadn't yet contacted Peta as promised.

Peta knew it was her fault, too. When they'd spoken at Marie's party, both women promised to keep in touch, then Peta had become involved in her own life and hadn't made the connection. No doubt Fran was a busy lady too.

After a productive morning in which she managed to secure an interview with both the paper and the editor of the magazine – who promised a full page spread with photographs – Peta headed out to the university campus where she'd arranged to meet Fran. It made sense to meet there as it was where Fran and Owen worked. It must be odd to work side-by-side with your husband, Peta thought as she found her way to the café Fran had nominated. She couldn't imagine anything worse than having worked alongside Tony all day, every day – not even in the heady early days of their relationship. Marie and Frank had done that too, still did. Not for the first time, Peta puzzled over their relationship. Marie was about to marry Drew Hamilton, but there still appeared to be a closeness between her and Frank – one that was difficult to understand.

It seemed odd to Peta, but perhaps it was Peta who was odd, and her relationships – Joy's, too, she thought with a pang. She was still trying to work out why Fran and Marie's relationships were so different from her own experience, when she saw the sign for the Banjo Patterson Café, or Banjo's as Fran called it, and turned towards it. As she walked along the pathway bordered with the tall red bottlebrush, Peta looked up at the clear blue sky. Despite the meeting with the ICL which lay ahead later in the day, a bolt of pleasure shot through her. It had been a good decision to come here to live, to leave the city and all the memories behind.

As she walked in, Peta was struck by the noise. Being lunchtime, the café was full of students and all of them seemed to be talking at the top of their voices. This, combined with the dull pounding of music coming from two speakers in the ceiling, threatened to burst her eardrums. She saw Fran seated at a table in the far corner and made her way toward her, weaving between tables filled with cheerful young people, who seemed intent on setting the world to rights over lunch.

'Sorry,' Fran said, when Peta joined her. 'I'd forgotten how busy – and noisy – it gets at this time during semester. Owen and I normally have a bite to eat in the office. But we do love their coffee and croissants.' She gave a secret smile which made Peta wonder what she was thinking. 'Anyway, classes start again soon and we'll have the place to ourselves. They'll turn the music down, too. Here's the menu. I'll go up and order when you've decided.'

Peta took the menu card from Fran, noticing the students were beginning to drift off. After a quick skim of the dishes on offer, she decided on roast pumpkin with fetta and olives on flatbread, while Fran chose the eggplant open grill with pumpkin, fetta, semi dried tomatoes and pesto. Peta ordered a cappuccino and Fran a peppermint tea.

'I'm glad we've finally managed to get together,' Fran said, once they'd been served. 'I've been meaning to call you ever since we met at Ann's. Life got in the way, as it does.' She gave a wry grin.

'I'm glad, too. I enjoyed our chat at Marie's party, brief though it was. You enjoy working here?' she asked, glancing around the now almost empty café to the campus outside.

'Love it!' Fran grinned. 'I started in the School of Education soon after I arrived in Granite Springs. That's when I met Ann. Then, after a trip to England – my mother passed away – I was asked to take on the position I have now. The School of Music and Drama didn't exist back then, and Owen still had to be appointed. He was a bit of a shock to everyone when he arrived, but has managed to become part of the university community and the wider community in town. He's taken over the choir, too. Do you sing?'

Peta shook her head. She remembered seeing a flier for the Granite Springs Choristers on the library noticeboard.

'And that's how you met?' she asked.

Fran laughed gaily. 'It certainly is. Can you imagine what I thought when I first saw him? He looked even more disreputable than he does these days, but underneath his untidiness, his habit of acting without thinking…' she smiled warmly, '…is the man I fell in love with. Sorry, but it was so unexpected. Sometimes I still have to pinch myself to prove it's real, he's real.'

Peta looked across at Fran, clearly happy with her Owen. They were around the same age, as was Marie. Two women who professed to have found love when they were what many would call *past their prime. Could it happen to her, too? Did she want it to?*

'What brought you to Granite Springs in the first place?' she asked, curious to know Fran's story, despite realising she risked being asked the same question.

Fran's eyes clouded over. She carefully placed her cutlery on the table and twisted her fingers together. 'It's not something I often talk about. I arrived here by chance, a lucky chance as it turned out, though I didn't think so at the time. I was in an accident and wakened up in Granite Springs Base Hospital.' She paused, her eyes taking on a faraway look. It was filled with grief, making Peta regret having asked the question.

'Sorry if I brought up bad memories for you.'

Fran shook her head. 'Not your fault. These days I don't think about it much, but there were years when the memory wouldn't go away, when… But enough about me. What about you? You seem happier than when we first met.'

'I am.' As she spoke, Peta realised she was if not happier, more content than she'd felt for years. 'You were right what you said when I met you at Ann's. Granite Springs does seem to have a nurturing effect.' She gave a nervous laugh. 'But you don't want to hear my story.' She pressed her lips together.

'Sorry, I didn't mean to be intrusive.'

Peta felt guilty. She couldn't keep silent about it forever. 'My daughter was killed.'

Fran's eyes widened. 'Oh, I'm so sorry. I didn't know.'

'No reason why you should.' Peta was pleased Ann hadn't revealed it to Fran, and Jo hadn't either. 'It happened just before we left Sydney. I had to get Lily away.'

'Oh! Lily's mother?'

Peta nodded, unable to say more.

'I'm so sorry, I know… no, I don't. I don't know what it would be like to lose someone you'd given birth to and brought up till…' Fran's eyes filled.

What had she done? Why was Fran so upset? For the first time when she'd thought of Joy, Peta wasn't the one in tears, though she wasn't far off. She hoped the staff in the café didn't look this way to see two middle-aged women weeping.

'Sorry,' Fran sniffed. 'It still gets to me. After all this time. I lost a child, too. Not like you. It was a miscarriage, but it meant I wasn't able to have another. For years I avoided women with children. It sounds silly, but…'

'Not at all.' Peta wanted to hug Fran. 'I'm sorry, too. It's a dreadful thing to happen, whatever the circumstances.'

Peta felt a tinge of regret as she said goodbye to Fran when lunch was over. They'd shared so much, discovered they had more in common than they imagined. Peta even forgave Fran when she again hinted about Frank, suggesting she'd like to see her as happy as she was with Owen.

As she drove back into town, the impending meeting with Brenda Kable was at the forefront of her mind. She hoped Lily hadn't spent the day worrying about it. When she arrived at the school gates, it was to see Eve already there. Today, she had Emily Rose with her.

'We're off to see Mum,' she said when Peta joined her. 'It's a surprise for the twins. We don't usually go out there during the week, but Mum rang to say one of the alpacas gave birth this morning and Col wants to show the cria off to the twins.'

'Cria?'

'That's what a baby alpaca is called.'

'I didn't realise Col intended to breed them.'

'He didn't.' Eve chuckled. 'They have an eleven-month gestation period and this one was pregnant when he bought her. But, once they've seen the little one, I'm willing to bet it won't be the last. Mum says he's over the moon. She's so cute.'

'Lily will be so jealous,' Peta said without thinking.

'Why don't you come with us?'

'I'm sorry. We can't. Lily and I have an appointment. But next time...'

'For sure. We'll no doubt be going out more often with this attraction.' Eve pretended to sigh. 'Here they come now.'

The three girls were running out together, so alike they could be taken for triplets until they got closer. Lily slowed at the sight of Peta.

'Let me take Lily off before you tell them,' Peta whispered. 'I'll never get her away otherwise.'

Eve nodded as Lily came over to hug Peta, her face falling as she remembered what lay ahead.

'It'll be all right,' Peta reassured her as they walked up Main Street and turned into the building which housed Brenda Kable's office. It was close to the one occupied by Slater and Ford Solicitors. Brenda Kable was a lawyer who specialised in family law. She had been appointed to Lily's case by the Legal Aid Commission, New South Wales. Peta hated the fact Lily was now considered *a case*.

Peta pushed open the etched glass door to enter a warm and friendly reception area. There were two comfy, cane two-seater sofas with padded cushions bearing a palm-tree motif and a low table with a collection of children's books and several pot plants. At any other time, Peta would have admired the décor. As it was, she barely noticed it, realising instead that her hands were clammy with sweat. The reception desk was manned by a young woman in her early twenties with a welcoming smile.

'You must be Lily,' she said as soon as they walked in, 'and Mrs Forrest.'

Lily nodded, clinging to Peta's hand as she had when they first came to town.

'Mrs Kable will just be a few minutes. Take a seat. Would you like tea or coffee while you're waiting, Mrs Forrest?'

'Thanks, tea would be lovely,' Peta replied, though her throat was feeling so tight she didn't know if she'd be able to swallow it.

She took a seat, and Lily squeezed in close to her.

Before the tea arrived, a door to one side of the reception desk opened and an auburn-haired woman came out and walked over to them.

'Hello, Lily. I'm Brenda Kable.' She crouched down to meet Lily's eyes. 'I'm going to steal you away from your grandma for a little while so we can talk. Will that be all right?'

Lily nodded without speaking.

Brenda stood up and addressed Peta. 'Please do make yourself comfortable. We won't take long. Did Jodie offer you tea?'

'Yes, thanks.'

'I may want to speak with you afterwards, but perhaps not today. Come with me, Lily?' she asked, holding out her hand.

With a fearful glance at Peta, Lily took it and went off through the open door.

Thirty-eight

'He's out on bail.' Marie was rearranging the cakes in the display shelves during a lull in customers. 'Rick. I don't know why Lucy ever got involved with him. Once you told Drew and me how you'd seen them together, we tried to make her see sense, but it was like trying to make water run uphill. She can be so stubborn sometimes. She's so like Dee.' Marie stopped what she was doing and sighed, remembering her sister. 'Why did she have to die?' she cried, reaching out for Frank.

He lent her his shoulder and patted her on the back.

'Sorry,' she sniffed and moved out of his reach. 'It just hits me sometimes when I least expect it. I wonder if I'm doing things right, if Dee would approve or if she'd be annoyed with me for allowing Lucy to…' Marie wiped her eyes with the back of her hand.

'You're doing a wonderful job. It's only natural Lucy wants to kick the traces from time to time. But she's a good kid. I only wish…'

'What?' Marie gave him a puzzled look.

'I've known her all her life, Marie. I can't just abandon responsibility now there's a new man in your life. I know her as well as you do. For most of her life I've been like a father figure to her. You can't expect me to leave her to her own devices without saying something, without trying to help.'

'Drew has a daughter. He understands.'

'Are you saying I don't?' Frank could feel the anger tempting him to say something he'd later regret. 'I have no intention of butting in where I'm not wanted. But she's my niece, too.'

Marie pushed her hair away from her face and looked perplexed. 'I'm not sure where this all came from. I only said Rick was out on bail.'

'Sorry.' Frank took a deep breath. He didn't know what prompted the outburst any more than Marie did. Maybe it was the news Rick was out on bail, maybe it had nothing to do with Lucy. Today was the day young Lily was meeting with the court person, and he knew Peta was worried about it. But he was concerned about Lucy, too. 'She's not going to see him again, is she?'

After he'd filled Marie in on the break-in to the café, he'd received a tearful phone call from Lucy.

'I didn't know he was going to do that, Uncle Frank,' she wailed. 'When he asked me about the café, I only thought he was interested in me, not that he intended to…' She broke down and sobbed.

Frank had tried to reassure Lucy he didn't blame her. It was all Rick's doing. He'd come down hard on the guy, and might have said a few things he regretted later – suggestions of what he'd like to do to him if he caught him on a dark night with no police around. When Lucy tried to defend him, he'd told her to get a grip and find a better boy to hang around with, one who'd respect her – and her family. There was nothing wrong with that, was there? But he'd come off the phone unconvinced she'd give him the flick. Surely she didn't intend to remain involved? The guy was a criminal.

'Who knows?' Marie shrugged. 'I seem to have lost the power to influence her, if I ever had it. But it did shock her to think he might have used her to find out where you kept the cash float.'

'Luckily, I'd taken it home with me. I suppose the mess he made was all a result of temper. He's a bit old to have a temper tantrum. What on earth does Lucy see in him?'

Marie considered. 'Well, he's older, and earning money which he's not slow to spend on her. He bought her those white leather pants and a satin dress for her formal.'

'I didn't know that.' Frank leant his arms on the counter. 'Does she intend to take him – to the formal?'

'I think she must do – or did. He may be locked up by then. It's in the middle of next month.'

'Hmm.'

The café began to fill up and they let the conversation lapse as Frank made coffees and heated food and Marie served their customers, her voice as bright and cheerful as usual as if their discussion had never taken place. But Frank knew Marie like the back of his hand. She was worried about Lucy, as worried as he was. But what could either of them do?

It was almost two, and the lunch crowd was beginning to thin when Frank heard a disturbance outside the café. Looking out he saw Lucy engaged in what appeared to be a dispute with... Rick. The anger he felt earlier boiled up again. He threw off his apron and was heading for the door when Marie grabbed his arm. He tried to shake it off.

'Let her be. Just watch. She can take care of herself. He's not going to harm her in broad daylight. Have some sense, Frank. What good would it do if you got into a fight in the middle of Granite Springs main street?'

Frank took a deep breath to calm himself, put his apron back on and went back to his spot behind the espresso machine. But he kept a weather eye on the couple outside as Marie continued to serve and chat with customers.

The pair tussled for a few moments, then Lucy pulled away from Rick's grasp and pushed through the door and into the café, her body heaving with anger. 'I can't believe it. He thinks because he's been released, we can just go on as before. Oh, Uncle Frank, I tried to tell him it was over, and he said...' she hiccupped, '...he said he knows where I live and will make sure I...' She broke into tears.

Frank was around the counter in a flash, even before Marie had taken in what was happening. He drew Lucy into his arms. 'No one's going to hurt you while I'm around.'

'But he said... he said it was all your fault and he'd see you got yours.'

'I'd like to see him try.' Frank wasn't a violent man. He abhorred violence in every shape and form. But where Lucy was concerned, he'd do whatever it took to keep her safe. 'What are you doing out of school at this time of day, anyway?'

'It's exams. I was having lunch with a group of friends when Rick rolled up and said he wanted to talk to me, then...' She broke down again.

Frank had forgotten the HSC exams – the end of school marathon the kids thought decided their future. They hadn't done much for him. He'd known he was destined for the café regardless of what his result might be. But they were important for Lucy. She was a bright kid, always done well at school, but if she was to get her coveted place at university in Canberra, she needed to achieve the requisite result. How dare that lout disturb her at what was, for her, the most important weeks of her life, the weeks which could determine her future.

'Luce?' Marie hurried over. 'What happened? What did he do to you? Tea?' She looked over her shoulder to Frank and gestured to the café kitchen.

'Nothing, Aunt Marie. He just...' She allowed herself to be led to a table and pushed into a chair. Marie sat down opposite, as Frank went off to make the chamomile tea he knew Marie intended. Although coffee was his go-to beverage for every situation, Marie had always preferred her herbal teas, and the camomile was the one she always brewed when she was upset, proclaiming its calming properties.

When he arrived back with the tea, Frank checked the only remaining table with customers and put the CLOSED sign on the door, before joining Marie and Lucy. The girl's eyes were still red, but she'd stopped weeping.

'What am I going to do?' Lucy wailed taking a sip of tea, before saying, 'It's too hot,' and putting the cup down again.

Frank and Marie looked at each other, neither willing to speak first.

The two customers left with a smile in their direction, and Al walked out from the kitchen. Seeing the CLOSED sign, he started to speak, then saw Lucy sitting there twisting a tissue in her hands.

'*Che cosa c'è?*' Al slid in next to Lucy on the bench seat and took her hand.

'Not now, Al.' Frank gestured to him to leave.

But Lucy said, 'It's all right, Uncle Frank. He'll find out anyway. That bastard, Rick, is out on bail and he won't leave me alone.' She turned to Marie. 'He even says he's still coming to the formal with me whatever I say. He wants to see me in the dress he bought. I can't wear it. I never want to see it again.'

Frank was delighted Lucy had finally seen sense, but hated to see her so upset. 'The dress?' he asked Marie.

'It's beautiful. White satin. Strapless. Split to the thigh. I did think it a bit old for Lucy, too sophisticated for a school formal.'

'No one else has one like it. The other girls would have been so envious.' Lucy started to sob again. Even though she said she wanted to discard the dress, it seemed she couldn't give it up completely.

'Pouf! It is only a dress. My sister. She is a *sarta* – how you say – a maker of dresses? I can have her send you one of her model dresses. It will be *esclusivi*. You will be the belle of the ball – you say that, yes?'

Lucy shook her head. 'I can't go,' she said dolefully. 'Everyone has a partner. It's too late. Rick knows that. That's why…' She started to sob again.

Al pulled his shoulders back and pointed to his chest. '*I* will go with you. How is it? You will be with a *gionanotto di bell'aspetto Italiano*. The other girls, they will be envious, no?'

Frank was amused how Al lapsed into Italian when he became excited.

Lucy gave a little giggle.

'I think my Elisa will not mind.'

'Are you sure, Al? It would be kind of you and I'm sure Lucy would appreciate it.'

'But what if Rick turns up, what if he tries to…?' Lucy turned pale.

'I can handle Rick. He is a little man to threaten a girl, *un codardo, un bullo*.'

Lucy was in no doubt what Al meant – a coward and a bully. She nodded.

'So, we go to this formal together?'

She nodded again.

'Okay. I will ask my sister.'

Glad to have that settled, Frank gave a sigh of relief.

'To approach you like that in the middle of your exams.' Marie shook her head. 'How did it go this morning, anyway? You were worried about this one.'

'It was good, better than I expected. Only a few more to go. It's okay, Uncle Frank,' she said as Frank's forehead creased. 'I'm not going to let that idiot mess me up. These exams are too important to me. Thanks, Al.' She turned to the young man with a wide smile. 'Wait till I tell Jess.'

Frank shared a glance with Marie. It still surprised him how resilient young people could be. Seeing how distraught Lucy was when she ran in, he thought she'd be in tears for the rest of the day. He'd never understand how Al's offer could cause such an instant change in her. Unless… no, she couldn't be interested in him. She knew he had a girl back in Italy, and she'd only just broken up with Rick.

'Well, now that's settled, we'd better clean up. Do you want to wait till I go home, Luce?' Marie asked.

'No.' Lucy peered out the window. 'Rick's gone now. I'll catch up with Jess and we'll head home together. I left her outside Mouthfuls.'

'If you're sure?'

'I'm sure. Thanks everyone. Sorry I was such a wreck when I came in.' Lucy jumped up, gave Marie and Frank a hug and disappeared out the door in a flash.

'Thanks, Al,' Frank said. 'Good of you.'

'It is no trouble. I think I will enjoy seeing this formal. Lucy will look good in one of my sister's dresses. She designs for the models in Milano.'

'You must let me pay for it. No, I won't allow Lucy to accept it otherwise,' he added, sensing Al was about to refuse.

It didn't take the three of them long to finish up in the café. Marie and Al left, Marie to go home and Al to send an email to his sister.

When Frank was alone in the café, he checked the time. Four o'clock. Today was the meeting Peta and Lily had with the ICL person. He'd heard of Brenda Kable and knew her to be a fair person, one who was able to win children's confidence. He wondered how Lily was faring, and how Peta was coping. He imagined her sitting there in the reception area waiting for her granddaughter to emerge, worrying about how Lily was, about what Brenda Kable was asking her. He could almost feel her anguish.

He decided to hang around till she returned.

Thirty-nine

Peta looked up with relief when the door opened and Lily walked out with Brenda. She'd been imagining all sorts of things and one glance at Lily's tight lips told her the girl hadn't enjoyed talking about herself.

'I may need to talk with Lily again,' Brenda said with a smile. 'And you, too, Mrs Forrest. Can I contact you?'

'Of course.' Peta rose, and Lily ran over to take her hand, her small fingers clutching Peta's for comfort.

'There, it wasn't so bad, was it?' Peta asked, once they were out in the street. She bit her lip. 'What did Mrs Kable ask you?'

'I don't want to talk about it,' Lily said, a mulish expression on her face. 'And I don't want to talk with her again. Do I have to?'

'If she wants to talk with you, there's nothing I can do to prevent it. It's the law. She seems to be a nice woman.'

Lily didn't reply.

Peta sighed.

'Can we go home now?'

'Of course.' Though the flat wasn't really their home. It was temporary, a place to stay until they could look for something more permanent. Peta didn't dare think what she'd do if she didn't gain custody of Lily.

When they walked past the front of The Bean Sprout, Peta had the urge to peer in to see if Frank was still there. She needed some of the brand of comfort he always seemed able to provide. But he'd have gone home long ago, so she averted her eyes and continued along the lane to the back of the café and the stairs up to the flat.

As soon as she opened the door, Lily flew past her yelling, 'Archie!' The cat stretched and padded over from where he'd been lying by the window and Lily flopped to the floor and buried her face in his fur.

Peta dropped her bag and headed for the kitchen where she started making tea. She was just pouring herself a cup of the camomile tea that always managed to have a calming influence on her when there was a knock at the door.

With her cup in one hand, Peta opened the door to see Frank standing there smiling. Her heart gave the now familiar leap. It was as if he'd read her mind. 'Frank! I'm so glad to see you.' She put a hand up to her mouth. Where had those words come from? She *was* glad to see him but hadn't intended to sound so... so desperate. Since Sunday, she'd thought about him a lot, wondering if she was ready for a relationship, while knowing she was lucky to have met him. 'You'd better come in.' She opened the door wider.

'Lily?' he asked, his voice a whisper.

She pointed to the living room, before leading him into the kitchen. 'Tea?'

'Coffee if you have any.'

'Of course.' She turned to the coffee maker, but Frank put a hand on her arm and stopped her.

'How are you? It must have been an ordeal.'

Peta almost fell into his arms. The relief at having another adult to share her anguish with was overwhelming. She trembled as he led her to a chair.

'You sit down. I can make my own coffee. And what are you drinking? Don't you have anything stronger?'

'Camomile. It's...'

'Calming. I know. You and Marie with your herbal teas. I think Magda Duncan has a lot to answer for with the brews she's introduced to the women of Granite Springs.'

'Who?'

'Oh, you haven't come across our famous masseuse. She's a lovely lady, lives out near Fran and Owen, and she's a bit... otherworldly. You'll no doubt hear about her before much longer. But I didn't come here to discuss tea, or Magda Duncan. How did it go today? I was thinking about you.'

'Lily won't talk about it. And she's adamant she doesn't want to go back.' Peta frowned. 'I don't know what I'll do if Brenda wants to see her again.'

'Did she talk with you, too?'

'Not today, though she said she may need to. I suppose it'll give me the chance to give my side of it before any court hearing. I'm not looking forward to it, to having to face some judge or magistrate and try to justify why I'm the best person to care for my own granddaughter.'

'It may not come to that.'

'I can only hope you're right. If Grant decides to defend the case, then I'll have no option.' She took a sip of the tea which wasn't having its usual calming effect.

When Frank turned back from the coffee maker, his eyes were full of compassion. He took the seat beside her and placed an arm around her shoulder. 'You shouldn't be doing this alone.'

Peta welcomed the contact but knew this was one thing he couldn't help her with. 'I'll be right,' she said, but didn't even manage to convince herself. She could feel the tears well up and swallowed in an attempt to suppress them. Frank's closeness, while comforting, did nothing to change her situation.

'Sorry.' She shrugged off his arm. 'I should see what Lily's doing.' She needed time to compose herself. She didn't want Frank to see her tears again, to think she was one of those women prone to break down at the slightest opportunity.

Out in the hallway, she took a deep breath and blew her nose, then entered the living room to see Lily still cuddling Archie. 'I think Archie may want to go out,' she said. 'He's probably been inside all day. Why don't you let him out and come into the kitchen for juice? Your Uncle Frank's here.'

'He is?' Lily brightened and freed the cat who sped across the room towards the outside door, where he stood meowing and looking pitiful.

Casting a glance into the kitchen where a much more cheerful Lily was now chatting to Frank, Peta let the cat out – Archie was still wary about using the cat flap Frank had installed for him – then made a trip to the ensuite to rinse her eyes and renew her lipstick before joining them.

'Lily tells me she told Brenda she'll run away if she's sent to live with anyone else,' Frank said, with a warning glance at Peta.

Peta sat down with a thump, not sure whether to be pleased or upset she'd confided in Frank rather than her. 'Oh, honey!'

'I thought you'd be angry if I told you,' Lily said, her face crumpling.

'Of course I'm not angry with you. But it was a silly thing to say. It wouldn't help anyone if you ran away. Where would you run to, anyway?'

'Back to you.' Lily adopted the stubborn expression Peta had learned to expect when her granddaughter didn't get her own way.

'You have to admit, this is a girl who knows what she wants. What did Brenda Kable say, Lily?'

'She told me she hoped it wouldn't come to that, and she would be "looking into all options and choosing the best one for me".' Lucy mimicked the solicitor so accurately it was all Peta and Frank could do not to laugh.

'I need to think about dinner.' Peta looked at the fridge as if it held the answer. She couldn't think straight.

'Let me take you both out to dinner.' Frank drained his coffee. 'We can eat early so we're not out past Lily's bedtime.'

Peta looked at Lily. When would her homework get done if they went out to dinner?

'Please, Grandma,' Lily pleaded. 'I only have some spelling words to learn. I can go over them with you at breakfast.' She gazed up at Peta, her eyes so like Joy's, it made Peta's throat tighten.

Peta felt herself weakening. It would be good not to have to work out what to cook, not to have to make dinner. 'Well…'

'Good. You haven't been to Granite Springs' famous Italian restaurant, have you?'

'I didn't know there was one.'

'Pavarotti's. Another Italian family who settled in Granite Springs around the same time as mine. Old Marco and my grandfather were good mates. Genuine Italian food. I should take Al there sometime, too.'

'How can I refuse?'

'You can't. Do you like pasta, Lily?'

'I love it, Uncle Frank.' She grinned, seemingly having recovered from the meeting with Brenda Kable.

Peta smiled, amazed yet again at Lily's resilience. Maybe things would turn out all right. She looked across at Frank, loving the way his eyes creased when he smiled, and knew she needed more time with this kind man.

'I do like a good spaghetti carbonara,' she said with another wide smile, the cares of the day slipping from her shoulders.

Forty

The next few weeks passed in a haze of delight for Frank. Since the fateful evening when he and Peta had made love for the first time, they'd fallen into a routine of sorts. Both were busy during the week, but Peta had taken to popping down to the café for coffee most mornings. Frank had learned to suffer Marie's teasing, even taking it in good humour.

Weekends were different. He and Peta had fallen into the habit of having dinner together on Friday evenings, along with Lily, who loved seeing her Uncle Frank and regaling him with all the news of her week, including the latest doings of the twins. Then, after The Bean Sprout closed on Saturday, he'd quickly become accustomed to meeting Peta and Lily at the park where they treated themselves to ice cream before heading back to either the flat or his house for a meal.

Frank couldn't believe how his life had changed. He sometimes had to pinch himself to make sure it was real. But he still felt Peta was holding back, not ready for the commitment he was eager to make. Marie was getting married, why couldn't he? It was the ideal solution. His home was too big for him on his own – he should have considered that when he agreed to buy Marie out. It was made for a family, always had been. When Peta and Lily came to visit, it was as if they *were* a family.

But it wasn't the only reason. He'd fallen in love with this woman who tied him in knots. He wanted to spend the rest of his life with her.

It was Friday, and all day, Frank had been looking forward to their evening together.

'Where is it tonight?' Marie asked with a wink, when the last customer left and he put the CLOSED sign on the door. 'Getting to be serious with Peta?'

'Mmm.' Frank didn't want to reveal his innermost feelings to her, although he knew she could read him like a book. They'd known each other too long for subterfuge. 'Give over, Marie. Some things are best kept private.'

'Private? From me? You must be joking. I told you Peta was right for you from the start. I'm only glad if you've come to the same conclusion.'

'It takes two.' He gave a heartfelt sigh. Maybe he could share his doubts with Marie. After all, for so long it had been just the two of them. She knew him better than anyone, knew his strengths and weaknesses, knew how he thought. 'I'm falling in love with her, Marie.' He drew a hand through his hair. 'But I don't know what she's thinking. There's a lot happening in her life at the moment and...' He shook his head. 'I don't know,' he repeated.

'Come and sit down.' Marie stopped wiping down the tables and gestured to one in the back corner. 'Sounds like you need some womanly advice.'

Frank joined her but wasn't sure what advice she could offer. He clasped his hands on the table, his throat tightening. He wasn't ready for the grilling he anticipated from Marie. But he was wrong.

Marie leant both arms on the table. 'I may be able to understand how Peta is feeling. I've been through it, Frank. With Drew. Everything seemed to be going well, when I got cold feet. Of course, I had Lucy to consider, but Peta has Lily. Has she...?'

'She knows I stay over on weekends – or they stay with me. She seems okay with it.' Could that be why Peta seemed to back off at times? Could she be worried about what her granddaughter might be thinking? No. He shook his head. 'She's a great kid. She likes me a lot. It's not that.'

'What else then? You said she had a lot going on. Want to tell me?'

'It's not for me to say.' Frank didn't know how he could divulge Peta's ongoing concerns with the court order to Marie. There were some things too private to share, even with her.

But Marie was continuing to speak. 'It was Fran who helped me, made me see it was a storm in a teacup, that I was worrying needlessly.

And she was right.' She gave a smug smile. 'Lucy is so happy with us.' She put a hand across to cover Frank's. 'I felt bad at the time, when you wanted us to get back together. But it was too late.'

'I know that now. But at the time... it was hard. I wanted to do the right thing by you and Lucy. I wanted...' He drew his hand away. 'I never thought I could feel this way again, Marie. It caught me by surprise.' He gave a rueful grin. 'Remember the old Frank Sinatra song about when you think you're past love?'

Marie chuckled. 'You're not old, Frank. Because if you are, then I am, too. And that, I refuse to accept. But to get back to you and Peta. Have you told her how you feel?'

Frank winced. 'Not yet. I wanted to...' The truth was he was afraid of being rejected. He spoke the truth when he told Marie he'd taken her rejection hard, but lied when he said he'd only wanted to *do the right thing by her and Lucy*. It was more than that. He'd still had feelings for Marie and had hoped the thing with Drew would pass and she'd turn back to the man she'd known and loved for years, the man who had never completely given up caring for her.

But it wasn't to be. And here he was, in love with another, and getting advice on his love life from his ex.

'Well, you should. We women are strange creatures, you know. We like to be told when a man cares for us.'

'But she must know.' Frank thought of all the nights they'd spent together, the warmth of her body, the passion of their lovemaking. Surely that said it all?

'Don't count on it.'

'Hmm.' It was certainly food for thought. Maybe he could broach the L word tonight. Marie was the only woman he'd spoken to of love until now, and here she was encouraging him to tell Peta he loved her. Life took some strange turnings.

'We should get on.' He rose. This conversation was at an end. The café had to be cleaned and tidied ready for next day, and he needed to go home to shower and change before coming back to see Peta and Lily.

'Don't forget what I said,' was Marie's parting shot.

*

Peta was looking troubled when she opened the door to Frank that evening. While showering, he'd rehashed what Marie had said and stiffened his resolve to follow her advice. He'd tell Peta how he was feeling, risk being shot down in flames. But the sight of her puffy eyes and woebegone expression sent all his good intentions to the wind.

'What's happened. Is Lily…?'

'She's at the twins' till tomorrow. We have the place to ourselves.'

But Peta didn't appear pleased they'd have the evening alone, something which didn't happen often. Even though he loved Lily as if she was his own, her presence did sometimes put a damper on their evenings together.

'I brought…' Frank held up the chilled bottle of chardonnay he'd picked up on the way. 'Why don't I pour us a drink and you can tell me what's up?'

Without waiting for a response, he headed to the kitchen to collect a couple of glasses before joining Peta in the living room. She was sitting on the edge of the sofa tearing a tissue into shreds. He poured two glasses and handed one to her.

'Thanks.' Peta took the glass but appeared distracted.

Frank sat down beside her and stretched an arm around her shoulder. 'You can tell Uncle Frank,' he said, his words managing to elicit a weak smile.

Peta clutched her glass in both hands and took a gulp of wine, then began to speak.

'I had a letter from the court today, or rather, Col Ford did. He called me in to a meeting.' She raised her head to meet Frank's eyes. He thought how pretty she looked, even with her eyes red and puffy. All his protective instincts came to the fore.

'I told you about how I had to apply to the court for the right to keep Lily with me. Now it seems Grant, Lily's father, plans to defend it and his sister is demanding Lily be with her. She's submitted a counter claim.' Tears started to slide down her cheeks. 'Sorry,' she sniffed. 'I promised myself I wouldn't fall apart on you.'

Frank tried to make sense of what Peta was telling him. 'Let me get this straight. You told me about this before. You're Lily's grandmother, but you need to apply for some legal order before she can live with you?'

'Yes. I applied to the courts for an interim and final residency order. I was worried her father might put a spanner in the works but hoped he'd see sense.'

'And his sister – Lily's aunt. Are they close?'

'She's barely seen Lily. When Joy was alive, she told me Celia was always too busy to visit and when she did, she had no time for Lily. Joy didn't think she liked children. She certainly didn't know how to speak to Lily.'

'Well, it would seem you have nothing to worry about.'

'I hope so.' But Peta's disbelieving expression belied her words.

Frank tightened his hand on her shoulder, feeling helpless. This was something over which he had no control. 'What happens now?'

'It means we have to go to court. When I hadn't heard, I'd hoped...' She sniffed and wiped her eyes with the sodden tissue.

Frank looked around to see if he could spy the box of tissues. He didn't want to leave Peta while he fetched a fresh one.

'I have a meeting with Brenda Kable in just over a week's time,' she said, sobbing. 'I was hoping that would be the end of it. But now...' she started to weep again.

Frank took the glass, which was in danger of tipping over, from her hand and put it down on the coffee table beside his own. Then he pulled her towards him, feeling her body melt into his embrace. He kissed her forehead, his lips moving to her eyelids and cheeks, still wet with tears. 'Maybe it won't be as bad as you imagine,' he murmured. 'And I'll be here for you. If there's anything...' Now wasn't the time to profess his love.

'Thanks, Frank. I don't know what we'd do without you. You've been so kind to us, so...' She began to sob again.

Frank felt helpless. He patted her on the back, wondering what to do.

After what seemed like an age, Peta straightened up. 'Sorry to subject you to my mess,' she said. 'I'll be right, now. It was just so unexpected. I thought... when we hadn't heard... Well, I was wrong, wasn't I? The bastard isn't done with us yet. But I won't let them get away with it. I can't lose Lily. I can't.' Peta's voice gained in strength.

'What will you do?'

'I don't know yet.' Peta rose to take a fresh tissue from a box Frank hadn't seen. She wiped her eyes again. 'I'm sorry,' she repeated. 'You didn't come here to have me dump my problems on you. What had you planned for this evening?'

Frank thought of the romantic evening he'd envisaged, how he'd intended to tell Peta he loved her, how he wanted to take care of her and Lily, how he wanted to fill his house with their laughter. 'Why don't we go out to dinner?' he asked instead.

Forty-one

Peta turned over to look at the man sleeping beside her. She'd been in such a mess when Frank arrived the previous evening. The news of Grant's decision to defend the case, plus Celia's counter claim had knocked her for six. All she wanted to do was curl up in a ball and cry her heart out.

Frank had been wonderful. He fed her wine, listened to her, taken her to dinner at The Riverside, then to bed. Once there, he'd done everything in his power to help her forget the Holmes pair and their plan to snatch Lily from her. And he succeeded. It was difficult to think of anything else when his lips were travelling down her body, when he was bringing her to climax after climax. But when their lovemaking was over, when they were lying side-by-side, when he had fallen asleep, it all came back.

Peta lay awake for hours. She heard the town clock chime midnight, one, two… Then she must have slept, but it wasn't a restful sleep. It was one filled with dreams of Lily being snatched from her grasp, of Joy lying in a pool of blood. She was glad to awaken to the peace and silence of her own bedroom, to feel Frank's warm, comforting body next to hers. For a moment she wondered what it would be like to waken like this every morning, to know there was someone there for her, someone who cared, someone who…

She couldn't think of the word *love*. But she knew, if she searched her heart, she was growing to love this man who made her feel as if she was the most important person in his world. But he hadn't said he loved her. And there was Grant and Celia Holmes to take care of before she could plan her own future. Please God it was a future with Lily in it.

Frank moved beside her. He opened his eyes. 'Morning,' he murmured, throwing an arm around Peta and pulling her towards him.

She inhaled his scent and, trying to forget the scenes which had disrupted her sleep, curled into him. This was real, Frank and her together. If only she could shut out the rest of the world.

'I guess I should get up. I have a café to open.' Frank loosened his grip and rolled away from Peta, leaving an empty spot where his warm body had been.

Suddenly Peta felt a shiver run up her spine. It was as if the empty spot beside her signified how empty her life would be if she lost Lily. 'I'll make you breakfast,' she said, rising to join him and dragging on her robe. She'd shower and dress later, perhaps even come back to bed and try to make up her lost sleep.

Neither talked much over the broccoli omelette Peta prepared and served with toasted rye bread. Peta was trying to work out what she could do to strengthen her claim to Lily, while she imagined Frank was mentally preparing himself for his working day. She sipped a cup of peppermint tea while Frank drank his coffee.

'Lucky I don't have far to go,' he joked, when he'd swallowed the last bite of toast and drunk the last drop of coffee. 'I'll see you when I finish?'

It wasn't really a question. She knew their weekend routine. She nodded, feeling tired. Her broken sleep was catching up with her.

'Why don't you go back to bed?' Frank suggested. 'Try to get more sleep. I'm guessing you didn't get much last night. I went out like a light. Always do.' He grinned. 'Did I snore?'

'Only a little.' Peta managed to smile. It wasn't Frank who kept her awake.

Once he'd gone, after exchanging a warm hug at the door, Peta dithered around, washing up and feeding the cat before deciding not to go back to bed after all. What she needed was some action to take her mind off her worries. She dressed in the leggings and tee-shirt she reserved for cycling, picked up her helmet, wheeled her bike out onto the landing and bumped it down the steps.

Minutes later she was on the road out of town. With the breeze in her face and the sun on her back, it was difficult to remain worried for long. She pedalled furiously, as if by doing so, she could drive away the fear that had been eating at her ever since she received Col's phone call. She'd known from his tone of voice it was bad news, but had to wait till she met with him to get the full picture.

There must be something she could do. Col had advised waiting, saying her position hadn't really changed. Brenda Kable would still write her report, indicate what she believed to be in Lily's best interests. The only difference was that she'd have to go to court. Only! As far as she was concerned it was huge.

Peta's mind was so filled with thoughts of what might happen with Lily, she barely noticed the car coming towards her. It stopped. Drawing to a halt, Peta shielded her eyes from the bright sun to see Col Ford peering out the open car window.

'I thought it was you,' he said. 'Don't often see you out this way. Everything all right?'

How could everything be all right? He must know the anguish she was suffering. 'Fine,' she lied.

'Now you've come this far, why don't you drop in to see Jo? I'm sure she'd like the company. She was baking this morning, so there should be something from the oven for morning tea.'

Peta looked around, suddenly taking note of her surroundings. In her confused state, she hadn't paid attention to where she was going or how long she'd been riding. The turnoff to the Fords' couldn't be far up the road from here. The thought of Jo's company held some attraction. 'Thanks, I might do that.'

'And take care. Don't worry too much. It'll all work out. You'll see.' With a smile and a wave, he was off.

Easy for him to say. Peta's feet found the pedals again. But it was good of him to be concerned.

When she arrived at Jo's, wheeling the bike through the gate to the home paddock, she saw three dogs lying on the veranda. They raised their heads lazily as she walked past, before deciding she didn't pose any threat and dropping them again. She leant the bike against the wall of the house, hung her helmet on the handlebar and knocked gently on the glass sliding door.

'Peta! What a lovely surprise. I didn't hear a car.'

'I'm on the bike. I met Col on the road, and he suggested I drop by.' She noticed another woman sitting at the table, her white hair forming a halo around a cheerful face. 'Oh, I'm sorry. You have company, perhaps…'

'Come in. This is my neighbour, Magda Duncan, soon to be Magda Turnbull. We were just discussing her wedding plans. Magda, this is Peta Forrest.'

'Hello, Peta, lovely to meet you,' Magda smiled.

Another wedding! What was it about this place? And Magda must be in her seventies. Then it struck her. Frank had mentioned a woman called Magda. 'Hello. I think Frank mentioned you. Frank Beattie. Don't you do massage?'

'*Massage with Magda.*' Magda grinned. 'So, you're the young woman I've heard so much about?'

Peta winced. What had she heard? She should never have come. She'd thought Jo would be alone.

'Oh, nothing bad,' Magda assured her as if reading her mind. 'Fran Larsen mentioned you were new in town and Jo brought the twins' new friend to visit me – your granddaughter, I believe.'

A wave of relief swept through Peta. She had a vague recollection of Lily babbling on about the woman with horses and two dogs. They must be the two greyhounds lying outside with Jo's dog. She really needed to rid herself of the suspicion people knew about the murder and were talking about her, pitying her. 'Lily, yes.'

'We're having a cup of peppermint tea with slices of my newly baked apple sponge. You'll join us?' Jo asked.

'Thanks, that would be lovely.' The smell of the newly baked apple sponge wafted up making Peta realise she hadn't eaten since breakfast, and the unaccustomed exercise had given her an appetite.

Sipping her tea, Peta began to relax as she listened to the chatter of the two other women. She was pleased not to have to explain herself to yet another stranger. But, somehow, sitting here at the scrubbed wooden table in Jo's cosy farmhouse kitchen, the Aga along one wall, she didn't feel as if she was among strangers.

She was almost finished her tea, her lip covered with crumbs from Jo's delicious sponge cake when Magda said, 'Life hasn't been easy for you recently.'

Peta stiffened, but Magda's tone was so matter-of-fact, she couldn't be annoyed. 'How did you know?'

'Oh, don't mind me.' The older woman waved a hand in the air. 'I sense things, and what I sense from you is a terrible grief.'

Peta swallowed the retort that came to her lips. How could she be angry with this gentle, elderly woman who was gazing at her with such compassion? 'But…' Then she remembered Frank had said something else about her – if she could just remember…

But Magda hadn't finished. 'There's more to come before it's over,' she said. 'But don't let it worry you too much. You're a worrier, I see. There's a silver lining ahead, and maybe wedding bells for you, too.' She chuckled.

The woman was mad. Did she have weddings on the brain? And who was she getting married to at her age?

Spookily, as if reading Peta's mind again, Magda said, 'I never thought to marry again, but when George fell ill last year, I realised life's too short to spend any more of it alone.' She nodded to herself. 'It's strange how things have a habit of working out. This time last year, I thought I was destined to spend my remaining years alone with my animals. Now I have my George…' her eyes sparkled, '…and both my granddaughter and his grandson are enrolled in the local university here in Granite Springs. They make a lovely couple too,' she murmured to herself.

'Oh, congratulations.' Peta wasn't sure if it was the correct thing to say, but it seemed to please Magda who grinned.

They chatted for a little longer then Peta stood up. 'Thanks so much, Jo,' she said. 'And lovely to meet you, Magda. Maybe I'll come out for a massage one of these days.'

'You will,' Magda said, with a certainty Peta didn't share. 'You have a surprise in store. Remember to follow your instincts; don't allow yourself to become discouraged; follow your heart – and all will be well.

Forty-two

Peta was exhausted when she returned home. But a shower soon revived her, and the sight of Archie stretched out in his usual spot in a pool of sunshine by the window helped her to forget Magda's weird words. Surely they were just the foolish and confused meanderings of an old woman? But there was something about her tone of voice, the expression in her eyes, that gave Peta food for thought.

Brushing them aside, she made herself a cheese and tomato sandwich and took it and a glass of water through to her study. She'd wasted enough time today; there was work to be done. She needed to mock up an advertorial for the local paper and a more sophisticated version of it for the Style magazine in Canberra. Then she wanted to make a list of other possible avenues to promote her business, and contact Danny again to check on the progress of his display homes.

It was close to three o'clock when she finally stretched her arms above her head. 'Time to pick up Lily,' she said to the cat, who'd joined her, choosing a spot at her feet for his afternoon nap. She debated checking her emails, then deciding there was no time, closed down her laptop, drew a comb through her hair and added a smidgeon of lipstick before heading out and driving to Eve's house where Lily had spent the night in yet another sleepover.

Eager to get back to her computer, Peta was glad to see Lily waiting for her at the door. There was no sign of Eve or the twins.

'The twins had to go out,' Lily informed her as she swung on Peta's hand. 'Can we stop for an ice cream? It's hot.' She made a play of wiping her forehead with her free hand.

Peta chuckled. 'Okay, but only a small one. You can have a snack when we get home.'

They stopped on the way by an ice cream van, and Lily was satisfied with the single salted caramel flavoured cone and happy to go the rest of the way home without complaint.

Once there, Archie greeted Lily with a loud meow. Peta settled the pair in the kitchen, Lily at the table with a bowl of her favourite noodles, and Archie with a treat which he took under the table.

She made her way back to the study, fired up her computer and opened her emails, sighing at how many had accumulated since the previous day. She quickly scanned the list, deleting the obvious scams, skimming those from suppliers who had responded to her queries, then…. There was one she hadn't been expecting, one she'd looked for in vain for weeks. She drew in a breath, opened the email from Miller Realty and began to read.

It had happened. It had actually happened. Rod Miller was writing to inform her he had an offer for her house – a good offer. Peta's eyes widened at the sight of the seven-figure amount. It was a lovely home, but she'd been wondering if Rod had been too optimistic in the sale price he recommended and, in her distraught state, she agreed to. But it seemed someone – an interstate buyer – had offered the full asking price. With no need to negotiate, she quickly replied instructing Rod to accept it, then leant back against her chair and closed her eyes.

'I've finished, Grandma. Can I go out on my bike?' Lily's voice brought Peta back to the present.

'Not on your own, sweetie, and I can't come with you right now. Why don't you find something else to play with?'

Lily pouted but recognised from Peta's tone there was no point in trying to change her mind.

When Lily had left, Archie padding behind her, Peta tried to work out what she needed to do. First, she knew there were documents to sign. Rod had offered to have them couriered down to her. But it didn't stop there. There was a house full of furniture and other personal items – everything she'd left behind in her haste to leave Sydney. Peta tapped on the desk with her pen. Not everything could be done at a distance. She knew she needed to be there to sort out what she wanted to keep from what could be discarded. She would have to go to Sydney.

There was a loud knock on the door and Peta could hear Frank whistling outside.

'Good day?' he asked, giving her a hug. 'You're looking more cheerful than when I left this morning, but where did that frown come from?' He stroked her forehead before dropping a kiss on it.

It was reassuring to feel his lips on her skin. Peta sank into his embrace, then drew away. 'I have to go to Sydney,' she said.

*

Frank's stomach began to churn. 'Sydney? What's happened now?'

'Oh, it's good news this time. I had an email to say my house there has sold. It means I can move on with my life – or it would if the business with Lily was settled.' Her eyes clouded over again. 'But I do need to be there to finalise things and arrange to have my belongings sent here.'

Frank's heart which had started pounding when he heard she was going to Sydney, slowed to a normal rate. Peta wasn't leaving for good. She'd be back. 'When do you intend to leave?'

'As soon as I can get everything arranged.' Peta appeared distracted. She drew a hand through her hair. 'I only just heard. I need to arrange with Ann for Lily… find somewhere I can store my furniture till I find somewhere to live…'

Frank's face must have mirrored his distress, because she added, 'I've been very grateful to have lived here, for all you have done for us, but it was always going to be temporary, you knew that.'

'Of course.'

He had known, but it was so convenient to have her here, to know while he was working in the café, she was only a few steps away, working upstairs. 'Is there anything I can do to help?'

'Perhaps you can recommend a storage facility here in Granite Springs, if there is one. I'm not in a mad rush to move, and it'll take some time for the sale to settle. It's been good for us, and I don't want to uproot Lily any more than necessary. If…' Her lips turned down and a bead of moisture appeared in the corner of her eyes.

Frank knew she was thinking of the court case, of the possibility

Lily would have to leave Granite Springs altogether. 'You're going to win this.' He knew she had to – for her sake and Lily's. He couldn't imagine what it would do to the little girl to be sent away from the grandmother she loved. He would miss her, too. He'd come to love her – her and her grandmother and even, in his wildest dreams, to imagine a future which included them. They'd be the family he'd always dreamed of.

'I can help you there. Harper's is a family firm, has been in Granite Springs for six generations. They'll see you right. Started out as removalists and the present generation decided to branch out into storage. Bert keeps the removal side of it going and Ian, the younger one, built a storage centre on the edge of town. You can see it driving in from the airport.'

'I've never noticed. I don't often drive out that side of town, and I suppose you only notice those things when you're looking for them. Removals. Do you think they'd do my removal, too? I had envisaged a Sydney firm, but it might be easier to use one from here.'

'I'm pretty sure they would. They go back and forth all the time. My guess is they'd be glad to have a back load.'

They were still standing in the hallway. This wasn't how Frank had envisioned spending his evening. He picked up the bottle of wine which he'd put down on the hall table when Peta opened the door. 'Seems like you have something to celebrate.'

'You're right. Come through to the kitchen and I'll get a couple of glasses. I planned a cold meal for tonight,' she said, as he poured out the wine. Sensing Peta's mind would be on her proposed trip to Sydney, Frank could see his anticipated romantic evening disappearing.

They had barely sat down, when she jumped up again. 'I should call Ann.' She disappeared in the direction of her study.

Frank sighed and took a sip of wine. Had he been mistaken about Peta's feelings for him?

'Uncle Frank!' Lily appeared at his shoulder carrying a wriggling Archie who quickly slipped from her arms. 'I didn't know you were here. Where's Grandma?'

'She's calling your Aunt Ann.'

'I love my Auntie Ann. Did you know I hadn't met her till I came to Granite Springs? Now I have a new aunt and an uncle,' she said smugly.

'Don't you have another aunt?' Frank asked, curious to hear what she might say.

'Aunt Celia?' Lily's lips pursed. 'Brenda asked me about her too. I hate her. She was mean to me.'

Frank was saved from responding by Peta's return.

'Here you are, honey,' she said to Lily. 'I've been talking to your Auntie Ann. I have to go up to Sydney for a few days.'

Lily's eyes widened with fear. 'Do I have to come?'

'No, honey. That's why I was calling Ann. You can stay with her while I'm gone. My house has sold, and I have to take care of some paperwork and arrange what to do with my things. I can bring back anything you want, too.'

Lily shook her head and disappeared.

Peta frowned. 'She gets worried when I talk about Sydney. I don't know what she'd do if...'

Frank stood up and pulled her into his arms, breathing in the fragrance that always surrounded her. 'It won't come to that, I'm sure.' He mentally crossed his fingers. How could he be sure? How could anyone know what the courts might decide?

'I hope you're right.' She sighed, making Frank wish there was something he could do. 'Here,' he held up her glass of wine, 'drink this and let's decide where to have dinner. I think you need to get out of the flat. It might help you feel better – concentrate on more positive things, like the sale of your house and the solace you've found here in Granite Springs.'

'Oh, Frank. I don't know what I'd do without you. Granite Springs has been all Fran told me it was. It has been balm to my soul, and you've been the icing on the cake. Without you, it would have been much more difficult for Lily and me to settle. Dinner sounds wonderful. I just need to get myself ready.'

When Peta disappeared in the direction of her bedroom, Frank sat down again and picked up his glass. As he rolled it between his hands, he reflected that maybe, just maybe, he had a chance with Peta, and the thought gave him a thrill of delight.

Forty-three

There were people everywhere, hurrying along, talking loudly, families with children, businesspeople carrying briefcases, young people with bulky backpacks and holidaymakers in brightly coloured clothes. Peta looked around the busy airport, so different from the one she left a few hours earlier. She'd only been gone a few months and had forgotten the bustle of the city she used to love.

With only hand luggage – she'd have all she needed once she reached home – Peta headed to the car rental section to pick up the car Frank had helped her book the evening before. She was glad she'd heeded his advice to fly rather than drive. It meant she arrived fresh, instead of spending two days on the road and reaching the city exhausted and frazzled.

Driving out into the city traffic, Peta realised how spoiled she was in Granite Springs where everyone was more relaxed. On a weekday morning, Sydney traffic was a nightmare in comparison. Managing to avoid a tangle of traffic on the way into the city, she was soon crossing the Harbour Bridge, the blue of the ocean lying far below dotted with the white sails of those who'd managed to escape work for the day.

Soon she was back in familiar territory, navigating the midday traffic on Military Road, then into the quieter street she'd lived in for more years than she cared to remember. A whiff of regret tugged her at the sight of the SOLD sign outside her home. It reminded her of the sign outside Vera's when they picked up Archie. Like Vera, it was time for Peta to move on. She stifled the emotion threatening to spill over into tears and got out of the car.

'Peta?'

Peta looked across the driveway to where a familiar face was peering across the hibiscus hedge. Tina Elliot had been her friend and neighbour for years. She should have contacted her to say she was coming back, kept in touch from Granite Springs. It had been easier to ignore all her Sydney contacts once she left, easier to put the past behind her and try to create a new life for herself and Lily.

'Tina!' Peta went across to the boundary. 'I'm sorry I haven't kept in touch. It's been…' She waved a hand in the air.

'I understood why you had to leave. You and your granddaughter. She's not with you?' Tina peered towards the car as if expecting to see Lily emerge.

'No, she stayed in Granite Springs with my cousin.'

'Granite Springs. That's right. I knew it was somewhere in the country, but I couldn't remember the name. I must say we were surprised to see the For Sale sign go up so soon after you left. We thought you'd at least wait till…' Her voice tapered off, clearly unwilling to mention *the trial*. This was another reason Peta had been so anxious to leave – the gossip mill might be bad in Granite Springs, but it was nothing compared to the idle chatter of bored suburban housewives. Tina was better than most, but was one of a group of what Peta had heard referred to as *Ladies who Lunch*. 'Are you back for long?'

'Only a few days. Just long enough to finish things up here.' She looked up at her former home. It was far too big for one person. She should have rid herself of the place years ago. But in the back of her mind, had been the notion it would be there for Joy and her children when they came to visit.

'Ron's off on one of his fishing jaunts,' Tina grimaced, 'so why don't you come round to dinner. It'll be just us girls and you can tell me all about life in Granite Springs. Around six?'

Peta smiled. She remembered how Tina's husband would disappear for days on end with his fishing mates to return full of tall tales but few fish. 'Thanks, Tina. It'll save me shopping right away. I'll see you then.'

Entering the house was like going back in time. It felt odd, as if she was stepping into the house of a stranger. Peta dropped her small case in the hallway, the scent of flowers drawing her into the large open living room overlooking the harbour. She took a deep breath. How could she have forgotten this spectacular view? But it no longer held the attraction for her it once had. She looked around. The cleaner Rod organised had done an excellent job. The place was immaculate with vases of fresh flowers sitting on both the coffee table and the buffet.

She headed into the kitchen which was also spotless. Curious, Peta opened the fridge to see it stocked with bread, milk, cheese and eggs. A packet of herbal tea and one of coffee beans sat on the bench by the coffee maker, and there was a note tacked to the fridge door with a Millers Realty magnet. It read *Welcome Home*. Peta smiled. This was definitely Rod's doing.

A cup of tea was exactly what she needed. She made a cheese sandwich while the water boiled, then strolled around the house, cup in one hand, sandwich in the other. It was all so familiar, yet it didn't feel like home any longer. Peta was suddenly struck by a yearning to be back in Granite Springs, to see Frank's face, his comforting smile, to feel his arms around her, his lips on hers. She sat down on the bed with a thump. She didn't belong here. She belonged in Granite Springs.

*

The afternoon passed quickly. Peta went to see Rod Miller as arranged and signed the necessary documents, then popped into the nearby bottle shop to pick up a bottle of Tina's favourite prosecco for dinner.

By the time six o'clock came around, she'd made a list of the items she wanted to keep and those she wanted to sell. This might not take as long as she'd anticipated. Peta was finding it fairly easy to decide to dispose of many of the pieces accumulated over the years which would have no place in her new and simpler life.

With a quick glance in the mirror, Peta drew a comb through her hair, added a touch of lipstick, grabbed the wine from the fridge and she was ready.

*

'Are you really planning to bury yourself away in a country town?' Tina asked, when they were enjoying their after-dinner coffee and finishing off the prosecco.

'It's a new start for me and Lily, Tina. I'm liking it there. It may not be for everyone, but it suits us.'

'Rather you than me.' Tina took a sip of prosecco. 'No news of Grant's trial, I suppose. You know that sister of his has been sniffing around?'

Peta stiffened. 'Celia?' Celia had been here?

'Is that her name? I recognised her from the paper. That article they did. She's deluded if she thinks he's innocent.'

'What was she doing here? She lives on the other side of the harbour.'

'No idea. She didn't get out of the car, just drove past very slowly. I was coming back from tennis when I saw her. I thought at the time, it was a bit odd. It was after the For Sale sign went up and before the house sold. Must have been a full month ago.'

Peta shivered at the thought Celia Holmes had been spying on her. Had she thought she was living there with Lily? Thank goodness for Granite Springs.

'He's her brother, I guess she loves him and can't believe he'd do such a thing. She...' Peta hesitated, but Tina knew the whole story. She'd been there the day Peta came home in floods of tears, hugging a sobbing Lily. She'd seen all the news items, heard the gossip, been there for Peta until it all became too much, and Peta fled to the comparative peace and comfort of her cousin.

'Oh, you poor dear!' Tina said, when Peta had finished explaining what was happening.

'I didn't tell you to get your sympathy.' Peta wasn't sure why she'd told Tina when she'd been at pains to keep it secret. Perhaps she was becoming tired of keeping things bottled up.

'Have you...? No, you wouldn't.' Tina sipped her wine.

'What wouldn't I do?' Peta asked in an amused tone.

'See him. Grant. Your son-in-law.'

'Visit him in prison? Why would I do that? I never want to see the bastard again.'

'Perhaps you could appeal to his better nature?'

'He hasn't one. He's a murderer. He killed my daughter.' Peta picked up her wine glass and drained it. 'Thanks for the dinner, Tina. It was good to relax, and to see you again. I'm probably going to be busy for the next couple of days but…'

'We'll get together again before you leave?'

'For sure.' But would they? Peta now regretted telling Tina about the custody case. She could trust her not to spread it around, but for her to suggest seeing Grant… She clearly had no idea how Peta felt about him.

Peta's phone rang as she was walking up her driveway. Her heart leapt when she saw Frank's number on the screen. She pressed to accept the call.

'Frank!'

'Hey what's up? You sound stressed.'

'It's nothing. Just a minute,' she said, fumbling with the key and opening the door. When she was inside and sitting in a comfortable chair, she put the phone to her ear again. 'Still there?'

'Of course.'

It was wonderful to hear his voice. It seemed ages instead of only a day since she'd heard it. How she wished he was here.

'How was the flight?'

'The flight was good.'

'But? I can hear there's a but.'

'Oh, Frank!' She curled up in the chair, tucking her feet under her, clutching the phone as if by doing so, she could bring Frank closer. 'You were right to advise me to fly. I'd forgotten about Sydney traffic. I was stressed when I finally reached home – though it doesn't seem like home. I've been away too long, I guess.'

'Everything's fine there?'

Peta could hear the concern in his voice. 'Yes. I've been in to sign all the necessary paperwork. The sale's going through. No problems there.'

'But there is a problem?'

'Not really.' Peta picked a thread which was starting to unravel at the edge of her shirt. 'I had dinner with Tina – she's a friend and neighbour. We got talking. It seems Grant's sister has been here – driving past. It's creepy. And she – Tina – suggested… No, it's too stupid.'

'Tell me. It's clearly upset you. What did she suggest?'

'She suggested I go to visit Grant in prison to *appeal to his better nature*. Can you imagine?' Peta trembled even thinking about it.

There was a pause. She could almost hear Frank thinking.

'Is it such a bad idea?' he asked.

Peta wished they were on Facetime, so she could see his expression. 'A bad idea? It's madness. Even if he agreed to see me, he's not going to change his mind.'

'You'd rather go through the whole court thing?'

'No. Yes. I don't know.'

'Think about it. What harm could it do? And if you could persuade him to change his mind, think what a relief it would be. He's been shut up there for months awaiting trial. It could be two years before that happens. He must know he's going away for a long time. And you say his sister barely knows Lily. I remember what Lily said about her Aunt Celia.'

Peta grimaced. She hadn't expected Frank to agree with Tina. She thought he understood. She'd relied on him to be on her side, to see her point of view.

'I suggest you get a good night's sleep. If you were out to dinner, I expect you had a few glasses of wine which may have clouded your judgement. It may all look better in the morning when you can think more clearly.'

Damn the man! Who did he think he was talking to? Her judgement wasn't clouded. Peta knew she'd feel exactly the same in the morning – tomorrow morning, every morning. She never wanted to see Grant Holmes again.

Forty-four

Frank grimaced as he hung up the phone. Peta sounded so upset, and he hadn't managed to do anything to help. He wished he wasn't so far away, that he'd insisted on going with her. But what excuse could he have had? There was no reason for him to travel all the way to Sydney when she was only going to settle up her life there. That was before her interfering friend suggested she visit her son-in-law in prison.

It didn't seem like such a bad idea. But when he said so, Peta became even more upset and their phone call went downhill from there. They had their first argument, concluding with her telling him he had no business sticking his nose into her life.

Frank sighed. He dearly wanted the right to have a say in her life. But now it appeared less likely than ever. Maybe he should have kept his mouth shut.

His train of thought was interrupted by Al's return home. In the past month, the young man had become more independent. Following Owen's suggestion, he had enrolled to audit a couple of subjects in the Performing Arts degree at William Farrer University and was loving it. As a result, he'd made friends among the students which saw him with such an active social life, Frank rarely saw him in the evenings.

'Hey, Frank!'

His English had improved too, becoming more colloquial as he aped his new friends.

'Al.' Frank was still puzzling over how his call with Peta could have gone so wrong.

'Can you guess?' Al threw himself down in the chair opposite Frank, with a gleeful expression. Without waiting for a reply, he continued, 'I have a part in the production in the Christmas performance of students.'

Frank roused himself to express interest. 'You have, Al? That's good news. What's the part?'

'Oh, it is a small one, but for me, good. It is to be an Italian visitor to the court. I think it was easy to cast me, yes? It is not so easy for an Australian to play the Italian.' He chuckled. 'My father, he would not be so pleased.' He frowned, then a beaming smile crossed his face. 'But my Elisa, she will be here to see me on the stage.'

'Your girlfriend? When is she due to arrive?' Frank sighed, remembering the difficult call he'd received from Al's father. The older Baldini had wanted a progress report on his son and an assurance he was no longer in communication with the *puttana* he'd been involved with back home.

Frank had tried his best to sound vague but, accustomed to being honest, he wasn't sure the other man believed him. There had been a heated exchange, leaving Frank with the impression Baldini blamed him for Al's bad behaviour. At least Frank's concern Lucy would transfer her affections from Rick to the young Italian were unfounded. She'd declared she was finished with men which had made Frank and Marie laugh.

'It is this week she will come. In the airplane on Friday. That is…'

'The day of Lucy's formal,' Frank finished for him.

'It is no problem. You will be here to entertain her, yes?'

Frank pulled on one ear. Friday. Peta had only planned to be in Sydney for a few days. Would she be home by then? And, if she was, would she want to see him? 'I guess,' he said.

'You guess? What is this?' Al looked puzzled.

'I mean yes. No worries.'

Al beamed. 'I will take Lucy to her formal, we will surprise all her friends, then I will come home to my Elisa.'

Al seemed to have it all worked out. Frank wished his life was as simple. Perhaps it had been when he was Al's age, before life caught up with him.

*

By the time Friday arrived, Frank still hadn't heard from Peta and had been reluctant to call her. Despite telling himself it was a storm in a teacup and her annoyance with him would soon blow over, he'd decided to let her cool her heels for a bit before getting in touch. But it wasn't easy. He pictured her in her Sydney harbourside mansion, becoming accustomed to the delights of city living again. Granite Springs might seem small beer compared to what she was used to. It had been all right when she was fleeing, consumed with grief. But now the worst of her shock was over, though she was still grieving. What if she changed her mind and decided to stay?

'Uncle Frank, you're not paying attention!' Lucy berated him. She had brought her formal dress into the café to give him a preview.

He had agreed to allow Al to drive her in the ute tonight, having tested – and been satisfied with – his driving. The young man was presently on his way to the airport to pick up his Elisa and they should be arriving shortly. Frank pulled back his attention to admire his niece who was parading in front of him wearing a knee-length garment in a shade of pale green with shoestring straps. Frank didn't profess to know much about women's clothes, but even he could see this was something out of the ordinary.

'What do you think?' She twirled in front of him, the skirt shimmering like a wave in the ocean.

Frank put a hand to his heart. 'You'll knock their socks off.' Where had his little Lucy gone? This was a grown woman with all the guiles that involved. She was a heartbreaker, for sure. He gave her a gentle hug, careful not to damage the delicate fabric. 'You look beautiful, sweetheart.'

'I wish…' she said tearing up. 'I wish Mum could have been here to see me. She used to tell me about her school formal and we'd joke about…'

'Hey! Don't cry. You'll spoil your pretty dress, and your eyes will be all puffy and red. She'd be so proud to see you now, to see what a lovely young woman you've grown into.'

Lucy sniffed, just as Marie walked in from the kitchen.

'Wow! Let me have a look. That dress is amazing. You look so like…' She stopped. 'Dee would have been so proud of you, Luce.'

'That's what Uncle Frank said. Do you really think so?'

'I do. You're going to have a wonderful time tonight.'

'Thanks. I'd better take the dress off now. You going to drive me home, Aunt Marie?'

Marie tipped her head to one side to give Frank a questioning look. There was still a lot of clearing up to do.

'On you go. I'll finish up here. It isn't every day you have a school formal.'

'Thanks, Uncle Frank. I need to be at the hairdresser at four, and…'

But he didn't wait to hear any more before hustling them out the door. He shook his head. He didn't think girls had gone to such trouble in his and Marie's day. All this talk of hair, nails, and makeup Lucy and Jess had been talking about for weeks. It almost seemed to take precedence over their exams. What did he know? He was only a man.

Back home, Frank found Al in the living room arguing with a dark-haired beauty with flashing eyes. They were speaking Italian, the words flying so rapidly he had no hope of understanding. But it didn't take a genius to work out what was going on. He heard the words *bastardo*, *puttana* and *danza* and guessed this was about the formal. The timing of Elisa's arrival couldn't have been worse. Clearly Al had made a mess of explaining, or maybe there was no good way to explain why he was taking Frank's niece to a school formal on the very day Elisa arrived.

The pair fell silent when they realised Frank was in the room.

'This is Elisa,' Al said. 'Elisa, you must meet Frank who has been so kind to me.' Al looked as if he wished the floor would open up and swallow him, or Elisa would disappear and appear again after the formal was over.

'Welcome to Granite Springs, Elisa. Al has told me so much about you.'

At this, Elisa seemed to soften and, smiling ingratiatingly, held out a hand. 'You are kind to have me stay. Al, he say so much. But this dance, this girl. She is your niece?'

'Lucy? Yes. Al kindly offered to go to the formal as her partner when she was let down. Her boyfriend…'

Elisa waved away Frank's explanation. 'So he tell me.' She glowered at Al. 'But it is so unfair. I am newly arrived, and he is to leave.' She pouted.

Al is going to have trouble with this one, Frank thought, feeling some sympathy for Al's father's views.

'I'll take your case to…' Al began.

'No! I do not stay here.' Elisa said. 'You will find me a hotel and I will see you tomorrow when you… this… *danza*… is over.' She swept out of the room imperiously and Frank could see her standing just inside the front door.

With an apologetic smile to Frank, Al followed her out. Frank heard a stream of invective greeting him. Poor Al.

When he returned, Al's face showed his confusion. 'Elisa,' he said, 'she is not happy. But… I cannot let Lucy down. I made the promise. I have *l'obbligo.*'

Frank almost laughed at the miserable expression on Al's face. He was caught between wanting to please Elisa and his promise to Lucy. Frank was glad Al had a conscience. Lucy would be devastated if he let her down at the last minute. She was so excited about the evening ahead. 'You've made the right decision, son. Give Elisa time to have a good night's sleep, get over her jetlag. She'll see it differently in the morning.' Frank wasn't sure she would, but there was no sense in giving Al any more than necessary to worry about.

Al sighed. 'I think so, too. Elisa, she always have the temper. She is a passionate woman.' He smiled as if remembering. 'But I have never seen her to be jealous. There is no need. Lucy, she is a schoolgirl. It is a school dance.'

'Sure. Now, why don't I get us something to eat, and you get ready for the dance. Forget about Elisa for now and just enjoy your evening.'

'I thank you.' Al appeared relieved and went off to change into the smart suit Frank had insisted he wear.

Frank was sure he and Lucy would make a handsome couple. He hoped Elisa's tantrum wouldn't spoil their evening. They both deserved to have fun.

*

Once Al left, Frank couldn't settle to anything. He couldn't help thinking about Peta, wondering what she was doing, when she'd be back. He had been quick to hand out advice to Al. But who was there to advise him? He poured himself a glass of merlot. What would he advise if it was someone else in his position? He took a sip, knowing exactly what he'd say to them. But could he take his own advice?

Knocking back his drink and pouring another, he took out his phone and, after clutching it indecisively for several moments, he plucked up the courage to make the call.

Half an hour later, Frank leant back in his chair, surprised by Peta's change of heart.

'I thought about what you said,' she told him. 'You were right. It can't do any harm to visit Grant. And if it might work, for Lily's sake, I should overcome my own feelings – my revulsion for him – and do it. I called the prison today.'

Frank couldn't believe what he was hearing. While he'd been regretting his words, wishing he hadn't spoken, Peta had not only decided to act on them, she'd actually done it and received permission to visit the man who'd killed her daughter. But it meant she'd be staying longer in Sydney. He wished he could join her, even offered to fly up on the late afternoon flight on Saturday without considering how Marie would feel about manning the café without him, but Peta had refused, saying she liked to think of him waiting for her back in Granite Springs.

By the time he hung up, she'd convinced him his dream of a future together might be possible after all. It wasn't so much what she'd said as her expression when she said she wanted to think of him there in Granite Springs – he'd made a Facetime call this time so he could see her face. Unless he was imagining things, Peta felt the same as he did.

Forty-five

It was late afternoon, the sun low in a clear blue sky. Peta heaved a sigh of relief as the plane touched down at Granite Springs airport. It had all been a waste of time. Grant had refused to reconsider, had been quite rude, making her wish she'd never entertained the idea he might see reason. She could have been back in Granite Springs days ago.

Once the removal had been organised, Peta had spent the next few days visiting old haunts, places like Frenchy's Café in Headland Park and Waterview Café in Waverton, and had spent one glorious afternoon wandering around Wendy's Secret Garden in Lavender Bay. She'd also made a quick visit to her favourite boutique where she chatted with the owner – another Celia, but one who was kind and helpful – and picked up a couple of summer dresses which would suit the weather when she got home. A foray into a children's shop which had popped up since she left, and the local bookshop led to the purchase of a few items for Lily, too.

Once she'd reaccustomed herself to the city traffic, Peta found it easier to get around, but the one place she avoided was Lily's old home. She couldn't bear to be reminded of what happened there.

To her surprise, Frank was waiting for her when she disembarked from the plane. Her homecoming would have been perfect, had it not been for the shadow of the upcoming court case and the memory of Grant's bitterness.

'Welcome back!' Frank hugged Peta tightly, regardless of the swirl of people around them.

So much for keeping their relationship secret. But, glancing warily around, Peta realised no one was paying any attention. They were all too busy with their own concerns. 'It's good to be back,' she said, breathing in the fresher country air. Despite the aircraft fumes, it was still a lot clearer than the pollution she'd left behind in Sydney.

'I know you have your car here,' Frank said, as they walked out to the parking lot together, 'but I wanted to be here for you.'

'Thanks.' Peta looked up into the deep brown eyes which were like pools of chocolate, eyes she could melt in. A warm glow started at her toes and flowed through her entire body. But it couldn't dispel the trepidation that was never far from the surface.

'Dinner? I booked a table at The Riverside. I want to hear all about it.'

Dinner at The Riverside sounded wonderful, but… 'Lily?'

'I spoke with Ann. I hope you don't mind, but I thought you might want a night to settle in. If I acted out of turn, we can…'

'No.' She'd been hesitant about what to tell Lily. It was probably best she didn't know Peta had been to see her father. But the morning's visit was so fresh in her mind, she knew it would be difficult to hide it. 'Dinner sounds good.'

They parted at Peta's car, after making arrangements for Frank to pick Peta up later. Driving into town behind Frank's battered ute, Peta's thoughts were filled, not with the man who'd been there to greet her, but the man she'd spent less than half an hour with that morning. Time in prison had done nothing to soften her son-in-law. But it had taken its toll. Gone was the handsome, devil-may-care doctor Joy had fallen in love with. In his place, was an embittered husk of the man he'd been, one who'd been ravaged by his months in Long Bay Correctional Centre, mixing with Sydney's most notorious criminals. The glossy veneer he'd shown to the world had disappeared. He scared her.

*

Entering The Riverside Restaurant was like entering a different world, a world far away from the dark one Grant Holmes and his ilk inhabited, a world away even from the lower north shore neighbourhood where she used to live.

'This was a good idea.' Peta turned to Frank as they were being shown to their table. 'How did you know?'

'I could hear the stress in your voice when we talked last night, and I guess the visit didn't go too well?' They were seated by this time, and Frank covered Peta's hand with his. 'Want to talk about it?'

Looking at the large hand on hers, feeling its warmth, Peta knew it would be so easy to slip into allowing Frank to take care of her, of her and Lily. He'd be good to them, and she was falling in love with him, but… She pulled her hand away as a waiter appeared with menus.

'We'll have a bottle of *Pipers Brook Pinot Noir*,' he said. 'Okay with you, Peta?'

She nodded, not caring what she drank as long as it was alcoholic. She felt wrung out by the day.

They spent a few minutes on the menu before Peta chose the pan roasted spatchcock and Frank the black angus grain fed sirloin. Then Frank leant his arms on the table and asked, 'How did it go? I didn't want to ask earlier as you looked a bit tense.'

Had she? Peta had tried to hide her feelings and thought she'd succeeded. Evidently not. She took a gulp of the wine, which had just been served before replying. 'It was horrible. The place is like a fortress – very forbidding. I've never been to a prison before.' She shivered, remembering the icy feeling down her spine as she walked into the grey, stone building. She was only visiting. She couldn't imagine what it might be like to be incarcerated there, to spend months, years, in that dark, inhospitable place.

Peta twirled the stem of her glass, finding it difficult to continue. 'It was the strangest feeling, to have to leave all my personal belongings behind and walk in to meet Grant.' She took a sip of wine. 'It was no good.' She shook her head. 'He wouldn't budge. I felt he was laughing at me for even trying to change his mind. He could have seen me right away, but he kept me waiting for days. It must have amused him to think of me worrying about it.' She rubbed her forehead. 'He looked terrible too – like the criminal he is. It was difficult to believe he's the same man who was Joy's husband and Lily's father. *Is* Lily's father,' she corrected herself.

'I'm sorry,' Frank said, his eyes filled with compassion.

'So, it'll be an appearance in court.' Peta tried to sound confident but knew her attempt fell flat.

'When do you see Brenda Kable?'

'The day after tomorrow. I knew I had to be back for that, so every day he delayed agreeing to see me, it felt like he was taunting me – as if he knew.' She grimaced. 'But enough of me. What's been happening while I've been gone?'

Frank sighed. 'Well, the good news is that Lucy's formal went off without a hitch. She looked like a film star. The dress Al's sister sent her was a big hit.'

'Oh, good. And the bad news?' Peta wasn't sure she could bear to hear any more bad news.

'It's not really bad news, but Al's girlfriend has arrived.'

'What's she like?'

'Angry.' Frank ran a hand through his hair. 'It was bad timing. She arrived on the day of Lucy's formal and – perhaps naturally – was annoyed Al was escorting Lucy to the dance.'

'Oh! She's staying with you?'

'That was the plan, but she stormed off to a motel. She's still there. Making Al pay for what she considers his disrespect and lack of consideration. It's crazy, of course. There's nothing between Al and Lucy.'

'You sure?' Peta was glad to have a topic of conversation that didn't relate to her. 'Lucy's a lovely girl and Al's an attractive young man.' She smiled faintly for the first time since they entered the restaurant.

'Lucy's only a schoolgirl. She still has a lot of growing up to do, whereas Al is more a man of the world.'

'And that makes him attractive to Lucy. Rick was older, too. Remember?'

Frank groaned. 'Don't remind me. But you're wrong about Lucy and Al. They're family.'

Peta raised her eyebrows. But perhaps Frank was right. He knew both of them better than she did.

'At least Rick is completely out of the picture, thank goodness.' He grinned.

Their meals arrived and she managed to force herself to eat a few mouthfuls of what was a deliciously cooked spatchcock, before laying down her cutlery. Suddenly, without warning, her own troubles bubbled to the surface, filling her mind and threatening to swamp her. 'I'm sorry. I'm not very good company tonight. I can't…' She pushed away her plate.

'It's fine. We can leave now.'

When they reached the car park behind the café, Frank made to open the door, but Peta put a restraining hand on his arm.

'Not tonight, Frank. I'd like to be alone.' Peta immediately sensed his disappointment, and almost changed her mind. But she had a lot to think about and it would be best done when she was on her own. While part of her longed for nothing more than to spend the night in his arms, to lose herself in the ecstasy of his lovemaking, another part wanted time to process what had happened in the prison, to consider how to proceed knowing the battle lines had been drawn, knowing Celia Holmes wanted custody of Lily.

Forty-six

Peta had been back in Granite Springs for two days. In that time, she'd caught up with Danny Slater to check on his building schedule, had a second meeting with the hotel project manager, and received enquiries from several local women who were keen to have their homes remodelled. *Forrest Interiors* was proving to be a success.

Her appointment with Brenda Kable was set for two o'clock that afternoon. She was not looking forward to it and had agreed to drop into The Bean Sprout afterwards to tell Frank how it went.

He was being so solicitous it made her want to weep. It was so long since anyone had cared enough for her to cosset and comfort her the way he did. She could love him for that alone, even if his lovemaking didn't send her into raptures.

Walking along Main Street to Brenda's office, Peta felt a twinge of alarm. No matter how often she told herself it was going to work out, she couldn't stifle the fear it might not. What would she do if she had to hand Lily over to Celia Holmes? The other woman was younger, which was no doubt in her favour, but she had no children of her own. And, from what Peta had heard from Joy – and from Lily – she didn't seem to like children, finding it difficult to relate to them.

She arrived before she was mentally ready, took a deep breath and pushed open the door.

The meeting went better than she expected. Brenda was adept at putting her at ease, and the cup of camomile tea made by her assistant helped Peta through the difficult conversation.

'Now I've spoken to both you and Lily, I'll be writing my report to recommend you continue to have custody of your granddaughter,' Brenda said, at the conclusion of the long interview during which Peta felt she'd bared her soul, but managed to refrain from tears.

Glad to leave the building and be once more in the street, Peta drew in a lungful of fresh air. She made her way along to the café which was just closing, Frank in the process of changing the sign on the door to CLOSED.

She fell into his outstretched arms. 'Oh, Frank! I'm glad that's over.'

'Was it so bad?' Frank held her at arm's length and peered into her eyes.

'Not really, but having to go over it all again, trying to explain why I took Lily away from Sydney without applying for the residency order immediately. It brought it all back. I'm sorry.' The tears she'd managed to suppress during the meeting began to gather. Peta could see Marie watching curiously from the other end of the café and blinked to hold them back.

'Take a seat. You need coffee.'

Gratefully, Peta slid into a bench seat and patted her eyes with a tissue.

By the time Frank joined her, she'd managed to regain control.

'Now,' he said, sliding into the seat opposite. 'Marie's going to do the clean up today. I can do the accounts later. What did Brenda say?'

'She was very nice, professional but friendly. It seemed to go on forever. She's good.' Peta recalled how, with very little prompting, Brenda had managed to get her to reveal more than she intended about her relationship with Grant and his sister, and with Lily.'

'Her report?'

'She says she'll recommend Lily stays with me. But she also warned me she doesn't have the final say. It's still up to the court.'

'Any indication when it will be?'

Peta shook her head, and took a sip of coffee, the warm liquid going some way to comfort her. 'I hope it's soon. At least I think I do.' It was hard living with the uncertainty, but was it better than knowing she was to lose Lily?

'How about I come around tonight and bring something for dinner?'

'Thanks. You seem to be continually picking up the pieces these days.' Peta smiled at the man who had changed her life.

'My pleasure. I love being able to help.'

Peta's phone rang. She glanced at the screen, about to ignore the call when she saw Col Ford's number. 'I'd better take this. It's Col. It could be the court date.' She smiled apologetically at Frank, who grasped her free hand and squeezed it.

'Col?' Peta began to quiver. This could be it.

'I need to see you urgently. I'm in the office. Can you come?'

'I'm in The Bean Sprout, I can be with you in minutes.' Peta put down the phone. 'He wants to see me,' she said to Frank. 'It must be the court date. I need to go.'

'I'm coming with you.' Frank threw off his apron and yelled to Marie, 'I'll be back. Lock up when you leave.'

Outside, Frank took Peta by the elbow and steered her along the road to the offices of Slater and Ford. She was a quivering mess and would probably have fallen without his support. Peta took a deep breath. She could do this. If she was going to get so upset at the mere thought of going to court, what would she be like when she was actually there? Allowing herself to give in to a fit of the wobbles wasn't going to help her or Lily.

'I'll be all right,' she said to Frank as they paused outside the solicitor's office, 'but thanks for coming with me.'

The look in Frank's eyes said it all. He was there for her, for as long as she was willing to be with him. The knowledge of his loyalty strengthened her and gave her the courage to push open the door – the second door she'd had to push open that day in a similar frame of mind.

'Go right in,' Dot greeted her. 'Col's waiting for you.'

With a weak smile to Frank, who took a seat in the reception area, Peta walked into Col's office.

Col looked serious. He waited till Peta took a seat, then said, 'I have had some disturbing news – a call from Long Bay Correctional Centre. They apprised me of your visit – not a good idea to my mind. But that's neither here nor there.'

Peta wished he would get to the point. She twisted her hands in her lap.

'It seems there was some sort of altercation between your son-in-law and one of the other prisoners. It's not clear what sparked it, or who started the affray, and a warder who tried to intervene was assaulted for his trouble. But the result is that Grant Holmes has been taken to the prison hospital. His condition is critical.'

Shocked, Peta stared at him. Grant had been attacked? She knew prisons were violent places. They must be. They were filled with criminals. But she hadn't expected this.

'How does that affect me?' she asked, with a tiny glimmer of hope.

'Well,' Col steepled his hands, 'it may not. But if he fails to recover, it may make a lot of difference. There is still his sister's claim, of course.'

'Of course,' she said, the flicker of hope disappearing. If Grant died, Celia would most probably be even more determined to gain custody of his daughter. 'When…?'

'It happened three days ago, not long after your visit. Perhaps seeing you triggered something in him causing him to lash out. We'll never know. I'm sorry, Peta. I know this doesn't make things any easier for you.'

Peta pulled herself together. 'And they think…?'

'They don't believe he'll recover, but if he does, he won't be the man he was. He sustained a serious injury.'

Peta swallowed the retort which came to mind that it was only what he deserved. It would be an uncharitable thing to say, but Grant Holmes didn't deserve her charity. 'What happens now?'

'Nothing, as far as you are concerned. Your court appearance will continue to be scheduled as before. And I may be apprised if his condition deteriorates, or if…'

He dies, Peta thought, wondering if dying was too good for him. 'Thanks for letting me know, Col, but, as you said, it doesn't really change anything. I suppose I should tell Lily,' she added, the thought suddenly occurring to her.

'Perhaps you might want to wait on that.' Col glanced at her sympathetically.

'Oh! You're right.' There was no sense in telling Lily her father was seriously ill, when the news of his death might soon follow. 'Thanks,' she said again, rising to leave and finding herself a little unsteady.

Frank rose as Peta emerged and raised an eyebrow. She shook her head and headed for the door without waiting to see if he was following.

Outside in the street, she took several deep breaths, before turning to Frank. 'Grant's been hurt – critical, Col says. He could die.'

'Wow! Does that…?'

'There's still Celia's claim.'

'Oh! Come back to the café with me.'

'No, I have to pick up Lily. She went home with the twins after school. I didn't know how long I would be with Brenda Kable. Later? You said…'

'Later.' Frank gave her a peck on the cheek and left her to go back to the café while she went to pick up her car.

Fortunately, Eve wasn't in a talkative mood, and Lily was eager to leave, having had some sort of argument with Livvy, so it wasn't long before they were on their way home. For once, Peta was immune to Lily's chatter, but her occasional, 'Well!' and 'Really?' seemed to keep the little girl happy.

'What's for dinner?' Lily asked, as they trekked up the stairs.

'Surprise. Uncle Frank's bringing it.'

'Uncle Frank. Good. He can help me with my maths homework.'

'I could help you with it.'

'But he runs the café. He knows about maths. It's decimals.' She groaned.

Peta laughed. How early stereotypes were formed. Lily had no inkling of the complicated calculations Peta did every day. But tonight, she was too exhausted to try to explain. Let Frank deal with Lily and her decimals. Peta remembered how Joy had trouble with them too. When she had more energy, she'd tell Lily.

Dinner turned out to be leftovers from the café – a mixture of chicken kebabs, slices of smoked turkey, and a wedge of quiche, along with an entire loaf of sour dough bread. Peta foraged in the fridge to provide an accompanying salad.

'I wish we could eat like this every day. It's like a picnic,' Lily exclaimed, finishing off the quiche with a sigh of contentment.

'You'd soon get tired of it,' Frank assured her. 'It's what I tend to live on.'

'Leftovers?'

He nodded. 'That's why I often eat out. After cooking and serving food all day, the last thing I want to do when I get home is cook for myself. It's different when I have someone else to cook for,' he added, as Peta opened her mouth.

The evening seemed to go on forever, but finally Lily went to bed, and Frank and Peta were able to do the same.

'I've been waiting to do this all evening.' Frank took her in his arms and carried her to the bed, covering her with kisses till all she wanted was more of him. With his strong body next to hers, inhaling the scent of coffee that seemed to seep into his skin, Peta's worries faded away and she lost herself in the thrill of his embrace.

Forty-seven

When Col called again only a day later, Peta feared the worst.

'He's dead,' he said without any preamble. 'I thought you'd want to know right away.'

Peta could hear the weariness in his voice. It couldn't have been easy for him, taking on her case. Even though he said he liked to keep his hand in, he was retired and had a herd of alpacas to take care of. 'Thanks for letting me know,' she said, wondering how she was going to tell Lily her father was dead.

She had no idea how the girl would react. Ever since they came to Granite Springs, Lily had refused to talk about her dad. Peta checked her watch. Almost time to pick her up from school.

When they arrived back at the flat, Lily immediately made a beeline for Archie as she always did.

'Lily.'

The little girl stopped teasing the cat with a piece of string and looked up.

'I need to talk with you, I have something to tell you.'

'If it's about that woman I had to talk to, I'm not going to talk to her again.' Lily pouted.

'No, it's about something else.' She drew Lily onto the sofa and put her arm around her. 'I've just heard some bad news – news about your dad.'

Lily put her hands over her ears. 'I don't want to hear anything about him ever again.' She tried to run away, but Peta held her firm.

When the little girl was still again, Peta took her hands from her ears. 'You need to listen to me. Your dad was in a fight in the prison. He was badly injured, and I just heard today...' she swallowed, '...he has died.'

Lily stopped wriggling and became very still in her arms. For a few seconds she didn't speak, then she said very quietly. 'Does that mean he can't ever hurt me like he did my mum?'

Peta nodded and hugged Lily tight, tears coming to her eyes. *What had the little girl seen?*

Lily slipped out of her arms and went back to where Archie was lying waiting for her to return. She picked up the cat, hugged him and began to rock him back and forth like a baby.

Peta watched them for a while before going into the kitchen to make herself a cup of tea and prepare a snack for Lily. It might take time, but Lily would get over this too. The young were so resilient. Now there was only Celia to worry about, and the court proceedings which might be scheduled any day now.

*

When her phone rang with an unfamiliar number an hour later, Peta answered expecting it would be a prospective client. Since the articles had appeared in the local paper and the Canberra magazine, she'd been inundated with calls, some merely curious but many turning into genuine commissions.

'Peta? Is this Peta Forrest?' The supercilious, drawling voice was unmistakable.

'Celia?' Peta was too surprised to wonder how Celia had got her number.

'You've heard the news, of course? My brother was innocent. He should never have been arrested and locked up in the first place. I thought... He'd have been released after the trial and he'd take care of his daughter, though I couldn't understand why he wanted to keep her – a reminder of his marriage. But now he's gone, and I don't want to be saddled with your daughter's brat. You're welcome to her.'

Peta's hand holding the phone became sticky with sweat. She began to shake. Was she hearing right? Had Celia just said...? 'You mean you're dropping your claim for custody?'

'Whatever. I'm seeing my solicitor tomorrow. There's Grant's estate to see to.' There was a sound like a sob.

For a moment Peta felt sorry for her. She'd lost her brother. Then her anger reasserted itself. Her brother was a murderer. The pair of them had conspired to steal Lily from her. Celia didn't deserve her sympathy but, 'I'm sorry for your loss,' she said, before ending the call.

Peta stood up, unable to believe what had happened. She needed to call Frank. No, she needed to call Col Ford. He'd know what to do. Her mind was in a whirl. Had she imagined Celia's call? And she'd called Lily, sweet little Lily, a brat, said she didn't want to be saddled with her. Peta couldn't imagine what Lily's life might have been like if Celia had won custody, and Grant been sentenced to life or as many years as made no difference. But there was no need to worry about that now. It was as if a great load had been lifted, a load which had been weighing her down ever since her first visit to Gordon Slater. She picked up the phone to make the call.

'We need to wait till we hear officially,' Col said, when he heard her excited account of the conversation with Celia Holmes. 'But sounds as if you're home and dry. It must be a relief, though a pity it had to turn out this way. I'll be in touch when I have something definite, but I think, from what you've told me, Lily will continue in your care. The decision will only be a formality. You can start to celebrate,' he said, before hanging up.

Peta's next call was a jubilant one. She heard Frank's yell of delight when she told him about Celia's call. But he became more serious when she recounted her words.

'What a bitch! But all's well that ends well. This calls for a celebration. Why don't you and Lily get your glad rags on and I'll take you both to dinner. Where's your pleasure?'

Peta thought for a moment before replying. 'The Italian, I think. It's less formal than The Riverside, and we're unlikely to bump into my solicitor.' She chuckled. She liked Col – and his wife, Jo – but she wanted this evening to be about her and Lily – and Frank, she thought with a flutter of desire.

She found Lily sitting on her bed, still cuddling Archie.

'Sweetheart,' Peta began, sitting down beside her and giving her a hug. 'I have good news.'

Lily didn't move her gaze from Archie.

'I had a call from your Aunt Celia.'

Lily's arms tightened around the cat.

'Everything's all right. You're going to stay with me, and you won't need to talk with Mrs Kable again.'

Lily's face brightened and she let go of the cat who immediately leapt down from the bed and shot through the door.

'Really?' she asked, a wide smile on her face.

'Really, and we're having dinner with Uncle Frank tonight to celebrate. You'll need to wash your face and take a comb through your hair – and why don't you wear one of those new dresses I brought back from Sydney?'

Peta went into her bedroom to take her own advice. By the time she heard Frank's knock on the door, she was showered, had applied her makeup and was wearing one of the new dresses she'd brought back with her, too – a strappy blue and white striped sundress with a handkerchief hem which made her feel twenty years younger. Though her mood could be a result of the news she had today.

*

'Thanks for a lovely evening.' Peta had finally managed to persuade a tired Lily to go to bed after Frank promised to take them both to the lighting of the Christmas tree in the town centre the following week. Christmas seemed to be steaming towards them at a rate of knots, and Peta had discovered that, like everything else in Granite Springs, Christmas was celebrated in style.

She leant back against Frank's solid bulk, his arm automatically going around her shoulders and drawing her closer.

'I wanted to make it special for you. You deserve it after what you've been through. But it's over now.' He leant his chin on her head, his lips on her hair. 'I know these past few months have been difficult for you. I haven't wanted to add to your burden.'

Peta waited.

'I'm not good with words.' He paused. 'Fact is, you've come to mean a lot to me, Peta. You and Lily. You're like family.'

Peta's heart leapt. *Was he going to say what she thought he was?*

He pulled away and took her hands in his. He kissed her fingers, then raised his eyes to meet hers. 'Damn it, Peta. I love you. I want to take care of you, to be a family – you, me, Lily. I rattle around in that big house. It needs the sound of children, laughter. It needs… I need… you.' He stopped, his ears turning red. 'Do you…? Can you…? Am I making a complete fool of myself?'

Peta laughed, but a gentle laugh. The butterflies in her stomach were skittering around, doing a jig, a jig of happiness. 'I love you too,' she said, putting her lips to his.

Forty-eight

Peta stood in the storage unit wondering what she was going to do with all her furniture when she and Lily moved into Frank's house. It already held most of the items he and Marie had bought when they built the place, and he'd told Peta she had a free hand to redecorate – as long as she didn't touch the kitchen.

Deciding to put it all off till another day, she pulled down the garage-style door and walked back to where she'd left her car. Peta could scarcely believe how much had happened in the past week.

First, there had been Frank's urging for her and Lily to move in with him right away. While it was tempting, Peta needed time to accustom herself to the idea. Although she knew she loved him and wanted to spend the rest of her life with him, she was in no immediate rush to move. Lily, on the other hand, was excited about moving into Uncle Frank's big house.

They'd finally decided to wait till after Christmas which was less than a month away. That would give her time to decide what to do with the accumulated belongings of over thirty years and set in motion her plans to remodel Frank's old house. She already had ideas which she planned to share with him.

It would be good to start the new year afresh – as a new family with Frank. Al had already moved out. Peta recalled the conversation with Frank only two days earlier.

'Where's Al?' she'd asked, when there was no sign of him in the house.

'He's moved out. He told his father some cock and bull story, but the gist of it is he and Elisa have found a place to rent together. It seems they thrive on the sort of ding-dong I saw when she arrived. I guess the making up is what turns them on.' He dragged a hand through his hair. 'It wouldn't do me.'

'Nor me.'

Peta was glad she and Frank – and Lily – would have the house to themselves. Three people were enough to make a family, and tonight they were going to see the lighting of the town Christmas tree together.

*

It was a hot and steamy night, and the crowds were beginning to gather when Peta, Frank and Lily walked along to join in the fun beside the war memorial where the huge Christmas tree stood.

'It's so big!' Lily exclaimed, hopping from one foot to the other. 'Look, Grandma! There are even fairy lights in the other trees.'

Peta glanced around to see what she was referring to and sure enough, along with poinsettia wreaths on the lamp posts, the trees which lined Main Street were strung with twinkling lights.

In the general excitement when the lights were switched on, Peta felt Lily grasp her hand tightly, an ooh of delight escaping from the little girl at the magnificent sight of the sparkling lights. On her other side, Frank's arm tightened around her shoulders. She turned her face up to his. They were a family – she, Frank, and Lily – all part of the new life she came to Granite Springs to create. Just as she created new interiors for other people, Frank had helped her to create a new life for herself.

'Uncle Frank... if you marry my grandma, will you become my Grandpa Frank?'

Frank was stunned for a moment, before meeting Peta's eyes with a grin. 'I suppose I will,' he said.

Peta felt her life was complete. When she moved here six months earlier, determined to create a new life for herself and Lily, she could never have imagined finding this man, discovering such happiness. She really had created a new life for herself, a better one than she'd ever dreamt of.

The End

If you've enjoyed Peta's story, I'd really appreciate it if you could leave a review. A few words will suffice, no need for a lengthy review. It will mean a lot to me and help other readers find my books.

Look out for the next book in the
Granite Springs series, *The Life She Regrets*.

Sometimes life provides a second chance.

Ann Baird has never forgotten her first love and the decision she made that brought her a lifetime of guilt and regret. She knows that some refer to her as a bitter old maid, yet underneath the stoic face she shows to the world, beats a kind and vulnerable heart.

Chris Thomas left Granite Springs in his early twenties. Despite building a successful life and business in Canada, the memory of the girl he left behind has always stayed with him. When an accident forces Chris to return to his native town, despite initial misgivings, the couple acknowledge the spark of their love remains.

As unexpected challenges threaten to keep them apart, will Ann find a way to overcome her guilt and grasp what fate has sent her way, or is it too late for a second chance?

You can order it here: getbook.at/TheLifeSheRegrets

From the Author

Dear Reader,

First, I'd like to thank you for choosing to read *The Life She Creates*. After reading *The Life She Imagines*, many of my readers wanted to know what happened to Frank. So, I hope you've enjoyed meeting Frank again and being introduced to Peta and Lily.

Having spent seven years teaching university and living in an Australian country town, and don an acreage, I've enjoyed writing a series with a rural setting and drawing on my experience of living in the country – with goats – and teaching in university. This is the seventh book in the series set in the fictional country town of Granite Springs and I'm thrilled by the response of you, my readers, to this series, how you tell me my characters are real people you'd love to have as friends. I feel they're my friends too, and they've become a part of my life.

If you'd like to stay up to date with my new releases and special offers you can sign up to my reader's group.

You can sign up here
https://mailchi.mp/f5cbde96a5e6/maggiechristensensreadersgroup

I'll never share your email address, and you can unsubscribe at any time. You can also contact me via Facebook Twitter or by email. I love hearing from my readers and will always reply.

Thanks again.

Acknowledgements

As always, this book could not have been written without the help and advice of a number of people.

Firstly, my husband Jim for listening to my plotlines without complaint, for his patience and insights as I discuss my characters and storyline with him, for his patience and help with difficult passages and advice on my male dialogue, and for being there when I need him.

John Hudspith, editor extraordinaire for his ideas, suggestions, encouragement and attention to detail.

Jane Dixon-Smith for her patience and for working her magic on my beautiful cover and interior.

My thanks also to early readers of this book –Helen, Maggie and Louise, for their helpful comments and advice. Also to Annie of *Annie's books at Peregian* and Graeme of *The Bookshop at Caloundra* for their ongoing support. A special thanks to John who helped me navigate the legal issues of obtaining a residency order.

And to all of my readers. Your support and comments make it all worthwhile. I'm thrilled you enjoy my more mature characters and that the situations they find themselves in resonate with you.

About the Author

After a career in education, Maggie Christensen began writing contemporary women's fiction portraying mature women facing life-changing situations. Her travels inspire her writing, be it her trips to visit family in Scotland, in Oregon, USA or her home on Queensland's beautiful Sunshine Coast. Maggie writes of mature heroines coming to terms with changes in their lives and the heroes worthy of them. Her writing has been described by one reviewer as *like a nice warm cup of tea. It is warm, nourishing, comforting and embracing.*

From her native Glasgow, Scotland, Maggie was lured by the call 'Come and teach in the sun' to Australia, where she worked as a primary school teacher, university lecturer and in educational management. Now living with her husband of over thirty years on Queensland's Sunshine Coast, she loves walking on the deserted beach in the early mornings and having coffee by the river on weekends. Her days are spent surrounded by books, either reading or writing them – her idea of heaven!

Maggie can be found on Facebook, Twitter, Goodreads, Instagram or on her website.

www.facebook.com/maggiechristensenauthor
www.twitter.com/MaggieChriste33
www.goodreads.com/author/show/8120020.Maggie_Christensen
www.instagram.com/maggiechriste33/
maggiechristensenauthor.com/